"Sawyer, have you be[...]
help with [...]

Eve was pretty sure she [...]
to hear him admit it.

He winced. "I might ha[...] [...] your way."

"Why would you do that?"

He rotated his neck like he was uncomfortable. "Trades-people are hard to find around here. And all the new development in the next town over has sucked up a lot of them."

"But why? And it's not just the inn." She gestured to the lake. "You're giving me swimming lessons, too. I mean, I know we're friends now, but why are you being so nice to me?"

He didn't say anything. Just stood there in his hard hat and stared down at the town while he gripped the balcony's railing.

Just when she was about to give up and suggest they go inside, he let go of the railing, grabbed her shoulders, leaned in and— Oh my God, was he going to *kiss* her?

Thunk.

Their hard hats bonked into each other.

PRAISE FOR JENNY HOLIDAY'S NOVELS

ONE AND ONLY

"The perfect rom-com."

—*Refinery29*

"A satisfying iteration of the contemporary bridezilla subgenre."

—*New York Times Book Review*

"When it comes to creating unputdownable contemporary romances, Holiday is in it to win it."

—*Booklist*, starred review

"Delightfully sexy and sweet, Holiday knows how to deliver the perfect combination of sexual tension and happily-ever-after."

—Lauren Layne, *New York Times* bestselling author

"*One and Only* is fantastic! A great start to a new series. Compelling characters, tons of heat, loads of heart. I highly recommend!"

—M. O'Keefe, *USA Today* bestselling author

IT TAKES TWO

"Jenny Holiday turns up the heat and the charm for a summer read more satisfying than a poolside popsicle.... It's hard to imagine finding a more delightful summer escape."

—*Entertainment Weekly*

"This is romantic comedy at its best, complete with clever, sexy banter, a vibrant cast of characters, [and] a wedding that is a character in itself."

—*Washington Post*

"Holiday combines class and sass with a hefty dose of humor.... This winning hero and heroine will take up residence in readers' hearts."

—*Publishers Weekly*

"[An] irresistible mix of lively, piquantly witty writing; sharply etched, marvelously memorable characters; and some completely combustible love scenes that are guaranteed to leave burn marks on readers' fingers."

—*Booklist,* starred review

THREE LITTLE WORDS

"A perfectly plotted emotional journey.... Intense, heartfelt, mature and sexy as hell."

—*NPR*

"Holiday adroitly combines all the requisite elements of a great rom com—scintillating, witty banter and incendiary sexual chemistry—and a pair of protagonists whose emotional complexity and realistic flaws lend a welcome measure of gravitas to this brilliantly executed romance."

—Booklist, starred review

"Combines pure fun with surprising depth. . . . Leavened with witty banter, Holiday's sweet-hot tale captivates."

—Publishers Weekly

"[The] HEA is reached with warmth, humor, steamy interludes, excellent friendships and really delicious-sounding food."

—BookPage

Mermaid Inn

ALSO BY JENNY HOLIDAY

THE BRIDESMAIDS BEHAVING BADLY SERIES

One and Only

It Takes Two

Three Little Words

mermaid inn

A MATCHMAKER BAY NOVEL

JENNY HOLIDAY

FOREVER
New York Boston

Copyright © 2020 by Jenny Holiday

Cover design by Elizabeth Turner Stokes
Cover illustration by Allan Davey
Cover copyright © 2020 by Hachette Book Group, Inc.

Meant to Be copyright © 2019 by Alison Bliss

Hachette Book Group supports the right to free expression and the value of copyright. The purpose of copyright is to encourage writers and artists to produce the creative works that enrich our culture.

The scanning, uploading, and distribution of this book without permission is a theft of the author's intellectual property. If you would like permission to use material from the book (other than for review purposes), please contact permissions@hbgusa.com. Thank you for your support of the author's rights.

Forever
Hachette Book Group
1290 Avenue of the Americas, New York, NY 10104
read-forever.com
twitter.com/readforeverpub

First Edition: January 2020

Forever is an imprint of Grand Central Publishing. The Forever name and logo are trademarks of Hachette Book Group, Inc.

The publisher is not responsible for websites (or their content) that are not owned by the publisher.

The Hachette Speakers Bureau provides a wide range of authors for speaking events. To find out more, go to www.hachettespeakersbureau.com or call (866) 376-6591.

ISBN: 978-1-5387-1651-9 (mass market), 978-1-5387-1652-6 (ebook)

Printed in the United States of America

OPM

10 9 8 7 6 5 4 3 2 1

For Lexi, who will be so very missed.
(Don't worry; she's not dead. She's just
in Pittsburgh.) I'll see you at the falls.

Acknowledgments

So many thanks to the dream team at Forever Romance for their work in launching this new series. Lexi Smail really earned her pay on this one, from when I sent her a not-very-well-thought-out paragraph to when I delivered a hulking, monster manuscript. Estelle Hallick started messaging me photos of mermaid knickknacks a year ago, making me wonder if she was somehow channeling Great-Aunt Lucille without even having read the book. Elizabeth Stokes delivered the pink cover of Evie's (and my) dreams. Leah Hultenschmidt swooped in and took over with the perfect mix of enthusiasm and sympathy.

Thanks, as always, to Sandra Owens for reading an early draft, and to Courtney Miller-Callihan for steadfast support and relentless cheerleading.

Thanks to Elizabeth Gabriel for helping me figure out what Eve's dream library job could be.

Finally, thanks to my Facebook reader group (join us: we're Northern Heat!) for *lots* of discussion about the ins and outs of getting locked in refrigerators.

Chapter One

Great-Aunt Lucille always used to say that life is twistier than the Miskwimin River, and Eve Abbott had always filed that adage away as cute but ultimately meaningless. *No one's* life was twistier than the Miskwimin River. It made so many zigs and zags on its way to its outlet in Moonflower Bay that tourists were always getting lost. Locals, too, if they'd had one too many at Lawson's Lager House. One second the river was behind you, then bam, there it would be in front of you, and you'd be scratching your head and thinking, "Didn't I just cross that sucker?"

So basically, you'd have to be living in a soap opera for your life to be twistier than the Miskwimin River. And Eve's life was most decidedly not a soap opera. If a water metaphor had to be made, it was a nice, linear canal. A man-made canal—a *woman*-made canal, thank you very much—that stretched out in a gloriously straight line as far as the eye could see. Eve's life was hard won. Predictable. Not *twisty*. Not even gently curved.

Lucille's life, though, *had* been twisty, and she had usually been the cause of the twists. For example, there was that time Eve's father—Lucille's nephew—idly suggested she start thinking about retiring, about selling the inn and moving to an old-folks home, because he thought she was "slowing down," and she'd responded by going out and getting her first-ever driver's license at age seventy-two.

Lucille must have thought Eve's life needed more twists. Because a few days ago, Eve had been contentedly living her life in Toronto, a plant-lady librarian living the dream, and today she was standing on the roof of the Mermaid Inn in Moonflower Bay because *she owned it*.

Eve could still see the eight little words that had upended her life so utterly: "Last Will and Testament of Lucille Frances Abbott."

Eve sighed. Well, at least she had found the source of her immediate problem—her immediate problem being that it had been raining *inside* when she arrived yesterday. There was a big bare spot on the tarred roof.

When Eve had gotten to town last night, she'd been glad about the rain—the outdoor kind—because it meant she hadn't had to interact with anyone besides Jason Sims, the lawyer who'd handled Lucille's estate. Eve didn't know Jason. He must have moved to town sometime in the past ten years. As he'd handed her the keys, he'd warned her that the Mermaid was a little the worse for wear. "Lucille couldn't keep up with it toward the end," he'd said, his words a dagger to Eve's guilty heart. Eve's determination never to set foot in Moonflower Bay again after that summer ten years ago had been matched by Lucille's devotion to the place. That meant Eve had only seen her beloved great-aunt a couple of times a year over the last decade, usually on holidays when Eve's father had driven to pick up Lucille and bring her to Toronto for the day.

Eve had spent the last decade telling herself that she could be a devoted great-niece from afar. She sent presents, and she and Lucille talked on the phone a lot. She knew things—she'd thought.

But Lucille hadn't said anything about having trouble maintaining the inn.

She hadn't said anything about her heart condition, either.

Or about leaving the Mermaid to Eve in her freaking will.

Okay, Eve knew nothing.

Except that she needed a plumber, stat. Or a roofer. Or...whatever kind of person you called when it was raining inside.

She started making a mental list. She was a librarian, and categorizing things came naturally.

Either that or her fondness for list making was about making her feel more in control of what remained, essentially, uncontrollable. Potato-potahto.

People to Call

1. *Plumber.*
2. *Roofer.*

Also, the most important one:

3. *Real estate agent.*

Preferably one from Grand View, the next town over, because she didn't need her business spread all over town. Everyone was always up in each other's business here. She wasn't getting mixed up in any of that. She was going to be in and out as quickly and efficiently as possible. Like a spy.

Or, you know, a scaredy-cat.

She pushed down a niggle of guilt at the idea of selling the place that had been Lucille's pride and joy, the place that had been Eve's own beloved summer home for so many years.

She told herself she wasn't feeling guilty so much as overwhelmed. Lucille was dead, and Eve was back in Moonflower Bay.

And it was grossly humid. Way too hot for this early in the morning. Way too hot for any time of day for a town on the shores of a massive lake. Time to get back inside to the air-conditioning.

Okay, well, one step at a time. Literally, because the first thing she needed to do was get off the roof. She made her way to the rear edge, intending to climb down the ladder she'd left propped against the back of the building, and...what the hell?

She squinted down at the parking lot, which was empty except for her rental car. The ladder was gone. Not fallen over. Gone. Like, not in sight.

She reached into her pocket. It was empty.

She peered over the edge of the roof again. Not that she had expected it to magically materialize, but there was still no ladder in sight.

What *was* in sight was her phone—which she'd left on the hood of the car. "Crap." She'd pulled it out to take some photos of a section of the inn's exterior brick. It looked bad enough that she should probably get it repointed before listing the place.

4. Bricklayer. Mason? Whatever: brick person.

But the to-do list aside, this was extremely not good. She was stuck on the roof with no way to call for help.

Except, was that ...?

"Mr. Andersen?" she called.

So much for lying low. Once Karl Andersen, the owner of Lakeside Hardware, realized she was here, so would the rest of the town. Back in the day, his store had pedaled more hearsay than hardware, functioning as a sort of unofficial town hall and as ground zero for a pack of meddling town elders. Some towns had beauty parlor–based gossip networks; Moonflower Bay had the hardware store.

Karl hadn't heard her. He had to be in his eighties by now. She upped the volume. "Mr. Andersen!"

He looked around exaggeratedly.

"Up here, Mr. Andersen! On the roof of the Mermaid!"

Tilting his head back, he regarded her silently. She was expecting surprise, incredulity, but he just smiled. "Eve Abbott. I heard you were back in town."

You did?

How was that possible? She'd told no one she was coming—she didn't have any friends here anymore. But perhaps she had overestimated Jason Sims's commitment to client confidentiality. And she'd *just* been thinking about how robust the town gossip network was.

She braced herself for questions. What was she doing here? Where had she been all these years? Why had she stopped visiting Lucille? What kind of monster great-niece was she?

But he only said, "What do you think of the new square? You should be able to get a good bird's-eye view from up there."

She glanced down. Moonflower Bay's historic main street ran perpendicular from the bay for about four blocks before it widened into an open green space the town used for a weekly farmers' market and for its two big annual festivals.

"It, ah, looks great." It looked the same as it ever had. And she knew this view. Every time one of the top-floor front rooms was vacant, she used to sit on its balcony and read.

Or sit on the balcony and talk for hours on end with He Who Shall Not Be Named.

Or sit and watch the Mermaid Parade from up high, which they also used to do.

Except that the last year she'd watched alone from the sidelines, and he'd turned out to be *in* it.

But no thinking about the Mermaid Parade. Time to lock the marching, waving mer-people back in the mental vault. Which probably wasn't healthy, but whatever. It had worked pretty well for her for the past decade.

"That's a new gazebo," Karl called. "The old one had been painted over so many times, it would no longer hold on to a coat of paint for more than a season."

He was right. The old gazebo used to be a magnet for love graffiti. "Jake + Kerrie 4EVR," that kind of thing. It's possible there was once a "He Who Shall Not Be Named loves Evie" on that gazebo, too, and it had been *carved*, not painted. That way, the carver had proclaimed, it would be "more permanent." Eve, embarrassed by how thrilled she'd been, had teasingly pointed out that *permanent* wasn't a concept you could have more or less of. It just was.

Or *wasn't*, as it turned out.

"Town council was deadlocked over what color to paint it." Mr. Andersen was still going on about the gazebo.

"There was a pink faction, if you can imagine it. They said it was 'raspberry.'" She could hear the air quotes. "It was supposed to be an homage to the festival. But it was *pink*. Bubble gum pink. Raspberries are *red*, I kept telling them."

Right. "Mr. Andersen, do you think you could—"

"You see Jake Ramsey's boat on its way in?"

That gave her pause. The concept of Jake Ramsey—he of "Jake + Kerrie 4EVR"—on a fishing boat was not unusual, but ten years ago he would have been on a fishing boat with his dad. The boat would have been referred to as *Arthur* Ramsey's boat.

But time marched on, didn't it? She'd left everything and everyone in this town behind when she'd fled on that horrible Labor Day weekend ten years ago. Arthur had probably retired. For all she knew, Jake and Kerrie had broken up, too, though that seemed impossible. If there was any couple in the world that was *permanent*, it was them.

Jake's fate would have to remain a mystery. If she asked a follow-up question, Karl would answer it. He seemed to find nothing unusual about carrying on a mundane conversation with her, a person he hadn't seen in a decade, while he was on the ground and she was on a roof three stories up.

"I don't see Jake. Mr. Andersen, I need some help. I'm stuck up here. My ladder seems to have gone missing."

"Missing?" He looked around, again in a comically exaggerated fashion. "How can a *ladder* go missing?"

"I don't know. I thought maybe it blew over, but I don't see it at all. I guess someone took it?"

"Not in Moonflower Bay."

That was the problem with this town. Everyone acted like it was the magical land of Oz, except with mermaids instead of Munchkins. Eve didn't bother to rein in her eye rolling since Karl couldn't see her eyes from down there. "Regardless, I had a ladder, and now I don't. I'm stuck. Any chance I could borrow one from the store?"

"You're awfully high up there, Eve Abbott. You're going to need a serious extension ladder to get down."

She nodded enthusiastically. "I would be in your debt."

"I'd better call the fire department."

"Oh, don't do that!" She had visions of Moonflower Bay's single engine pulling up to the Mermaid, sirens blaring. That would be the end of her get-in-and-get-the-hell-out-of-Dodge plan. As it was, she'd been spotted, and Karl's gossip network would work fast. "They're volunteers! They don't need to be pulled from whatever they're doing when a ladder will—"

"I'll call the police chief," he said, more to himself than to her, as he turned away. "Chief Collins will know what to do."

Chief *Collins*?

Yes. She could totally see that being a thing.

But also: *no*. A thousand times no. *Eight hundred million* times no. In addition to the fact that she was wearing yoga pants so old and ratty that they were almost transparent and a T-shirt that said, "Keep Calm and Ask A Librarian," there was also the part where she hadn't seen He Who Shall Not Be Named for ten years.

Also, you know, the part where the last time she *had* seen He Who Shall Not Be Named, he'd had his tongue down Jeannie Wilkerson's throat on the Mermaid Christmas float in the parade.

Her hands started shaking enough that she probably should be concerned about her ability to climb down a ladder, but no way was she letting Karl call the police. She would rather have the *actual* Voldemort rescue her.

"Don't call...him!" She couldn't say his name, even in an emergency like this. "Maybe we do need the fire engine!" She ran to the front of the building, tracking Karl's progress down the sidewalk toward his store, which was on the other side of Main Street. "Mr. Andersen! You *really* don't need to bother the police. I'll figure something out!" She would rappel down this building with a rope fashioned from her own clothing if she had to.

"Back in a jiff!" Karl called as he disappeared into his store.

Alone again, she surveyed the town she used to love. The inn was four blocks up from the water, but she was high enough that she could see both town beaches, the closer of the two with its pier and red-and-white lighthouse.

She and He Who Shall Not Be Named used to sneak into the decommissioned lighthouse and climb to the top at sunset. They would watch the sun set from the pier first, then make a game of scrambling up the old, rickety stairs. If they were fast enough, they could see a slice of a "second" sunset. They usually didn't make it when they had his sister, Clara, with them—which they often did. Clara's little legs had been too short. But it was always fun to try, and the three of them would arrive at the top laughing and panting.

She had forgotten about that.

It should have been a good memory, but thanks to him it was tainted. She'd lost the lighthouse when she lost him. She'd had to lock it in the vault with the mermaids.

A frisson of anger made her shiver, even in the oppressive heat.

Interesting. Her usual method for dealing with thoughts of He Who Shall Not Be Named was to...not think them. Shove them away. She didn't even allow herself to think his *name*, for God's sake.

But where had that gotten her? Standing on a roof, literally shaking she was so afraid to see him.

But why? *He* was the villain in this story.

And to her great surprise, now that she was here, she was spectacularly angry at him.

She smiled. Anger was unfamiliar, but she could work with it. If she was stuck in this town for a little bit, anger was better than fear. Anger was armor.

So she looked down again at the town she used to love and waited for the boy she used to love to come and rescue her. And when he did, she would call him by his name.

Sawyer Collins.

When Sawyer got the call that someone was stuck on a roof on Main Street, he tried to send his deputy chief to deal with it, but Karl Andersen wasn't having it.

"Son, this is a job for the chief."

"It's probably a job for the fire department," he countered. "What building is it?" Main Street was lined with brick buildings that made a smooth façade against the street, but they were of differing heights, ranging from two to four stories.

"Not sure exactly."

"You're not sure? Didn't you see this person? Isn't that why you called?"

"Come see for yourself. It's hard to explain."

"I'm going to send Deputy Chief Powell." Whatever it was, Olivia would sort it out. Sawyer was exhausted after being on duty all night. It had rained steadily, which usually would have meant a calmer shift, but last night had also been a full moon, which in *Moon*flower Bay was big business. His sister, Clara, was working this morning, which meant the house was empty. He planned to sleep all day.

"Sawyer," Karl said in his I'm-your-boss tone. Never mind that Sawyer was twenty-eight years old and hadn't worked at the hardware store since he was a teenager. "Just come yourself." He hung up.

Sawyer pushed back from his desk with a growl of frustration.

"What's up, Chief?" Olivia, his newish deputy, looked up from a pile of paperwork.

He hesitated. If he told Olivia that Karl had called him directly and was insisting that *he* specifically answer a call, she would kick up a stink. She was trying to professionalize their small, four-person force. To get people to call the station and not Sawyer personally. To get them to accept that a woman could be as good a cop as a man. He agreed with her on all fronts. But he was so tired—summer evenings in the beach town always kept them on their toes, but with last night's full moon they'd had six drunk and disorderly charges. Right now, doing Karl's bidding was easier than doing battle with him—and was the fastest path home to a soft bed.

"Someone's stuck on a roof on Main Street. I have to run some errands anyway," he said to Olivia—*lied* to Olivia. "I'll check it out and go home from there."

"Sounds good. Call me if you need me."

When he got out of the cruiser downtown, he scanned the roofs of the buildings on both sides of Main. No sign of anything out of the ordinary.

The bells on the door of Andersen's Lakeside Hardware jingled, and its proprietor appeared. "Hey, Chief. Let me show you to your damsel."

"Deputy Chief Powell could have handled this," Sawyer said, preparing a speech on how damsels could rescue damsels. Or something.

Karl ignored him as he headed for the passageway on the far side of Lawson's Lager House. "Beautiful day, isn't it?"

It was not a beautiful day. It was sweltering, muggy, and overcast. "It's going to rain some more," Sawyer countered as he followed.

Most of the buildings on Main Street were flush against each other, but there was a narrow passageway between Lawson's and Pie with Pearl that functioned as a shortcut from Main Street to the parking lots behind the businesses. It *also* functioned as a spot for covert activities of all sorts, as evidenced by the condoms and cigarette butts that littered the gravel beneath his feet—more indications that last night had been an especially rowdy one.

"Nope," Karl said. "It'll clear up. It's gonna be one of those picture-postcard days that remind you how lucky you are to be living in the greatest town in Canada."

Sawyer rolled his eyes, but only because Karl, who was leading the way through the narrow passage, couldn't see him. He reminded himself that Karl, though prone to hyperbole, especially in his self-appointed role as chief town meddler, wasn't wrong. Sawyer had gone through his phases of hating Moonflower Bay. Well, okay, one big phase. But his sense of feeling trapped by it had faded over the years. Anyway, it had never been the town doing the trapping. He had dear old Dad to thank for that.

Some days, when his job ground him down, Sawyer got cranky. But this little town on the shores of Lake Huron was home. Its residents, even the sometimes-maddening ones like Karl Andersen, were his responsibility. The town *itself* was his responsibility—he made a mental note to come back and clean up the passageway after he'd caught some shut-eye.

They emerged into the parking lot behind the bar. It was owned by his buddy Ben Lawson, and Sawyer idly wondered if he could go inside after this call and stick his mouth under one of the taps. Yes, it was eight in the morning, but he'd been on all night, so technically it was happy hour for him.

"She's up there." Karl pointed.

"On Lucille's building?" Sawyer frowned. He'd had some concerns about the building standing empty in the week since Lucille's death. Lucille had been a collector of antiques. She had a lot of junk, too, but there was some valuable stuff mixed in among the mermaid knickknacks. The place didn't have an alarm, and though he'd just been thinking what a great town this was, it had its share of the usual small-town problems, addiction and unemployment chief among them. That, combined with the tourists they attracted in the summer, had him keeping a closer eye on the inn. "I don't see anyone. How long ago did you spot the person?"

There was no answer. He looked around. Karl was gone. He looked back up at the roof, which still showed no signs of being populated. Dammit. Did he need to start worrying about Karl's mental state? The man seemed invincible, but he was eighty-seven and a widower who lived alone.

Still, Sawyer should probably make sure there wasn't actually anyone stuck on the roof. That was a long way up.

"Good morning!" he shouted. Karl had been right about the weather clearing up. The gray sky of earlier was fading, and the sun was starting to peek out from behind a cloud. "Moonflower Bay Police here. Is anyone up there?"

And then he knew. He *knew*. Before he saw her.

Like every good cop, Sawyer had learned to trust his instincts. He could puzzle out a crime based on not a lot of evidence. But this wasn't that. This was a deeper kind of knowing. This was his body leading the way. Or, more accurately, his body giving out on him. He sagged back against a car, not trusting his suddenly weak legs to keep him upright. Or to run away, which right then actually seemed like the sensible option. He opened his mouth to draw a breath, but nothing happened. He just stood there—*sagged* there—moving his mouth like a witless fish.

Then she stepped into view, and Sawyer's suffocation began.

The sun was fully out from behind its cloud now, and it backlit her. He had the absurd thought that it had come out from behind that cloud for the sole purpose of shining on her, like she was an angel who required illumination.

But if she was an angel, she was an avenging one.

It was Evie Abbott.

The only girl he'd ever loved.

A sudden, sharp pain in his chest added to the feeling that his body was shutting down.

When Sawyer thought about heartbreak, he remembered it less like breaking and more like emptying. Because when Evie had left town ten years ago—when he'd *pushed* her out of town—he hadn't experienced it like his heart *breaking*. It had been more like his heart *draining*. Like all the happiness and life inside him had flowed out like the river rushing toward the bay. He'd been a fish then, too, flopping around in an emptied tank until all that was left was the dry, scaly shell of something that had once been alive.

The upside, if there was one, was that once your heart was empty, it was *empty*. Smart Evie, Evie who valued accuracy and precision, once told him that there was no such thing as "more permanent." That night, the night he'd carved their names into the gazebo, into the town itself, felt closer to him now than last night's shift.

"There's no such thing as 'more permanent,' Sawyer," she'd teased. "That's like being kind of pregnant. You're either pregnant or you're not. A thing is either permanent or it's not."

A heart is either empty or it's not.

And his was empty.

He'd *thought*.

The great, gaping pain inside his chest suggested that he had been wrong. That there was a lot more damage left to be done. More emptying to endure.

And he very much feared that Evie Abbott was here to finish the job.

Chapter Two

$\mathscr{C}\!\!\sim$

$\mathscr{A}$nger, it turned out, was a strangely enjoyable emotion. Eve let it flow through her as she looked down at Sawyer Collins. She cracked her knuckles. She wanted to punch him. Damn, she *should* have punched him, back in the day. Actually, she should have scrambled right up onto that stupid Christmas float, shoved aside the mer-elves, broken the vacuum seal between his and Jeannie Wilkerson's mouths, and pushed him off it.

"Evie?" Sawyer called.

Things Eve Was Pissed Off About

1. That Sawyer was leaning casually against her car three stories down, squinting up at her. The way he almost didn't even seem to recognize her, his delayed "Evie?" betraying no surprise—no emotion at all, really.

"Don't call me Evie," she snapped. The old nickname rankled. He was the only one who had ever called her Evie, and he had lost that privilege.

"Okay," he said slowly. "Are you stuck?"

"What do you think? I'm just hanging out up here for fun?"

"How'd you get up there to begin with?"

"I had a ladder. It's gone now."

He looked over his shoulder. "Hang on a sec."

Like she had a choice? She took advantage of his absence to add an item to the Pissed List.

> *2. That twenty-eight-year-old Sawyer Collins*
> *was eight hundred million times more*
> *attractive than eighteen-year-old Sawyer*
> *Collins had been.*

It wasn't fair. Eighteen-year-old Sawyer Collins had been cute, with his shaggy, dark-brown hair and his eyes the same color as the bay on its bluest day, but there had been a boyishness about him that was no longer in evidence— shorn away with his hair, perhaps, which today was just this side of a buzz cut. His beard was almost as long as the hair on his head.

His beard.

Eve had never had a thing for beards. She was immune to the whole lumberjack-chic aesthetic that seemed to be a thing these days on the covers of the romance novels she shelved at the library.

> *3. That she was getting the feels from Sawyer*
> *Collins's beard.*

But she hadn't really gotten a good look at him. She was three stories up. His beard, like all beards, was almost certainly gross up close.

When he reappeared, he was dragging a ladder. Hers, from the looks of it.

"Where did you find that?" she called down.

"It was in the passageway between Lawson's and the *Moonflower Bay Monitor* building. I noticed it on my way here, but Law is having some work done out back, so I assumed it was his."

"All right. Lean it against the building."

He went still and did that puzzled-looking thing again, like she was someone he only vaguely remembered and he was trying to summon the relevant details.

> *4. That Sawyer Collins was looking at her like*
> *he didn't remember that she had let him into*
> *her heart. Into her body.*

"Thanks for your help." The thanks felt strange in her mouth now that she was Angry Eve, but her priority was to get rid of him. "I'll take it from here."

"You're three stories up."

"And I'd like to be three stories *down*. But for that, I need a ladder."

He leaned the ladder against the edge of the building. *Finally.*

But then he stepped onto the first rung.

"Maybe you didn't hear me. I need to come *down*. I don't need company up here."

"You're three stories up," he said again.

"As has been well established."

"I'm coming up to help you down."

"I don't need your help." The protest was automatic, and its petulant tone made her wince.

>   *5. That she sounded like a child. Which*
>   *suggested he was getting to her, and that was*
>   *not what she wanted to communicate.*

She was still getting used to this anger thing. She tried again. "Your assistance is not required. You're dismissed." There, that was better. Icier.

He kept coming.

"What are you going to do?" she sniped. "It's not like you can carry me down."

"No." He reached the top, and he stopped with his head above the roof, the rest of his body still on the ladder.

>   *6. That his beard was not gross.*

"But I can stick close to you, and we can make our way down together."

"That doesn't even make any sense!" Crap. There was the petulance again. She cleared her throat and made a conscious effort to speak in a lower register. "So, what? If I fall, I take you down with me?"

That didn't seem like a bad idea, actually.

He shot her a look she couldn't interpret other than to note that it didn't look casual. At least she'd finally inspired something other than mild curiosity. "Something like that." He made an impatient come-here sort of gesture. When she didn't move, he said, "Evie Abbott, get your ass on this ladder."

She got her ass on the ladder, because she really didn't have a choice. But she did snap, "*Don't* call me Evie."

7. That Sawyer Collins looked at her ass all the way down—she could feel it—and there wasn't a damn thing she could do about it.

What she *could* do was use her feet. The moment they hit the ground, she stepped away from him.

"How long are you, ah, in town?" he asked.

"A week. Just long enough to get this roof fixed and the place listed for sale. I have to get back to Toronto." She studied his face. She was pretty sure he was relieved. Asshole. She wanted to revise her answer, tell him she was moving right in, staying for good. Just to irritate him.

"I'm sorry about Lucille," he said. "I remember—"

"You know what, Sawyer?"

He raised his eyebrows. Maybe he was surprised she'd interrupted him. The old Eve—*Evie*—would never have done that. She would have hung on his every word, anxious to hear every thought in his head.

"Shut the hell up."

"Ow!"

Eve, who had been trying to heft her suitcase into the closet of the room she'd decided to move into, yelped when a mermaid figurine fell on her head.

Ironically, she had decided to settle in this room because it was the only one that didn't contain a creepy *life-size* mermaid. Last night, after discovering it was raining on the third floor, she'd crashed in the room closest to the front desk. But when she'd awakened in the middle of the night and shuffled out of bed to hit the bathroom, she'd run into a five-foot-tall mermaid perched near her door. Her sleep-addled mind had catalogued it as an intruder, and she'd screamed bloody murder.

It was possible she might have broken the bedside lamp.

By using it to attack a fiberglass mermaid.

Which was now a pile of fiberglass mermaid shards.

Seeing the inn in the bright light of day had been... something.

The Mermaid Inn had always contained mermaids, of course. The whole town was a little mermaid crazy—hence the Mermaid Parade every Labor Day weekend. As a kid, she'd adored the little mermaid touches here and there: the mermaid mugs the guests used for their morning coffee, the curio cabinet in the parlor that contained Lucille's collection of mermaid figurines, the green-painted metal coat hooks shaped to look like mermaid tails.

But it seemed that in the decade Eve had been away, Lucille had gone full-on mermaid crazy. That, or a giant tidal wave had engulfed the place and barfed mermaids all over it.

You couldn't go a step without running into a mermaid, sometimes literally. They were on pictures on the walls in every room. They were on pillows on the furniture in the parlor. There were mermaid coffee table books and mermaid calendars. There were signs in the dining room that said, "Please do not feed the mermaids" and signs in the bathrooms that said, "If your thighs touch, you're one step closer to being a mermaid."

And there were little mermaid figurines *everywhere*—and they were *glued down*.

She got it—sort of. She remembered Lucille's frustration when guests would steal the mugs, for example, or the hand towels, which Lucille had personally embroidered. So she supposed that if you were going to exist in a universe that contained mermaid figurines on every last surface, those mermaid figurines needed to be glued down.

The only mermaids *not* glued down were the giant fiber-glass ones that stood like sentries outside the guest room doorways, probably because they were too big and/or too ugly to steal.

The figurines were one thing. They could be chiseled off their surfaces and thrown away. But the inn itself was falling apart. What had once been charmingly vintage wallpaper was now a peeling mess. The floors needed refinishing. The ceilings were spiderwebs of water stains.

But, she reminded herself, those things didn't matter. They were problems to be solved by the new owner. She would have to deal with the indoor rain, but she could do that in the week she'd taken off work. She would fix the Mermaid's roof and sell it, and her money problems would be over.

She smiled. She and Lucille had always shared a love of fairy tales, and now it seemed that Lucille was Eve's fairy godmother, waving her wand from beyond the grave and making Eve's pile of student debt disappear. She might even be able to get a less crappy apartment.

She rubbed the bump on her head as she surveyed the room she'd chosen. It was the only room without a mermaid guardian. Or a pile of mermaid shards. Though the first-floor back room did not contain a life-size mermaid, it *did* have a ledge above the dresser lined with keepsakes. Including a figurine of a little girl mermaid that Eve had hit when she swung her suitcase over her head to stash on a shelf in the closet. Unlike the rest of the inn, the figurines in here were not glued down, and the girl had fallen and bonked her on the temple.

It was possible she'd been slamming her suitcase around a little too vehemently.

That was Sawyer's fault.

She picked up the statuette and inspected it. The girl

looked sad. She sat with her tail tucked under herself as she stared wistfully into the distance.

Hmm. Eve spun in place, looking more closely at the room. On the far wall was a print of the Little Mermaid, but not the Disney version. The mermaid was floating in moonlit water gazing at a prince, who was standing at a stone balustrade.

This print used to hang in Lucille's bedroom, and the sight was a jolt. Suddenly Eve was eight years old, curled up in Lucille's bed, holding back tears as Lucille read the story of the mermaid who gave up everything for the prince she loved, only to watch him marry another.

Lucille had championed the original version of the story—the tragic Hans Christian Andersen one—and though she'd tolerated young Eve's obsession with the Disney version, she'd made sure to leaven it with exposure to the original.

It occurred to Eve that Lucille's love for fairy tales—the traditional ones, like from Andersen and the Grimm brothers—was probably what had turned her into a reader. She would even go so far as to say it was what had set her on her career path. She'd wanted to be a librarian for as long as she could remember, and she'd done it. Lucille probably deserved a lot of the credit for that.

Lucille had raised her as much as her parents had. Maybe more, in the ways that counted. Eve was close to her parents and adored them, but they weren't readers. Which wasn't a knock against them, it was just that they had always been too busy making ends meet to curl up and read to her. Lucille worked hard, too—none of the Abbotts had ever been wealthy—but maybe when you lived where you worked, it left more time for fairy tales.

Returning the figurine to its ledge, Eve discovered half a dozen other mer-girls, all of them rather sad looking, none of them glued down. Each one triggered a *ping* of recognition. She knew these girls. They used to sit in the cabinet in the parlor.

The most unsettling thing about being here—well, *one* of the most unsettling things—was that this room aside, none of the decor in the inn today was very Lucille-esque. Lucille had been into mermaids, of course, but the hard-core kind. Selkies and sirens and even more obscure variations from different mythologies. The types that were more likely to be found luring men to a terrible death—spinsters unite!—than singing and frolicking with their underwater friends.

The inn used to reflect that stance. The mermaid touches had been subtle and sometimes even a little bit spooky. But now cartoon Ariels, fiberglass statues, and jokey inspirational signs had taken over. It seemed that a lot of the old stuff—the real stuff—had ended up in this room.

This must have been Lucille's room. In the past she had occupied a room on the third floor, next to the tiny one in the back that had been Eve's. But of course it made sense that Lucille would have moved to the main level as she'd aged and become less mobile. Eve's throat tightened.

And to confirm that this had been her aunt's room, four photos sat on the ledge next to the mer-girls. The first was of Eve and Lucille "marching" together in the Mermaid Parade—Lucille had pulled mer-Eve in a wagon, tails being not quite the thing for marching. She remembered how hard they had worked on that costume, painstakingly sewing sequins onto the tail Lucille had made. The next photo was of Eve in Paris, where she'd done a semester abroad—another lifelong dream that Lucille had planted in her mind. "When else in your life are you going to get to try out another place like that?" Another was Eve's formal university graduation portrait.

She moved on to the last picture, and her breath caught. She and Sawyer were picking raspberries. Eve was showing off for the camera, grinning and holding up red-stained fingers. Sawyer was smiling, too, but he was looking at her. Adoringly. He was looking at her *adoringly*—there was no other word for it.

She felt anew the empty space inside her, the shape of what she had lost. She had dated in the last ten years, even had a couple genuine boyfriends in there. But she was pretty sure none of them had ever looked at her like that.

But, she reminded herself, the space inside her wasn't empty anymore. It was filled with anger. Powerful anger. *Satisfying* anger.

She turned a more analytical eye on the photo. Unlike with the others, she couldn't pinpoint exactly when this one had been taken. They'd had so many days like that, so many Raspberry Festivals. She scooched the edge of the photo up from where it was tucked into the frame. Lucille had had one of those old-school cameras that printed the date on the photo. It told her this shot was from her last summer here. The summer they'd started sleeping together.

Everything between them ratcheted up several levels of intensity that summer. The fun, the love, the loyalty. The sense that it was the two of them—often with Clara in tow—against the world.

She turned the picture to face the wall. Her eyes burned.

She was a little disgusted with herself. Was she really getting all weepy over a teenage betrayal? She was a big girl. She'd had ten years to get over it. She *was* over it.

It was just that she had loved him *so much*.

And now, she reminded herself, she was angry at him *so much*.

She set down the photo. She didn't have time for this. She had a roof to fix and a funeral to plan.

Sawyer was surprised to find his sister in the kitchen when he got home, which was inconvenient on account of the melt-down he was about to have. Normally he'd be glad to see Clara, but he was barely holding it together at the moment.

Her wide-eyed look as he paused on the threshold wasn't helping. She had a summer job at a grocery store out on the Bluewater Highway near Grand View, and she'd been scheduled to work at seven this morning.

"What happened? Did he come to the store again?" Though Sawyer understood that it was important, both socially and financially, for Clara to have a job, he hated that it was located outside his jurisdiction. The officers who patrolled Grand View knew about Charles Collins's history—Sawyer had made sure of it—but still, the idea of someone else getting the call if anything happened didn't sit easy with something in him.

"No, no!" She popped up, and the addition of a grin indicated that her eyes had been wide with something good, something other than fear. And, rationally, what were the odds? Charles hadn't bothered them for a long time. It had been a year since he'd shown up at the store while Clara was working.

Sawyer needed to chill out.

About this, at least. The other source of this morning's agitation? He did not foresee any chilling on *that* front anytime soon.

Clara dragged him to the dining table. "I swapped shifts with someone, because I got some great news yesterday that I wanted to tell you in person." She made a silly jazz-hands gesture as he sat. "You are going to be so surprised!"

He'd had more than enough surprise for one day, but okay. "Hit me."

"Do you remember that national essay contest I entered for Canada Day?"

Kind of? He hated to admit it, but one of the amazing things about Clara as she grew up was how self-regulating she was. He had the idea that other teenagers required more maintenance. That you had to nag them to do their homework and remind them about university application deadlines. But not Clara. She was so driven, so self-sufficient, that he was guilty of tuning out some of the details related to her many ambitions. Not the big ones. He knew she wanted to go to the University of Toronto and study engineering. But she was always applying for scholarships and entering contests, even though she had another year of high school yet to finish—it was hard to keep track of it all. "Of course," he lied.

"So remember how the topic was, 'If you could advise the prime minister on one major policy change, what would it be?' I wrote this thing about vaccination policy. You remember that measles outbreak last year?"

He *did* remember that. He'd been the first responder on a 911 call for a kid who was having seizures because of what turned out to be measles-related encephalitis. Sawyer had decided they couldn't wait for the ambulance, so he'd loaded the kid into the back of his cruiser and made the longest ten-minute drive of his life to get to the hospital.

"I wrote this thing proposing changes to the federal exemption policy, blah, blah." Clara slammed her hands down on the table, her mouth open wide like it always was when she was excited. "And I won!"

Well, hot damn. "That's fantastic!" They high-fived, and pride surged through him.

"I thought for sure the winner would be someone writing about something a lot sexier," she went on. "Like residential schools or climate change or something."

Sawyer's heart squeezed. Only Clara would call climate change "sexy."

"I'm so proud of you, Clare Bear." Proud and amazed. He wasn't really sure how he'd managed to raise such a person.

"There's more! They want the top three contestants—that's number three, number two, and *me*—to be on *The Agenda* this fall!"

The Agenda was a politics show on the Ontario public television station, a fact he knew only because he sometimes watched it with Clara. His own teenage years had not included *The Agenda*. And not only because he'd been more interested in making sandcastles and picking raspberries with Evie, but also because he wasn't naturally the brainiac his sister was.

"So we'd have to go to Toronto for filming. Can we? Please, Sawyer?"

Clara was about to enter her last year of high school. And given the nature of his work—long shifts, often overnight—she spent a lot of time on her own. She was responsible and mature, and he trusted her. All of which was to say that she didn't need his permission, much less his chaperonage, to go to Toronto to be on TV to talk about her science policy essay. Oddly, although he stressed about her at the grocery store in the next town over, he didn't worry about her farther afield. Probably because Charles, who didn't have a driver's license anymore, didn't have the wherewithal to get much farther than Grand View.

But since she was still asking his permission like she thought she required it, he wasn't going to tell her any of that. "Of course. Maybe we'll stay overnight, make a trip of it."

"Yay!" She bounced in her chair. "Okay, I know you want to go to sleep. Since I begged off work, I'm going to the beach." He furrowed his brow, and she read his mind. She usually went to the beach with her friends. "It's nine in the morning. He won't be there."

"Maybe he will. Maybe he won't." Charles was known for his habit of strolling the town's beaches with a metal detector.

And his habit of going ballistic when angry.

"Besides," Clara said, "it's a summer weekend. It will be crowded."

By which she meant any threat an encounter with their father might present would be neutralized by the presence of tourists.

He squelched his instinct to lecture Clara about not letting down her guard. He'd taken her and moved out when she was seven and he was eighteen. So she didn't remember the worst of it. Which had been exactly the point of getting her out of their childhood home. Clara's sense of their dad was more about the series of confrontations they'd had with him over the years that they'd been on their own.

But as he'd just been thinking, they hadn't had one of those for a long time. "Okay. But call me if you need me. I'll leave my phone on."

"Don't do that. Go to sleep. I'll call Law if I run into trouble."

"Or Jake. Call Jake." Both of his friends would come to Clara's aid in a heartbeat, but Jake was built like a linebacker.

"Sawyer. I'm not a kid anymore. I'll be fine."

She would be fine, yes. But would he?

After she left he heaved himself out of his chair and started the coffee maker—sleep was no longer in the cards for him. Hadn't been since he'd seen Evie on that rooftop. She had jolted him awake, and who knew how long it would last? He might never sleep again.

Chapter Three

❧

*W*hen Eve answered the bell at the front door early that evening, she was expecting Jason Sims. They had an appointment to go over Lucille's will.

What she got instead was an elderly woman with blue hair. And not pale, old-lady-blue-rinse blue. No, this was an *electric*-blue bob.

"Eve Abbott!"

"Pearl?"

The woman looked like the Pearl Brunetta Eve remembered, the Pearl Brunetta who owned Pie with Pearl, the bakery next door to the Mermaid. And judging by the pie she was holding, she probably was.

The blue hair was throwing Eve off, though.

"Honey!" Pearl pushed her way inside, set the pie on the front desk, and enveloped Eve in a hug.

The hug did not stop. It just kept going. "Okay, um..."

Eve tried to pull back, but Pearl only squeezed her harder. "What can I do for you?"

That question partially dislodged Pearl. She pulled back enough to look Eve in the eyes. "Honey, no. What can *I* do for *you*?"

Eve wondered if there was a polite way to say, *What you can do is leave me alone.*

Pearl answered her own question, and thankfully, she let go of Eve as she did so. "I can bring you pie, to begin with. Mermaid pie! I started thinking that what you need here is a signature pie."

"Oh, I don't—"

Pearl took Eve's hand and towed her over to the desk. "It's a bit odd to do a lemon pie with a double crust, but I wanted to do the scales, so I needed a top one." There was indeed an intricate fish-scale pattern made out of dough on the top of the pie. "There are other ways to communicate the mermaid theme, of course, but what am I going to do? Dye coconut cream aqua and stick a plastic mermaid on the crust? No. I like to be more subtle."

Eve eyed Pearl's extremely not-subtle hair.

"Anyway," Pearl went on, "it's a work in progress. Try it and give me your feedback. I know Lucille wasn't in the habit of serving food at cocktail hour, but who doesn't like a piece of pie? Or I could do mini ones, and you could give one to each guest when they check in. The minis have been getting really popular. Everyone says they're very Instagram-able."

"Pearl." Eve didn't know how to break it to her. "I'm not going to need a signature pie, because I'm not going to be running the inn. I'm going to sell it."

"Oh." Pearl's brow furrowed like she was confused.

"Hello? Eve?" Pearl had left the door open, and Jason stepped through it.

"Hi, Jason. Come on in. Pearl, if you'll excuse us, we're going to go over Lucille's will."

"Oh!" Pearl perked right up. "*Oh.*" She smiled. "Yes, I'll be going, then." She blew a kiss at Eve. "Ta-ta."

"Sorry everything's a bit dusty." Eve led Jason to one of the bistro tables in the dining room and used her sleeve to wipe the back of his chair before he sat. Jason Sims was like an action figure of a lawyer. His hair was freakishly perfect, and he was wearing a pinstriped suit. He looked way too done up to be sullying himself among the dusty mermaid schlock. "I would have been happy to come to your office."

"You have enough on your plate. It's easy for me to come here, and I'm done for the day." He slid a stack of papers across the table. The top one read "Last Will and Testament of Lucille Frances Abbott."

She had seen it before, in a scan Jason had attached to an email. But even so, being confronted by the words like that, so sharp and final, black on heavy, crisp white paper, made something pinch in her chest. She sucked in a breath.

"It's a lot to take in, isn't it?"

He had no idea. He was talking about the will, about the finality of death. There was that, yes, but there were also little land mines everywhere she turned in Moonflower Bay. Driving into town earlier today after a trip to Grand View to meet with a Realtor had taken her past the Twistee Freeze, a faded, 1950s-era ice cream stand shaped like a giant ice cream cone. Lucille used to take her there in the evenings. They would get cones and sit on the picnic tables nearby and watch the first stars come out.

Later, she and Sawyer would do the same. Neither of them ever had much money, so they'd get small, plain cones. Or if Clara was with them, Sawyer would forgo a cone entirely in favor of getting one for his sister. Eve always used to try to get him to share hers, but he never would. He would say he wasn't hungry, but she knew it was a lie. He was always hungry.

But she also knew that sometimes, pride was more important than hunger.

"Lucille loved this place," Jason said, drawing her from her memories.

"Yes. I did, too." *I* do*, too?* She wasn't sure. The past and the present were getting all muddled.

"Lucille thought carefully about what to do with it. She considered selling it about five years ago, when she was starting to face the notion that running it was getting to be too much for her."

"We were always urging her to hire a manager." Did that sound defensive? Eve still felt terrible that she hadn't realized how poorly her aunt was doing toward the end.

So maybe she sounded defensive because she *was* defensive?

She should have been here more. She should have been *here*, period.

A flare of anger erupted in her chest. God *damn* Sawyer.

"As was I," Jason said. "She did hire a cleaning service, but she held on to the day-to-day management until the end. She had quite the independent streak, didn't she?"

"You can say that again. If you tried to get her to do something she didn't want to do, she would put up shields and just not hear you."

It hit Eve that she could have been talking about herself. Why had she not thought about the Twistee Freeze all these years? Because she'd blocked it out, along with the lighthouse and everything else about this town.

But, she reasoned, shields were not inherently bad things.

Shields protected you. They made it so you could keep putting one foot in front of the other and get on with your life.

"In the end, she decided she wanted you to have the place," Jason said.

"Yes. I'm flattered by her generosity." She really was. The money from the sale of this place was going to make a *huge* difference in her life.

"As I told you when we first spoke on the phone, when she went into the hospital, she had me cancel all her bookings through the end of June, but you'll want to have a look at her book beyond that so you know what to expect."

"Oh, I'm not keeping the place. I made arrangements to have the roof fixed yesterday, and if there's enough time before I have to go back to work I'm going to get some of the exterior brick repointed. Then I'm putting the place on the market." So the bookings, along with the peeling wallpaper and stained ceilings, were going to be someone else's problem.

"Well, see, she really wanted *you* to have it," Jason said. "That's why she kept your room."

Dammit. Eve had visited all the rooms except for the one Jason was referring to. She had gotten as far as the closed door before she turned tail—her old room was another thing that lived in her vault. She wasn't even sure why, just that the mere idea of her old room freaked her out. "I appreciate that. But my life is in Toronto. I have a job there." And she had an even bigger job *prospect* there. "I have..." *Plants. I have a sensitive palm tree that needs me. I am very important and in demand in the botanical community.*

"You're a librarian, right? Lucille was so proud of you. She always said how you two were so much alike."

"I don't know about that." They *were* both spinsters; she'd give him that.

There was also the shield thing.

And the fairy-tale thing. She'd *just* been thinking about what a big influence Lucille had had on her.

Crap. She might as well just start calling herself Lucille Junior.

Well, whatever. She was proud to be Lucille Junior. But that didn't mean she had to live Lucille's life. Lucille had been a devoted Moonflower Bayer. Eve was a city girl. She liked Toronto. If her landlord would just let her put in the Little Free Library she'd been lobbying for, she would like Toronto even more. Anyway, the point was, she could be Lucille Junior, urban edition. Which she *would* be as soon as she got rid of the inn.

Jason moved his hand like he was going to touch her arm. She pulled away before he could make contact. What was happening here?

"I wonder if you could get a part-time job at the library here. Maybe you'd enjoy that. It's not like you would personally have to run the inn. You could hire the manager Lucille always refused to."

Huh? "But I'm not going to open the inn." Had he not heard her the first time? "I'm just here long enough to get the place sold."

"Well, see, that's the thing."

She was starting to get a bad feeling about this. "What? *What's* the thing?"

"I sent you the first page of the will, but there's a...clause."

Oh, crap. She was getting a *very* bad feeling about this.

"I didn't want to tell you this over the phone, or ambush you last night, but things are a little more complicated than you just inheriting the inn free and clear."

"Complicated how?"

"The inn is yours...but you can't sell it for a year."

By the time Sawyer dragged himself into Lawson's Lager House, he had been awake for twenty-eight hours. But at this point he was better off staying up and going to bed at a "normal" hour.

And he needed to be around his friends. Clara was always telling him that he and Ben Lawson and Jake Ramsey had a "bromance" going on, and honestly, Sawyer had no problem with that interpretation. They helped him look out for Clara. Hell, they looked out for *him*, even though he didn't like to think of himself as the kind of person who needed looking out for.

Festival weekends aside, Sawyer didn't work Fridays—one of the perks of being chief—so unless he had something going on with Clara or mermaids had taken over the town, he generally passed Friday evenings at the bar with his buddies. The three of them had been friendly in high school, but it had been in the years since graduation that they'd become close. You sat next to a man at a bar for however many hundred Fridays in a row, and that man became your family. So if that was a bromance, he was all for it.

He eyed the bar in question and sighed. Law was at one end arguing with Maya Mehta. Which meant it would be a while before he got served. He pulled out the stool next to Jake. "Hey."

Jake nodded.

Maya's voice carried from the other end of the bar. "All I am asking is for you to have the band start fifteen minutes later so my patrons don't have to listen to your dubious brand of rock and roll spilling out onto the sidewalk as they're arriving for a civilized night at the theater. Don't bands always start late anyway? Because their sensitive artistic souls are so unpredictable?"

"Why can't you start your play fifteen minutes early?" Law countered. "Then everyone will be inside by the time the band starts."

"Because, *Benjamin*, the theater starts at eight o'clock. Not seven forty-five."

Sawyer shook his head. There was a time when he would have tried to intervene in the ever-festering low-level feud between Law and Maya, who ran the theater two doors down. Much of small-town policing was about peacemaking—smoothing over grudges and helping people find common ground. But those two were beyond help.

"Where's Amber?" Amber was one of Law's employees, and she was usually behind the bar with him on weekend nights.

Jake shrugged. Jake was not much of a talker. He was more of a doer. Which he demonstrated by getting up, walking behind the bar, and pulling a pint for Sawyer.

"Thanks, man." Sawyer chuckled as Jake's presence behind the bar was seized on by a pair of women a few stools down.

"Can you make us cosmos with extra cherries?" one of them asked.

Jake blinked. "No."

"Okayyy ..."

The woman's incredulous tone must have carried across the bar to Law, because he stopped bickering with Maya and came over.

"Sorry, sorry." He made a shooing motion at Jake. "Get out."

When the cosmos were made, Law made a beeline for Sawyer. "So I hear Eve Abbott is back in town."

Jake whistled, drawing Sawyer's attention. His eyebrows were slightly raised, which for Jake was the equivalent of the shocked-face emoji.

"What's got Maya so worked up?" Sawyer countered. He needed to divert Law from the topic of Eve's surprise reappearance.

"So I hear Eve Abbott is back in town," Law said again, undeterred, and Jake snorted.

Sawyer rolled his eyes. "And?"

"What is she doing here? How long is she staying?"

"Why are you asking me?"

"Because you were basically Mr. Eve Abbott for a while there."

"When I was a *teenager*!" Dammit. His protest had been too vehement. This was the dark side of the bromance, of having people in your life who knew your shit. You couldn't be selective about what shit they knew. He started over. "I haven't spoken to Eve Abbott in ten years. I don't know what she's doing here, but it probably has something to do with Lucille's death."

"Maybe she's the executor of the estate," Law said.

"Maybe." Sawyer became extremely interested in a baseball game playing on a TV above the bar.

"Maybe she inherited the Mermaid."

"Maybe." Wow, a double play by...whatever team that was.

"Maybe *who* inherited the Mermaid?" Maya slid over from her spot at the other end of the bar.

"Eve Abbott." Law wordlessly refilled Maya's wineglass. "She's back in town."

"She *is*? Oh my God! But of course she is, with Lucille

having passed." Maya turned thoughtful. "Hmm. If Eve's inherited the inn, I wonder if—"

"Whatever you're thinking, don't," Law said.

"What is *that* supposed to mean?"

"You have your plotting face on. You'll suck Eve into whatever it is you're plotting against me."

"I'm not plotting against you, *Benjamin*. I know it's hard for you to understand, but not everything is about you." She turned to Sawyer and Jake. "Anyway, Eve Abbott is back! I always liked her back in the day."

"I gotta go." Sawyer pushed back from the bar. If everyone was going to keep talking about Evie, he needed to get out of here.

"*Everyone* liked Eve back in the day," Law said, and when Sawyer laid down some cash for his unfinished pint, he added, "Some of us more than others."

Eve saw Jason Sims out, legal jargon making her head spin. She wasn't sure she'd caught all of what he'd said after he'd dropped the bomb on her, but she had heard one thing loud and clear. A year.

A freaking *year*.

She had also heard the figure he had cited for property taxes and basic bills to keep the inn going over the course of that year.

She was stuck. If she couldn't sell the inn for a year, she would have to reopen it just to afford its upkeep.

But there was no way *she* could run it. She had a job in Toronto. She had a mountain of student debt she was chipping away at with an ice pick. Soon she would be applying for another job, a bigger one she had a good shot at that would pay enough to turn her ice pick into a shovel.

She would have to hire someone to run the inn.

And add that person's salary to the mountain.

Little crackles of panic raced up and down her spine.

"Oh, Eve," Jason said as they stood in the open doorway. "One more thing. Lucille said to tell you she left your room the way it was."

She nodded mutely and closed the door behind him.

That was the second time he'd referenced her room.

Well, crap. Given that she had no earthly idea what to do about the disaster her life had become in the last five minutes, maybe it was time to go upstairs and face the stupid thing.

She wondered why Lucille hadn't renovated it into something reasonable. That would have been the logical thing to do, once it became clear that Eve's absence from town was permanent.

Could she just go up there, open the door a crack, and throw a lit match inside?

No. No matter how she decided to handle the inn, she was going to have to deal with the room. Since she was already on the verge of a meltdown, why not get it over with? She could have a multitasking meltdown.

She climbed the stairs like she was marching to her death. There were two large guest rooms in front and three smaller rooms in back on the third floor. Lucille used to occupy one of the back ones, but judging by Eve's detective work that morning, she had moved to the first floor at some point. But back in the day, they'd slept in neighboring rooms—all the better for marathon fairy-tale reading sessions.

The corridor was familiar. Eve's body made the turn by muscle memory. Her hand automatically floated up and slid along the textured velvet wallpaper, just like it always had.

And there it was. The scratched oak door with the little

wooden sign that said, "Eve's Room." She laid her hand on the crystal doorknob that was always a little loose.

And stood there.

Okay, this was dumb. It was just a room.

She pushed open the door and...it was not just a room. All the circuits in her body fired at once. Tears surged to the corners of her eyes. Blood rushed to her head.

She swiped at the tears, took a deep breath to counter the dizziness, and stepped inside. Or did she step back in time? It was the same thing. The room was unchanged, just as Jason said. Pale-pink walls, hot-pink ceramic tile floors—*hot-pink* tile floors. As an adult, she marveled that Lucille had given her—at age *nine*—free rein to redo the room however she wanted. Heck, as an adult, she marveled that Lucille had kept a room for her year-round, even though she spent only two months a year here.

She stepped farther in. The double bed that took up most of the floor space was the same. It was covered with a black-and-white-checkered quilt—teenage Eve had tried to temper some of nine-year-old Eve's extreme devotion to pink with what she'd thought of as more mature decor choices. That was why there was only one poster of Ariel left on the wall— teenage Eve hadn't wanted to *totally* eviscerate nine-year-old Eve's vision—among the more "mature" Eiffel Tower prints that comprised the room's second generation of art.

And there was the vanity with its photographs stuck into the edge of the mirror. The vanity was black to match the bedspread. Sawyer had helped her strip it—it had originally been pink—and repaint it.

The bookshelves that covered one wall—also made by Sawyer, who'd had a serious woodworking hobby but not much of a venue to indulge it—were the same color. If she looked closely, she had no doubt she would find her beloved old books. The Grimm brothers, but also *The Sisterhood of the Traveling Pants*. Harry Potter.

She did not look closely.

She wasn't sure why she was so freaked out about this room in particular. Maybe because it had been *hers*. Her parents' house in Toronto was a tiny one-bedroom bungalow. Her "bedroom" had been an alcove off the living room that her parents had curtained off. They had been scrupulous about respecting her privacy, but there was no door. You couldn't knock on a curtain.

This place, however, had been *hers*.

She had spent so many hours in this room with Sawyer when they were kids. Back when he was her best friend. They would play board games with Clara and listen to music and make plans to spy on the guests.

Once he became her boyfriend, Lucille had barred him from the room. Of course, that hadn't stopped them from sneaking up every chance they got. They couldn't hang out at Sawyer's place, and Lucille was often busy with guests.

So when they wanted to be alone, this was where it happened.

She looked back at the bed. That was where—

All right. *Enough.*

She wasn't a child anymore. She no longer lived in a pink fantasyland.

She went to the small ledge mounted on the wall near the door. All the rooms had one. When they turned over a room, they left the key on the ledge for the next guest.

Her key was there. Finally, something going her way on this wretched day. She picked it up and, with a strange calmness settling over her, left the room. She locked the door, stuck the key in her pocket, and went downstairs.

By the time she reached the main floor, she knew what she was going to do next.

It was time to head to Lawson's Lager House for Operation: Get Shitfaced.

Slightly Shitfaced, she corrected herself. Operation: Get *Slightly* Shitfaced.

Operation: Get Shitfaced Enough to Temporarily Forget the Clusterfuck Her Life Had Become in the Span of One Short Hour but Not So Shitfaced That She Was Incapacitated Tomorrow Because Drinking Would Not Remove the Need to Un-Clusterfuck Her Life.

The bar was two doors down from the inn. She walked quickly, keeping her head down. She didn't want to see anyone. Obviously she was going to have to—the funeral was the day after tomorrow. But for now she felt like a raw, exposed nerve masquerading as a human. She felt like—

The heavy wooden door to Lawson's swung open just as she was about to grab the handle. Startled, she took a step back.

Dammit. Sawyer.

He was not in uniform. He was wearing an old London Knights T-shirt and a pair of faded jeans that somehow managed to hang loose on his hips *and* fit him to perfection. Despite the casual-bordering-on-sloppy vibe—or maybe *because* of it?—he looked *amazing.*

"Evie?"

Okay, good. All he had to do was open his mouth, and she suddenly didn't care how amazing he looked. "What part of 'Don't call me Evie' do you not understand?"

"Sorry. Habit. I wanted to say—"

"Are you leaving?" He had looked like he was. "Because if not, I am."

"I am. I'm just—"

Wordlessly, she spun around and started back toward the inn. She wasn't doing this with him. Maybe she could find some of that gross brandy Lucille used to drink.

"Okay, I'm leaving, Evie. *Eve.* I'm leaving."

She waited a few beats before turning. Sure enough, he was retreating down the sidewalk with his hands in his pockets.

Soon she was settling in at the bar that, like so much else in this town, was unnervingly familiar. Not that she'd spent much time here. It was a true bar. They didn't really serve food beyond frozen pizzas they heated in a toaster oven. But she and Sawyer used to come to trivia night, which had been open to all ages.

She glanced around. As in the Pink Room of Pain, nothing had changed. Dartboards still hung on wood-paneled walls. Neon signs advertised various kinds of beer. The old jukebox sat in the far corner.

Thankfully, she didn't recognize any of the patrons. She was *not* in the mood. She did not need someone freaking out over her the way Pearl had.

"Ms. Abbott. Long time no see. What'll it be?"

"Hi, Law." She did know Ben Lawson, but he *didn't* freak out over her appearance. From him, "Long time no see" could mean ten years, or it could mean ten days. That was Law for you. He had always been chill. "Got a good IPA?"

"Sure do. This one's local." He pulled the pint, set it in front of her, and rested his elbows on the bar and his chin on his palms. Maybe she'd spoken too soon. Was he cueing up a freak-out? Or at least a chilled-out Ben Lawson version of a freak-out?

No. He just looked at her, his expression inscrutable.

"Eve Abbott?! Is that you?" The screech from her left

was loud enough that she physically jumped. "Oh. My. God. *Eve!* I heard you were back in town!"

Eve turned to face her accuser and was pleasantly surprised. "Maya?"

Eve and Maya had been friendly if not explicitly friends back in the day—Maya was a little younger than Eve, and Eve had been pretty wrapped up in Sawyer. As a young teenager, Maya used to direct plays out on the village green. Eve had once let herself be cast as Puritan Number Four in a production of *The Crucible* that had gone over like a lead balloon, *The Crucible* being not quite the theatrical experience that tourists who were otherwise in town for raspberry picking, mermaid tail fittings, and beach frolicking were looking for.

As Maya moved over several stools to sit next to Eve, Law grabbed her wineglass from where she'd been sitting and set it in front of her. Without speaking, he topped it off. Maya didn't seem to notice. "*Eve.* We were all so *gutted* by Lucille's passing. Everyone loved Lucille *so* much." Maya had a melodramatic way of speaking—probably an occupational hazard, if she was still in the theater business. But the sentiment seemed genuine.

Maya laid a hand on Eve's arm. Unlike with Jason Sims, Eve allowed it. Something in her chest hitched.

"I'm just so surprised to see you," Maya went on. "Though I don't know why. Clearly you're going to be here. I mean, Lucille is *dead*."

There was another hitch in Eve's chest, a bigger one that came out like a gasp. She was just so…utterly and completely overwhelmed by the bomb that Lucille's will had exploded in her life.

By being back here at all. By the Twistee Freeze and the pink room and…everything.

"Aww, crap. That came out wrong. I'm sorry." Maya slung an arm around Eve's shoulders, and Eve felt like the Wicked Witch of the West melting, except instead of water being the culprit, it was just a little bit of human kindness. "How long are you staying?"

Wasn't that the million-dollar question? She wished she could answer it. Not just because she wished she *knew* the answer, but because she was...about to burst into tears.

Nope. Not *about*. She *was* bursting into tears.

"Oh, sweetie." What had been an arm loosely draped over her shoulder became a full-on hug as Maya hopped off her stool, stood next to Eve's, and wrapped her arms around her. As much as Eve had resisted the hug from Pearl earlier, she went right in for this one, hiding her face against Maya's neck. She tried to get a grip on her emotions but failed miserably as another sob shuddered through her. Maya hugged her tighter, and after a few seconds said, "Let's snag one of the booths in the back."

Eve nodded. She was down with anything that would make her meltdown less public.

"Benjamin." Maya spoke over her shoulder as she steered Eve away from the bar. "We're going to need shots. Lots of shots." Once they'd settled into one of the wooden booths that lined the back of the bar, she said, "All right. Tell me what's wrong."

"I..."

"Spit it out." She made a hurry-up gesture. "You'll feel better."

"I got snot all over your neck."

There was a pause, and Eve was about to apologize, but Maya threw her head back and let loose a laugh so infectious that Eve couldn't help but smile through her tears. When she recovered, Maya blotted her neck with a napkin.

"That's okay. That's the most action I've gotten in—" She abruptly stopped speaking when Law arrived with two shot glasses.

"Ladies." He set down two disgusting-looking bright-green shooters.

"Thanks," Maya said, "but I'm not sure what part of 'lots of shots' you didn't understand. We're going to need a second round ASAP." Law departed, and Maya slid one of the shooters to Eve. "Bottoms up."

"I am going to regret this."

"Nah. Look! You've already stopped crying!"

"True." Eve clinked her glass against Maya's and drank. Wow. "Sour."

Maya must have agreed, because she shuddered as she set the glass on the table. "Okay, so what's up, buttercup? Why the tears? I mean, beyond the obvious 'Lucille's dead' thing. I feel like there might be more going on?"

"I'm . . ." Eve looked around. She hadn't told anyone. Not even her parents. She'd started to call them but had decided to wait until she saw them in person for the funeral.

But she needed to tell someone, suddenly. It felt too big for her body, this knowledge, this *burden* Lucille had left her.

Well, *clearly* it was too big for her body if it was causing her to break into spontaneous sobs at Lawson's Lager House. She took a deep breath. "I inherited the Mermaid Inn, and I was going to sell it, but I just found out there's this wackadoodle clause in Lucille's will that makes it so I *can't* sell it for a year. But I can't afford to *keep* it for a year, either."

Maya blinked rapidly. It *was* a lot to take in. "Are you *kidding* me? Because I had the *best* idea the other day, and I was thinking what a shame it was that Lucille had passed. I mean, it's a shame that she passed regardless, but I feel like she would have been really into this idea." She slapped the table. "Are you ready for this?"

It was Eve's turn to blink. "Um, maybe?"

"Murder mystery theater *in* the Mermaid."

"Pardon me? Murder what?"

"Well, so I'm the artistic director of the Moonflower Bay Theater Company, right?"

"There's a Moonflower Bay Theater Company?" Eve remembered Maya directing those plays on the green, but nothing beyond that.

"Yes! This summer will be our second anniversary. We do most of our shows in the old movie theater."

That was actually a nice bit of news. The town had a grand old art deco movie theater that used to show classic films, but it had been shuttered when Eve was sixteen. She remembered going to *Casablanca*, the last movie they showed before closing, with Sawyer.

"Every summer we do a big musical. We're sold out the whole run—the tourists love it." Maya sniffed. Clearly her taste did not align with that of the tourists who paid her bills. "Then, in the fall, I do a real play. That one's usually outside, like in the old days."

"Like *The Crucible*?"

"Yes! And don't take this the wrong way, but you made an excellent Puritan."

"But I was just an extra. I didn't have any lines."

"You had a real presence, though."

"Puritanical presence?"

"*Exactly.*" Maya smacked the table again, missing Eve's attempt at humor. "Anyway, I've been thinking about adding an annual murder mystery play to the docket. Tourists would go bonkers for that." She snorted derisively. "But for it to be really immersive, we would need to stage it some-where other than the theater. A run-down inn would be the *perfect* place. Patrons could go from space to space as they try to solve the mystery. Like, was it done with the lamp in the library or the candlestick in the kitchen?"

"I wouldn't say the Mermaid is 'run-down' per se," Eve said. Yes, every inch was covered in mermaid detritus, and the Pink Room of Pain was like a cherry on top of the whole monstrosity, but that was not the same as "run-down."

Hold on. Was she getting defensive again? She thought again about the peeling wallpaper and the water stains.

The Mermaid *was* run-down. It was *beyond* run-down. It was a dump.

"Oh, no, I didn't mean *run-down*–run-down," Maya said. "Just that it's got character. And oh! We can do a play where the victim is a mermaid! It can be *supernatural* murder mystery theater."

"Her aunt just died, and you're scoping the place al-ready?" It was Law, back with two more shots—orange ones this time.

Maya opened her mouth and raised a finger as if to shake it at him—there was definitely no love lost between these two. But then she closed her mouth and retracted the finger. "You're right." Law raised his eyebrows, and she added, "*Once.* You're right *once.*" She shooed him away. "I'm sorry—truly. I get kind of single-minded about the theater. It's my job, but it's also, like, my life." She rolled her eyes self-deprecatingly.

"It's okay," Eve said, and suddenly it was. Even though she didn't think she was down with murder mystery theater at the Mermaid, she felt better. Maya's enthusiasm and general air of optimism were contagious.

"We're here to talk about you," Maya said. "And your *inn*."

"I have no idea what to do about the inn, but I don't think I'm going to solve it tonight."

"Cheers to that." Maya slid Eve one of the orange shots, and they tilted their heads back. It wasn't sour like the first one. In fact, it was the opposite—disgustingly sweet. Like if Orange Crush and sugar cubes had a baby.

"*Uck.* He's doing this on purpose." Maya glowered in the direction of the bar before returning her attention to Eve. "Is there really not a way to sell it if you want to? You hear about these kinds of stipulations in wills, but, like, only in soap operas."

"I know! And usually there's a letter or some dying wish that gets passed on."

"And there wasn't?"

"Nope." Nothing. She had expressly asked Jason Sims about it, and he'd just said, "Lucille said you would figure it out."

"And you and Lucille weren't estranged? She never said anything about this?"

"We weren't estranged. I didn't see her as much as I should have." *Because I'm a selfish idiot, and instead of telling Sawyer off I just shut my mouth and fled.* "But she came to Toronto for holidays, and we talked on the phone a lot."

"Huh."

"I could challenge it, I suppose, but Jason Sims seems to think it's airtight."

"Well, yes, but he probably wrote it. And no offense, but Jason Sims isn't maybe the finest legal mind of our generation."

Eve chuckled. "Is it weird that he kind of looks like he should be in *The Sims*, the video game?"

"Oh my gosh, yes! His hair looks like it's made of plastic!"

"Maybe I *should* get a second opinion."

"Definitely do not accept legal advice from a video game avatar without getting a second opinion."

Eve wasn't sure it would matter. Could she turn her back on Lucille's express wish? She felt again the regret of having allowed her pride to keep her from having a more meaningful relationship with Lucille this last decade. She should have overcome her fear of running into Sawyer and visited more. She should have overcome her fear and visited *once*. Then at least this would have come as less of a shock.

Maya got to her feet. "I'll be right back. I'm going to go get us something decent to drink. You want to share a bottle of wine?"

"Sure." Why not? She'd already had half a beer, a vile green shooter, and an orange syrupy thing. What could go wrong?

Chapter Four

❦

What could go wrong, it turned out, was that she could end up locked in the refrigerator at A Rose by Any Other Name.

"Oh my God! No! You have the key in there with you!" Maya, on the other side of the glass—the normal, inside-the-floral-shop side—clapped her hands over her mouth. Then she cracked up.

"What?" Oh, crap, she did have the key. She'd taken it from drunk and clumsy Maya, who hadn't been able to get it into the lock, opened the fridge herself, and gone inside to get the flowers Maya wanted. And then, apparently, let the door close behind her with the key still in her hand. How completely ridiculous. Eve futilely rattled the definitely locked door, but she was giggling, too.

She was drunk. Just a little. Not as much as Maya, and not so much that tomorrow would be a write-off. But she was, apparently, tipsy enough to have endorsed Maya's idea that they should raid her father's shop for flowers so they could go to the beach and chuck them into the bay.

And tipsy enough, apparently, to get herself locked in the fridge in the process.

It was a town tradition—the flower-throwing thing, not the getting-locked-in-the-fridge thing. The idea was that if you went to the beach under a full moon and threw a moonflower into the water and made a wish, it would come true. All the merchants on Main Street grew moonflowers in gardens and pots. Every fence or post was host to the climbing vines. It was almost too much—was this a town or a movie set of a town? But Eve had to admit that strolling Main Street in the evening, when the night-blooming flowers were open, had always been magical. It had seemed easy enough, back then, to believe that the flowers had wish-granting properties—as a fairy-tale enthusiast, Eve had always been on the lookout for magic.

"There's another key, right?" Eve asked. She watched in real time as Maya's mirth turned to horror. It seemed to happen in slow motion, her tendency toward the theatrical magnified by her inebriation as she transitioned from one emotional extreme to another. "You don't have another key?" This was not good. "Why is this case even locked, anyway?

"An amaryllis is not a cheap flower." Maya, rummaging around in a drawer behind the cash register, answered Eve's unspoken question.

Amaryllis? Weren't they here for moonflowers?

"And my father does a fair bit of business in rare orchids," Maya went on. "So at any given time, he's got several grand worth of flowers in there."

That struck Eve as funny—so maybe she was doing the tipsy, emotional-back-and-forth thing, too. "You gotta beware of those organized orchid crime rings."

Maya sputtered with laughter as she yanked open another drawer. "I'm almost certain my dad doesn't keep a key here overnight." She looked up. "Because, you know, you can't leave a key just lying around on account of the organized orchid crime rings." They both giggled some more, but then Maya sobered—metaphorically only. She lurched toward the case and bumped her head on the glass.

"Ow!" Eve yelped in solidarity.

"I'm okay!" Maya held her hands up like she was being robbed. By a member of an organized orchid crime ring, perhaps? The prospect made Eve crack up anew.

"Okay," Maya said through her laughter even as she rubbed her head. "I'm gonna have to go to my parents' house and wake them up. I'll have to take a taxi, though, or find someone to drive me."

"How long is that going to take?" Eve suddenly registered how cold it was inside the refrigerator.

"Hello?"

Oh no. *No.* She knew that voice. What was *up* with this guy? Was he *everywhere*?

Well, he was the chief of police, so maybe?

He Who Shall Not Be Named.

But no. She was using his real name now.

"What?" Maya paused in her rummaging, her brow furrowing. "He who shall what?"

Oh, crap. Had she said that out loud?

Maya looked over her shoulder, confused, until Sawyer stepped into the store. "Sawyer?" She turned back to Eve. "Were you talking about Sawyer?"

She was speaking in that super-loud way drunk people do when they lose control of the volume button, and Eve wanted to die. To just curl up and slowly freeze to death in the refrigerator.

"Hey, Maya."

He stepped into the circle of light cast by a lamp on the cash desk—Maya hadn't turned on the overhead light, so it and the light inside the refrigerator were the shop's only sources of illumination.

"Burning the midnight oil? I was passing by and saw the light on and wanted to make sure everything was..."—his eyes found Eve's—"okay."

Well, at least if he was just realizing she was here, he probably hadn't heard her using his pseudonym.

"I'm so glad you're here!" Maya exclaimed. "Eve's locked in the refrigerator!"

"I can see that." His eyes did not leave Eve's as he stepped forward and tried the handle. "You don't have a key?"

Eve held up the key in question.

Sawyer rolled his eyes and tried—unsuccessfully—to open the door.

"My parents have another key," Maya said. "You want to keep Eve company while I go get it?"

Eve had hugged herself when Sawyer came into the shop. It had been an instinctive, protective gesture, but now that the coldness had sunk in, she was shivering. She ran her hands up and down her bare arms.

The movement drew Sawyer's attention. Wrinkles appeared on his forehead as he raked his gaze down her body and back up. She told herself his attention was assessing, clinical. He was trying to figure out how to get her out of here. That was a *professional* gaze.

It just...didn't feel that way.

He came right up to the glass, and for a minute it looked like he was just going to...what? Smash through it? She wasn't sure, but there was such determination on his face. She was tempted to take a step back, but why? He was merely taking stock of the situation. He was doing his job. She stood her ground.

Suddenly he dropped to his knees to look at the lock. But because she hadn't stepped back, that put his face…in a certain region.

Not really, though. *Because, hello, there was a pane of glass between them!*

It was just that the picture they made, him kneeling with his face level with the juncture between her thighs, was bringing actual, physical heat to…that juncture, despite the chilled air around her. She ordered herself to stay still, not to squirm. *Your juncture is immune!*

He extracted something from his belt.

"Oh!" Maya exclaimed. "Is that a lock pick? How FBI of you!"

"Nope. Just a Swiss Army knife."

It was one of those ones with a bunch of different tools, and after fiddling with it for a moment, he inserted a tiny screwdriver into the lock and wiggled it around. Just like that, with a *snick*, the lock gave way. The door was on a track, and he pushed it to the side, removing the barrier between them.

He did not get up. Just stayed there on his knees, looking up at her. His eyes were…doing something. Sparking? Sparkling? Apparently the evening's booze buffet had robbed her of her vocabulary.

"Yay!" Maya was celebrating. "I don't care what you say, Sawyer, that *was* very FBI. And I won't have to wake my parents, so wins all around!"

He still wasn't making any move to get up. He was just spark-sparkling up at her while her juncture burned. What was he waiting for?

"Oh, hang on!" Maya shrieked. "You two used to date, didn't you? I just remembered!"

That little nudge down memory lane was apparently what he'd been waiting for, because he reared back—enough that he had to reach out and grab the counter to steady himself. He was on his feet a second later, like he couldn't get away from that reminder—from *her*—fast enough.

The pain that sliced through her chest was almost as strong as the pain that had doubled her over that day at the parade. The day she'd watched him glide by on the Mermaid Christmas float, his presence on the Wilkerson family store's float a shock, then a knockout punch.

But she swallowed the pain. "It was never serious," she lied. She needed to minimize it before he did. What do they say? History is written by the winners.

"Right." He was a good ten feet away now, but he was still looking at her. Just as the silence was getting uncomfortable, he repeated, "It was never serious."

Well, that stung. Even though he was only agreeing with her.

At least she'd said it first.

Not serious, his ass.

He knew why she'd said that. It was a protective measure. A logical one, given what he'd done to her. But it was a complete and utter lie. They had been on the path to forever, and they both knew it.

"Grab two flowers!" Maya ordered as Evie moved to exit the refrigerator.

"We're not still doing it?"

"We sure as hell are."

"It's not even a full moon!"

"Pshaw." Maya waved a hand dismissively. "Details."

"It's not going to work if it's not a full moon!"

Hearing them argue about the finer points of the local

superstition made Sawyer wonder if grown-up Evie still believed in fairy tales and magic.

"Well, it's not going to hurt!" Maya declared. "And the full moon was last night, so we're close enough."

"All right, all right!"

He smiled at the way the women bickered like old friends. That was Maya for you. She knew everyone. If anyone was going to roll out the welcome wagon for a newcomer, it was Maya.

Not that Evie was a newcomer.

And not that she was staying.

A fact he was thankful for, given the way she glared at him as she stepped out of the refrigerator.

"Wait," she said to Maya as she set the flowers on the cash desk. "These aren't moonflowers."

"They're sort of..." Maya lowered her voice to what she probably thought was a whisper, but she was too drunk to achieve subtlety. "Decoys."

"Decoys? What?"

He stepped in to explain. "A few years ago, the wishing thing got so popular that everyone's flowers were getting stolen. There'd be none left by midsummer. And since moonflowers grow on vines, florists can't really sell them cut, like other flowers."

"So my dad did this presentation to the town council suggesting that he start importing amaryllises." Maya cocked her head. "Amarylli? I never know what the plural is."

"The Heritage Preservation Commission, which decided the *actual* moonflowers on Main Street were under their purview, had plaques made encouraging people to buy their flowers here, rather than take them from Main Street," Sawyer said.

"The town actually passed an ordinance making the theft

of a live moonflower finable by up to five hundred bucks!"
Maya finished.

Evie seemed out-of-proportion aghast at this story. "So
what you're telling me is that the town is engaged in an
organized effort to defraud tourists."

"It's not fraud! Nothing in here says moonflowers!"
Maya tapped the glass in front of the big bucket of flowers
inside the cooler. There was a sign on it that said, "Wishing
Flowers."

"Wishing flowers." Evie scoffed. "So it's just a coincidence that an amaryllis looks remarkably like a
moonflower?"

Maya performed an exaggerated shrug, and Sawyer
chuckled. Evie was right: the town was basically conspiring
to protect its blooming Main Street by tricking unsuspecting
visitors into using the wrong kind of flower for their wish
making. The whole thing was, frankly, absurd. But that
was Moonflower Bay for you. A town full of professional
meddlers.

When Evie, still seemingly wildly offended, shot him a
look of disgust, he said, "Hey, I don't make the law; I just
enforce it."

"So you honestly write people five-hundred-dollar tickets
for stealing a flower?"

He smirked. "When I feel like it." In other words, when
drunk tourists got lippy. He'd never issued one to a local.
But no one knew that. He had to hold on to the upper hand
where he could.

He held the door for them. Evie glared at him again.
She and Maya spilled out onto the sidewalk, and they were
already on their way when he cleared his throat to get their
attention. Maya looked over her shoulder.

"You want to lock the door?"

"Oh, right!" She lurched back, and after an unsuccessful attempt to fit her key into the lock, Sawyer took it from her and finished the job.

"Thanks, Chief! You saved the day!" She blew him a kiss. "We can steal the real thing if you like," she stage-whispered to Evie as they set off down the sidewalk. "I'm just trying to be a good citizen, but we stole these amaryllises from my dad, so we're basically criminals either way."

He followed them. After about a quarter block, Maya turned and called over her shoulder, "You're dismissed, Chief!"

"Ignore me." He would try to make himself unobtrusive, but they were tipsy enough that he couldn't just let them hang out on the pier without keeping an eye on them. He would even refrain from writing them tickets if they stole some authentic moonflowers.

"You're not invited!" Maya yelled.

"And you're not sober!" he yelled back.

"Is that a crime?"

"Actually, I could arrest you right now for public drunkenness, but I personally think tolerating me lurking in the background so you don't fall in the bay and drown is your better bet. But it's up to you."

Maya threw up a hand in a gesture he chose to interpret as one of surrender and kept walking—but quietly, which he chose to interpret as victory.

He'd been watching Evie the whole time. As Maya had argued with him over her shoulder, Evie had stared straight ahead. Her posture was not easy. Her back was ramrod straight, and she marched with a kind of robotic gait.

He took some twisted comfort in the fact that though she was epically pissed at him, that was not an "It was never serious" posture.

As he walked, he marveled anew that she was back in town. After he'd left the bar, he'd gone on a walk, not wanting to go home and face Clara and her questions about why he was home so early. He hadn't had a conscious plan, but his feet had carried him to the elementary school. He'd met Evie on the playground there the first summer she'd come to stay with Lucille. His mom had still been alive then, Clara not yet born. Life as he knew it had yet to be upended. And while Mom had chatted with Lucille, Sawyer and Evie had circled each other. She'd been shy. So he, having recently discovered puns from a joke book he got out of the library, swung himself up on the monkey bars and called, "Wanna hang out?" It had worked. She'd smiled and joined him, and they made up a game called "How long can you hang?" which was exactly what it sounded like. They'd laughed and made faces as they'd hung facing each other, each trying to get the other one to laugh and let go.

And then they'd grown up together. Become friends. Best friends. And then more.

The thing that hurt the most was that when he'd sent Evie away, not only had he lost his girlfriend, he'd lost his best friend.

He'd been overcome for a minute there, back at the flower shop. He'd been kneeling in front of her, and once he'd achieved his aim of unlocking the door, he'd just been...stunned. It wasn't lost on him that both times he'd seen Evie since she'd been back, she'd been towering over him. Larger than life. Illuminated. By the sudden, unexpected appearance of the sun when she was on the roof of the Mermaid, then by the light in the refrigerator in an otherwise dimly lit store.

And she was so *angry* at him.

Which shouldn't be a surprise. It was the natural conse-quence of what he had done.

He had wanted to stay on his knees. To take her hands and explain that everything he'd done had been for her own good. *No explaining*, he'd promised himself back then. He *couldn't* explain himself then, or she wouldn't have left. She would have turned down her scholarship and turned her back on her dreams.

But what about now?

Maybe he *could* explain. He had tried to, earlier, outside the bar, but she wouldn't listen. Still, he held out hope that maybe he could find a way to apologize while she was here.

And, in so doing, find out if it had all been worth it. Had she gone to college, studied abroad, made something of herself? She looked like she had.

But what did that even mean? She looked great. Her face was the same creamy pale—she'd always sunburned easily—but it had slimmed some as she'd grown into her adult features, her already prominent cheekbones becoming even more so. Her light-brown hair was long, like it had always been, but instead of the braid she'd always worn, it hung in layers down her back.

He shook his head. Her appearance had nothing to do with the answers he sought. He couldn't tell anything about her academic or professional accomplishments from the way she looked.

Main Street ended at "the little beach," which was the town's not-very-original name for what was, in fact, the smaller of its two beaches. The women started crossing it, heading for the pier. As he trailed them, his attention was drawn by some movement near one of the lifeguard stands. While most of the stands were just elevated platforms, this past summer, a local artist had convinced the town council to let her convert one of them into a functional art project. She'd built a small deck surrounding the platform, with stairs up from the beach. On the platform was a structure topped with a miniature version of the old lighthouse.

It was cute, and the lifeguards loved it because it functioned as a shed they could keep supplies locked up in, but from a policing perspective, it was a pain in the ass. They were forever catching people doing questionable stuff up there. Teenagers drinking. Hell, adults drinking.

And, of course, doing what Art Ramsey and his wife Jamila Johnson were doing at this very moment.

He sighed. He wasn't on duty, and if they would just be more subtle about their interludes, he could look the other way. But no. They hadn't even bothered to break into the shed part of the structure like most self-respecting public sex havers did. At least they were dressed. Mostly. "Hold up!" he called to Maya and Evie.

He switched on the flashlight he kept on his key ring—he carried it and the knife he'd used to spring Evie from the refrigerator because there really was no such thing as "off duty" when you were the chief of police in a small town—and coughed while aiming the flashlight at the sand in front of the couple, trying to get their attention without making them feel like they were being ambushed.

A masculine curse and a feminine giggle were followed by the sound of clothing being adjusted. He waited a few seconds before walking around to the front of the stand. "Evening, folks."

Art took a step away from his wife, as if it would somehow obscure the fact that they'd been caught in the act. "Sawyer. Son."

Art Ramsey—Jake's dad—*was* kind of a father figure to Sawyer. Before he retired from fishing, he used to bring

Sawyer a cooler full of cleaned and filleted fish every month or so. Sawyer and Clara had had a lot of fish dinners over the years. He appreciated that the town had looked after him and his sister both before and after they struck out on their own—things would have been pretty grim otherwise—but it made his job today a little tricky. When you had to bust your father figure for public fornication, things got awkward.

"Hello, Chief." Jamila's voice was a little too singsongy. "We were just moon…"—she looked around, belatedly realizing that the moon was mostly obscured by the shed— "gazing," she finished lamely.

No one had known what to make of it when Art, a widower, had started dating Jamila, a teacher at the high school. She was almost twenty years younger than Art, so the narrative that had initially settled around their romance was that she was a gold digger after his money. Or, more accurately, his late wife's money. But then Pearl and Karl and company had gotten involved—or, knowing them, they'd probably been involved from the beginning—and that was the end of that rumor. A year later, Jamila and Art were married and lived simply, squeezed into Art's small house in town.

"May I suggest you take your moon gazing inside?" Sawyer smiled, but only because it was dark and they couldn't see.

"Yes, of course." Art made his way down the ladder— Sawyer couldn't help but note that his second marriage had put a literal spring in his step—and reached up to guide his wife down. He was happy Art was so happy— the Ramseys had had more than their share of tragedy in recent years.

Sawyer glanced around. Miraculously, Maya and Evie had waited for him and were just setting off again for the pier. "They are *adorable*!" Maya said, loudly enough that he inferred she was talking to him.

"You wouldn't say that if you caught them going at it everywhere you turned."

"That was Art Ramsey—Jake's dad—and his new wife," Maya explained to Evie. "Though not that new anymore, I guess."

"What happened to Jake's mom?" Evie asked.

"She died. Breast cancer."

"Oh no."

There was real anguish in Evie's tone, and Sawyer had a sudden flashback to her chatting with Jake's mom at the annual art fair that was part of the Raspberry Festival. Jake's mom had done a series of abstracts she'd entitled *Magic*, and they had captured young Evie's imagination. She had loved the paintings, but she couldn't afford any of them. But then Jake's mom had given her one at the end of the festival, a small piece that hadn't sold. Evie, delighted, had hung it up in her room at the inn.

He'd forgotten about that. Which was alarming, in a way, because he wouldn't have thought he was capable of forgetting anything about Evie Abbott.

"I always liked her." Evie looked up at the sky as she walked.

"I know," Maya said. "Happily, Jamila is awesome, too. Everyone likes her, even Jake. No evil-stepmother stuff there." She whistled. "And damn, I hate to say it, but I think Art likes her in a way that's maybe a little more *intense* than with his first wife."

They'd reached the pier. Sawyer stopped at the base of it and watched them walk out to the end. Since the rain had cleared out this morning, the weather had remained fair. Big and silver, the moon hung low, and it was reflected on the lake's still, black surface, a rippled river of diamonds. Karl's picture-postcard day had become a picture-postcard night.

He could hear the women murmuring, but out of respect for their privacy, he didn't try to make out what they were saying, just let their voices—Evie's voice; Evie was *here*—wash over him. Maya retracted her arm like a pitcher and hurled her flower into the lake. Evie extended an arm over the water, her flower cradled in her palm. As she stood there, pausing to conjure her wish, he could almost believe she had the power to freeze time. That the moon and the bay alike had paused, waiting silently as they prepared to grant her heart's desire.

He had a wish, too. It wasn't a fantastical, impossible, out-of-his-league wish. He hadn't bothered with those since Evie left town. No, this was just a small wish. But it was *strong*. It flowed through his body, making him want to move, to run, shake all his limbs to try to release it into the wild. But he didn't have a flower—an amaryllis or the real thing—so all he could do was stand there and let his wish consume him.

He wanted to know what Evie was wishing for.

Wishes Eve Abbott Considered While Sawyer Collins Stared at Her Back

1. That Sawyer Collins was not, in fact, staring at her back.

But that seemed unlikely. He was stuck to her and Maya like glue. It appeared that Sawyer's old caretaking ways—they'd been directed mostly at Clara back in the day—had widened to include the whole town. It was his job, she supposed, but she'd also bet that he took his job really, really seriously.

She turned around and glared at him.

"Wow," said Maya. "If looks could kill."

"It was never serious," Eve said again.

"Liar."

2. That she could go back in time and make "It was never serious" true.

"Do you remember Jeannie Wilkerson?" Eve asked Maya.

"The Wilkersons used to have that Christmas shop, right? Jeannie was the youngest kid, I think, but she was still older than us— *Oh.* Yes. I *do* remember. The parade..."

Eve made a strangled noise. "Ugh. Does *everyone* remember that?"

"Not *everyone*," Maya said diplomatically.

"But the whole town goes to the Mermaid Parade! He *made out* with her on the Mermaid Christmas float!"

"It wasn't that big a deal."

Eve snorted.

"Hey," Maya said firmly. "If it wasn't serious, then its demise wasn't a big deal, right?"

Right. So Eve needed another wish.

3. That she could toss Sawyer in the lake?

No, no. She discarded that one immediately. If she tossed Sawyer into the lake, when he got out, he'd be all wet and shivery.

4. That she could stop thinking about Sawyer Collins being all wet and shivery.

Which in turn made her think about what that stupid beard would look like wet.

Ugh. What was *wrong* with her? If there was anything grosser than a beard, it was a *wet* beard.

"What are you waiting for?" Maya teased. "Divine revelation?"

"Okay, okay, just give me a sec."

Time to get serious. The thought of which had the opposite effect: it made her smile. Because the idea of getting serious over this silly, irrational tradition was a contradiction. She didn't even have the correct kind of flower for this superstitious ritual that wasn't even real.

So she should use the first thing that came to mind. Go with her gut.

5. That she could sell the inn right now?

No. She *did* wish that, but it seemed rude, somehow, to make an *official* wish that directly went against Lucille's own firmly held one.

"Come on!" Maya urged. "My buzz is wearing off, and my bed is calling me!"

"You're the one who wanted to do this!" Eve protested, but she did it with a smile. She liked Maya. Even though she'd only been reacquainted with her for a few hours, she felt like a real friend. "Can you blame me for trying to make sure this moon mojo doesn't accidentally curse me?"

"I'm about to turn into a pumpkin." Maya started walking backward.

It came to her all at once, so simple, given that she was standing in front of one of the Great Lakes, that it made her gasp with both its obviousness and its perfection. She'd wanted this for a long time. She hadn't felt its absence as keenly in Toronto as she had all those summers here, mostly because in Toronto she didn't have a view of a body of water every day. But now that she was back, *it* was back, the wanting. Wanting mixed with embarrassment. And fear, of course. Always, when it came to this, fear.

But this wish was overdue. And even better, it wasn't really a wish. A wish was just a hope. A passive request to God or the universe or whatever for stuff to happen to you. That whatever came around the next bend would be pleasing. But, as she had so recently reminded herself, her life wasn't twisty. It was straight and predictable, and, more to the point, it was that way because she had *made* it that way. So yes, she'd make this her "wish," but really, it was more of an intention. A pledge to do this thing. A vow.

I wish I could swim.

Chapter Five

❧

𝓔ve did get a second opinion about the will. After waking up with a hangover and a bunch of mixed-up feelings that Sawyer had stirred up in her the night before, she called a friend who worked at the law school library in Toronto. She gave Eve a referral to an estates lawyer who told her, via a telephone consultation, that Lucille's will was probably contestable in court.

Two words there had given her pause: *probably* and *court*.

The day after *that*, she got several more opinions. Unsolicited ones.

From, seemingly, every citizen of Moonflower Bay.

At her aunt's wake.

"Those balconies out front have got to go," Karl Andersen said as he handed her a jar of homemade pickles. "Despite what everyone thinks, they are not original to the building. They were added sometime in the early twentieth century. If you ever want to get this building listed on the historical register, they'll have to come off."

"Oh, come on, Karl." Pearl appeared on Eve's other side. "She doesn't need to worry about the *balconies*. The bigger issue is getting rid of all the crap in here and classing up the joint. She can charge a lot more for the rooms if she gets rid of some of this"—she patted the head of one of Lucille's glued-down mermaids—"junk."

"Oh, but I'm not going to open the inn," Eve said.

Pearl seemed not to have heard her as she shooed Karl away and added two pie boxes to the growing pile of food on the table in the inn's dining room, where Eve was, in theory, hosting a postfuneral open house.

In practice she wasn't hosting anything. She was 100 percent on the defensive.

"I say this with love," Pearl said, fondling a wineglass that had "Drink Like a Fish" written on it along with a picture of a mermaid, "but this place has gone downhill."

Eve did wonder about that. "I remember some of this mermaid stuff, but not like this. Lucille thought of mermaids as these fantastical, mythical, borderline-scary creatures." She picked up—or tried to, but of course it was glued down—an Ariel figurine that couldn't have been more different from the sad mer-girls in Lucille's bedroom. "She loved the original fairy tale."

"That's right!" Pearl said. "I had forgotten that. The tragic story of the mermaid who gave up her voice to come to land for the love of a man."

"And her tail," Eve added.

"Yes! And walking on legs was like walking with knives shoved into her flesh at all times." Pearl's chipper tone was at odds with the gruesome images her words conjured.

"But then it was all for naught because her prince betrayed her and married another, and instead of murdering him, which was the only way to get her old life back, she decided to throw herself into the sea," Eve said.

Pearl frowned. "I thought she became some sort of magical spirit being?"

"Yeah, well, she kind of did. There was this surprise loophole where if she performed three hundred years of good deeds for humanity, she'd get her soul back. *Three hundred years.*"

"It's funny," Pearl mused. "I definitely remember Lucille's obsession with those dark fairy tales, but she kind of dropped it in recent years."

"Hence the Disney explosion?" Eve asked.

"Hmm." Pearl looked around like she was assessing the inn with new eyes. "I think there are two things going on here. One is that people kept giving her this junk. She kept talking about wanting to renovate, but I think she was getting too frail to actually do it."

Guilt complex: activated. "And the second thing?"

"Some people get more rigid and cranky with age, but some of us stop caring about all the crap you young ones worry about and just have more fun. Maybe Lucille just decided to lighten up a bit." She put her hands on her hips. "Regardless, some of this junk has got to go. A theme is cute, but this is *not* a theme. This is a sledgehammer to the skull. When you reopen—"

"I'm not opening the inn." She had decided this morning. She would take on more debt if she had to, in order to pay the bills until she could sell.

"—you want people to be charmed, not overwhelmed. You want—"

"Pearl."

"Sorry, what?" Pearl had been slowly spinning in place, but she stopped and looked at Eve—finally.

"I'm not opening this place. I'm selling it." *When* she was selling it remained to be seen, but she *was* selling it.

Pearl blinked. "But I thought..." She closed her mouth, seeming to think better of what she'd been going to say. Some more blinking happened. "Eve, will you excuse me?"

"Of course." Eve looked around for S—*No.* She looked around for her *parents.*

She'd thought earlier that the whole town had come to Lucille's wake, but that wasn't entirely correct. The whole town had come except for Sawyer Collins. Not that she cared.

Not that she *wanted* him here.

She wanted her *parents.* Because theirs were the opinions she cared about, more than the lawyers', more than the town busybodies'.

She got her wish, but not for another hour. Not until she'd accepted casseroles and carrot cakes and fended off opinions about plumbing and parking.

She collapsed onto a stool at the big island in the kitchen as her mom portioned the remaining food into freezer bags.

It was strange having them here. Her dad was Lucille's nephew and the person who had always taken care of her affairs, since Lucille didn't have kids. But he'd been in his twenties when Lucille bought the inn. And Eve's parents worked a lot—which was why they'd sent Eve here in the summers. So they'd never really spent time here aside from the odd weekend visit.

Having them here was like having them in her home. Except not. Because this wasn't her home. Her home was a tiny apartment in Toronto.

Her dad laid a hand on her shoulder. "How are you doing?"

For the second time in as many days, Eve burst into tears. She was just so *overwhelmed.*

They hugged her, one from each side, and let her cry. Eventually she calmed down and told them the story of the will. What it said. What the fancy Toronto lawyer said.

"Sweetie," her mom said, "you know we're behind you, whatever you want to do." She looked at Eve's dad. "Maybe we can loan you the money for the lawyer, and you can pay us back when you sell the inn."

"No way." It was a generous offer, but she was *not* taking their money. Her parents weren't at risk of being out on the street or anything, but they didn't have extra money rolling around. They had worked hard their whole lives—they still did. Her mom was a seamstress, and her dad was a security guard at a condo building.

"I once looked at Lucille's will," her dad said, "and there was nothing in it about you except a minor bequest."

"But that was probably fifteen years ago," her mom said. "Eve was just a kid then."

"The lawyer here says she redid it nine years ago," Eve said.

"Right about the time you stopped spending summers here," her mom observed.

"Mm-hmm," Eve said vaguely. Her parents didn't know about Sawyer. Well, they knew she'd dated him as a teenager, but nothing beyond that.

It had been Lucille's idea for Eve to start coming to Moonflower Bay, and Eve's parents had readily agreed. Child care in the summer was expensive, and Lucille was free. But as Eve had gotten older, her parents had started to grumble about how spending the whole summer with her aunt meant missing important opportunities. Like that summer she was sixteen, when she'd been admitted to a prestigious summer program but hadn't wanted to go. They'd had a huge fight, which wasn't normal for them.

Her parents were determined—dead set *determined*—that she would get the higher education they hadn't.

Eve had won that particular battle, but not before her parents had accused her of letting a boy come before her studies.

So despite the fact that they were close, she'd clammed up on the topic of Sawyer—especially since she'd been contemplating staying in Moonflower Bay for good, instead of going to university.

All this meant she had never told her parents exactly what Sawyer had meant to her. That he'd been her first love.

She'd certainly never told them that he'd been her *only* love.

Sure, she'd thought she loved the handful of crushes and boyfriends she'd had in the intervening years. But those guys had all . . . worn off.

Sawyer had not worn off.

Worse, even once he was gone, once she'd physically left, he'd retained his power over her. She had let him keep her away from Lucille, from the inn, for *ten years*. Which made her hopping mad. "Well, whenever Lucille redid her will, she clearly wanted you to have the inn," her father said. "*Have* it. Run it. She wouldn't have put that clause in otherwise."

"So just because she wanted me to uproot my life and become a small-town innkeeper, I have to do that?" Eve hated the way her voice got high and shrill when she was upset. She made a conscious effort to speak more calmly. "I have a life, Dad, and it's in Toronto. With you guys. At the library."

"I know," he said quickly. "I know." He waved a dismissive hand.

Crap. Her father so rarely had an opinion. The strong, silent type, he was usually just there in the background, being quietly supportive of both her mother and her. He let them decide pretty much everything—what to watch on movie night, when everyone should take off work for their annual family staycation.

All this was to say that on the rare occasion that Dad *did* issue an opinion, she and her mom paid attention.

Or, in cases like this, when he clearly had an opinion but was censoring himself, Eve felt duty bound to drag it out of him.

"Dad," she said softly, "tell me what you're thinking."

"Well, the will says a year, right? You can't sell it for a year."

"Right."

"And you've already established that in order to sell it at all, you'll need to get some work done."

"I'm just doing the roof. And maybe some repointing of the brick." That was it. The Realtor had come by yesterday and given her a list of improvements she thought would pay for themselves, but that was a slippery slope she wasn't going near.

"Look," her dad said. "I'm not telling you what to do, but what if you *were* to fix the place up?" He looked around the shabby kitchen. "Spend a year restoring it. It could be great again."

He...might not be wrong. She could feel herself approaching the aforementioned slope. "You mean, like hire someone to renovate? Like a contractor who can be my eyes and ears in town? I guess I could come back one or two weekends a month."

"You could," he said blandly, in a way that suggested that was not what he'd had in mind. "Or *you* could take it on as a project. A tribute to Lucille. Maybe you don't want to become an innkeeper, but if you fix it up, then when you *do* sell at the end of the year, the place will be worthy of her."

Eve looked at her mom for her thoughts. She grimaced apologetically. "She *did* take care of you for so many years." She tried to straighten the grimace into a smile but didn't quite succeed. "And maybe it would be a fun change of scenery?"

Her parents' logic was sound, but it didn't hold up against the fact that doing all this—spending a year doing what Lucille wanted, honoring her wishes, blah, blah—would have to happen *in* Moonflower Bay. Moonflower Bay was not "a fun change of scenery."

"And more pragmatically," her mother added, "won't it make that much more money if it's ready to go as a high-end inn?"

Eve tried to consider what they were suggesting separately from her *emotions* about what they were suggesting. A year *wasn't* that long, when she thought about it objectively. She could take an unpaid leave from work. It might actually work out pretty well on that end of things. Eve worked as a branch librarian, but she had her eye on a new job in the central administration, but it wasn't going to be posted for several months.

But…the money. No salary plus all the expenses Jason had laid out *plus* the cost of a renovation?

Not to mention being in the same town as Sawyer for a year.

But hadn't she just been regretting that she'd let him keep her away for so long?

Yes, she should stop doing that.

She tilted her head up. She wasn't sure what she was expecting. A sign from the universe?

A chunk of plaster fell out of the ceiling.

The little prodding of guilt that had been popping up here and there the past few days was suddenly starting to feel more like a bulldozer—a bulldozer dangerously near her slippery slope. She sighed. "Well, I guess I'll give it some thought."

When Jake showed up at Sawyer's house, he was wearing a suit.

"Wow." Sawyer raised his eyebrows. "Look at you all cleaned up."

"It's my funeral suit."

Aww. Sawyer felt like an ass. He remembered now that Jake had bought that suit for his son Jude's funeral three years ago. "Right."

"Just came from the Mermaid."

"Right."

Jake looked at him pointedly.

"I was on duty until seven." Working the shift he'd added to his schedule specifically so he'd have an excuse not to go to Lucille's funeral. Evie was here for a week, and she clearly didn't want to see him. Even though he felt terrible for not paying his respects, it seemed like the least he could do.

Jake sat next to Sawyer on the couch. "What are you watching?"

Sawyer flipped his phone over. What he was watching was a YouTube tutorial on how to build a canoe, but Jake did not need to know that. Not yet, anyway. He was pretty sure he was going to need Jake when it came down to it. Sawyer used to like noodling around building stuff when he was younger, but Jake was actually good at it. He was always fixing stuff in town or building sets for Maya's plays.

Sawyer had started the canoe that last summer Evie was in town. Since she didn't swim, he'd had the idea that maybe she could experience the lake on a boat. How much had he loved playing around in the shed in his backyard, Evie perched on a stool talking to him—or just reading a book? Doing her thing while he did his?

It had made him feel normal. Happy.

But then she'd left—then he'd sent her away—before the canoe was done.

Though it hardly mattered. The damage his father had done to it was probably irreparable.

"You ever think about starting a carpentry business?" he asked Jake, verbalizing the thought as it popped into his head.

"Why would I do that? I'm a fisherman."

"Except you hardly ever actually fish." He'd all but stopped after Jude died, after Kerrie left.

Jake stood up. Sawyer had gone too far.

You had to be careful with Jake. He had never gotten over Jude's death. Sawyer and Law had learned that trying to get Jake to do anything he didn't want to do—come out to social events, think about dating—only caused him to retreat. If you pushed too hard, Jake disappeared for a while. Didn't show up at the bar the next Friday night.

Sawyer lifted his hands in a gesture of surrender. "I was only thinking if you declared yourself in business, you could actually—call me crazy—charge people money for all the work you do around town."

Jake paused with his hand on Sawyer's front door. "I gotta go."

Okay, then. Sawyer turned his phone back over and restarted his video.

* * *

After seeing her parents off, Eve went in search of Maya, who was the closest thing she had to a friend in Moonflower Bay.

She'd been planning to do this alone, but suddenly she wanted company.

Maya lived above Jenna's General Store, she'd said. Sure enough, next to the store entrance was an unmarked door with a buzzer.

"Yep?" came a tinny voice from the intercom.

"Maya? It's Eve."

"Eve! What's up?"

"Do you want to walk down to the lake with me?"

Soon they were strolling down Main Street toward the water. Eve had been in Jenna's store a fair bit since she'd been back—in addition to souvenirs and fudge, Jenna had an espresso machine—but she hadn't really been beyond the store.

Which was why she was totally unprepared for another memory to surge up and clobber her. She physically stumbled as she spotted the fountain. But there it was, the same as ever. And there it was inside her head, too. Something that had once delighted her. "I forgot about this thing. Does it still work?"

"Sure does," Maya said.

It was a drinking fountain shaped like a giant fish—a piranha of some sort. To drink, you had to stick your head inside the fish's toothy head. She remembered tittering with nervous laughter as she and Sawyer would visit when they were little. Even though she knew it was fake, it always felt weird to subsume your whole head inside the fiberglass creature. "It seemed a lot bigger and scarier when I was a kid."

And she remembered that while Lucille would tell her to

buck up when she was scared, Sawyer's mom would always comfort her.

Sawyer's mom was fuzzy in Eve's memories, partly because she'd died when they were young, but partly because, although she knew he missed her terribly, Sawyer had never really talked about her.

Being here was like playing Whac-a-Mole with her memories. The fountain, Sawyer's mom, the Twistee Freeze, the lighthouse.

All these things she'd thought she'd forgotten. But it turned out they were still inside her somewhere. She didn't like the idea of all these memories just lying in wait, dormant. Ready to surge up and engulf her with no warning.

"What ever happened to Clara Collins?" she asked, though she had no idea why. She had just been thinking about how she didn't want to muck about in Moonflower Bay memories.

But she had always had a soft spot for Clara.

Maya raised her eyebrows. "Why do you ask?"

"No reason."

"No reason, my ass!"

"I was just thinking about how she used to like this fountain." Which was *true*. Long after Eve had gotten over her fear of the fountain, she and Sawyer had visited with Clara in tow.

"Well, she's about to start her last year of high school. She's a great kid. Super smart, but also one of those annoyingly well-rounded people. I cast her in a lot of my plays."

Eve was genuinely happy to hear it. Her newfound Sawyer-directed rage did not extend to Clara.

When they arrived at the beach, she asked, "Can we walk out on the pier?"

"Sure." When they reached the railing at the end, Maya leaned over it. "The funeral was nice."

Eve didn't answer, just got out the urn.

"Though I have to say, I'm not sure if—Holy crap! What is that?"

"Lucille."

"What?"

"She wanted to be scattered in the lake, but she didn't say how. Like, should I take her out on a boat? Should it have been part of the service?" Eve's voice cracked—it felt like something inside her was cracking, too—but she soldiered on. "Should I invite her friends?"

"Aww." Maya slung an arm around Eve's shoulder. "What do *you* think?"

"I think if she cared about details, she would have specified. She just said to cremate her and spread her ashes in the lake. I can imagine her adding, 'And don't make a big deal about it.'"

"Well, what are you waiting for, then?"

"I'm going to stay for a year and renovate the inn," she whispered, realizing she wasn't answering Maya's question at all. She had no idea why she was whispering, except that saying it out loud felt like trying to talk through a mouthful of rocks.

Maya ran with the abrupt change of subject. "Wow."

"I have no idea what I'm doing," Eve said. "How does a person with no money renovate an inn?"

"That's what YouTube is for. And we'll help you."

"Who's 'we'?"

"Me! I'm pretty handy, you know. I run that theater on a shoestring. And Jake Ramsey can build anything. And Pearl and Karl and Eiko and all Lucille's old friends. I mean, they'll want you to stay forever—God forbid anyone ever leave Matchmaker Bay, where they pull the strings—but you can exploit that. Karl owns a hardware store! That will be handy."

"*Matchmaker* Bay?" Eve asked.

"Yeah, those old folks have gotten really aggressive with their meddling, so some of us started jokingly calling the town Matchmaker Bay."

That was actually pretty funny. It didn't change her circumstances, though. "Even so, I *really* have no money— I'm taking a leave from my job. You can't renovate an inn without money. I can't do *everything* myself, even if I have a pack of meddling elders helping me."

"That's what lines of credit are for."

She did own the place free and clear—she wasn't accustomed to owning things—so she probably *could* get a loan against it.

This was all so deeply, deeply unsettling.

When she didn't say anything for a few moments, Maya said, "Okay, what else you got?"

"What do you mean?"

"Technical knowledge. Money. If we're listing roadblocks, what are the rest of them? Tell me, so I can plow them over for you." She angled her head so she could look Eve in the eye. "Unless you don't *want* me to. In which case, screw Lucille, she's about to be ashes in Lake Huron, let's get you back to Toronto." She smiled. "I would miss you, but I will totally come up with a list of roadblocks a mile long if you want me to."

Something in Maya's cheerful relentlessness—and her loyalty, despite the fact that they'd only recently gotten reacquainted—made Eve want to tell the truth. "Sawyer. Sawyer's what else I got."

"Ah." Maya nodded and, without missing a beat, said, "Okay, well, the answer there is exorcism."

"I'm sorry, what?"

"Exorcism."

Eve laughed incredulously. "As in 'Get thee behind me, Satan'?"

"*Exactly.* I mean, look. It sounds like Sawyer looms pretty large in your personal mythology. But he's just a man. Which will probably be made abundantly clear if you spend a year here. He'll turn out to be a normal, unremarkable dude. You won't be able to figure out what you ever saw in him. If you're spending a year here, semi-against your will, why not look at it as an opportunity? Redo the inn, *un*do Sawyer."

"An exorcism." Eve tried out the word. It sounded like…not a bad idea. If she could cut Sawyer down to size, maybe she could also walk around this town without water fountains and ice cream stands giving her panic attacks. She shot Maya a tentative smile. "It's just a year, right?"

"Yay! Renovation with a side of exorcism, here we come!" Maya clapped her hands. "Okay, now, are we tossing Lucille in the bay or what?"

"Not now." Eve pulled back from the railing.

"Why not?"

"I don't know. It just doesn't feel right."

Maya shrugged. "Okay. You're the boss." Eve put Lucille back in her bag, and they turned back toward town. "Hey, you know what would be really cool?" Maya exclaimed. "Murder mystery theater at the half-renovated Mermaid! Just think of the murderous possibilities! Rickety scaffolding, vats of cement, power tools." She clapped. "This is going to be the best year ever."

Chapter Six

❧

$\mathscr{A}$ week later, having filed the necessary paperwork to secure a leave from work, given notice to her landlord, and packed up Flounder—the rest of her plants were under her mother's guardianship for the coming year—Eve was on her way back to Moonflower Bay in her brand-new-to-her car, which was enough of a junker that she wasn't convinced it was going to make it.

She stopped in Grand View for groceries. Last week she had lived on snacks from Jenna's General and the food people had brought to the wake, but a girl could only eat so much casserole. If she was really doing this—*moving to Moonflower Bay for a year!*—she needed real food.

"Oh my gosh! Eve Abbott?" The checker paused with the scanner in her hand, which she'd been aiming at Eve's loyalty card for the chain, which displayed her name. "I heard you were back!"

The girl looked like she was in her late teens. She had

long, mahogany hair and...*Crap.* Eyes as blue as the bay. Maybe Eve *would* have been better off subsisting on a diet of frozen tuna noodle casserole and chicken supreme. But no, they were bound to run into each other at some point.

"Oh, I'm sorry!" the girl said. "I recognized your name, but you probably have no idea who I am."

"Clara Collins." Clara Collins all grown up. It was uncanny.

"Yes! Impressive—I was only seven when you left town. But old enough to remember how down in the dumps my brother was about it."

Uh, what? Eve opened her mouth to ask a clarifying question but was preempted by Clara's continuing speech. "That was smart on your part, though. Sawyer's a terrible boyfriend."

"I'm not sure I follow."

"He works all the time, and such odd hours, too. He can never hold on to a girlfriend."

"Has Sawyer had a lot of girlfriends?"

Not that she cared. Realizing that she was leaning forward and furrowing her brow pretty intensely, she ordered herself to adopt a posture more in line with a person who did not care about Sawyer's slate of girlfriends past.

Clara tilted her head, considering. "Not really. Two, I think? And not serious ones. Neither of them moved in with us or anything."

"Yeah, I can't imagine your dad really going for that." Not that Eve knew Charles Collins that well. She'd only met him in person a handful of times. She and Sawyer always hung out at the inn or in the town's various nooks and crannies, often with Clara in tow.

Except that time they'd been at his house at the wrong time. Why had they been there to begin with? Hanging out at Sawyer's house was not something they did.

The memory exploded in her head, making her gasp.

The canoe.

How could she have forgotten *that*?

That canoe had meant more to her, back then, than any-thing. Sawyer was making her a *boat* out of *nothing*. No one had ever done anything like that for her before.

It was like the time he carved his declaration of love into the gazebo, but *more*.

It had been set up in his backyard. That's where he worked on it—but only when his dad was at work.

He had gotten his father's schedule wrong that day.

The rest of the memory came pouring in. Charles's rage. Him swinging a garden shovel at the half-finished canoe. Running inside with Clara. Calling the police.

Icing Sawyer's black eye later in the kitchen at the Mermaid.

She had to work to slow her breath. As much as Sawyer had broken her heart—as much as she hated him—she still didn't like to think of him suffering as he had that day. As he had every day, really, even if most days hadn't ended with black eyes.

Clara didn't seem to notice her distress, though. "Oh, no, Sawyer and I haven't lived with my dad for almost ten years. Sawyer got an apartment when he enrolled in the police academy, and later he bought a house." She smiled ruefully. "It's a lot more peaceful than living under Charles's roof—or so I gather. I don't really have a lot of memories of my dad."

Eve looked at Clara again. Really looked. She seemed… healthy. But what did that mean? She would be seventeen. All seventeen-year-olds looked healthy. "So you're headed into your last year of high school?"

"Yep."

"You know what you want to do after that?"

"I want to go to the University of Toronto and major in some kind of engineering—either computer or electrical."

"Wow. That's really..." *Specific.* "...impressive."

"I mean, if I get in." One of Clara's shoulders lifted and fell, but it seemed like she was performing a shrug more than she was actually shrugging.

"That's false modesty, isn't it?"

She grinned. "Totally. I have a 4.0 GPA, and I'm super into science. And science policy. And acting. Do you know Maya Mehta?"

"I do!" That might have come out a little too vehemently, but now that she was going to be in town for a year, she was glad she had a friend.

"Maya cast me as the lead in the fall play," Clara said.

"What's it going to be this year?" Eve thought back to her time as Puritan Number Four.

"*Medea.*"

"As in Greek tragedy Medea who murders her children in cold blood to get back at her cheating husband?"

"That's the one!"

"I see Maya hasn't lost her penchant for light, crowd-pleasing drama."

"You should come! But I guess you'll be gone by then. I heard you're selling the inn?"

"I am, but not for a year. I'm going to do a pretty major reno before I put it on the market, so I'm going to..." The words hovered in her throat. It felt big, to actually say them to someone other than Maya. It would make it that much more real.

And as long as it *wasn't* real, she could still take her rust bucket of a car and turn around and go home.

But no. She was here for a reason. She was here to honor Lucille's wishes.

And for an exorcism. Of this lovely young woman's brother, in fact. She cleared her throat. "I'm going to stay for a year."

"Oh, wow! That's fantastic!" Clara looked genuinely thrilled. Then, her eyebrows traveling almost all the way to her hairline, she looked even more thrilled, though Eve would have thought that impossible. "So you can come to the play!"

"I can." She found she was looking forward to it, infanticide and all. She wanted to see Clara as Medea. She wanted to support Maya. Maybe there was a role for her as Greek Citizen Number Four—okay, no, she wasn't going that far.

But look at her. Day one and was she sort of... integrating herself?

Maybe Lucille was right. Maybe life *was* a little bit twisty.

Sawyer was at the hardware store when Clara texted him. Eve Abbott came into the store earlier this morning, and she's staying in town for a year! Also, Lucille's funeral was last weekend?! How did we miss that? We should have been there—I felt like a huge jerk.

"You okay, Chief?" He looked up to find Olivia frowning at him.

Olivia was coming off duty, and he was going on. They often met at Lakeside Hardware for the changeover. It was a good spot to shoot the breeze for a while and tap into the town gossip network.

The answer to Olivia's question was no. He was not okay. What had happened to getting the roof fixed and selling the Mermaid? Followed, presumably, by getting the hell out of town?

He unclenched his jaw. "Yep. Fine."

Olivia wasn't buying it, judging by her lingering look.

He ordered himself to be cool, but heat traveled up his neck.

"Where's everyone else?" he asked by way of diversion. There was a hardcore group of four town elders who congregated at the store every morning for coffee. They all owned or were retired from local businesses and had been sharing coffee and conversation every morning for as long as Sawyer could remember. But only two were in attendance this morning—Karl, the proprietor of Lakeside Hardware, and Pearl, who got up early to get the baking started at Pie with Pearl, then stopped in at Lakeside after handing things off to an employee.

"Eiko's out looking at a crop circle near Hensall."

Eiko Anzai owned the *Moonflower Bay Monitor*, and though she was constantly professing a desire to retire and hand the newspaper off to a new editor, she was often out chasing down the news—or, when there wasn't any, inventing it.

"It's just kids pulling a prank," Sawyer said. "The Ontario Provincial Police looked into it last week." Not that facts would stop Eiko from putting it on the front page.

"And Art is checking in on Carol Dyson," Pearl said, accounting for Art Ramsey, the other missing member of their quartet.

Right. Carol had just had hip surgery. He made a mental note to check in with her daughter, who cut hair at Curl Up and Dye, the beauty salon Carol owned, to see if she needed anything.

"I brought her a lemon meringue yesterday," Pearl said.

Olivia, who had been listening silently to the conversation, took a step back, judging—correctly—that the chatter was ramping up and that she'd better escape while she could. When she reached the car door, she raised one hand in a sign-off salute to Sawyer. He nodded, relieved. Not that he wanted to get rid of her per se, but his immediate aim was to try to figure out how the hell he was going to survive this coming year.

"Carol says the recovery is steady but slower than it was with her other hip." Pearl blew out a breath. "Getting old sucks."

"It's better than getting dead," Karl said.

"Hear, hear." Pearl lifted her coffee mug and clinked it against Karl's. "Speaking of getting dead, I saw Eve Abbott driving into town on my way over. She has a sporty little red car, but it looks like it's about to fall apart."

A spike of panic pierced Sawyer's gut. "How do you get from 'getting dead' to Eve Abbott?" He forced his voice to be calm. Surely if something had actually happened to Evie between when his sister saw her and now, Pearl would have led with that.

"Because Eve Abbott is here because Lucille Abbott is dead," Pearl said with her characteristic forthrightness.

Of course. The core circle of four here used to be a circle of five—Lucille had been the first of them to pass away.

The chimes on the door jingled, and Art Ramsey joined them in the patio furniture display the group always occupied for their morning chats. Accepting a mug of coffee from Karl, he said, "I need a screw."

"Really?" Karl said. "I thought you were doing okay in that department."

Pearl snorted, and Sawyer chuckled.

Ignoring the ribbing, Art produced an old, rusty screw from his pocket. "This one is stripped. And it's kind of a weird size, I think?"

Karl took it from him, put on his reading glasses, and examined it. "This is a brass screw."

"Yeah, but the replacement doesn't need to be brass."

"This is from your bed, isn't it?" Karl peered at Art over the top of his glasses. "You have a brass bed."

"You and Jamila broke your bed! Ha!" Pearl pointed at Art and in the process sloshed some of her coffee over the edge of her cup. "Shoot! Look at that. You get laid; I get stained." Pearl was a younger-than-her-years widow, and she was perpetually on the prowl.

"I told you I can set you up with—"

Pearl cut off Karl's attempt at matchmaking. "And I told *you* I'll never date anyone in this town." She stood, blotted her blouse, and *tsk*ed. "And to think, I did blueberry pies this morning and managed to come out of *that* clean."

"We need to talk about the Anti-Festival," Art said.

"You're just trying to distract us from the fact that you and Jamila literally broke your bed," Pearl teased.

"Possibly." Art suppressed a smile. "But has anyone considered that if the Mermaid doesn't reopen by then, we need to find a new venue for the town sleepover?"

"Oh, crap!" Pearl exclaimed. "I hadn't thought of that!"

"Well," Art said, "I *just* heard on my way in that Eve Abbott *isn't* selling the place. At least not right away. She's going to stick around and renovate it."

Pearl whipped her head up from where she was still working on the stain on her blouse. "Oh my God, Lucille actually did it!"

The three of them shared a conspiratorial look that Sawyer couldn't quite decode.

"Let's go." Karl stuck his head around the corner of an aisle to shout at an employee—the employee who actually ran the store while Karl ran the gossip network. "I'm going out for a few minutes!"

They reminded him of a smaller, slower, more geriatric version of *Ocean's 11*.

Which probably meant he should follow them.

Eve was swarmed—there was really no other word for it—by elderly people as she unloaded her car behind the inn. Karl Andersen, Art Ramsey, and Pearl Brunetta appeared out of nowhere, and they were all talking a mile a minute. Something about a...sleepover?

"I'm sorry, what?" She shifted her grocery bags to one arm so she could fish the inn keys out of her purse.

"Sawyer," Pearl said, "take her bags."

Sawyer? What? She looked around, and there he was, leaning against the edge of the inn's deck watching the scene with amusement.

But Pearl's command made him snap to attention. "Yes, ma'am." He was by Eve's side in two seconds, trying to pull the bags out of her grasp. She resisted—she didn't want Sawyer carrying her stuff—which resulted in a tug-of-war.

"Give him the bags," Pearl ordered.

Pearl had a way of making people do what she wanted—she always had. Underneath all that pastry flour was a spine of steel.

And what she was currently trying to do was get Eve to agree to participate in something called the "Auntie Festival" that was scheduled for the first weekend in October? And they seemed to need the inn for a town sleepover?

Town. Sleepover. What was this? Had she teleported into an episode of *Gilmore Girls*? Or maybe *The Twilight Zone*?

"Everyone sleeps at the inn? How would that even work?" There were only ten rooms—eleven if you counted the Pink Room of Pain.

She wasn't doing it. And she wasn't giving Sawyer her bags. They'd paused their tug-of-war while she spoke to Pearl, but with a swift, sharp tug, she succeeded in wrenching them from his grasp.

"Well, not everyone," Art said. "It tends to be younger folks. Last year, Lucille designated the main floor for teenagers—and tucked the adults away in the upper rooms."

"So you're saying my aunt turned the upper floors of this place into hookup central?"

"That is not at *all* what he's saying." Pearl sniffed like she was offended. "People bring sleeping bags." But then she grinned. "Though that *is* an interesting idea."

"I keep *telling* you that Dennis Bates is ready and waiting for me to fix you two up," Art said.

"The *only* reason to date Dennis Bates is that I might be able to sit in the bridge and have my revenge on people I don't like by raising it when they drive up."

Eve had to laugh at that. Dennis Bates, she remembered, operated the little lift bridge that traversed the river near where it emptied into the bay. There was a marina a ways up the river, and when taller boats came and went, the bridge had to be raised.

"However," Pearl continued, "as tempting as that is, it would require me to actually date Dennis Bates, so that's a hard no."

"If you would just—"

"Right, so." Eve got the sense that this argument might go on for a while, so she interrupted them. She needed to get her stuff into the inn—and herself off the hook for this weird sleepover thing. Not to mention away from Sawyer. She eyed him. He was looking at her with a weird, intense expression. "I have some news."

That got their attention, which, even though it had been

her aim, suddenly felt a little disconcerting. As at the grocery store, it had been hard to say the words. Every time she said them, she made it a little more real. And this time Sawyer was present to hear them.

She took a deep breath. They were going to be so surprised. "I've decided to stay in town for a year. I'm going to renovate the Mermaid."

"We know, dear," the woman said. "That's why we're here. If you're staying, you'll be here for the Auntie Festival."

"Wait. What?" How could they know?

Sawyer chuckled. "News travels fast here."

Soon they were all talking a mile a minute at her about the renovations. Where would they be in a month? Could she pause them for the festival? Was she going to have guests in during the reno or close entirely?

"The thing is…" Eve said, trying to get their attention. It didn't work.

She had Sawyer's attention, though. He hadn't stopped looking at her the whole time, in fact. "Let the lady speak," he barked, peevishly enough that it shut everybody up.

"Right, so." She shifted in place, feeling like she was back in school, giving a presentation to a not-very-friendly audience. "I have no idea what state the inn will be in by the first weekend of October." As if that were her only objection to the idea of throwing open the doors of the Mermaid and literally inviting the entire town to spend the night. That still made no sense. "So I don't think I can commit to this."

There was a brief moment of silence, but she could *feel* them regrouping.

"Sawyer."

The greeting came from someone else, someone farther

away, and it wasn't very loud. But it was enough to make Sawyer whip his head in its direction.

Just as on that terrible day, her instinctive reaction as Charles Collins approached was to shrink back. Sawyer noticed and moved to stand between her and him. Which, if she thought about it with her rational mind, made no sense. Charles wouldn't actually harm her. She hadn't even really thought he would that day ten years ago. No, he had reserved that treatment for Sawyer.

Charles looked the worse for wear. He was like a faded version of Sawyer. Instead of Sawyer's thick, dark-brown hair, Charles's was a lighter brown shot through with silver. Instead of deep lake blue, his eyes were milky baby blue. But it went beyond that. Eve had only ever witnessed one of his physical rages back in the day, but it had been enough to strike the fear of God into her. Now, though, Charles seemed diminished. Defanged. Almost...sad?

"I got Clara a birthday present," he said.

Sawyer didn't say anything. He just stood there, waves of unease radiating off him. Clara had said that she and Sawyer hadn't lived with their father for almost ten years. It was abundantly clear, though, that Charles had not lost his power over his son.

"I was hoping to give it to her next month." He took a step closer to them, and Sawyer tensed even more. It was like he was braced for battle but confused at the same time. She was seized with the desire to move in front of him, to protect *him*, but that was absurd. That would be ineffective—and there was the part where she was *mad* at him.

She looked at the older folks for a cue. Pearl was making small, jerky pointing motions at Karl, like she wanted him to do something, but Karl seemed as frozen as Sawyer.

Well, damn. She was mad at Sawyer, but she didn't want him to suffer.

Well, she did kind of want him to suffer, but not like *this*.

So she took that step out from behind Sawyer—or tried to. He stuck out an arm to block her. She hooked her bags over his wrist. "Are you taking my stuff inside, or aren't you?" He glanced at her, the spell broken. "I need help with Flounder, too."

Sawyer set Evie's plant on the floor of the kitchen and her groceries on a counter. He hated this feeling. It was like he was a teenager again, cowering before his father. Even more than that, he hated that she'd seen it.

But he *wasn't* a teenager anymore. And one of the things that differentiated boys from men was that men took responsibility for things. Men had manners. So he turned and said, "Thank you."

She looked up from unpacking her groceries. "For what?" Her eyes were the same explosion of color he remembered. He supposed they were technically hazel, but that didn't seem like a strong enough word. They were made up of little shards of every color eyes could be.

But they were expressionless, which unsettled the hell out of him. He cleared his throat. "For rescuing me out there."

She made a dismissive gesture. "It was too hot out there. Flounder needed to come inside." She leaned over and fluffed the leaves of the potted tree.

"Isn't that a tropical plant of some sort? Isn't heat its natural environment?"

She made a show of rolling her eyes. Which was at least better than the blankness from a moment ago.

"What?" he asked.

"I was *trying* to not call attention to the fact that I manufactured an excuse to get you to come inside with me, but you're either too upstanding or too stupid to run with it."

Oh. He didn't know if she was complimenting him—he could handle being called upstanding—or razzing him. She *did* tend to make him feel stupid. Either way, he was here, and this was his chance to apologize.

"Evie." She shot him a withering look. He kept forgetting. "*Eve.* I wanted to tell you how sorry—"

"*Anyway,*" she practically shouted as she cut him off. "Flounder is a cat palm. He's tender. He doesn't like change."

Dammit. He really, really wanted to apologize, but not if it meant talking over her. He sighed and went over to examine the plant, trying to think how to regroup. "Cat palm? Did you make that up, or is it a real variety of palm?"

"Real variety of palm."

"And you named yours Flounder." Flounder was a fish who was Ariel's best friend in the movie *The Little Mermaid*.

"I tried to get an actual cat, but it turned out I was super allergic. I had to give it back. So I got this instead."

That was so her. Despite his unease, he smiled.

At a tree. Named Flounder. A cat tree named after a fictional fish.

He had lost control of himself. This was not how the chief of police acted. "So, a year? You're staying a year?" He wasn't sure if he wanted her to confirm the rumor or deny it.

"Lucille had a clause in her will saying I couldn't sell this place for a year."

So she wasn't staying because she wanted to. She was staying under duress.

Of course she was. Why else would she stay?

But it seemed like a surprise move by Lucille. He had talked a fair bit with her toward the end of her life. He would stop in to check on her, like he did with most of the single old folks in town. She'd never said anything about leaving the inn to Evie, much less this one-year thing. But that must have been what Pearl meant when she referred to Lucille as having "done it." The question was... "Why?"

"I have no idea. I was talking to Maya about how, if this was a movie, there would be a letter along with the will. You know, 'If you're reading this, I'm gone. Now let me outline all the ways I'm going to eff up your life.'"

He was seized with a kind of sadness that she regarded a year in Moonflower Bay as "effing up her life," but why shouldn't she? She no doubt already had a full life in Toronto. "No letter?"

"Nope. So I have no idea why she did this to me."

"This town isn't so bad," he said weakly.

She ignored him in favor of rummaging in one of her grocery bags. "Anyway, it will go fast." She produced a calendar. It was the iconic milk-themed one that Canada's dairy farming association produced every year—they gave them out at grocery stores. She flipped it open to August. There were a bunch of black X's through two weeks' worth of dates. "I'm crossing off the days since Lucille died." She pointed to the picture and recipe at the top of that month's page. "And look! I can also learn how to make three-cheese scalloped potatoes!" Her voice was high and infused with artificial enthusiasm. He was pretty sure she was talking to herself and not him.

"I had nothing but respect for Lucille," he said quietly, "but if you sell the place, she'll never know."

"But I'll know."

"Right. Of course."

Her shoulders slumped, but just for a moment before she rolled them back and straightened her spine. "Sawyer?"

"Yes?" Was she maybe not so angry at him anymore? She'd done him a good turn, and that had been followed by a full minute or so of conversation that had not involved yelling.

"Why are you still here? Rescue complete. Now get out."

Ah. No such luck.

Chapter Seven

❦

*E*ve sucked in a breath as she stepped onto the beach at Paradise Cove and eyeballed the Ramsey cottage, which sat at the far end of the inlet. She wasn't sure if she was breathless from the trek in or because of what was about to happen.

You had to know Paradise Cove was there to find it—it could be reached only on foot, and you had to scramble over and around a rocky outcropping to reach it—and the townspeople kept its existence to themselves. The beach here was technically private property, but back in the day, at least, Mr. and Mrs. Ramsey had been fine with townspeople intrepid enough to make the trek in using it.

She was counting on that still being the case. She eyed the dark cottage. As far as she remembered, the Ramseys kept a house in town and used the cottage as a retreat of sorts, and as an art studio for Jake's mom. She had no idea if anyone occupied it these days, since Jake's mom's death.

Regardless, she was glad no one was around today. She did not need an audience.

She dropped her bag on the sand, slipped off her sandals, and turned to face her beautiful, watery nemesis.

She took a deep breath. She could do this. Moonflower Bay faced west, so sunrises weren't spectacular like sunsets were, and this little cove was extra sheltered from the morning sun. But there was a different kind of beauty here, a subtler one. The sky was just beginning to lighten, black giving way to a diffuse blue. Mist swirled on the surface of the lake, and waves lapped the sand gently. The rocky wall behind them—the limestone that formed the cove—created a sense of coziness.

All right. All she had to do today was wade in. Get her feet wet—literally *and* metaphorically. The beach around here was pebbled at the water's edge. As you approached the lake, at a certain point the sand would start to give way to tiny rocks that hurt your feet. She knew this pain. It was a good pain. You had to walk over the rocks to get to the sand again, which reappeared once you were about knee deep in the water.

She stopped walking when she hit the second band of sand. The water was up to her knees. Even though wading had never been a problem for her—her brain classified wading as fundamentally different from swimming—her heart was clipping along at a pretty good pace. It was partly because she knew this was her last day of just wading.

But it was partly because of the wrenching surprise of yet another revelation. Another of the sucker punches this town kept walloping her with. But this one was bigger than the fountain or the lighthouse or the canoe. This was the lake itself. The blue lake that was so big it might as well have been an ocean.

She *loved* this lake, even if she was afraid of swimming in it.

And she loved the little town on the shores of this mighty lake.

This place had made her.

She always told people she was "from" Toronto, and it was true in the sense that she'd been born there and had attended school there. But the summers she'd spent in Moonflower Bay with Lucille had had an out-of-proportion impact on her.

The epiphany brought tears to her eyes. It filled her chest with regret, regret for all the years she'd pretended she was done with this place. That it didn't matter to her. That she could just ignore it and carry on with her life. Why hadn't she summoned some of the anger that seemed to be coming so easily now and had it out with Sawyer? Gotten to a place where she could coexist with him in the same town?

Regret and love and fear swirled together, creating what felt like a riptide inside her that was so strong she doubled over.

"Eve?"

She stood so fast from her crouch that she felt like a marionette.

"Are you okay?"

It was Jake. Who, judging by the footprints behind him, had just come from the cottage.

"Yes! Yes, I'm fine. I'm sorry. I shouldn't be here." She swiped at her eyes and started walking back toward the shore.

He held up a hand. "Don't mind me. I'm on my way out."

"But it's your beach."

"You're always welcome here."

What a curious thing to say, given that he hardly knew

her. He was a year older than Sawyer, and by the time she left Moonflower Bay, he'd been working on his dad's boat. He'd had an apartment he shared with his girlfriend Kerrie. She had thought of him as an adult. "That's really nice of you, but I don't want to disturb you or your family."

"Dad and Jamila live in town full-time now, and my brother moved to Alberta. And I'm on my way out, so you're not disturbing me."

"What about Kerrie?" She glanced at the cottage. "Will she mind?"

"Kerrie's not around anymore."

"Oh, I'm..." She'd been going to say she was sorry, but she wasn't really sure, given the way he had phrased it, if he meant they had broken up. And if they had, whether *sorry* was the correct response.

So she ended up standing there awkwardly. There had been a few instances like this, when she was hit with some knowledge from the decade she'd been away—like when she'd found out about Jake's mom's death, actually—and ended up feeling like a jerk. She was missing a lot of knowledge. She finally settled on, "So you're out here by yourself now?"

"Yep. Took the plunge and moved out here full-time."

"I came out here because..." *I'm trying to teach myself to swim because I made a moonflower wish but it wasn't really a wish; it was more like a vow.* "I wanted to be by myself. It's the parade today, and..." *They're setting up on Main Street and I can't bear to be around anything to do with that stupid parade.*

"This town can be a lot," he said.

Exactly. He understood. Jake didn't talk much, but he had perfectly summarized her swirling thoughts. Hmm.

Was it possible Jake was a low-key guru, full of wisdom? She decided to test him with a little bit of truth. "It turns out even though I thought I hated this town, I'm also sort of…remembering what I always liked about it." *What I* loved *about it.*

"This place'll get under your skin."

"You going to the parade later?" she asked.

He smiled—a little sadly, she thought. "Nope. Going out on the boat."

"Good fishing."

"Not that boat." He pointed at a canoe stored on a rack next to the cottage.

"Oh." She started to walk in toward the shore. "Well, I should get back."

"Stay," he ordered as he turned back toward the house. "And come back anytime."

"All right, so what we have going for us is that it's not a full moon."

"Amen to that." Olivia held up her coffee cup.

They were at the station, and Sawyer was briefing everyone on the day ahead. The Saturday of the long Labor Day weekend was by far the craziest day of the year in Moonflower Bay.

Also the anniversary of the worst day of his life.

"Hear, hear." This came from Joel Pinter. Dominic Keyes raised his coffee cup. Dom and Joel made up the balance of "everyone" on their four-person force.

"And with the Mermaid Inn closed, we'll have fewer overnight guests than usual," Sawyer said.

"But if they're staying outside of town, we'll have a lot of drunks getting in their cars," Patty, their dispatcher, pointed out.

"True." Other than the Mermaid, and the handful of residents who Airbnb-ed their places, there was one motel on the edge of town. Beyond that was a strip of chain hotels out on the highway. "So let's keep our wits about us."

Two hours later, unable to heed his own advice, Sawyer almost crashed into the high school marching band while they were performing a lurching version of "Under the Sea," because he had caught sight of Evie standing up ahead along the parade route.

"Chief!" Olivia shouted.

"Sorry, sorry." He hit the brakes and slowed to a stop while the majorettes did their thing. It felt like the batons they threw high into the air were hurtling through his intestines.

Sawyer always drove a squad car in the Mermaid Parade. Olivia was riding shotgun, it being her first year on the force, and Joel and Dom were patrolling on foot. He'd thought about having Olivia drive today, as part of his quest to bolster her credibility in the eyes of the townspeople—and in Dom's eyes, frankly, because he was being a dick about being passed over for deputy chief. But he *always* drove in the Mermaid Parade. He was the chief. It was tradition.

In truth, though, he made sure to be *in* the parade so he didn't have to *watch* the parade.

He had bad associations with this parade and, this year even more than most, no desire to be here at all.

And now he was stopped twenty feet from Evie.

He tried not to look, but it was like his eyeballs were made of metal, and she was made of magnets. She was as pretty as always. She was wearing a sundress, and her hair was piled high on her head in some kind of updo that looked so precarious it kind of made him uneasy. He didn't like the in-between-ness of it. It was done up but about to fall down. He missed the tidy braid of her youth. He wanted—

"Chief?"

He swung his attention to Olivia. She was pointing in front of them. The band had moved on, and there was a noticeable gap between it and them. Right. He hit the gas a little too hard—what was the *matter* with him?— and Olivia inhaled sharply as the car vroomed forward. He got himself back into the snail's pace required by the parade.

There was going to be no avoiding Evie. No avoiding the fact that this wasn't the first time he'd been in the Mermaid Parade and Evie had been on the sidelines. Except that time, he'd been *trying* to be seen. Performing a very public betrayal. Today, by contrast, he would like nothing more than for a sinkhole to open up and swallow him whole.

As they drew closer, he could see that all the beauty he'd been admiring from farther back contrasted with her demeanor. Should he take comfort in the fact that she didn't look like she wanted to be here any more than he did? Her lips were pursed, and she was looking off to the side, like although her body was in attendance, she was determined her mind would be somewhere else. Probably lost in one of her fairy tales.

They were closing in on her. His body—his entire being—was seized with an overwhelming desire to flee. He glanced behind him. They were being followed by the big marquee float, the one transporting this year's mer-king and mer-queen. The king was Karl Andersen, as always. Everyone always voted for Karl since the whole parade had been his idea twenty years ago. The queen changed from year to year. It was usually a high school girl, the contest functioning almost like an extracurricular homecoming queen competition. But this year the queen—the reluctant queen—

was Maya. She was sitting on her clamshell throne rolling her eyes, with her signature Converse high-tops clearly visible beneath her tail. As part of their ongoing war, Law had masterminded a write-in campaign to get her elected to the coveted post, purely because he knew it would annoy her. Though Maya normally did not shy away from the spotlight, she hated anything that smacked of "letting Law win," whatever that meant.

Sawyer swung his attention back to the band. The majorettes were dressed as mermaids, too, and they twirled batons made to look like tridents.

Even if he could manufacture some excuse to get out of here, it was physically impossible until they got to the next cross street. He was stuck in a gaggle of crazy people dressed as mermaids.

Under other circumstances he might have found it comical. Instead of getting the hell out of Dodge, he had no choice but to inch along at two miles an hour in a squad car decorated with mermaid decals and blue and green balloons. The world's least macho getaway car.

Maybe she wouldn't notice him, despite the fact that he looked like he was driving the Barbie Dream Car: Mermaid Edition. She always could get lost in a daydream. She'd be lying on the beach and you'd say, "A penny for your thoughts," and she'd say, "I was just thinking about if there was any chance my Hogwarts letter got delayed and it might come on my twelfth birthday?"

But no. She'd seen him. As they rolled past, Evie looked at him like she thought he was the devil.

And, really, in her story, he kind of was.

"Hey, can I ask you a question? What is this Auntie Festival everyone keeps talking about?"

Eve had made it to the end of parade day. She and Maya were sitting on a sofa in the parlor at the Mermaid watching *The Exorcist* on Maya's computer. "Homework," Maya had said.

"I don't remember that festival," Eve went on. "I swear, this town has gone festival mad. But you couldn't come up with anything better than aunts? And why not uncles, too?"

Maya laughed. "Anti-Festival. *A-N-T-I.*"

Huh? "Because *that* makes so much more sense? What, are you celebrating your collective orneriness?"

"Mmm." Maya studied the screen. "Father Damien is kind of hot, in a shaggy 1970s way, don't you think?"

"I don't know. If he's hot, I think it has more to do with the forbidden priest thing."

"Collective orneriness is not so far off the mark," Maya said, returning to the festival conversation. "The Anti-Festival started as a joke a few years ago. The marquee events—the parade and the Raspberry Festival—have gotten *really* big. And the moonflower thing, too. All this stuff used to be kind of homespun and local, but it's really taken off. Which is great—God knows I need tourists to come to my shows. But it can get old. At some point, someone— probably Pearl—said, 'I wish all these tourists would go away.' The grumbling somehow turned into a town party— just for locals—the first weekend of October."

"That's the point at which the seasonal businesses shut down."

"Yeah." Maya returned her attention to the movie. "Do you think all these effects seemed super cutting edge at the time? I feel like I could make stage vomit at least that convincing on my tiny budget." She shrugged and reverted to their parallel conversation. "The festival happens out back behind the businesses on the north side of Main.

There's some fund-raising stuff, but it's strictly for town causes—the library, the food bank. But also—and beware the meddling matchmakers here—a bachelor auction."

"That all sounds kind of painfully cute. You'd better hope no tourists catch wind of it, or you're going to end up accidentally creating a real fall festival."

"I think everyone is pretty invested in keeping it on the down low. I have to say, auction aside, it's actually a good time."

"But Pearl is all over me to open the inn for a town sleepover? Isn't that a little weird?"

"It's a lot weird," Maya agreed cheerfully. "That part came about a couple years ago because Lucille didn't want anyone drinking and driving, so she offered free rooms. So many people took her up on it that it became a group sleepover. Who knows with this town? You do something twice, and suddenly it's a tradition, cast into stone tablets as town lore. If you don't want to do it, just tell—"

Thunk.

Something crashed against the front window.

"Now *that* is a special effect," Maya said.

Thunk.

"What *is* that?" Maya asked.

"Whatever it is, it's about to break my windows." Eve got up to have a look.

"Which is why perhaps you should consider moving *away* from the windows," Maya said.

"I can't just let people break my inn."

"*Your* inn? Aww. Look how fast that happened!"

Eve didn't respond, because she'd opened the curtains to reveal a pair of men fighting. Like, *fighting*. The kind of fighting you saw in movie versions of bar brawls.

She shrieked and recoiled as one jammed his head into

the other's stomach. The force propelled them both against the Mermaid.

Maya joined her at the window. "Oh my God."

"Right? We should call—"

Someone screamed. A woman had appeared on the scene, and she was yelling at the men. It was hard to tell if she was egging them on or exhorting them to stop.

"Where's my phone?" Eve looked around the room. "We have to call the police."

"No we don't," Maya said. "Because here comes your prince of darkness."

"He's not my prince of *anything*. He's..."

Eve had never had a thing for men in uniform. Historically.

Of course, she had *also* never had a thing for beards. Historically.

But...*something* was happening to her as Sawyer strode up to the fight and shouted, "Police! Break it up!"

Tingly things were happening.

"It's just like on TV!" Maya opened the window an inch so they could hear better.

Sawyer's announcement didn't seem to have had any impact on the fight. Now that the window was open, the sickening thwack of flesh on flesh carried into the inn. Eve felt a flicker of fear. What if they *did* break a window? What if they broke each other?

What if they broke Sawyer?

But by the time she had finished thinking these thoughts, he was...handling it. He waded right in and grabbed one of the guys and moved him to one side.

"Oh *my*," Maya said.

"Clara!" Sawyer said urgently, looking over his shoulder—presumably at his sister, but she was out of Eve's visual range. "Go home."

"Jesus Christ, Sawyer, you think I'm a threat to my own daughter?" one of the men snapped.

Oh God. It was Charles Collins—she hadn't even registered that because his back had been to her.

Without stopping to think, she raced to the door and flung it open. "Clara!" She motioned to the girl, who was standing partway down the block, to come inside.

Sawyer glanced at her, then back at Clara. "Go inside." His voice was low and, on the surface of things, controlled. But Eve heard the urgency in it.

He returned his attention to her. "Evie. *Eve.*" Ah, crap, she felt terrible that he was stopping to correct himself in a situation like this. "Call the station. I need another officer here. If you don't get through for some reason, call 911."

She nodded and held his gaze for a moment. She knew, somehow, that he was remembering the same thing she was. That summer day in the backyard of his house, working on the canoe. Charles appearing seemingly out of nowhere, drunk and ranting about his late wife, yelling about little Clara having killed her.

No-longer-little Clara jogged over, eyes wide and cheeks pink. Eve stepped partway out the door and extended an arm to shield her the last little way. Which was dumb, because it wasn't like her arm was going to do anything if Charles became violent. If anyone was going to be doing any shielding, it was the man with the badge and gun.

She closed the door behind Clara, who crumpled forward. Eve caught her. She was shaking.

"Oh, sweetie." Eve turned the catch into a proper hug.

It was a familiar hug, even though Clara was all grown up. The way she burrowed her head under Eve's chin was *exactly* the same. As a girl, Clara had been easy with her affections, which, from the vantage point of adulthood,

Eve found rather remarkable. She'd had no mother—and effectively no father. But when she skinned her knee, she'd run to Sawyer or to Eve in search of comfort. The sharpness, the *suddenness*, of the memories had a lump rising in Eve's throat.

"I'm calling the station," Maya said quietly.

"I hate it when this happens," Clara whispered.

Eve led her to the sofa. "Does it happen a lot?"

"No. I've never seen him get violent like that."

"He hasn't threatened you or anything?" Eve wasn't sure why she was getting involved. This was not her business anymore.

"He sometimes shows up where I am and kind of…tries to patch things up. But Sawyer tells me not to be alone with him, so I always sort of freak out when I see him. But I don't think he would actually hurt me."

Eve wasn't so sure about that. "He did hurt Sawyer. You know that, right?"

Clara's eyes widened even more. "No. I mean, I get that he has an anger problem. And an alcohol problem. But I didn't know that. What happened?"

She shouldn't have said anything. It wasn't her place to tell Clara the story if Sawyer hadn't.

Maya must have picked up on Eve's discomfort. "Olivia and Dom are on the way." She smiled at Clara, who was still standing, and patted the spot next to her on the sofa. "Come on. We're watching *The Exorcist*."

"You're watching what?"

"*The Exorcist*?"

Clara sat and squinted at the screen.

"Classic American horror movie in which a girl gets possessed by a demon—as one does. And her mother and a bunch of priests try to exorcise it—as one does."

Clara still looked confused.

"You know, the one where her head spins around—"

Eve closed the computer just as the girl on the screen started vomiting and levitating.

"Right." Maya got up and examined the DVD collection Lucille kept on top of the old TV in the room. "*Splash*! Let's watch *Splash*."

"I don't think I know that one, either," Clara said.

"Classic rom-com about a mermaid who rescues a man, and then many years later he rescues her?" Suddenly Maya cocked her head and squinted at Eve like she was trying to figure something out.

An hour later Sawyer arrived to pick up Clara. Eve stopped the movie and let him in. His eyes went right to his sister. "You okay?"

Clara popped up from the sofa. "I'm fine. You?"

"Yeah, yeah. We broke it up easily. Just took some time to sort it out. The woman was high on meth, and it turned out she's manufacturing it over in Grand View."

Eve sucked in a breath. She hadn't meant to sound shocked, or disapproving. It was just that meth was something she had, until now, only read about in newspapers.

Sawyer glanced at her, and must have gleaned her meaning. "Welcome to small-town Ontario."

"Is Dad on drugs, Sawyer?" Clara asked quietly.

"I don't think so. At least not tonight. It actually sounds like the woman and her boyfriend started it."

"Do you think—"

He held up a hand. "Let's talk about this at home."

"Right." Clara darted a glance at Eve and Maya—it was as if she'd forgotten that she and Sawyer had an audience—and her face turned pink. "It's so embarrassing," she muttered as she moved toward Sawyer. He pulled her into a hug.

She had probably meant the observation for her brother's ears only, but Eve heard, and her heart broke a little. Clara seemed mature beyond her age—Eve supposed you had to be when you didn't have functional parents—but she was still a teenager.

After a few moments, Sawyer pulled away from his sister and made eye contact with Eve. He looked at her really intensely and said, quietly, "Thank you, Eve."

He got the name right this time. That was...good. That was what she wanted. Right?

"No problem," she croaked.

"We'll get out of your hair." Sawyer slung an arm over his sister's shoulder. His biceps were too big, objectively speaking, for the sleeves of his shirt.

And...she was getting the tinglies over that uniform. *Dammit.*

"Come on, Clare Bear."

Eve stifled a sigh as she saw them out. So, okay. Maybe she was going to have to do a little exorcism on her wayward tinglies, too.

"Why don't we ever talk about Dad?"

Sawyer had said they would talk at home, but clearly Clara didn't want to wait that long. "We talk about Dad."

"No, we don't," she said firmly. "You tell me to stay away from him. You freak out if he comes within a mile radius. I get that he was a bad dude. I mean, I *guess.*"

He tightened his grip on the steering wheel. "He *was* a bad dude."

"So you say."

"Clara." Her name came out like a warning.

Which she ignored. "We talk about Mom. We have that picture of her on the mantel. But we never talk about him.

It's like I have a dead mother and a hole where there's supposed to be a father."

He didn't mean to wince. At least not outwardly. But did that ever sting.

"Oh, Sawyer, I'm sorry. That's not what I meant."

He glanced at her as they rolled to a stop at a stop sign. Her eyes were filling with tears. "It's okay." And, really, she wasn't wrong. When it came to their father, his approach had always been to stonewall. Keep him away from her. And she was right in that when that didn't work—like that time he'd shown up at her store drunk—Sawyer tended to lose his goddamn mind. When he actually thought about it with his higher intelligence and not his animalistic brain, he could admit that maybe that wasn't the best way to handle things anymore. Clara was almost grown up.

He could still remember feeding her at night when she was a baby. Pearl, Eiko, Lucille, and Carol Dyson had taught him how after Mom died. They'd known, somehow, that in all the ways that mattered, Clara was going to belong to Sawyer rather than to Charles, and so they'd shown him what to do. They'd rotated through when Charles was on nights at the packaging plant—back then he'd still been nominally employed. And once things had stabilized a bit, the whole town had pitched in. Fish from Art Ramsey. Hand-me-downs from neighbors. Free cleanings from the town dentist.

But Clara wasn't a kid anymore.

He turned right at Sarnia Street and headed for the bridge. They lived on this side of it, but since it didn't seem like they were going to be done talking anytime soon, he thought he'd keep driving.

"Where are we going?"

"You know what? I think it's easier to talk about this

stuff in the car." He shot her a self-deprecating grin. "It gives me something to do with my hands."

She smiled back, and his heart squeezed.

They wound through the forest toward the road that followed the shoreline on this part of the lake, and he took a deep breath. "I think they were going to get divorced. I think she was staying only until she had you." He had never said those words out loud to anyone, not even Evie. And he'd told Evie so much.

"Why do you think that?"

"Because I'd hear them fight. And she would say these cryptic things to me sometimes. He'd be ranting, throwing things, and she'd say, 'Next summer is going to be so peaceful.' I mean, I was only a kid, but I remember the things she said, and as an adult I look back and wonder. It seems pretty clear she was gearing up to leave him."

"Or to murder him."

He looked over, alarmed. She winked. He chuckled. "Hey, if you change your mind about engineering, I think you have real potential as a homicide detective."

He'd been aiming to make her laugh, but it didn't work. She looked out the window. "Did he rant a lot?"

"Yeah."

"About what?"

"You name it. What was for dinner. How they were going to afford a second kid." She sucked in a breath and he examined her face, trying to decide if she was ready to hear more. Oddly, now that they'd started, he found himself wanting to lay everything out. He spoke gently, though. "And then, after Mom died, he got it in his mind that it was your fault."

"Well, it kind of was."

"*No.*" So much for gentle. But he couldn't let that interpretation stand. "You can't think that."

"Well, if she never had me, she'd still be here. That's just common sense."

"*No.*" He wanted to pound the steering wheel, but he held himself in check. "She wanted you so much. She used to sing to you in utero. 'Sweet Caroline.' But she'd change the lyrics to make it 'Clara-line.'"

"*You* used to sing that to me."

"Because she did it first."

He could see that had thrown her for a loop. She'd thought the song had originated with him.

"Anyway," she said, "I'm not disputing that she wanted me. I'm just saying that when someone dies in childbirth, it's not logical to say that it wasn't the child's fault."

"It isn't *anyone's* fault. It's a thing that happens. Shit happens. People die."

"Did he hit her?" she asked quietly.

He took a deep breath. They would be returning to this "It's my fault" business later, but for now it seemed best to answer her questions as honestly as he could. "Not that I know of. But you can hurt people pretty badly without laying a hand on them."

"Did he hit you?"

He hesitated. "Yeah. After she died, he used to knock me around some, but it wasn't that bad until one time…" God. His throat felt like it was closing.

"Until one time when it was that bad?"

He cleared his throat. "Yeah. He kicked my ass, basically. He was getting worse. Drinking more. His rants were longer—and meaner."

"So we moved out."

"So we moved out." She made it sound so easy, but he still remembered the state of perpetual panic he'd been in as he'd looked at apartments and secretly packed their stuff.

"He seems more pathetic than scary to me these days. But maybe that's just because I'm older."

He considered that. It was true that they hadn't had an incident in a year. Charles hadn't bothered them, and he hadn't done anything that had required Sawyer's attention in a professional capacity in that time, either. And tonight he had passed his Breathalyzer. His story of having been caught up in a brawl because he was in the wrong place at the wrong time had been corroborated by witnesses.

Still. "I can't risk anything happening, Clare Bear. Maybe I've been wrong not to talk about him, and hell, I'll talk about him all you want going forward. I just... I don't trust him." He pulled over, cut the engine, and turned to her. "Look. If this was a movie, this would be the part where I realize that you're not me, where I tell you there's nothing stopping you from having a relationship with him if you want to. Maybe you'd go do that and find out he's changed."

"But..." she prompted.

"I can't do that."

"It's okay. I don't want that. I just want..."

"What?"

"I just want us to talk about it sometimes. About them. About the past. Rather than pretend it never happened."

He nodded. "Yeah. Okay. I can do that."

She leaned over the center console and hugged him. He hugged her back, his eyes stinging. He was going to miss her *so much* next year.

Chapter Eight

The next week Sawyer was at the bar for his customary Friday-night hangout with Jake and Law. It had been a blessedly quiet week. The Labor Day long weekend with its mermaids, majorettes, DUIs, Charles Collins encounters, and painful heart-to-heart chats was behind him. Clara had started her last year of high school, and aside from a "soul-crushing amount of calculus homework," everything was fine on that front.

He usually looked at Friday nights as a chance to chill out, but tonight the guys were on his case—about the canoe. He'd moved on from YouTube and gotten it out of the shed it had spent several years in and set it up in the garage—and asked Jake to help him finish it.

"But why now, all of a sudden?" Law asked.

"No reason," he lied. Well, it wasn't a total lie. Obviously it had to do with Evie's return—the boat had been for her initially. But he honestly couldn't articulate why her appearance had suddenly triggered an intense desire to finish it.

Law had been a couple years ahead of Sawyer in school, so maybe he didn't remember how intense Sawyer's relationship with Evie had been.

"This is about Eve Abbott, isn't it?" Law asked.

Dammit.

"Why have you been dragging that thing around all these years? Your life was total chaos there for a while. You lived in an apartment when you and Clara first moved out. What did you do with it then?"

"He stored it at my parents' house," Jake said.

"Well, damn, Sawyer. You—" Law's attention was drawn by something behind Sawyer that inspired a gleeful grin. "Maybe we can ask *her* about it."

Sawyer's heart rate kicked up as he turned on his stool.

She walked up to the bar wearing a beach cover-up. Her hair was up in another of those maddening, unstable-looking topknots, but it was damp. The heat was making little wisps curl up along her hairline.

She looked like an ad for sunscreen. If ads for sunscreen featured angels sent to earth to dazzle all the grubby, beer-swilling mortals.

She came up to the bar and issued a bland "Hi" to all of them. Her eyes did not linger any longer on Sawyer than on the others. Had he been expecting them to?

In addition to looking like an ad for sunscreen, she smelled like one, all sea breeze and coconut. He tried not to sniff too overtly, but he must not have succeeded because Law shot him a quizzical look.

She handed a credit card to Law. He ran it and passed over a cooked pizza. "We don't usually do takeout, but I found these old boxes in the back. It's too big for the pizza, so be careful it doesn't slide around too much."

The sight was a jolt to Sawyer's system. Lawson's Lager

House was mostly about the lager. Though, to be fair, Law had developed a pretty impressive wine and cocktail list, too, since he'd taken over from his dad. Still, he didn't do takeout, probably because there was no reason anyone would want to buy a frozen pizza when you could cook one at home for half the price.

These were the same pizzas Law's dad used to run across to the hardware store for Sawyer to take home at the end of his shifts. John Lawson had probably bought the boxes just for that purpose—they were probably the same actual boxes. Like the fish that Jake's dad used to give him, the pizzas had sustained Sawyer and Clara during some rough years. He cleared his throat.

"Don't take this the wrong way, Eve," said Jenna Riley, who was sitting a few seats down. "But you can do a lot better than that crappy pizza. No offense, Law."

"None taken."

Evie smiled. "Well, I was craving pizza. I was going to run into Grand View, but my crappy car had other ideas."

"Did you take it to my brother's place?" Jenna asked. "He'll sort you out."

"Yeah, don't take it to PartsPro out on Bluewater," Law said. "They'll take you for a ride."

"Noted," Evie said. "But it's not really a repair. The battery is dead because I, in my infinite automotive wisdom, left the interior light on for three days. I need to call someone for a jump—does he do that?"

"I have jumper cables," Law said, beating Sawyer to the punch—he'd been about to say the same thing. "I'll get my truck and meet you out back in ten."

"Wow, pizza *and* car resuscitation—that's really nice. Thank you." She transferred her attention to Jake. "And you, too. Thanks again."

"What's she thanking *you* for?" Sawyer asked as Evie left in a cloud of coconut. "And why is her hair wet, do you think?"

"She's been swimming in the cove," Jake said.

What? He knocked over his beer. "She's been swimming in the cove?"

"Yep."

Law appeared with a bar cloth, and Sawyer took it from him, trying to modulate his tone as he mopped up. "Since when?"

"Not sure. Ran into her there about a week ago, told her to make use of it whenever. Seen her back a couple times since then."

"And you've known all this time?" Sawyer's voice had risen an octave. Which was not a good look. He paused and cleared his throat. "Why didn't you tell me?"

"Why would I? What business is it of yours?"

"She doesn't know how to swim!"

"That's pretty obvious." Jake chuckled like this whole thing was *funny*. "I think she's trying to teach herself."

Law set a fresh pint in front of Sawyer. He wore a bemused expression Sawyer couldn't decode.

"What?" Sawyer asked.

"Nothing."

"*What?*" When he didn't get an answer—Law turned and grabbed his keys—Sawyer turned back to Jake. "Can you call me next time you see her there?"

"Why would I want to get involved in your little soap opera?"

"My little *what?*" Though he did realize how dramatic he probably sounded asking Jake to call him. Jake did not have a cell phone and basically never used the landline at the cottage.

Jake smirked and shook his head. "Forget it. Yeah. I'll call you."

"Can you guys watch the bar for a bit?" Law asked. "I'm going to go jump Eve." He cracked up, and Jake chuckled, too. "Assuming that's okay with you, Sawyer."

Dammit. This was the downside to the bromance. These assholes could read him like a book.

When someone knocked on the door of the inn, Eve looked up from her spreadsheet. The Mermaid was closed—she'd posted a sign on the front door saying as much. And it wasn't Maya. Maya's knock was a lot more exuberant than this one. She smiled to think that she'd gotten to the point where she recognized Maya's knock.

But if the door knocker ignoring the sign wasn't Maya, Eve was wary. She had spent the week since the parade trying to get organized for the renovation. She'd gotten the line of credit, but she was going to try to do as much as she could herself.

She swung the door open. "Clara?"

"Hi, Eve. Am I interrupting anything?"

"No, no. Come on in. How are you?" She had worried about Clara after last week's incident with her father.

"Oh, fine." Clara must have heard the concern behind Eve's question, though, because she added, "Really. Sawyer and I had a big chat and cleared up a lot of things."

Eve was dying to know more, but since none of the "things" Clara referenced would have anything to do with her, it wasn't her business. "You want some lemonade?"

"From Legg's?"

"Yep."

"Heck yes!"

Legg's Lemonade had been on the beach since the 1920s,

serving burgers and fries and its famous lemonade. Both Clara and Eve had been mad for it back in the day. It had been a rare treat back then, but since she'd been back, Eve had gotten in the habit of buying a jug every couple of days.

In the kitchen, Clara dumped a stack of glossy paper on the island while Eve got down some glasses.

"What's all that?"

"University brochures."

"U of T engineering, right?"

"Well, yes…"

There was something unsure in the girl's tone. "But?" Eve queried.

"I'm having cold feet."

"About which part? About university in general?" There was something strangely, uncomfortably familiar about this. Was this how Sawyer had felt when Eve had had this same conversation with him?

"No. About everything else, though. What to study. Where to go. Even if I do want to do engineering, I could do it at the Mississauga suburban campus. Maybe that would be better? Like, not as dramatic a change as moving from here"—she waved her arms around—"to a humongous city. But also, engineering. I *thought* that was what I wanted to do." Her voice was rising, and she started talking faster. "But I won this essay contest recently. It was about federal policy, and I think I might really like political science. And then I think of Maya, who has this really cool, creative job. And that's just all the stuff I already know about! I mean, what if what I really want to do is, like, dig up dinosaur bones or something that I've never even thought of? I'm seventeen years old! How am I supposed to know what I want to do with the rest of my life?"

Eve slid a glass of lemonade across the island. "Breathe. And drink."

Clara smiled sheepishly but did both. "I'm sorry. I shouldn't be dumping this on you. I just thought, you went to U of T, right? And you're, like, smarter than pretty much everyone else in this town—no offense to everyone else."

"Let's go into the parlor and sit." There was a plastic mermaid doll "standing" on the table between their two chairs. Eve grabbed her by the head and pulled to make way for their drinks. She had learned that the glue holding everything down was old and brittle. Once she'd freed the doll, she tossed it across to a small sofa that was littered with similar crap she'd pulled up. "Anyway, about school. I don't think you *have* to know what you want to be when you grow up. That's what university is for. Partly, anyway."

"But I have to apply to a program. And a school."

"So apply to them all. Put off the decision."

"Can I just do that?"

"I don't see why not. But my larger point is that whatever you decide, you can change your mind. It sounds like you have great grades and extracurriculars. What's the worst that happens? You apply to one program and you end up transferring to another?"

"Yeah, but money's going to be tight. I'm not going to have time to waste."

"I hear you on that. This place"—she pointed to the ceiling to indicate the inn—"is going to pay off my student loans." *If it doesn't bankrupt me first.* "But it's not like you're going to get halfway through an engineering degree and decide to run off and join the circus."

Clara looked thoughtful. "You said earlier that university was partly for figuring out what you wanted to be when you grow up. What's the other part?"

"The social part. And I don't mean parties and stuff like that so much as—I know this is going to sound cliché—widening your horizons."

"Meeting new kinds of people."

Clara had said that last bit with a strange sort of vehemence. Eve eyed her. "Yes."

"I want to meet those people."

"And you will. So in that sense, it doesn't matter where you go."

"But if you want to meet certain sorts of people you need to go to places they're likely to be."

Hmm. What was going on here? Eve was about to ask, but Clara heaved a sigh. "This is all good advice. You're making me feel much better. Thanks."

"No problem. Come by anytime you want to talk."

"I will take you up on that!" She picked up her phone and started texting. "But not now. I gotta go soon. I'm meeting my brother."

"So…" She shouldn't ask. Clara looked up, her eyebrows raised. "How was it, growing up here…with your brother?"

She shrugged. "I don't know. I mean, I know Sawyer raising me when he was a kid himself is not that normal, but to me it's normal."

Eve had so many questions. She wanted to know about this apartment Clara had referenced before. How did Sawyer afford it? When did he go to police school? How did he *do* it all? It wasn't like she would have expected Sawyer and Clara to be living in the gutter, but they were so clearly thriving. But she couldn't say that, so she settled for, "I was a bit surprised he's chief of police at his age. How'd he manage that?"

There was a rap at the front door, and Clara hopped up. "You can ask him yourself. I told him to meet me here."

Oh, crap.

"Hi!" Clara swung the door open to reveal an off-duty Sawyer. He was wearing those same perfect jeans and a black T-shirt.

Eve, by contrast, was wearing the infamously ratty yoga pants and a shirt that said, "Librarian: The Original Search Engine."

"Sawyer, Eve wants to know how you became chief of police at such a young age."

A startled look flickered over Sawyer's features, but he recovered quickly and one corner of his mouth turned up. "She does, does she?"

Eve rolled her eyes. She didn't deny it, having decided that to do so would be less dignified than to just own the fact that she'd been asking about him.

"The answer is nepotism."

"What?" She laughed in spite of herself.

"You remember the old chief?"

"I do not. I didn't really have encounters with the long arm of the law." Wait. Was she *teasing* him?

"You're forgetting that time he busted us in the lighthouse."

Ohhhh. "Right." And was *he* teasing *her*?

"Anyway, *I* did have encounters with the long arm of the law." His gaze flickered uneasily to Clara. "*We* did."

"We *did*?" she exclaimed.

"Well, Dad did. The old chief was a guy called Maurice Allen. He used to book Dad for stuff from time to time, back when we were still living with him."

"He *did*?" Clara's eyebrows had climbed up to the top of her forehead.

"We're supposed to be talking about this stuff now, right?" He glanced at Eve. "Sorry. I'm working on my"—

he made joking air quotes—"'communication skills' with my sister."

Clara made a go-on gesture.

"So Maurice would check on us. Give me pep talks. He's the one that suggested I go into policing. He hired me fresh out of the academy. And when he retired a few years later, I suddenly found myself in front of the town council being offered the job of chief."

"That's not nepotism," Clara said vehemently. "You're *good* at your job."

Sawyer ruffled her hair and glanced at Eve. "Anyway, what are you doing here, Clare Bear?"

"Eve is giving me advice about school."

"Well, thanks." He looked around at the disaster that was the parlor. "Hey, you need recommendations for contractors?"

"Yeah, probably, but I'm going to try to do some stuff myself first." She hesitated over the rest. But it wasn't like Sawyer didn't understand being short of cash. "I'm broke until I sell this place. I got a line of credit, but the last thing I want is more debt."

He cocked his head. "*More* debt?"

"Student loans. They're still dogging me."

"I thought you got a scholarship."

"Oh yeah, for undergrad. But it only covered tuition, not living expenses or books or anything. And then I went to grad school."

He furrowed his brow. After a pause, he said, "I can help you." She was about to object when he said, "Jake and I recently started a carpentry business."

"You *did*?" Clara was starting to sound like a broken record.

Sawyer ignored her. "We're just getting it going, so

we're looking for testimonials. We'd work for the price of materials."

That was a strange offer. What was even stranger was that her first instinct wasn't to immediately shut it down. To lash out at him. The anger that had turned on like a neon sign being plugged in when she first saw him was starting to...flicker.

It wasn't extinguished entirely, though. "But I don't need a carpenter, at least not yet. I'm talking about pulling up carpets and painting and stuff."

"I can do that."

Maybe he could, but she wasn't going to let him. But she didn't want to get into it with Clara there. So she just smiled and said, "We'll see."

The swimming was going well. Eve had been visiting Paradise Cove a few times a week for a couple of weeks, and she was at the point where she could walk out until the water was up to her boobs. She could spread her arms and lean back. She just couldn't seem to make herself actually lift her feet off the ground and float, which, according to *Learn to Swim in Five Easy Steps*, was supposed to be her first big milestone.

So maybe it wasn't going well in terms of the actual *outcome*. But she was coming to love the time she spent in the water. There was something about being immersed in the big blue lake under the big blue sky that was good for the soul. Eve had mentally written off Moonflower Bay when she and her broken heart had skipped town. But a lot of good things had happened here, and, as she was finding out, those things were still there inside her head, hiding under layers of heartbreak she'd hastily papered over them.

She jumped a little when she heard someone enter the water.

It was probably just Jake, but she didn't need an audience for her pathetic attempts to teach herself to swim. She turned, intending to head back to shore.

And came face-to-face with Sawyer.

Who was, from the look of things, spitting mad.

"Evie Abbott, what the hell are you doing?"

What she was doing was standing there staring at him with her jaw hanging open because he was walking into the water in his cop outfit.

Once he'd gotten her attention, he stopped with the water at his knees. She let her eyes move upward. He was wearing one of those short-sleeve cop shirts that she'd always thought were stupid, because button-down shirts in short-sleeve format just were. But on Sawyer, it was...not stupid. It fit him to perfection, with the exception that it was, as she'd noted the other night, a little snug around his biceps. Sawyer had always been strong, but he'd never had those defined muscles before.

He started walking again, probably because she was just standing there like a dodo. "Evie. What are you doing?"

I am ogling you, but purely for exorcism purposes. A know-thine-enemy sort of thing.

When he didn't answer, he emitted a dissatisfied growl and picked up the pace.

"I'm swimming!" she said quickly.

"You don't know how to swim." He did not sound pleased.

"How do you know I didn't learn?"

He kept sloshing toward her.

"Okay, okay!" She held up her palms. "Stop. You'll ruin your outfit."

He furrowed his brow, but he stopped moving. He was about ten feet from her, and all his splashing had made his...juncture wet. Which had a highlighting effect.

"Uniform," he corrected.

"What?"

"This is a uniform, not an 'outfit.'" He made air quotes.

"What's the difference?"

"The difference is dignity."

Eve tried—unsuccessfully—to smother a giggle.

One side of his mouth quirked up, too. "Have you learned how to swim? Tell me you learned to swim sometime in the last ten years, and I'll back off and leave you alone."

Clearly the answer was to lie. "I have not learned how to swim." She made a vague noise of frustration. "Dammit."

He quirked an inquisitive brow.

"My mouth can't lie to you even though my brain is telling it to."

He started walking again.

"I'm getting out!" She started toward him. "Anyway, I was fine. I've got to the point where I can go in quite a ways and..." It was still so embarrassing. What kind of adult didn't know how to swim? What kind of adult who'd spent *ten summers on the shores of Lake Huron* didn't know how to swim?

Well, there was no point in sugarcoating it. He'd seen it before. So she finished her thought. "I've got to the point where I can go in quite a ways and not have a panic attack."

"Still, it's a bad idea to be out here by yourself." He turned and pointed to a sign on the beach that gave a disclaimer about the beach being unguarded.

"I'm swimming at my own risk." Or, more accurately, *not* swimming at her own risk.

"Well, then you're being stupid."

"Am I breaking any actual laws? Or are you just here in a nonprofessional, paternalistic capacity?" She tried to plug that neon sign back in, to summon some anger.

He sighed. "Look, I know you hate me, but—"

She sighed, too. "I don't hate you." To her surprise it was true. Newly true.

"Well, if you don't hate me, I'm not sure why. You certainly have reason to."

She blinked, shocked.

"I'm just worried about you out here by yourself," he said softly.

His gentle tone poked at something vulnerable inside her. "I just hate that I still can't swim. I always intended to tackle it once I was back in Toronto. But I always had a reason not to. And now I'm back here staring at this giant lake every day, and it's like…"

"Suddenly being face-to-face with your failures in a way that means that you can no longer pretend they don't exist?"

And…*wow*. "Exactly. I've been thinking hey, if I'm stuck in this town for a year, I might as well accomplish something."

Something softened on his face, to match his gentled tone. "So how's it going?"

Her first instinct was to lie, but again, her mouth did not get the memo. "Uh, not super well?"

"Well, how do you learn to swim without a teacher?"

"From a book called *Learn to Swim in Five Easy Steps*?"

He let his head fall back like he was appealing to the heavens for divine patience. In her defense, she *did* realize how dumb that sounded. "Look, I'm not stupid. I only ever come out to practice in calm weather. I'm just trying to work up to the point where I can pick up my feet and float."

"All right. Come on."

He was right. It was stupid to be alone in the lake when she didn't know how to swim. She started walking, but he brushed past her. "Aren't you going the wrong way?"

"Come out and float. I'll hold you." They had swapped positions. He was farther out in the water than she was, and he'd turned back to look at her. When she didn't move, he said, "Come on. My *outfit* is already wet anyway."

Her brain considered the offer.

Ways Eve Abbott Should Respond to a Drenched Sawyer Collins Offering to Hold Her in the Water While She Floats

> *1. No.*
> *2. Hell no.*
> *3. I would rather drown and have my body borne away by rabid mermaids who break my limbs on the rocks and set fire to my hair even though I'm not sure how that would work, but if anyone can light a fire in the water, it's mermaids.*

Her renegade mouth opened and said, "Okay."

It should have been weird, but it wasn't, mostly because he started talking right away, as he led them into deeper water.

"I never really got the chance to thank you for what you did for Clara. The school advice, but mostly taking care of her the night of the parade. I should have just told her to go home, but I get a little overprotective when it comes to her and my father."

This could go one of two ways. One, she could brush it off, and they'd be done talking about it. For some inexplicable reason, she went for number two, number two

being compassion. It was like now that she was apparently
done being mad at Sawyer, she wasn't sure what should fill
the space the anger had taken up. "Obviously I don't know
what the last ten years have been like, but it seems to me
that if you're overprotective, you have your reasons."

His eyes did something she couldn't quite figure out. It
sort of seemed like they were ramping up to do that sparkling
thing. Which made her panic a little. For many reasons, not
least of which was that she didn't want to drown because
his eyeballs had put the whammy on her. So she reverted
to option one. "Anyway, it really was no problem. Clara is
great." She clapped her hands. "Okay, if we're going to do
this, let's do it."

Maybe he should have thought about this a little more
thoroughly. Because the thing was, Sawyer hadn't had Evie
Abbott in his arms for ten years. And now not only did he
have Evie Abbott in his arms, she was wet. And wearing a
bathing suit.

And doing exactly what he said.

And, stupidly, what he'd said—because he was a damn
idiot—was, "Lie back in my arms, and let's see if we can
get you floating."

She—the actual, physical fact of her in his arms—was
a shock. But also not. Because she was, simultaneously,
familiar.

He knew, in some kind of bodily, bone-deep way, how
to hold Evie Abbott. In general, you had to hold her lightly
enough that you weren't holding her *back*. But, depending
on the circumstance, you might also have to, temporarily,
hold her tight. Be a bolster, a place to anchor.

But he had learned this over time, through experience.
Through trial and error. Last time they'd been together in

the water like this, he'd held on too lightly. They'd been, what? Fifteen? Not dating yet—officially still in the friend zone, but hanging out a suspicious amount. He, of course, had been in love with her.

But then, had he ever *not* been in love with her?

He hadn't understood, back then, how deep her fear of water went. He hadn't held tightly enough. He had learned from his mistake, though. Even though she'd never wanted to try swimming again, there had followed plenty of opportunities to hold Evie Abbott. He had become an expert at holding Evie Abbott.

So much of an expert that he'd known exactly what he had to do to get Evie Abbott to stop holding *him*.

But, as it related to swimming in particular, he sent his mind back to the last time. They'd been wading at Sandcastle Beach. It had been a perfect summer day, sunny and hot. So hot that if you sat on the beach for too long, you'd end up sweaty. He'd known she couldn't swim. When it came up, she'd always be self-deprecating about it, making fun of herself as the city girl who had never learned. He'd lured her out farther than usual that day, pledging to hold on to her. Getting her to feel buoyant in the water had been his goal, and at first it had seemed like it was working. She'd been nervous—he could tell by the way her pulse fluttered at her throat—but, judging by the set of her lips, determined.

Then he'd made his mistake. Thinking she would be fine—he was touching her so lightly that he wasn't actually doing any of the work of keeping her afloat—he'd let go. And she'd *freaked out*. It was like she'd turned to stone and started sinking immediately. He'd grabbed her, of course. She hadn't been in any danger, but her fight-or-flight instincts had kicked in and she'd started flailing and screaming. It had only lasted a few seconds—he'd carried her to shore—but he would never forget it.

The lifeguard had come over to check her out. There were people everywhere, and her skin had turned as pink as the bathing suit she'd been wearing. He'd tried to talk to her about it. She kept saying she was embarrassed, that she wanted to be in the lake but wasn't brave enough—and she would shut down any further attempt at discussion. And the longer they went without talking about it, the harder it was to bring up.

So he'd started building the canoe. He'd taken what little she had said—she wanted to be in the lake but she was afraid—and acted on it the best way he knew how. Of course, he could have just borrowed a rowboat or had Jake take them out, but for some damn reason, he'd gotten himself fixated on *personally* making her a boat. Some guys gave their girlfriends letter jackets or promise rings. He was going to give Evie a boat. It was going to say what he couldn't: That it didn't matter if she could swim. That her fears had no bearing on how much he loved her. That he wanted, always, to smooth the way for her.

"Don't let go," she said.

Her voice shook him out of his memories. "I won't," he vowed. Whoa. That had come out too intense sounding, like he still was the teenager pouring all his emotion into a stupid boat. He cleared his throat and tried to sound less like a creeper. "I won't let go unless you tell me to."

"This is stupid. I'm a grown woman. I shouldn't be this afraid of water."

"Fears aren't rational."

"Some of them are."

He wanted to ask, so badly. But if he couldn't ask back

then, he definitely couldn't now. "Just lie back and look at the sky."

"That sounds like the outdoor version of 'Lie back and think of England.'"

He chuckled. Evie had always been funny. Not everyone saw it, because she had a dry sense of humor that only came out when she was comfortable with someone.

He was stupidly proud to have witnessed it—then and now.

"Yeah, lie back and look at the sky," he echoed, letting himself take a deep breath of that same coconut sunscreen aroma that had clung to her at the bar a few weeks ago. "That's what I tell all the girls."

He winked to show he was joking, and she smiled up at him. Something happened in his chest. It was like a twisting and an untwisting at the same time, which was impossible.

But it was also impossible that Evie Abbott should be here. In Moonflower Bay, in the lake, in his arms.

Sawyer had only ever wanted one woman in his arms. And now she was there.

If only he could say everything he wanted to say to her, but he'd lost that right.

Chapter Nine

❦

"Well, this is a piece of junk." Law whistled as he strolled into Sawyer's garage.

It was Saturday morning, and Sawyer had made the mistake of inviting Jake over to consult on the canoe. And telling him that they were starting a carpentry business whether he liked it or not.

And that he'd offered their services to Evie for the inn.

He had a lot to catch Jake up on, was the point, so that he didn't end up looking like an idiot if Evie cross-referenced any of what he'd said. Sawyer did not need to give Evie any reason to get mad at him again. It was only just starting to feel like she was thawing a bit.

He had *not* invited Law, but of course here he was anyway, settling into a lawn chair and sipping coffee while Jake and Sawyer assessed the boat. "What happened to this poor excuse for a boat?"

"My father came at it with a garden shovel."

Law whistled. "Recently?"

"No. Ten years ago."

"Well, if you want to build a canoe, you're better off starting over than trying to salvage this."

He wasn't wrong. The shovel had created several holes with rough, jagged edges that, because of how long the boat had been in storage, were now rotting.

The thing was, he didn't *want* to start over. He wanted to finish this boat. He just didn't know how to explain why— even to himself.

Jake saved him from having to. "Sawyer started building this canoe for Eve ten years ago. When she left town, he put it away. So the boat is a metaphor, I'm pretty sure."

If Sawyer weren't so irritated, he would have gaped at Jake. Jake was not the sort of guy who talked about metaphors. Hell, Jake was not the sort of guy who talked, period.

"Ah," Law said, like he wasn't at all surprised that Jake was speaking of metaphors. "Let me ask you something. That last summer Eve was here, you two were the poster children for young love. You were in each other's pockets twenty-four seven. But then all of a sudden you were making out with that other chick in the Mermaid Parade."

"Jeannie Wilkerson," Jake said.

"Shhh!" Sawyer hitched his head toward the yard. The three of them were in the garage, but the door was open, and he'd just heard Clara. She was headed to the beach.

They all waited a moment until the sounds of Clara moving through the yard disappeared.

"Right," Law said. "Jeannie Wilkerson. So what was going on there?"

"A lapse in judgment," Sawyer said stiffly. "I wasn't thinking."

"I think you *were* thinking," Law said. "I think you did it on purpose. Because you had never even looked at Jeannie before, and you were crazy for Eve." Sawyer started to object, but Law talked over him. "Oh, shut it. You were crazy for Eve, and the whole town knew it. So the question was, if you pulled that stunt on purpose, why?"

The truth came slipping out so easily that he suddenly wondered if some part of him had invited them over here to talk about this shit. "Because Evie was talking about not going to university."

"Aha," Law said triumphantly. But then, bastard, he didn't say anything else. Just looked at Sawyer expectantly.

He tried to explain, though he had no idea why. Maybe they'd just worn him down. "Becoming a librarian was all she'd ever wanted to do. She needed to go to school for that. And she was going to be the first person in her family to go. It was a huge deal."

"Okay. So what I'm not getting is how that translates into you making out with Jeannie Wilkerson. Could Eve not have gone to university nearby? Western is an hour away. She was smart enough to get in there."

"She was talking about not going *anywhere*, though. About moving *here*." Now that he'd started talking, Sawyer was overcome with the desire to make them understand. "She had a scholarship at U of T, and there was a study-abroad program she wanted to do. She was going to walk away from all of that. She started looking for full-time jobs. *Dead-end* full-time jobs. She knew Lucille would never sign off on her not going to school, so she was talking to Barbara Northridge—remember, she owned the diner before Sadie? Back when it was a dive that kept failing health inspections?" Law nodded. "She was going to wait tables there."

"And you couldn't just let her make her own mistakes?"

Law asked. "So she slings crappy coffee for a few years. Is that the end of the world?"

"I couldn't just let her give up everything for me."

"That's awfully big headed," Jake said. "Maybe she just liked it here."

They didn't understand. He shook his head. "No. She was worried about me and Clara. That last summer there was this...incident with my dad. I tried to keep her away from him—just like I did with Clara. But I'd miscalculated one day, and we were at my house while I thought my dad was at work." They'd been working on this very boat, in fact, but he didn't want to say that for some reason. "My father showed up suddenly, drunk. He had wanted me to do some damn thing around the house that I hadn't done."

"Well, you were a little busy raising his daughter for him," Law said, and though this conversation was turning out to be unexpectedly wrenching, Sawyer appreciated the loyalty.

"What happened?" Jake asked.

"He went into a rage. He screamed all the usual garbage at Clara about how it was her fault Mom was dead, and then he laid into me. I had to yell at Eve to run inside with Clara, which she did."

Law whistled.

"Yeah. It was bad."

"So Eve decided to stay and save you," Law concluded.

"And you decided to make her go to save her," Jake added.

A crash from the yard had him on his feet. He'd thought Clara was long gone. But, okay, they were supposed to be talking about stuff now. Not necessarily Evie stuff, but Clara was mature beyond her years. He could explain this.

He stuck his head out around the open door that led to the yard. "Clara, I—"

It was not Clara.

Evie.

"Hi!" Her voice bordered on hysterical.

He made a frantic gesture at the canoe, and God bless his asshole friends, they quickly moved to cover it with the tarp it had been under for the past decade.

"Hi!" Eve said again, her voice so high she sounded like she'd been sucking on a helium balloon. "We're…" She looked around like she was trying to remember where she was. Her attention snagged on a stainless steel water bottle she must have dropped—that was what he'd heard.

"How long have you been standing there?"

She didn't answer because Clara and Maya appeared from inside the house, each of them holding one end of a cooler.

"I thought you were going to the beach," he said to Clara. *I thought you were already gone.*

"We are," Clara said. "We're gonna spend the day going over my school applications."

"And eating," Maya said. "For me, it's mostly about eating. These two brainiacs are going to do the school stuff."

His mind was all muddled. How much had Evie heard?

She just kept staring at him, her mouth hanging open. She had heard *something*.

Well, shit. He could make this worse, or he could try to make it better.

"Get in the car," Sawyer said.

Some part of Eve registered that his voice was low and commanding, but another part of her could barely make sense of what he was saying, his words seeming to reach her through a thick fog.

"*What* is going on here?" Maya dropped her end of the cooler, put her hands on her hips, and moved so she was standing between Sawyer and Eve.

Sawyer ignored her. It was like he hadn't even heard her. He pointed at a Subaru parked on the gravel drive at the end of the yard, "Get in the car, Eve."

He called her Eve on the first try again. It continued to be...unsettling.

"Hold on, now, Sawyer." Maya, bless her, got all up in his face. "You can't just—"

He still wasn't listening to her. Or maybe he was, because he gentled his tone and tried again. "Eve. Please, will you get in the car? I promise I won't take up very much of your time." He turned to his sister, whose mouth was frozen in an O of astonishment. "I'll drop her off at the beach."

Eve felt like she had that day at the Mermaid Parade, like even though she couldn't get her brain to properly process what was happening, life was about to take a sharp twist. If she let it.

She got in the car.

She waved off Maya's barrage of questions—Was she okay? Did she want company?—even though she appreciated them. "Call me if you need me!" Maya shouted as Sawyer started the car.

They drove in silence for a few minutes while Eve adjusted to the idea that Sawyer had *not* left her for Jeannie Wilkerson.

Was it wrong to be relieved about that? Because she was. But she was, simultaneously, *pissed*. The thing that had driven her away hadn't even been real?

He pulled up to the elementary school.

Here went the Whac-a-Mole memory game again. They

used to come here all the time—as kids with Lucille and Sawyer's mom and later, when they were older, with Clara.

Sawyer came around and opened her door for her. Maybe because he was chivalrous like that—or maybe just because she wasn't making any move to get out on her own.

She sat for a few moments while he stood there with the door open. She should get out. She'd come this far.

"You've come this far. Come on."

She almost laughed—he had always known what she was thinking—even as dread pooled in her gut.

He led her to the monkey bars. Of course he did.

She didn't even have time to get her bearings, to try to compose her face into some kind of not-embarrassing arrangement, to get her mole-whacker ready, when he said, "I'm sorry."

She had no idea what to say to that. A simple "I'm sorry" wasn't enough, was it?

But she didn't *have* to say anything, because he kept talking. "I think."

"*Excuse* me?"

"I *think* I'm sorry" was definitely not enough.

"You went to library school," he said. "Which is what? Like more school after you got your undergrad degree?"

What was *happening*?

"So that's five years of school total?" When she didn't answer, he said, "Humor me. Please."

"Six," she said warily. "Four years of undergrad and two years for a master's of information science, which is what they call library school these days." She wasn't sure why she added that last bit. It wasn't relevant, even if it did make her seem fancy. She was a master of information.

"Which is why you have student debt."

"Yes."

"And then you got a job as a librarian?"

"I did. I had a few offers, actually. I almost went into corporate taxonomy, because I had a job offer land in my lap, and—" Again with the extra stuff. Why? Maybe because she wanted him to know that she had been in demand. Which was kind of pathetic. She was supposed to be exorcising him, and she was pretty sure you weren't supposed to care what your own personal demon thought of you.

Her stupid mouth, unswayed by logic, kept going. "I admit I was seduced by the money, but I decided to stick with public libraries, which is what I always imagined myself doing."

"I remember."

Yes, they had talked about it. They had talked about *everything*.

Except that wasn't really true, was it? They'd talked about the little things. They had *not* talked about the big things. Like heartbreak, for example. That had just happened, and then there'd been no more talking *at all*.

"Listen, Sawyer—"

"I remember you always wanted to do a semester abroad, too. Did you do that?"

She failed to see the point of trotting out her entire life history. "I'm going to go." She turned and started walking away.

"Last question!" he called after her. "I promise." He arrived at her side.

She sighed. "I did. A year in France."

He smiled. "So then I'm not sorry."

"*What?*" She marveled now that she'd thought the other day, at the beach, that she was running out of anger toward him. It turned out there was some left after all. Being dragged out here so he could apologize was one thing.

Being dragged out here so he could actively *not* apologize was another.

"I'm sorry I hurt you, but I'm not sorry you left. You never would have done all that if you'd stayed here."

Rage surged inside her, hot and spiky. Her first impulse was to censor herself, but what if she just said what she wanted to say? "Fuck you, Sawyer. That wasn't up to you! You *broke* me!"

Ugh, she shouldn't have said that last bit. It was more truth than she wanted him to know.

He took a step back and nearly tripped over his own feet. "Well, I couldn't leave it up to you. You would have made the wrong decision."

It wasn't just anger that was back, it was pure, electric rage. "You. Pompous. Ass." She was done here. *Done.* She turned and started walking away.

He jogged after her. "I should have tried harder. I should have made you see."

"Made me *see*?" She picked up the pace, but he adjusted his, too. "Like you were an all-knowing adult, and I was a child who wasn't capable of seeing what was right in front of my eyes?"

"Well you sure as hell weren't capable of seeing..."

He'd been yelling before he cut himself off midthought. The first time he'd yelled at her since this argument began. The first time he'd yelled at her *ever*. They'd had heated words, ten years ago, when they'd been arguing about her university plans, but there had been no actual yelling. And then he'd just...given up. She'd won him over. She'd thought.

She stopped walking and whirled to face him. "*What*, Sawyer? What wasn't I capable of seeing?"

"That I wasn't worth it," he finished quietly.

He might as well have punched her. She gasped as if he

had. Tears stung her eyes. She didn't know what to say. Her first instinct was to contradict him, to say that he *was* worth it. Her second was to agree with him. Both felt equally true. Because two versions of Sawyer were getting muddled in her mind. She decided on the truth. "I thought you were. Back then." The tears that were threatening started to spill over. She didn't want him to see, so she started walking again.

"Don't cry," he said softly as he fell into step beside her. "I'm definitely not worth that."

That was true. She slowed down.

Except it *wasn't* true, even if she was angry at him. She hated that he thought that about himself—back then and now. That he wasn't worth people's tears, or loyalty.

"Look." His voice sounded tired. Resigned. "I'm sorry I hurt you. Know that I did it because I—" His voice cracked. "Because I loved you. If I made a mistake, it was because I loved you."

She'd reached the edge of the playground. She stopped walking. Because she *couldn't* walk anymore. It was all she could do not to double over. Everything she'd believed was wrong.

"I didn't come back here for ten years because of what happened. What I *thought* happened. I missed out on so much of Lucille's life."

"I am sorry about that. I didn't...think through all the consequences of what I was doing."

Had that been his fault, though? Or hers?

Or some combination of the two?

She sighed. "We should have..."

"Talked about it. Instead of me deciding to arrange things so you would leave, we should have talked about it."

"Well, we did. Kind of."

"But did we really?"

He was right. They had argued, but that had consisted mostly of them stating their positions. There hadn't been a lot of discussion about what was in their hearts. About fear and worthiness and regret. "I know that this is a lot to take in," he said. "And I know you probably need some time, but I was hoping that since you're going to be in town for a year..." His voice had gone scratchy, and he paused to clear his throat. "I was hoping we could be friends."

"Friends?" she echoed dumbly. Well, what had she expected? *Loved* was a past-tense word.

"Well, or at least not not-friends."

"Not not-friends?" Was she a parrot?

But more importantly, was this it? Her chance at exorcism? She thought about what Maya had said about cutting Sawyer down to size. She had imagined it more like watching him over the year and coming to realize she hadn't missed out on anything after all.

Maybe it wasn't about exorcising him so much as it was about forgiving him.

And maybe also forgiving herself? For letting him keep her away from her aunt and the lake and the town that she had loved so much?

She looked at him. Hard. He looked so different with the beard. He looked so grown up. But she could still see the kid Sawyer inside. The kid who had always tried to do the right thing, even at great cost to himself.

Something unclenched in her gut. It felt like...relief?

Exorcism complete?

It seemed so. She looked at him now without the old fear and shame *and* without the more recent anger.

It definitely hadn't been like the Hollywood version of an exorcism. Nobody's head had spun around 360 degrees. No incantations had been uttered. No holy water had been required—unless you counted the lake. Which, actually, she probably should. She squinted at him. "So you want to be friends. Or not not-friends."

He looked at her for a long time. She startled when he turned around and jogged back to the playground. He ducked under the monkey bars and grabbed one. He was so tall that he had to lift his legs off the ground. "Wanna hang out?" he hollered.

She laughed.

And joined him. There really was no reason not to.

She wasn't as tall as he was, so while he had the lower part of his body tucked into a crunch position, she only had to bend her knees to hang. "Okay. Not not-friends."

"Really?" His face lit up. There were little lines around his eyes that hadn't been there when they were kids.

She smiled. "We'll see how it goes."

Chapter Ten

❧

As the end of September approached, the renovation was well underway. It was going better than expected.

Mostly because Pearl kept sending Sawyer over to "help." From her vantage point at the bakery next door she had a ringside seat for the reno. It had taken Eve a while to figure out why Sawyer would mysteriously show up with, for example, a sander exactly when she was getting ready to rent one.

"Just go with it," he'd said when she'd protested. "Pearl and company are total meddlers, but you can exploit that."

"Maya said you guys call this town Matchmaker Bay now? Is Pearl sending you here because she's trying to get us back together?"

"Yeah, probably, but I'm immune to her meddling."

She was, too, she'd rushed to assure him. Which was true, for the most part.

It was nice to see him around the inn again. He'd been

there when she'd found Lucille's old mermaid coat hooks hiding in a drawer in the parlor, and he, as delighted as she was at their reappearance, had given her a high five. She'd forgotten how much she had always *liked* Sawyer.

The other thing that was going shockingly well? Swimming lessons. Also with Sawyer.

As she left the hardware store with a handful of paint chips, she pulled out her phone to text him. I'm headed to the cove in about half an hour.

He'd asked her to let him know when she was going swimming. He couldn't compel her to, he'd explained—as she had pointed out, technically she *was* swimming at her own risk—but he thought someone should know when she was there. "I'm not going to tell anyone," he'd said, anticipating her objection. "But if I know you're going, I'll check in with you later to make sure you're not dead. Give me that much? I'm the chief of police—it's basically my job."

She'd agreed, but only to get him off her back.

So she would text him, and he would show up. Stand there on the shore while she did her try-but-not floating thing. If he had to leave before she was done—he was often on duty—he would extract a promise that she would text him when she was finished. She had to grudgingly admit that there was some logic to his thinking.

Today, when she got to the cove, he was waiting. And he was not on duty, judging by the fact that he was sitting on a beach towel and wearing swim trunks.

Oh no. She wasn't prepared for this. He hadn't gotten in the water with her since that first time.

He sprang to his feet when he caught sight of her. "All right, let's do this."

"Do what?"

"Don't take this the wrong way, but you standing there and willing yourself to float isn't going to work. It's almost October. It's going to be too cold to swim soon."

"So, what? *You're* going to will me to float?"

"Forget floating." He strode to the edge of the water and gestured for her to follow.

"Ow." She stepped gingerly when she got to the pebbled stretch. She kept meaning to pick up a pair of water shoes. "My city girl feet aren't toughened up yet."

Wordlessly he picked her up and started walking. She opened her mouth to object, but nothing came out. She'd been noticing how her mouth often said things around Sawyer that her brain did not want her to say.

She seemed to be having the opposite problem right now.

It was just that his arms felt so *good*. Familiar. Comfortable.

Instead of setting her down once they cleared the pebbled part of the beach, he kept going.

Stop. Put me down, her brain said.

Her mouth stayed closed.

He did eventually put her down, but not until they were deep enough that the water was up to her belly button.

"Okay," he said gruffly. He was all business. "Do this." He lifted his arms out of the water and made a motion like a breaststroke, but a really fast one. He looked like a cartoon dude trying to take flight.

Laughing, she followed suit.

"Faster," he urged. "Form doesn't matter. Just keep your fingers closed and get your arms moving as fast as you can, like a propeller."

She sped up and laughed harder.

"Good. Now turn the whole thing ninety degrees and kick really hard, too." He laid his hand lightly on her upper back, not pressing down but indicating that he wanted her to tilt her body into the water. "Don't think, just go! Go!"

She went.

And sank.

But at least she didn't panic when it happened.

He was at her side before she fully righted herself. "Okay, again."

She tried again to the same end.

"Again."

"What's that saying about how insanity is doing the same thing over and over and expecting different results?"

"Humor me," he said.

She sighed and started her propellers again, and...

She was swimming! Extremely inelegantly and tossing up a ton of water as she did so, but still! She was moving her body through the water, her brain crackling with a mixture of concentration and excitement.

"Yes!" he shouted. "Keep going!"

She went about ten feet before she was so exhausted that she had to stop.

But on second thought, maybe it wasn't exhaustion that had her breathless so much as exhilaration.

Which Sawyer seemed to share, judging by the way he was whooping and pumping his fist.

"I did it!" she exclaimed.

"You sure as hell did!" He started splashing over to her. He held his arms out, and without thinking she stepped into them. She realized at the last second that he had actually been holding up his palms in a double high-five gesture. She tried to stop her forward momentum, but it was too late.

He adjusted, and his arms came around her as if a hug had been his plan all along. He even lifted her off her feet and twirled her around like they were a couple in a movie. And oh, once again: those arms. Strong and sure and dangerous.

And there was his beard, rubbing against her cheek. It was as soft as it looked. She didn't have experience with beards. Her exes had been clean shaven. She had always thought beards would be coarse to the touch. Scratchy. But she could deep condition the hair on her head every day for the rest of her life and never get it as soft as Sawyer's beard.

Things started to get awkward. There was no call for them to be standing in the lake hugging, and they both seemed to realize it at the same time. She pulled away from his embrace, intending to free herself, but he was holding on more tightly than she'd realized and he stumbled forward as she started to tip back. He grabbed her, resulting in a tighter embrace than they'd started with.

"Ha!" She fake laughed. It *sounded* fake. Ugh.

"Yeah, uh..." He succeeded in setting her down and patted her arm. His face had gone all weirdly serious. "There you go."

Sawyer realized with a start that he would never touch Evie again.

He could feel the grin sliding off his face as he set her back on her feet.

There might be incidental contact, now that they'd made up. Forearms brushing accidentally at the bar, that sort of thing. But this was the last time he would ever have Evie Abbott in his arms. He should have paid more attention.

He reminded himself that everything was good. She had learned to swim. They'd made up. They were not not-friends.

So why did he feel so *bereft*?

They slogged out of the water in silence. He wanted more

than anything to pick her up again and carry her over the rocky patch. He might have, too, if she'd made any noises of discomfort, as she had on the way in. But she was silent, so he let her suffer. Let *himself* suffer.

"How's Garretson doing with the new bathrooms?" he asked as they were drying off, in an attempt to distract himself with mundane conversation.

"How did you know I hired Marco Garretson?"

Oops. Should he tell her the truth? That he was abusing his position and reputation in town to make sure she got the best tradespeople in to do the stuff that was beyond his abilities? No. It was hard to say why, but he felt like she wouldn't appreciate it. He was going to take his not-not-friends achievement and quit while he was ahead. "I saw his truck outside the inn yesterday. He did some work on my place a few years ago." There. That was reasonable, right? It was also another partial truth. A not-lie, perhaps, for his not not-friend.

She accepted his excuse. "I'm surprised how easy it's been to get people lined up. I thought I'd have to book them in for slots down the line, but it's like they just magically appear when I need them. I hadn't even really thought beyond the plumbing, but then I found a note in the mailbox from this tiler guy who said he heard I was doing bathrooms and could he come in and quote? I took him up on it. I figure I probably *could* lay tile myself, but the results would be horrendous."

Sawyer dried his face next so he could smile into his towel. He was no better than Pearl. But he didn't care.

"All right." She hoisted her beach bag up, but he intervened. He grabbed it and slung it over his shoulder. "Oh, so not not-friends comes with bag-carrying services?" she teased as they started walking. She'd been getting a lot of mileage out of the not-not-friends thing. It had become a joke as he wormed his way into her renovation.

"It sure does."

He wasn't sure why he'd let himself get so wrapped up in the reno, except that it felt like a sort of penance. He meant what he said at the park. He wasn't sorry he'd run her out of town—even if that made him a dick. But he was sorry he'd hurt her. Broken her. *Broken.* God. The word still made the hairs on the back of his neck stand up.

So yeah, if he could help her now, he would. Even if it sent her away again. But it wouldn't be like last time. There would be no breaking. She would just be going back to her life in Toronto. Paying off her debt. Hell, he was still trying to figure out how he was going to pay the mortgage *and* Clara's tuition, so he understood what a gift Lucille had given her there.

"You miss your job in Toronto?" he asked suddenly.

"I guess so." She looked over her shoulder at him.

"You guess so?"

"Well, I enjoy my job." Her expression turned quizzical, like she was trying to figure something out. "But it's not like I'm sitting here pining for it."

"I always pictured you doing story time, recommending books to people."

"That's pretty much what I do—well, that plus a lot of behind-the-scenes stuff that the public doesn't see. But actually, I have my eye on another job. I want to get into collections development."

"Collections development?"

"Deciding what the system should buy. It sounds like being a glorified shopper, but it's more than that. It's about matching resources with community needs—and not just books. You can't just—" She stopped. "Sorry, you don't want to hear this."

He did. But to say so felt too grasping.

"Anyway, it works out. I'm on an unpaid leave. And sometime this upcoming spring or summer, a couple new positions are going to open up in collections development, and not to sound too cocky, but one of them is *mine*."

"Yeah?" He kind of liked Cocky Evie.

"Yeah. They're doing a bit of a re-org, and an old mentor of mine from school—she was a part-time professor—is creating new selector jobs. That's like for people to be the buyers in certain subject areas."

"And one of them is yours."

She grinned. "Pretty much. See? You're not the only one getting jobs via nepotism."

He chuckled and they hiked back toward town. He even got to touch her again. He extended a hand to help her over the little outcropping that bordered the cove, and she took it.

He looked at her hand, her pale-pink-painted nails jutting out from his larger fist. He made a note of the way it felt— soft and smooth.

This time—the real last time—he paid attention.

Clara was knocking at the door. Eve was at the point where she recognized three knocks: Maya, Sawyer, and Clara. Maya was a bunch of staccato raps. Sawyer was a couple thudding pounds. Clara was four quiet, steady knocks.

She put down her paintbrush and went to the door.

"I decided on engineering at the downtown campus!" Clara practically shouted.

"Hello to you, too," she teased.

"Sorry. Hi, Eve! I decided on engineering at the down-town campus!"

"Well, great."

"Also, I'm gay."

"What?" *What?*

"I was thinking about what you said, and I think it makes sense to apply to the hardest program—that's engineering." She was talking really quickly, almost manically. "And then I can transfer to the Faculty of Arts and Science if I end up wanting to do political science."

"Hang on. Rewind." They were still standing in the doorway. "Actually, come in." She led Clara back to the kitchen and poured her a lemonade.

Clara ignored it in favor of burying her head in her hands. "Oh my God. I did not mean to blurt it out like that. I had a whole speech prepared."

Eve smiled. "Do you want to give it now?"

"No," Clara said miserably.

"Clara." Eve laid a hand on her arm. "This is good news."

"What do you mean, good news?"

"Well, I'm getting the sense that maybe this is a secret that's been weighing on you?" Clara nodded, but she still looked miserable. "It's not a secret anymore. That's good!"

"But you're not going to tell anyone, are you?" Clara asked urgently.

"Of course not. Not if you don't want me to."

"I don't want you to," she said quickly.

"Have you told Sawyer?"

"No."

Eve wanted to laugh at the vehemence of that *no*. "I think you could."

"Not yet. I just…I wasn't going to tell anyone. I mean, it was all theoretical anyway."

"Theoretical?" Eve asked.

Clara made a face. "It's not like I had a ton of prospects around here."

"Ah. I see."

"I was going to go away to school and, you know . . . maybe meet people."

"Is this what you meant about meeting specific sorts of people?" That conversation all of a sudden made a lot more sense.

"Yeah." She ducked her head like she was embarrassed. "That's partly why I think the downtown campus is best."

"I think you're right."

Her head whipped up. "You don't think I'm weird? Or gross?"

"Of course not! You're just you. This is part of who you are." She hesitated. "And I'm pretty sure your brother will think the same thing."

"I can't tell him yet."

"Okay." Eve could respect that. She used to run a LGBT teen book club at the library, and one of the things she'd learned—both in her training and on the job—was that you had to respect people's timelines for coming out. "Just out of curiosity, why are you telling me now?"

"Well, so I was going to wait on account of it being theoretical . . ."

"But it's not theoretical anymore!" Eve grinned.

"Oh, it is! It is! There's just . . . maybe a prospect of it not being." She looked around like she was checking for hidden cameras, lowered her voice, and whispered, "There's a new girl at school."

Eve clapped her hands. "Awesome."

The misery returned. "Not awesome. Because what do I *do*?"

"Talk to her?" Eve suggested. "Be bold and just ask her out?"

"How did you and my brother do it?"

Good question. "I don't know. He was just always there. He was...inevitable."

Until he wasn't.

"Eve." Clara folded her hands under her chin like she was praying. "I just got overcome with the idea that I had to tell *someone*—it just suddenly felt like I couldn't keep it in anymore—and I thought of you. But *please* don't tell Sawyer. Not yet."

Eve's heart twisted. "I won't, sweetie. I promise."

She was flattered by Clara's trust. And impressed by her self-awareness. She'd made intelligent, logical decisions about college, and she was going to blossom there. Eve felt proud to have played even the smallest role in how well Clara had turned out.

But really, that claim to fame belonged to Sawyer. The guy who did hard things in service of other people.

Chapter Eleven

❧

"What happened to Jeannie Wilkerson?" Eve asked as Maya turned in to one of the marinas upriver from Moonflower Bay.

"Why?" Maya asked.

"I was just...idly wondering what happened to her."

"You are such a liar! You were not"—Maya made air quotes with one hand while the other stayed on the steering wheel—"idly wondering."

Busted. "Well, Sawyer's all exorcised, right? We're friends now. Kind of." She wasn't going to try to explain the not-not-friends thing. "Still, it's not like I can ask *him*."

Maya parked and cut the engine. "Well, Jeannie was already in college when the kissing debacle took place, right? She was just back for the summer. I think she must have gone back to school, and that was that."

"And where is she now?"

"She's back in town, and she's coming on this boat ride."

Adrenaline made Eve surge forward, and her seat belt engaged.

"Just kidding! Gotcha!" Maya reached over and unbuckled Eve's seat belt. "I don't know where she is. She went to school at Dalhousie, so maybe she's still out east? I haven't really heard anything about her. Her parents got divorced and sold the store—probably about seven or eight years ago now. Her mom moved to Windsor, but her dad is still in town. But I haven't seen or heard anything about Jeannie for years."

Eve tried to be casual, but she was massively relieved. It wasn't like there had actually been anything between Jeannie and Sawyer. She just didn't love the feeling that she might run into Jeannie at any moment. "Thanks."

"But...you know Sadie Saunders?"

"I don't think so, why?"

"She owns the diner out on Oak Road."

Eve's body jerked.

Maya's eyes narrowed. "What?"

"That diner used to be owned by a woman named Barbara."

"Yeah," Maya said. "Nice woman, but it was a total hole back then."

"Toward the end of my last summer here as a teenager, I had gotten myself a full-time job there, and I was going to move here permanently."

"What?" Maya shrieked.

"Yeah, I decided I was going to stay." For some reason she hadn't told Maya any of this. After her big blowout with Sawyer at the playground, she'd just reported that they'd made up.

"What happened?"

"Jeannie Wilkerson happened."

Maya narrowed her eyes. "Oh. My. God. All the pieces fall into place. Let me guess. Sawyer was not thrilled about this plan of yours."

"Not initially, no. He thought I should go to college as planned. But he got over it pretty quickly. Because, you know, apparently he'd hatched the whole Jeannie Wilkerson plan in order to dislodge me."

"He does have that whole protective, noble-self-sacrifice thing going on, doesn't he?"

"Yep." Eve sighed. "On the one hand, it's maddening. He just unilaterally decided what was best for me. I wasn't a child. Well, I *was* a child. But you know what I mean."

Maya chuckled. "I do. But on the other hand, he was kind of right, wasn't he? You would *not* have made a great career waitress."

Eve didn't like to think about that. "So what about Sadie? She owns the diner now? Why do you bring her up?"

"Because if you're going to get all territorial about Sawyer, *she's* the one you have to worry about. She has a massive crush on him."

What? As of a few minutes ago, she had never heard of this Sadie person. "First of all, I'm not territorial. Second of all, he always hated that diner. It was a total cesspool."

"Not anymore!" Maya trilled. "Sadie's cleaned it up, and now it's as cute as a button. And she serves great food."

Well, crap. "I still fail to see your point."

A car pulled into the spot next to them and beeped.

"Oh, look, it's Benjamin and your boyfriend," Maya teased.

"Shh! He's not my boyfriend! We're friends." Or not not-friends. Whatever.

Maya snorted. "Okay, then, time for a friendly boat ride."

* * *

It *was* a friendly boat ride. It turned out that when you were not not-friends with a guy, you could find yourself on a boat with him, cruising down the Miskwimin River on a gorgeous Friday afternoon and have a surprising amount of fun.

There was a group of late-twenties and early-thirties Moonflower Bayers who hung out socially, and Maya was their ringleader. Today, she had sweet-talked everyone into playing hooky in favor of a cruise on Law's boat.

Also in attendance were Olivia, the deputy chief of police, and Jenna and Jordan Riley, siblings who owned, respectively, Jenna's General Store and Moonflower Motors.

And Sawyer. Sawyer was here.

Which was fine, because they were not not-friends.

The only person missing was Jake, who had protested that since his job had him on a boat all the time, he had no desire to also socialize on one.

"I'm not sure that's true, though," Maya said—they'd been talking about how she couldn't convince Jake to come. "He doesn't really fish anymore, and besides, he and Kerrie used to kayak all the time back when he *was* fishing full-time."

"But that was before," Law said.

"Before what?" Eve asked. "I've been wondering what happened to Kerrie."

"She moved to Guelph," Maya said after a few beats of uncomfortable silence. "She was commuting there for work the last several years she and Jake were married, so I think it just made more sense for her to move there once she...didn't have anything keeping her here."

"So they got divorced?" Eve asked. She was met with more silence. "Sorry. None of my business."

"No need to apologize," Sawyer said. "It's not like it's a secret."

"It's just so tragic," Jenna said. "It's almost like the town has an unspoken agreement not to talk about it, even when Jake isn't around."

"Jake and Kerrie had a baby," Jordan said.

"Four years ago now," Jenna said when Jordan didn't elaborate. "He died when he was almost one—the flu. Like those cases you read about in the paper. The one-in-a-million person who dies from the flu."

Tears sprang to Eve's eyes. "That's terrible."

"Jake and Kerrie's marriage didn't survive," Maya said softly. "And Jenna's right. No one really talks about any of it."

"Jake never got over it," Law said. "Not really."

"Well, I don't know how you would," Eve said. "Is that why he's so quiet all the time?" She looked at Sawyer. "We didn't hang out with him that much in the summers, but you guys were friends, right?"

It wasn't lost on her that she'd just referred to her past with Sawyer like it was no big deal. Also not lost on her: the small smile he shot her that seemed like it was meant for her alone. "He's always been quiet. Not shy, just not a guy who had a lot to say. But he's even more so now."

"He's, like, existentially quiet now," Maya said.

The group fell into a melancholy-tinged silence. It contrasted with the beauty around them. The Miskwimin River was bordered by forest on both sides. Most of the leaves hadn't turned yet, but there would be the odd overachiever tree, its scarlet or yellow leaves standing out like jewels against the green. They had driven to a marina outside of town and boarded the boat there and were motoring back toward town and the lake. As they approached the bay, they had to slow because the lift bridge was down. They could have cleared it in their motorboat, but there was a big sailboat in front of them.

The bridge was operated out of a tower on one end.
The tower was glassed in so the operator, usually Dennis
Bates—though Jake had been known to fill in for him
from time to time—could see in all directions and control
the bridge according to the demands of both boat and
motor traffic.

Because Eve lived downtown, and the little beach and
Paradise Cove were on the downtown side of the bridge, the
bridge didn't figure that much into her day-to-day routine. But
she had the sense that it could be annoying for people who
lived on the other side. And Sandcastle Beach, the big beach,
lay on its other side, so things could get quite jammed up at
the peak of summer.

Today, though, there seemed to be no reason the bridge
shouldn't be lifting to let the sailboat through.

Except maybe that Dennis Bates was currently distracted.

"Is that Pearl up there with Dennis?" Eve exclaimed.

"It is!" Maya stood to get a better look at the tower. "I'd
recognize that blue hair anywhere!"

"Careful," Law warned. "I wouldn't want you to fall in."

"Oh, shut up, Benjamin." Maya squinted at the tower and
broke into a grin. "That is totally Pearl. Ha! Methinks the
lady doth protest too much."

"You know," said Jenna, "Dennis is going to be in the
bachelor auction this year. Maybe it's time for *our* generation to do a little meddling."

"I am all for that," Law said. "Karl talked me into being
in it, too, and I don't even really know how it happened."

"Are you going to be in it?" Eve asked Sawyer, though she
immediately regretted it. What did she care? Maybe cute-as-
a-button Sadie would bid on him. Didn't matter to her.

Thankfully, he ignored her question and turned to Law.
"We can't go too far out with both Olivia and me on board.

Joel's on duty, but Dom's out of town, so we need to have someone within arm's reach if Joel needs backup."

"Joel will be fine," Olivia said.

"In fact, pull up to the pier, and I'll get off. That way I won't be cramping your style, and you all can go out as far as you like."

"We won't go out so far that we won't get a cell signal," Law said.

"Thanks, but I think I'm just going to bail. Clara will be home from work in an hour, and I should really have dinner with her. She's been busy between school and work."

"Damn, Sawyer. If it's not the town, it's Clara," Maya said. "What would we all do without you?"

Law navigated the boat to the pier that jutted from the little beach. Even though it was daytime, and a weekday close to the end of September, there were two women Eve didn't recognize standing on the pier holding flowers. And they weren't the amaryllis impostors Maya's dad sold.

"Uh-oh," she said, getting her not-not-friends mojo back. "Good call on getting out here, Sawyer. Looks like you might have some tickets to write."

It struck her that her ability to distinguish, at a glance, between the real and fake wishing flowers could be interpreted as a sign that she was getting pretty comfy in Moonflower Bay. That was an unsettling thought.

Sawyer paused, one foot on the boat and one on the pier, and shot her what she could only call a smoldering glance—it was that eye-sparkling thing again. What was up with that?

Before she could figure it out, he was on the pier smiling at the criminal tourists. He did not write them tickets. He mimed tipping a hat at them and said, "Hope you ladies are enjoying your time in Moonflower Bay."

And then he was gone.

He should have just stayed on the boat.

Sawyer didn't actually need to worry about Joel. And he didn't have dinner plans with Clara. She had a calculus study group meeting at their place. But he had needed off that boat.

Because, for one insane second, when Evie had asked him about the bachelor auction, he had imagined that he'd detected a note of jealousy in her voice.

But that was crazy. That was his deepest teenage yearning talking.

Sawyer's careful examination of Evie in the time she'd been back had revealed that even though she was back physically—geographically—they lived in two different worlds. She had gotten the education she was supposed to get. She had become the librarian she was supposed to become. He'd overheard her the other day in a deep discussion with Maya about the plays of Tony Kushner. Sawyer wasn't knocking himself, but he had no idea who Tony Kushner was.

And even *that*—the two-different-worlds thing—was beside the point. Because if, hypothetically, he could somehow talk her into...what? Dating him? Sleeping with him? The point was, there was no way on God's green earth that he would ever be able to say goodbye to Evie Abbott again. He wouldn't survive it. That wasn't hyperbole. He'd done it once. He could not do it again. If he knew anything with certainty in this world, he knew that. Evie Abbott was the only person he'd ever shown his whole, true self to. She'd been his one shot. His person.

So he needed to remind himself that she was going to *leave* when her year was up.

He *couldn't* go showing himself to her again, only to have her leave again.

He just couldn't.

Chapter Twelve

$\mathcal{E}$ve was beginning to think maybe Moonflower Bay *did* have magical properties. That would explain why the reno continued to clip along so amazingly well—*someone* had to be casting a spell for everything to be coming together under budget and ahead of schedule like this.

"Whoa." Maya spun in place in the newly painted dining room the Saturday morning of the Anti-Festival. "They did the crown molding, too."

"Yeah, I guess they did." She hadn't noticed, to be honest. "They" was Sawyer and Jake, who were increasingly on-site offering the services of their carpentry business. She had painted the parlor herself, but they had wrested her paintbrush from her and taken over the rest of the main floor. They hadn't spoken about the molding, but it did indeed appear to have a fresh coat of bright white that really popped against the very pale blue she'd chosen for the walls.

"Hello, hello! I come bearing pies!" Pearl appeared from

the kitchen brandishing her phone. "Look what I found! Adorable mermaid bedsheets, but they're *classy* instead of cartoony."

Eve and Maya huddled around Pearl's phone, but before Eve could make out what she was supposed to be looking at, a notification popped up and Maya snatched the phone away. "Pearl Brunetta. Are you on *Tinder*?"

Eve chuckled. She was impressed. She had met her last boyfriend, a few years ago now, at the library. And the one before that had been a blind date arranged by friends. Who was the old lady here, again?

"Are *you* on Tinder?" Pearl asked Maya. "Or Hinge or Bumble or one of those new ones?"

"Yes," Maya said, "but—"

"So don't give me your ageist, double-standard bullshit."

Maya handed back the phone. "You're right. I'm sorry."

"Why should Art be the only one in my age bracket getting any?"

"You're right," Maya said again. "I'm used to people of a certain vintage being kind of technologically inept. But clearly that isn't the case with you."

In addition to being a little old lady who made pies, Eve had learned that Pearl was a champion gamer. She'd reached Champion's Road in Super Mario 3D World. Eve had no idea what that meant, but apparently it was impressive.

"But what about Dennis Bates?" Maya asked, winking at Eve.

Pearl made a frustrated, strangled noise. "Will everyone stop with Dennis Bates?"

"I don't know," Eve teased. "I have it on good authority that you were in the lift bridge with him."

"I heard he's going to be in the bachelor auction today," Maya added.

"Well, good for him," Pearl declared. "I hope someone who appreciates boredom and silence bids on him." Eve noticed Pearl didn't address her presence at the bridge. In fact, she turned to Eve and said, "What about you?"

"What *about* me?"

"Are you going to bid on anyone?"

"No." *Eight hundred million times no.* "There's no point, really, in getting into something with someone. I'm only here for a year."

"And given how smoothly this reno is going, maybe not even that long," Maya said. "You could be back to Toronto early to wait out the remainder of the year."

What? Eve hadn't considered that. But it was true. There would be nothing keeping her here once the reno was done.

Wow. She needed a moment to adjust to that reality.

But Pearl wasn't going to give her a moment. She narrowed her eyes and looked around. "Hmm. The reno is going remarkably quickly, isn't it?" But then, seeming to change her mind about what she wanted to talk about, she said, "Did I mention I brought pie?"

"You told me I didn't have to feed people," Eve protested when they entered the kitchen to find Pearl's signature pie boxes stacked two deep across the kitchen island.

The "problem" with how well the reno was going was that she hadn't been able to get out of the Anti-Festival town sleepover thing. The main floor was almost done. When she'd cleared the furniture out for the floor refinishing, it had been "suggested"—aggressively and frequently—that if she held off on bringing it back, the big, empty space would be perfect for the sleepover. She'd tried to wiggle out of it, but resistance was futile when you were up against Pearl, Karl, Art, and Eiko.

"You're not *feeding* people," Pearl said. "You're just giving them a little treat. You can't have a sleepover without a midnight snack."

"And/or a midnight tipple," Maya said. "I have twelve bottles of wine being delivered a little later."

"You guys, I only have one functioning bathroom at the moment. We need to be *de*hydrating people."

"Wine and lemon pie?" Pearl asked, brazenly ignoring Eve.

"It's some kind of late-harvest Riesling," Maya said. "Benjamin ordered it for me from his wholesaler. He said it pairs well with lemon." She rolled her eyes. "Who knows. He's probably pranking me, and it will be terrible."

"He's going to be in the auction, you know," Pearl said.

"Well, good for him," Maya said. "Since you're in the market, why don't *you* bid on him?" Pearl started to argue, but Maya turned to Eve and said, loudly, "Let's go check things out."

The festival was in full swing out back. There was a stage set up, and a local band was playing. There was a face-painting booth, a "cake" walk featuring more of Pearl's pies, and various carnival-style games.

It was a gorgeous day. The sugar maples that would be fire-engine red by the end of the month were starting to pinken. There was a not-unpleasant chill in the air—Law's employee Amber was running a stand out back of the bar that was selling hot cider and mulled wine, and it looked like it was doing a brisk business.

They rounded the corner of the stage, and there, of course, was Sawyer. He was speaking to Eiko.

"I can't," Sawyer was saying to her. "I'm on duty. I'm in uniform."

"Oh, pish. No one cares about that. Your uniform will probably up your price."

"Well, *I* care about it. I'm *working*, Eiko."

"Poor Sawyer," Maya whispered. "Eiko's all over the place trying to pre-matchmake the auction."

Eve wondered who Eiko had in mind to bid on Sawyer. Sadie of the cute diner and tasty food, perhaps? "And here I thought she wasn't as bad as the rest of them."

"Oh, she is. If it seems like she's not, it's because she's not retired yet like her coconspirators. She owns the newspaper and basically writes and produces it by herself. But that also means she has her nose in everybody's business, like, *professionally*. Then she reports back to Pearl and Karl and Art, who execute the meddling."

As if on cue, Eiko turned her head. You could practically see the gears turning as her eyes slid from Eve to Maya.

"Gotta run!" Maya chirped. "Love ya!" And she was off.

Eiko furrowed her brow as her gaze followed Maya.

Eve seized on the break in Eiko's attention to try to extract Sawyer from her clutches. "Sawyer! Come quick!"

He hadn't seen her yet, but at the sound of her voice, his head whipped up. Oh no, she'd genuinely alarmed him. Eiko was still watching the departing Maya, so Eve shot him a quick wink. His expression relaxed.

"There's a . . ." What? She cast her mind around for a plausible story. ". . . mermaid emergency," she finished lamely.

"If you'll excuse me." He tipped an imaginary hat at Eiko. "Enjoy the festival."

He closed the distance between them, and he was clearly working hard not to laugh. Her heart did a fluttery thing.

He led them quickly and purposefully through the crowd, with a posture and at a pace that allowed him to return the greetings everyone lobbed at him without getting drawn into conversations. The way he could manipulate the crowd like that was impressive.

His phone rang as they entered the kitchen.

"Joel," he said. "What's up?" There was a pause while he listened. "I'm at the Mermaid Inn." Another pause. "For what? Something legit, or something designed to trick me into being in the auction?" He scratched his beard absently. What was it about that beard that was so compelling? It was just hair. On a face. It was just—

He glanced at her, and she realized her mouth was hanging open. She turned and straightened some pie boxes that did not need straightening.

"Yeah, well," he said, "if it's Karl asking, I highly doubt it's legit." Another pause. "I'm *busy*." Pause. "A mermaid emergency," he said without missing a beat. His deadpan delivery cracked her up. She turned to him, and he winked. "I'm going to be a while. Handle Karl, will you?" Pause. "Yeah. Yeah. Okay."

He set his phone on the kitchen island and blew out a breath.

"It's hard out there for an eligible and gainfully employed gentleman, eh?"

He chuckled. "You know how Maya's nicknamed this town Matchmaker Bay?" She nodded. "This is like Christmas Day for the matchmakers. It's their biggest day of the year." He looked around. "Thank you for rescuing me. Again."

"No problem. That's what not not-friends are for."

He shot her a grin. "No chance of an upgrade to friends?"

"Nope," she teased, though in truth they had kind of spontaneously upgraded. She thought about the last few weeks, about him coming over after long policing shifts to paint the dining room. About his sister *coming out*. About how Eve had, without really meaning to, knit herself back into the lives of the Collins siblings.

It was weird. But nice. Also a tiny bit awkward.

Okay, it was *a lot* awkward.

Things had never been awkward in the old days. But now, whenever they found themselves alone, she usually ended up feeling really...cringey.

> *Ways Being Friends with Sawyer Collins*
> *Was Super Awkward*
>
> *1. Friends don't get caught staring slack-jawed*
> *at friends' beards while getting the tinglies.*
> *2. Well, that was it, basically. For now. She*
> *was certain to come up with something else*
> *next time.*

He stroked his beard and looked away, shuffling from foot to foot. He felt the weirdness between them, too, she was pretty sure. "I didn't realize you were doing any work in the kitchen."

"I wasn't going to since it's not a public part of the inn, but the tiler I got for the bathroom had this extra backsplash tile he wanted to get rid of, so he made me a great deal."

Was it her imagination or was Sawyer suddenly trying to suppress a smile? "What's with all the pies?"

"Pearl. She's bent on developing a signature pie for the inn. I keep telling her there's no point. I'm not going to be here once it reopens."

"Right. You'll be back in Toronto. Doing collections development."

She wasn't sure if he was asking a question or making a statement. She decided to treat it like a question and answer it, even if only for herself. "Yes. I will be back in Toronto." She pointed to the calendar she'd bought the day she'd accepted she was staying. It was now mounted on the wall by the door, and she'd kept crossing off the days.

He looked at it for a long time before transferring his attention back to her. "You like Toronto? I mean, besides your job."

Did she? She didn't not-like it.

Kind of like she and Sawyer were not not-friends?

"I've been trying to get my landlord to let me set up a Little Free Library in the lobby of my apartment building." Which, she was aware, went exactly zero percent of the way toward answering his question. "Do you know what those are?"

"Those little boxes where people leave and take books, right?" She nodded. "Yeah, there's one near my house."

"But none here downtown."

"I guess not."

"I think some Little Free Libraries are exactly what this town needs. I mean, I don't think Main Street, with its cascades of moonflowers and its charming little stores, is cute enough."

She had been trying to lighten the mood, but he squinted and examined her face so intensely that it started to heat up.

Gah. She had to get him out of here. "So you want to escape out the front door?"

He shook his head like he was trying to rouse himself from a trance. "Good thinking."

She followed him through the dining room, which was littered with sleeping bags and camping pads various people had dropped off for the sleepover. She really should move them all into a pile in—"Oof!" She tripped over one, and Sawyer grabbed her elbow. As she righted herself, he slid his hand down her forearm, painting a swath of goosebumps as he went. He reached her wrist, rotated his hand so their palms were touching, and just...didn't let go.

Everything about his hand was the opposite of her hand. Hers was cold, which she hadn't realized until she had his warm one for contrast. His was big. Hers was small. His was rough. His hands hadn't been callused when they were kids. She knew that because she'd spent hours holding them. She wondered how grown-up Sawyer had gotten all those calluses. Maybe the carpentry side gig?

Regardless, there was something about the juxtaposition between the callused, work-roughened hands and the silky, smooth beard she'd felt at the cove when they were swimming. She could imagine circumstances in which such different textures in such close proximity could be... interesting.

"Eve! Eve, are you in here?"

It was Maya.

She dropped Sawyer's hand like it was a grenade.

"Oh my God! Hide me!" Maya came tearing in from the kitchen. "The auction is underway, and when Law was on the block Pearl kept trying to physically raise my hand for me—and let me tell you, that woman is stronger than she looks."

Eve cracked up.

"Ha ha. I know everyone thinks it's *hilarious* to stick us together because we hate each other, but it isn't. Because we *actually* hate each other."

Eve wasn't so sure about that, at least as it related to Law's feelings on the matter.

"*Then,*" Maya said, her tale of woe gaining steam, "I tried to distract her by saying that the whole concept of a bachelor auction was sexist. I mean, the women are supposed to make picnic 'hampers' to share with the men? What is this? The nineteenth century? *Anne of Green Gables*? But then she just *agreed* with me and told me they'll do bachelors *and* bachelorettes next year, and she tried to appoint me head of the committee!"

Eve patted Maya's arm. "What do you say we take one of Pearl's pies upstairs and hide out until it's over?"

"I say *yes*. I want to talk to you about this idea I have for a kids' theater program. Or maybe a summer camp."

Good. A little pie. A little chat about *someone else's* life. She turned to Sawyer. She was aware that she was supposed to say something, but suddenly she did not know any words. There was another item for her list.

3. He made her forget how words worked.

"I'll, ah, see you later," he finally said.

"Right. Yes. See you later."

How much later? When?

It didn't matter, she told herself. It wasn't like she had a Sawyer calendar. She wasn't crossing off the days until she would see him again. She would see him "later."

Whenever that was.

That evening, several hours into the town sleepover, Eve's phone dinged. It was a text from Sawyer. Hey, is my sister there?

> *Eve:* Yep.
> *Sawyer:* Is she alone?
> *Eve:* I'm not sure what you mean by "alone."
> She's with like 30% of the town.
> *Sawyer:* Is she . . . getting cuddly with any-
> one? She isn't answering my texts.

She lifted her head to survey the space. Clara was in the far corner of the dining room. She was watching a movie with a girl Eve didn't recognize. Ha! Was this Miss It's Not Theoretical Anymore? Clara was resting her head on the girl's shoulder. It could have been platonic, but if you were in the know...Eve's face felt like it was going to crack from smiling too hard.

> *Eve:* She's watching a movie with a friend.
> They each have one earbud in, and they're
> huddled together over a phone. Probably the
> friend's, so my guess is she just didn't hear
> hers.
> *Sawyer:* Is this friend male or female?

Did he suspect something? As far as she knew, Clara had still not told him, but Sawyer was pretty perceptive. Maybe he had figured it out.

> *Eve:* I have reached the limit of my comfort
> with spying on your sister.
> *Sawyer:* Thanks for nothing.

He had added an emoji, though, the one with the tongue sticking out. She stuck her phone into her back pocket and surveyed her domain. Maya, who was playing cards with Jenna and sipping her sourced-specially-for-her-by-Law wine, was waving in an attempt to get her attention.

"I am sorry to have to tell you this," she said when Eve arrived at her side. "But Art and Jamila went upstairs a few minutes ago."

"Really?" Eve had strung rope across the base of the

stairwell. There was major work going on up there, and she'd agreed to the sleepover only on the condition that it happen on the first floor only.

But had she really expected a rope to keep those two out? "Ugh. Thanks." She walked toward the stairs but paused, uncertain. The idea of bursting in on them was supremely unappealing. But so was the prospect of getting sued because a wire came loose and they got electrified in flagrante delicto.

Well, she knew someone she could ask.

She got out her phone. I think Art and Jamila are getting it on upstairs. The demolition guys are in the middle of taking walls down, and they said not to have people up there. What should I do? It turned out to be kind of handy to be not not-friends with the chief of police.

The reply came right away. I'll come over.

> **Eve:** You don't have to do that. Just give me some...pointers.
> **Sawyer:** Pointers for breaking up public sex?
> **Eve:** Okay, yeah, come over.

He was, no doubt, gunning for an excuse to anyway, so he could spy on his sister firsthand. Speaking of...she picked her way through the crowd in the parlor and tapped Clara on the shoulder. She startled and pulled away from her friend, a look of horror dawning on her face, like she hadn't realized how cozy she'd gotten.

Eve leaned in and whispered, "Just wanted to let you know your brother's on his way over."

Clara scooted away from her friend and shot an intense look at Eve. "You won't—"

Eve pantomimed zipping her lips, winked, and went back

to the base of the stairs to find Sawyer already there. "That was fast."

"I got off at eight—everything's wound down outside—and I was just over at Law's."

He was indeed no longer in his police outfit. Uniform. Whatever.

He was wearing a plain white T-shirt and those damn jeans. What was it about Sawyer that inspired the coexistence of contradictory states of being? Loose and snug. Hot and cold. Soft and rough. Hate and...not hate.

He gazed up the stairs. "So what are we looking at?"

"Maya saw them go upstairs a while ago. So I guess all the evidence we have is circumstantial."

"Oh, with them, the evidence always points to one thing." He mounted the stairs and gestured for her to follow.

She stopped him at the first landing and pointed at the hard hats lined up on the windowsill. "Everyone's supposed to wear hard hats and steel-toed boots upstairs."

He grabbed a hat. "We're going to fudge it with the foot-wear." He turned and set the hat on her head. He cocked his head and looked at her for what felt like slightly too long. "How is it that you look good in a hard hat?"

Her cheeks heated. It was like there was a dial that controlled her body temperature, only she didn't know where it was located. Maybe it was actually a remote control that Sawyer possessed.

They went up one flight, but there didn't seem to be anyone on the second floor. She pointed to the stairs that led to the third. As they approached the top, he started talking in a fake, singsong way. "Oh, wow, you've really made a lot of progress up here."

They paused, as if by silent agreement, and listened. Sawyer pointed toward the front of the inn. Yep. Art and

Jamila were definitely in one of the two front rooms. They probably thought they were being quiet.

They were not being quiet.

"Let me show you the new bathroom!" she trilled, adopting his strategy of overly loud talking to try to alert the lovers to their incoming visitors. She opened the door to the second bath, which had the toilet and vanity installed but no tiling or finishing done, and waved inside like a game show model. The gesture must have looked as exaggerated as it felt, because Sawyer muffled a snicker. She stepped inside and played up her *Price Is Right*–style arm waving.

His eyes danced. Those eyes. The laughter in them was contagious. "Two bathrooms side by side? My, what an interesting choice."

"Yes!" she practically shouted. "Ideally I'd put a bathroom in each room. I'm going to do that on the second floor, but it's not going to work up here for complicated plumbing reasons that made sense to me at the time but I can't explain now. But we worked out a way to squeeze in a second hallway bathroom."

"That was a good compromise." Sawyer winked as he resumed his overly loud speech. "Having more than one bathroom up here will definitely make it easier for guests." He was hovering in the doorway, one hand on either side of the frame. He leaned back and glanced down the hallway. When his attention returned to her, he rolled his eyes and shook his head, indicating that the lovebirds had not vacated.

Eve swallowed another giggle. "Exactly. Consumer expectations around privacy have changed since the early days of this inn." Maya should see them. They deserved Academy Awards.

"Yes. Consumer expectations. Very important." He made a silly face.

She shook with silent laughter. When she recovered herself, she waved dismissively. "Okay, they're not getting the point," she whispered. "We're going to have to go in there."

She made to move out of the bathroom, but Sawyer stuck out an arm, blocking her way. "Wait. They're making a break for it," he whispered as he pushed farther into the small room, pressing close to her with his stupid chest and his stupid jeans and his stupid beard. He stroked the sink. "Hmm. Marco did a great job here. I knew these tiles would work for a kitchen, because—"

She suddenly realized what had been happening. The truth arrived in her head so fully formed that she felt like an idiot for not seeing it sooner. *He* was why everything was going so smoothly with the reno. He hadn't seen Marco Garretson's truck parked outside; he'd *sent* her Marco Garretson. And the "leftover" tiles that were now magically being used in her kitchen? She'd bet the farm they were also his doing. "Sawyer."

He held a finger to his lips and gestured behind him with his other hand. Sure enough, she heard whispers, followed by the creak of footsteps on the exposed underfloor of the hallway. The tryst was over.

"Do you think they heard us?" Jamila whispered.

"No, no," Art assured his wife.

Eve had to clap a hand over her mouth to keep from laughing out loud. Sawyer closed his eyes and looked down. His shoulders were shaking.

They waited a few moments, until the footsteps on the stairs faded. Her stomach hurt from all the suppressed laughter. But she still needed to know what he was up to.

So when she was sure the coast was clear, she laid a palm on his chest and pushed him out into the hallway. "Sawyer, are you meddling in my renovation?"

"No!" His denial sounded as theatrical and manufactured as their previous dialogue had.

"This is why the right sort of tradespeople just magically show up at exactly the right time, isn't it? You're as bad as Pearl!" She didn't know if she was annoyed—here he was again, doing what he thought was best for her—or touched. Because it did kind of rock to have everything going so smoothly.

"I better go have a look at the crime scene," he said before she could decide how to feel.

The front rooms on this floor were the inn's biggest. Because of that, and because they had balconies overlooking Main Street, they'd been in demand back in the day. Eve had loved them, too, and on the rare occasions they hadn't been occupied, she would set up shop on a balcony to read or simply watch the world go by.

And she often hadn't been alone.

As she followed Sawyer into one of the rooms, she was hit with contradictory sensations. There was the relief of no longer being crowded in the too-small bathroom. But there were also memories, memories like mousetraps threatening to annihilate her if she stepped wrong.

Sawyer inhaled sharply. Was he similarly affected?

To mask her unease, she walked swiftly inside, brushed past him, and came to a stop at the French doors. But of course that didn't help, because it put her right in front of the balcony they used to canoodle on.

"I'll be right back," he said.

What? She was standing here trying to stave off a freak-out, and he was casually headed off on a bathroom break?

She stepped out and grasped the railing. She felt herself slipping into that place—that place where this town seemed to keep *putting* her—where she was caught in a confusing whirlpool of nostalgia and pain. Perched up here, she and Sawyer had had a view of the town but been apart from it. It had felt like it was them against the world.

"I thought we should have a toast."

She jumped. He was back. Too soon.

"Sorry. I didn't mean to startle you." He was holding one of Maya's bottles of wine and a pair of plastic cups.

Why not? It had been a long, strange day. She stepped aside to make room for him on the small balcony. He took up so much more space than she remembered.

He poured two glasses, handed her one, and lifted the other. "To the end of festival season."

"Well, you still have to watch your sister star in *Medea* tomorrow."

"Yeah, well, in overhearing her running her lines, it seems like she spends a lot of the play cursing men. I don't want to come off like the Neanderthal older brother, but I think I'm down with that."

So much for her theory that maybe he'd figured out Clara's secret. "Well, big brother, I don't think you have to worry about Clara. She seems like a really responsible kid."

"She is. And she hasn't really shown any interest in boys."

You don't say?

"Although, the other day when I came home, she was having what she had previously described as a calculus study group. It turned out to be just her and one boy. Some kid I don't know." He curled his lip.

Eve had to bite her tongue to keep from laughing. "Well, calculus is hard. I don't think most people take it in high school. It's probably a challenge to find people to study with."

"I know, I know. And it's not like she's not allowed to date. She just hasn't seemed to want to."

Don't laugh. Don't laugh. Don't laugh.

"And less than a year from now she won't be living with me anymore anyway. It's just..."

"Hard to let go?" Regardless of his big blind spot, he was a good brother.

He made a sheepish face. "Something like that."

They were still standing there with their wine. She lifted her glass. "To little sisters. To Medea." They clacked their plastic cups together. "Wow," she said. "I don't really know wine, but this is great."

"Yeah, Law is pretty knowledgeable about wine and craft beer. The lists of both at the bar definitely punch above their weight."

"But this isn't on the list. He ordered it just for Maya."

He swirled the wine around in his cup. "Hmm. You know, sometimes I think he likes her, despite their battles."

"Isn't that usually how it works? A boy pulls a girl's hair because he likes her?"

He shrugged. "I never really went in for that method."

"True." They'd gone seamlessly from "hanging out" at the monkey bars to entering the annual sandcastle competition to being boyfriend and girlfriend. She'd never had to wonder about his feelings. "I don't think Maya likes Law, though. Her disdain seems genuine."

"I think you might be right, at least judging by the fact that she never tries to make him be in any of her plays the way she does everyone else."

"Exactly."

"I thought you were in *Medea*, too," he said.

"I was supposed to be one of the Phoenician women. But I talked my way out of it because of the sleepover."

"I'm surprised she gave up that easily. The only way I get out of it is that my work schedule never meshes with the rehearsal schedule." He grinned. "I make sure of it."

"I *may* have told her she could use the Mermaid for murder mystery theater as my way of getting out of it."

He whistled. "That was brave of you."

"Well, it's looking like the place will be done early." She shot him a look. She was mostly grateful for all his help, but she still felt weird about it. "So the place will just be sitting empty."

"You won't open it for the remainder of the year?"

"I don't think so. I mean, I will admit that part of the rationale for doing this reno is to fetch a higher price when I sell. So in that sense, if it's done early, opening it would make sense. But I don't know that I want to bother doing it for a few months." She felt a little guilty because clearly the spirit, if not the letter, of Lucille's will was that she should actually run the place. But the late Lucille was going to have to settle for a reno. Pearl had told her several times that Lucille would approve of the work she was doing, so that made her feel a little better.

"Yeah, that's smart. There have been developers sniffing around some of the historic properties around the towns on this part of the lake. Most people looking for second properties want beach access, of course, but there's a little condo project going up in Grand View downtown where some douchebag bought up the old post office and tore it down."

"Tore it down? You mean someone could buy this place and turn around and tear it down?" That had literally never occurred to her. "Then why am I spending all this money and energy on renovating it?"

She felt like an idiot that she hadn't thought about the prospect of a new owner not keeping the Mermaid as an inn. Or not keeping the physical building at all. But of course she couldn't sell the place and dictate how it was going to be used after the fact. Or could she? She would ask Jason. Maybe she *should* take the balconies off and see about getting it listed as a historic property.

Sawyer cleared his throat, drawing her out of her thoughts. Okay, well, she wasn't going to solve any of this now.

They contemplated the view. Main Street was empty, which made sense given that everyone was around back for the Anti-Festival. But it was a gorgeous night. The sun over the lake was turning the sky orange, and it was cool and breezy with that crisp scent of autumn in the air.

"Sawyer, have you been sending tradespeople here?" She was pretty sure she knew the answer, but she wanted to hear him admit it.

He winced. "I might have sent one or two your way."

"Why would you do that?" Was it because he felt guilty? In order to be able to decide how she felt about his meddling, she needed to know the answer to that question.

He rotated his neck like he was uncomfortable. "Trades are hard to find around here. And all the new development in Grand View has sucked up a lot of them. There's one guy in the area who's a total crook—I think the douchebag developer used him—and I didn't want you to get mixed up with him."

"But why? And not just the inn." She gestured to the lake. "The swimming, too. I mean, I know we're not not-friends now, but why are you being so nice to me?"

He didn't say anything. Just stood there and stared down at the town, while he gripped the wrought-iron railing like it was the only thing between him and certain death.

Just when she was about to give up and suggest they go inside, he let go of the railing, grabbed her shoulders, leaned in, and— Oh my God, was he going to *kiss* her?

Thunk.

Their hard hats bonked into each other.

Chapter Thirteen

⌒

*T*he next day, as he was getting himself settled in a lawn chair in the audience for *Medea*, Sawyer's face was still burning. His mouth was talking to Law, but his mind was freaking out.

What the hell was the matter with him? What had he been *thinking*?

Well, he *hadn't* been, clearly.

Thank God for those hard hats. They were supposed to protect against falling debris, against physical danger. Turned out they were also good at protecting weak-willed men from making epic mistakes.

He looked around anxiously, not sure whether he wanted her to be here or *didn't* want her to be here. She made him feel like a bumbling teenager. Which was weird, because he hadn't felt that way around her back when he *was* a bumbling teenager.

"Hello?" Law was waving his hand in front of Sawyer's face.

"Sorry. Yeah?" He leaned back in his chair and slouched down.

"Are you hiding?"

He sat up straight. "No."

"She's helping with the costumes, so she's not even here."

"Who isn't here?"

Law snorted.

He glanced around to make sure no one else had heard them talking. Karl was next to him on the other side, and Eiko and her husband Kensi were next to Karl. They seemed absorbed in their own conversation.

"Hey." Law was greeting Jake, who was arriving on his other side. "Sawyer is freaking out about Eve."

Sawyer glared at Law. "Will you *shut up*?"

The corners of Jake's mouth turned up.

"Testing. Testing." It was Maya, standing on the temporary stage Jake had built for the day. They'd held the bachelor auction on it yesterday, and now it was decorated with fake columns he supposed were meant to evoke ancient Greece.

"Can everyone hear me?" Maya called.

Law rolled his eyes, but he moved forward so he was sitting on the edge of his chair.

"Thank you all for coming. As you know, the fall play is always a labor of love for me."

Sawyer tuned her out and let his attention wander over the crowd. If Evie was helping with costumes, what were the chances she would stay in the curtained-off area that functioned as a backstage?

As if she had heard him summoning her—not that he *was* summoning her—the curtains parted and she slipped out. He ordered himself to chill. Except she was on her way over. He looked around. The chairs next to him were empty now.

Karl, Eiko, and Kensi were nowhere to be seen. Pearl, who had appointed herself usher, was escorting Evie his way.

She sat next to him and immediately leaned over and whispered in his ear, "I asked Pearl to seat me next to you."

Oh God. Should he apologize for the almost-kiss? He'd left suddenly—and awkwardly—last night after it had happened. Or hadn't happened.

Or maybe she wanted to sit next to him because she *didn't mind* that they'd almost kissed? If that was the case, he had a whole other set of problems. He could *not* get into anything with her. She was *leaving*. He needed to *remember* that.

"You know," she whispered, "this play is about a lying jerk of a dude who cheats on his wife." She cracked up. "And then Medea gets her murderous revenge."

"It is?" He'd heard Clara practicing and had intuited that this Medea lady was not a fan of men in general, but he hadn't known about the murderous-revenge part.

"So I started thinking maybe you had it too easy. I mean, you just apologized, and I said okay? You got off *easy*." She laughed again—cackled, really.

She was kidding, but she also wasn't wrong. In his wildest dreams he could never have imagined a scenario in which he was sitting next to Evie at a town play because they were friends again. "Eve, I—"

But Carol Dyson walked out from behind one of those columns and started talking about a ship and a golden fleece.

And so Sawyer found himself watching his sister star in the story of Medea, the spurned woman bent on revenge against her cheating, no-good husband, with Evie Abbott sitting next to him.

When his sister lamented, "'Of all creatures that can feel

and think, we women are the worst-treated things alive,'"
he started to get a little uncomfortable. He shifted in his
chair to put some distance between Evie and himself.

She moved over to compensate. He could *feel* her looking
at him. He could *feel* her smirk. She was effing with him.

When Clara shouted, "'You vile coward! Yes, I can call
you that, the worst name that I know for your unmanli-
ness!'" he moved over again.

Evie followed.

Maybe, instead of murdering her children to get back at
her husband, Clara/Medea should come out into the audience and put *him* out of his misery instead.

"Will you get off me?" Law not-so-subtly whispered as
he shoved Sawyer. "I love you, man, but I don't want to
cuddle with you."

Well, crap. He looked at Evie, who was gazing at him
and looking extremely amused. She must have seen something in his face that made her take pity on him, because
she whispered, "Relax. I'm not going to murder anyone.
Probably."

He rolled his eyes. But he made himself as small as
possible, positioning his body in the exact center of his
chair so that no part of him touched any part of Evie while
he watched his sister commit righteous bloody murder to
avenge all womankind.

Eve led the standing ovation.

Wow. People teased Maya about her intensity. She
even made fun of herself sometimes—she wasn't above
mocking her own single-minded devotion to her theatrical
pursuits. But that had been one impressive play. Yes, it
was a little handspun, with its togas made from bedsheets
and its particleboard set. But everything else, everything

important—the script, the acting, the pacing—had been first rate.

Eve also had to give herself a standing ovation for *her* acting skills.

She'd decided after yesterday's weirdness, after beard lusting and maybe-possibly-almost kissing, that she was *not* cool with the new awkwardness that seemed to be settling between her and Sawyer. So she'd decided to just be done with it. Perform the role of not-awkward friend as fully and enthusiastically as she could. Which, she had decided from watching Sawyer with Law and Jake, meant giving him crap.

And it was working. On her, anyway. She'd started out acting, but ended up having genuine fun harassing him during the play. Genuine, *friendly* fun. He didn't seem like he was having as much fun as she was, though. Ha.

She turned her attention back to the stage, where, after several curtain calls, the actors dragged Maya up on stage. Eve sneaked a glance at Law. She was pretty sure he was clapping louder than any of them.

When the applause died down, Medea bounded over to them.

"You were *fantastic*." Sawyer swept Clara into a hug, heedless of the "blood" all over her costume. "In a totally terrifying way."

He caught Eve's eye over Clara's shoulder and grinned. She smiled back. His pride was contagious.

"You were great, Clara," she said when Sawyer had let her go.

"Hey, Eve! Thanks! I haven't seen you lately—I've been working a million shifts at the store. But I wanted to ask you if you think I should apply to live in one of the campus residences, or if I should look for an apartment. Everything is so expensive in Toronto, it's hard to know what to do. Where did you live when you went to school?"

Sawyer was gesturing behind his sister's head, but Eve couldn't interpret his meaning.

"I lived at home through university to save money, so I'm not going to be much help in that department," she said, keeping one eye on Sawyer. "But why don't you go have a look around? There used to be a campus housing service that posted apartment listings." Sawyer started making slashing gestures with his hand across his neck. He clearly didn't like the idea of her living off campus. "Or…" He nodded vehemently. "You can tour the various residences, can't you? You should go check them out." Sawyer was now smiling and nodding exaggeratedly and making a keep-going motion with his hand. She pressed her lips together so as not to smile. "I think it would be fun to live right on campus." That earned her an exaggerated thumbs-up.

"Maybe we could go and check out a couple of them, Sawyer?" She turned to Eve. "We're going to Toronto next weekend."

"They're going to Toronto next weekend because Miss Clara won a national essay contest, and she's been invited to be on some smarty-pants TV show to talk about it," Law said.

It was cute the way Law exuded as much pride in Clara's accomplishments as Sawyer. These Moonflower Bayers could get all up in your business, but they stuck together.

"That's great," Eve said, and she meant it.

"So can we go early, Sawyer? I'm doing fine in all my classes, so I don't think skipping out on a Friday for something like this is that big of a deal."

"I wish we could, but Olivia's going to be out of town, so I'm on seven to eleven on Friday. Maybe we can do it another time?"

"I could take you," Eve's mouth said. Her brain kicked in belatedly, and she was just about to overrule her mouth when Clara's eyes lit up. She glanced at Sawyer to see if they were still playing charades. He was looking at her skeptically.

"I *have* been meaning to go back for a weekend," she reasoned out loud. "I haven't seen my parents in forever, and they've been on my case to come home for a visit." Which was true.

"*Really?*" Clara exclaimed. "That would be so amazing! And you're from there, so you'll have all kinds of insider info." She turned to her brother. She must've been able to tell, as Eve could, that Sawyer was not 100 percent down with this plan. "Oh, come on, Sawyer. *Please?*"

Eve shot Sawyer an apologetic look. She'd been trying to do his bidding, with the charades, but she'd ended up backing him into a corner.

"I guess I can add a night to the hotel and meet you there on Saturday." He narrowed his eyes at her. "Are you sure you don't mind?"

"Not at all." She was looking forward to hanging out with Clara—and maybe getting an update on Miss Not Theoretical. "And don't extend your reservation. Clara and I can stay at my parents' place. We'll leave here early Friday morning, check out some residences during the day, and then do something fun."

"Oh! Oh!" Clara was practically vibrating with excitement. "Can we go to the Science Centre?"

"We sure can." She shared an amused look with Sawyer. Their girl was such an adorable nerd.

No, wait. *His* girl. Not *their* girl.

Whoa. Where had *that* come from?

Later that evening Sawyer and Jake were in his garage working on the canoe when Law showed up. He was carrying a bottle, which he proceeded to open with a corkscrew he pulled from his pocket.

"Wine?" Sawyer asked. That was unusual.

"Cider. French style, but local. I'm thinking of adding it at the bar. Let me know what you think."

"Well, aren't you getting fancy?" Sawyer said.

Law shrugged. "Just trying to keep up with the times." Once everyone had started drinking, he eyed the canoe critically. "Is that pink paint?"

It was indeed pink paint. They were painting a hot-pink stripe around the entire boat. That had always been the plan, and Sawyer saw no reason to change it now.

"Eve's favorite color," Jake said when it became clear that Sawyer wasn't going to answer.

"What *the hell* is going on with you and Eve?" Law said. "And *don't* say nothing."

Sawyer sighed. "I tried to kiss her, and things are getting weird."

Law cracked up.

"Well, that's helpful."

"What do you mean you *tried*?" Law asked.

"I was about to do it, but it didn't work out."

"You're going to have to get a little more specific than that."

And so Sawyer found himself telling Law and Jake about the kiss that wasn't, and about how things had been awkward between them since they made up. "What's the matter with me? It was like somebody else was inside my body, manning the controls. Thank God for those hard hats. That would've been an epic mistake."

"You sure about that?" Law asked. "It sort of seems to me like if there was a kiss that was a mistake, it was that one you planted on Jeannie Wilkerson all those years ago."

Nope. They weren't going there again.

Still, he could use some advice. He'd been wondering if the reason Evie had been so odd at the play was that she was annoyed at him about the almost-kiss. "What do I do? Apologize? I'm not totally sure she realized what my intentions were. What would I say? 'If you thought I was trying to kiss you, I'm sorry about that'? 'But if you didn't, let's just pretend we never had this conversation'?"

"Well, if it will stop you from making a fool of yourself every time you lay eyes on her, maybe you *should* apologize."

"Or..." Sawyer and Law swiveled to face Jake. Because Jake so seldom spoke, when he did have something to say, people tended to listen. "You could forget all the talking and kiss her."

Yeah, so much for listening to Jake. "Are you crazy? I can't do that. If I do anything, which I'm not at all convinced I should—"

"Shut up." Law held up a palm. "Let the man speak."

Jake shrugged. "Nothing more to say, really. I just think if you almost kissed and it's been weird, maybe you should see what happens when you *actually* kiss."

"You know what?" Law grinned. "He's right."

"She's leaving in ten months." He had seen the X's in her calendar, concrete reminders that she was counting the days.

"So?" Law said. "Ten months is a long time. And you don't have to marry her."

"We're not the same people we used to be."

"What does *that* mean?"

It meant that Evie wanted to work in collections development and not corporate taxonomy, and he barely even knew what those phrases meant.

When he didn't answer, Law said, "Dude. You don't even have to *date* her, if you know what I mean. Just put yourself out of your misery."

What they didn't understand was that he *couldn't* do it again—"it" being have Evie and give her up. Be with her and then not. It was like this theory Jake had about air-conditioning. He hated it. It could be burning up outside, and he wouldn't turn it on in his car—and he didn't have it in his cottage at all. He said that going in and out of the heat was worse than just being continuously hot.

Sawyer could survive breaking up with Evie Abbott only one time, and he'd already done it.

He was gearing up to try to explain this without sounding like an idiot when Jake held up a palm, just like Law had done before. Sawyer's words died in his mouth. Jake speaking really did have that effect.

"*Sawyer.*" Not only was Jake talking, he wasn't even bothering to disguise the impatience in his voice. "Kiss the girl."

Chapter Fourteen

❧

*W*hen Sawyer showed up at Evie's parents' house to pick up Clara, he found her in a tizzy because she had fallen in love with one of the residences at the University of Toronto.

"Oh my gosh, Sawyer! Wait until you see it. It's this old, Gothic building. It's so *awesome*! It's a Trinity College residence, so I have to get *into* Trinity, but oh, I loved it!"

"You'll get in." According to everything he had read, Trinity was the most competitive undergrad college at the university, but they would be idiots not to want Clara. In addition to having a mind-boggling GPA, she was the world's greatest teenager.

"We also visited the housing office," Evie said. "We looked at a lot of listings, but it seemed like apartments are *really* expensive—and pretty far from campus." She winked at him—Clara couldn't see her because she was still jumping up and down in front of Sawyer. That wink told him Evie had steered his sister toward on-campus options.

Which made him want to kiss her.

Which made him think of Jake telling him to kiss her.

Which was something he'd been thinking about lately. A lot.

"I met this girl named Lynn on the tour." Clara was talking a mile a minute. "She was visiting with her parents from Nova Scotia. We totally hit it off. She's going to study biology. I'm thinking I might ask her if she wants to room with me, assuming we both get in."

"She seemed like a really cool girl," Evie said. "And her parents were great, too."

Sawyer hadn't realized that the residence tour was going to be such a formal thing. He probably should have been there. But he also found himself not really minding that Evie had taken on a quasi-parental role. He trusted her judgment.

"And after we did the campus stuff, Eve took me to the Science Centre!" Clara was on a roll. "There was an exhibition on black holes that was *awesome*. And then we had dinner at this adorable little place called the Ladybug Café, which was *awesome*."

"Awesome," he deadpanned. Clara missed the joke, but Evie didn't. Her eyes twinkled. "You ready to go, Clare Bear?"

"Yep."

"And do you have something to say to your host?"

Clara responded by throwing her arms around Evie. "Thank you! I had the best time. I'm so excited to come here next year."

"I had the best time, too." Evie appeared to be hugging Clara just as hard as Clara was hugging Evie. "Break a leg at the taping!"

And then Sawyer took his sister to the TVOntario studios and watched as she was made up, briefed, and ushered onto the same set he had seen so many times on television.

He watched her speak passionately and intelligently about vaccination policy.

He reminded himself that everything he had done, he had done for a reason.

Evie had gone to library school, and Clara had turned into a girl genius whose future was bright.

This was the way everything was supposed to turn out.

Hey, how did the taping go? What are you guys up to?

Sawyer grabbed his phone from the nightstand. His stomach did a funny flipping thing when he saw the text was from Evie. The taping went great. What I am up to is flipping through TV channels in my hotel room because Clara ditched me.

The phone rang. He switched to the TV guide channel, set the remote down, and answered the phone. "Hey."

"Ditched by the teenager!" She sounded almost gleeful.

"Yeah, she and Lynn wanted to go out to dinner. I spoke to her parents on the phone. There didn't seem to be any reason not to let them. It's not like they won't be able to do whatever the hell they want come next fall."

"Aww, you're freaking out, aren't you?"

"I am not freaking out," he lied. "I'm just sitting here trying to decide between"—he examined the listings scrolling on the TV—"*Keeping Up with the Kardashians* and . . . *House Hunters International*. This is why— Oh, *hang on*."

"What?"

It took him a moment to say it, because seeing the title pop up in the listings felt a little like being zapped with a cattle prod. "*The Little Mermaid* is on. At eight. On the Disney Channel."

"Oh. My parents don't have cable."

"Come over and watch it with me here."

Silence.

Yeah, there was making up and being not not-friends, and then there was watching *The Little Mermaid*. Some things were best left in the past.

But then he opened his goddamned mouth and said, "Come on. You love this movie. I'll run out and get snacks."

More silence.

All right. He would tell her the truth. But only some of it. The whole truth would scare her. The whole truth scared *him*. And more importantly, the whole truth was useless. Because, he reminded himself for the millionth time, her life was here. In Toronto. Deciding between collections development and corporate taxonomy. Where she didn't have to make little X's on the calendar to try to make time go faster. "I'm getting a pretty unsettling preview of what empty-nesting is going to be like. I could use the company."

She sighed. He had cracked her. "Is there a pool in that hotel where I can try out my new swimming moves?"

"There is."

She sighed again, but it was an overdramatic, jokey one. "I suppose since we're not not-friends, I pretty much have to come."

"Exactly. You don't have a choice. It's in the fine print: when your not not-friend is having an empty-nest panic attack and watching *The Little Mermaid*, you're contractually obligated to show up."

"You really are a good guy, aren't you?"

He wasn't sure what to say to that. Maybe he was; maybe he wasn't. He tried.

The resulting silence that spun out should've been awkward. So many encounters between them lately had been. But strangely, this one wasn't.

When she finally spoke, her voice was soft. "You've done such a good job with Clara, Sawyer. She really is the most remarkable person."

He wasn't sure he could speak. "Thanks," he finally managed after the silence between them went on a beat too long. "I tried really hard."

She cleared her throat. "You know what, Sawyer?"

"What?"

"You're upgraded."

"What?"

"We're not not not-friends anymore." She snorted. "Which is maybe the most ridiculous sentence I have ever uttered. But the point is you're upgraded. We're friends."

"Friends," he echoed, wondering why the word, which should have signified a victory, sounded clangy and out of tune when it came out of his mouth.

"Friends," she said firmly. "I'll be there in half an hour."

Chapter Fifteen

❧

$\mathcal{S}$tanding outside Sawyer's room, Eve ordered herself to feel friendly things. *Not* tingly things. If it took her a few moments of standing there to get all the things unjumbled and properly sorted, so be it.

"Ahh!" She jumped when the door swung open. She wasn't ready. The tingly things had not yet fully receded in favor of the friendly things.

And his raspy "Hey" was not helping matters.

Nor was the dimly lit room, or the fact that he was wearing a pair of swim trunks and nothing else.

"What do you think?" He turned around and wiggled his butt—also not helping. But she laughed when she realized his white trunks had a giant red maple leaf on the ass. "I didn't bring my swimsuit, so when you said you wanted to use the pool, I ran to the gift shop. They were having a massive blowout on their Canada Day stuff."

"Well, I have my suit on under my clothes, so I'm ready when you are."

Soon she was standing on the steps in the shallow end of the pool, holding the railing in a death grip.

"This is your first time in a pool?" Sawyer asked gently, coming to stand next to her.

She shook her head. "I don't know what my problem is. This is a tiny pool. You can see the bottom. Way less scary than that enormous lake."

"Want me to hold you?"

Yep. Yep, she did. For many reasons, only one of which was the whole fear-of-swimming thing. "Nope. I got it."

In order to make herself feel like less of a liar, she let go of the railing and started walking. At the edge of the shallow end, she paused and put her hands out, like she used to do in the lake when she was just standing there, willing herself to float.

"Oh no you don't. Wishing doesn't make it happen."

Damn him. He knew her too well.

He was coming toward her. As much as she wanted him to touch her, she couldn't let it happen. So she gave a little shrieky war cry, lifted her feet off the ground, tilted her body forward, and started paddling.

"All right!" He was leisurely breaststroking alongside her as she huffed and flailed inelegantly.

She stared intently at the far edge and kept moving. Visualizing herself at the end.

And then she was there.

"All right!" he said again. He lifted his hand for a high five, and she slapped it.

And then they did it again—back to the shallow end.

And again back to the deep end. She was rewarded with

a display of seemingly genuine delight from Sawyer at the end of every lap.

Could she ever have imagined this, back on the roof of the Mermaid? That she'd be *swimming*? With *Sawyer*?

Life had been pretty damn twisty lately.

When Eve came out of Sawyer's bathroom half an hour later, she was so exhausted, she felt like she'd swum the English Channel. And hungry—she was *starving*.

As if he could read her mind, Sawyer tossed her a bag of Flamin' Hot Cheetos.

"You remembered."

"Of course." He winked. "I'll be right back—just gonna change quick."

He disappeared into the bathroom, and Eve considered her seating options. There was a little table at the far end of the room flanked by two chairs, and there were two double beds. The angle to the TV from the table would be extreme, and more importantly, if she sat there, would it seem like she was avoiding him? This was a friendly movie viewing, right? She didn't need to sit in Siberia.

She sat on one of the beds.

He emerged and sat on the other.

There. No problem. They were easy. They were breezy.

He turned on the TV. "We missed the first ten minutes."

"It's okay," she deadpanned. "I've seen this movie once or twice before."

"You don't say?" He kept his eyes on the screen, but his lips quirked up.

Hers followed like they were attached to his via some unseen force. It was kind of funny, in retrospect: the city girl who couldn't swim, obsessed with the tale of the Little Mermaid. But it wasn't really about the swimming. It was the idea of being of one world but wanting to live in another one. Of what you might give up to do so. Of whether, once the sacrifice had been made, it had been worth it.

She thought about what he'd said when he invited her over. He had made sacrifices, too, to get to this point where he was preparing to see his sister off to university. "So you're nervous about the looming empty nest?"

"Yeah, there's that. But I'm also worried about the money. Even though I've been trying to save for this since she was a kid, I'm stressing about it."

"I don't suppose..." She shouldn't ask. It was none of her business.

"What?"

"Well, technically, if she applies for loans or grants or anything, it's your father's financial situation they take into account." She was betting that Charles Collins's finances were a lot less rosy than Sawyer's. "So that could actually be good?"

"I have legal custody."

Wow. She had imagined Sawyer taking Clara and leaving and that being the end of it. "Impressive."

"Margaret Thompson helped me. She was the lawyer in town before Jason Sims. We drew up a petition. Charles didn't fight it. A judge agreed with me. It was actually remarkably easy."

"I remain impressed."

"Anyway, we don't have to talk about this. We're missing the movie."

She waved dismissively at the TV.

"But how will we know if Ariel gets her voice back?" he asked.

"Spoiler: they live happily ever after, and everyone can talk."

"Well, anyway, Clara's eighteen now—it was her birthday last week—so I guess she technically has custody of herself."

"Did you let your dad give her that present?"

"I did not."

"Sorry," she said quickly. "None of my business."

"No, sorry, I didn't mean to sound harsh. I just—" His phone dinged from the nightstand. A smile blossomed as he picked it up.

She wanted to ask him what it was, but of course that was none of her business, either. She got a thrill, though, when he walked over and showed her a picture. It was of Clara and Lynn, with a filter on it that made them look like cats. They had their arms around each other, and the word *roomies* had been scrawled across the picture.

"Aww," Evie said. Clara clearly hadn't told him her *other* big news yet, though. If she had, surely he would have—

Sawyer plopped down on her bed.

Why was he doing that? He was still looking at the phone affectionately, so maybe he hadn't realized?

"What's with the cat thing, though? I want her to project herself as the capable young woman she is, not a cat." He looked up from the phone and made an apologetic face. "No offense to any cat lovers who might be present. Or cat palm lovers."

"None taken. I mean, I love cats, even if they don't love me back, but I don't want to look like one. It's the mysterious ways of the youth, I suppose."

"Lynn and her parents seem good, right?"

She understood that he was looking for reassurance. "Yes, for sure. I think Clara probably couldn't have done better on the roommate front."

He blew out a breath and turned to her. "God, Evie. I'm a wreck. What am I going to do now?"

She knew he meant the question in the big, existential sense. But she didn't know how to answer it in that sense. So she pointed to the TV and said, "Now you're going to watch *The Little Mermaid* for the eight hundred millionth time."

He kissed the girl.

How could he not? For one thing, he had a chorus of animated sea creatures egging him on.

He wasn't really sure why he was suddenly listening to cartoons when the same advice from his best friends had fallen on deaf ears.

It probably had something to do with the fact that this latest opportunity presented itself while he was lying on a bed next to Evie Abbott—and not wearing a hard hat.

And his defenses were down. Way down, thanks to all this empty-nest talk. So when Evie was sitting there with her shoes off, cross-legged in the same position she used to watch movies in as a girl, braiding her damp hair? And yet was, so clearly, no longer a girl?

He had nothing. He was a goner.

"Sha la la la la la," sang the cartoon creatures.

"Oh!" she exclaimed on an inhalation, then held her breath.

He had startled her. She had been so engrossed in the movie, she hadn't sensed his approach until they were nose to nose. He stopped with a millimeter of space between the tips of their noses, not wanting to just plant one on her. Well, he wanted nothing *more* than to just plant one on her, but it was possible this kiss would be unwelcome. So he paused. Assessed.

Maybe he had cartoons on the brain, but her face looked like an illustration of the concept of desire. Her cheeks pinkened and her pupils dilated as he watched. Her mouth formed a little O of shock.

She had not exhaled. He moved forward a bit more but turned his head, so his lips were barely resting on her cheek. "Breathe," he whispered.

He felt the hot, rushing exhalation against his own cheek. Hot Cheetos and her. Which should have been ridiculous but was instead very, very sexy.

"This is a bad idea," she said, but one of her hands floated up and hovered over one of his cheeks.

"I know." Speaking of cats, he felt like one, seized as he was with the desire to press his cheek, his chin, his whole face into her touch. He held himself back, barely.

"I'm only in Moonflower Bay for ten more months," she breathed.

"I know." His face was on fire. He could feel each individual strand of beard hair, electrified like a wire, straining toward her touch.

"We're *friends*. We just upgraded." The hand came down.

"I know," he bit out, and *damn*. Live wires was right—it was only the lightest touch of fingers on his beard, but she might as well have grabbed his dick directly.

She was right, though, about all of it. Evie Abbott was not for him. Not even for ten months. If they did this, when she left, he would not survive. That sounded like hyperbole, but—

The girl kissed *him*.

Just as he was about to pull away, she clamped her hands on his cheeks and planted her mouth on his. *Opened* her mouth.

He had no defenses against this.

Like everything about his reintroduction to Evie—swimming with her, watching her braid her hair—it was familiar, yet not. The hands were the same, one planted on either cheek, like she always used to do. It was like she was hanging on, making sure he wasn't going anywhere—spoiler alert: as ill-advised as this was, he wasn't going anywhere—and he loved it now as much as he had then. But his beard under her fingers reminded him that he was older. *They* were older.

Some things were the same, but some things were different.

Same: The lips. Sweet and soft. Different: The pressure. So much more of it. She explored, her tongue sliding against his in a way that made him groan. There was a self-assurance here, a taking of the lead, that was new.

There was also a new sound: a sort of hybrid between an exhalation and a low moan. It made him realize that she'd always been quiet before when they'd been intimate. She had gotten a little breathless from time to time, but that had been the extent of it.

He liked that sound. He liked the grown-up version of kissing Evie Abbott. He alternated kissing with gently scraping his teeth over the pulse fluttering at her throat. He was trying to make her make that noise again, but he wanted it heavier on the moan this time.

Then another sound: the unmistakable slide of a key card being inserted in a door.

The unmistakable sound of reality crashing in on them.

Evie heard it, too, somehow, even though the noises she'd been making should have drowned it out.

She hurled herself away from him, so hard he grabbed for her to make sure she didn't fall, or crash into the nightstand.

But she bucked her torso dramatically to twist out of his grip and catapulted herself onto the other bed.

Clara was struggling with the door. Both of their key cards were being a little persnickety, a fact he was grateful for now.

"That was not a *friendly* activity," Evie whispered urgently as she smoothed her clothing.

He picked up the remote and raised the volume on the movie, as if singing sea creatures could magically cover the fact that Evie looked exactly like someone who had just been thoroughly kissed. Her skin was pink and blotchy, her hair was messed up, and her lips were slightly swollen. She had only half finished braiding her hair.

He grabbed a pillow and set it on his lap. "It's okay. We just overcalibrated for a second there."

"Overcalibrated?"

"Yeah. On the friendship thing. You upgraded me, and we overcalibrated. No big deal. Things will settle down." *Please let things settle down.*

She shot him a look as Clara burst into the room. "Hi! Oh! Eve, hi!"

Sawyer cleared his throat. "Hey, kiddo."

"*The Little Mermaid*!" Clara dumped her bag and perched on the end of his bed, her eyes never leaving the TV. "I love this movie!"

Chapter Sixteen

⟲

*T*hings did not settle down.

Sawyer had been hoping the whole making-out-in-Toronto thing had been about the fact that they'd been in *Toronto*. Away from his daily life in Moonflower Bay. In a placeless hotel room far from his usual responsibilities.

But a month later, firmly ensconced back in his routine, he had still not recalibrated.

"Jake." Maya sighed theatrically. "Why is your hair so beautiful?"

It was a Friday in November, and Sawyer was hanging out at the bar with Jake and Law. Some of the wider crowd had also assembled: Maya, Jenna, Jordan.

Jake—who did have great hair, objectively speaking—shrugged.

"I feel like you should get some of the credit for the man-bun trend," Maya said. "You were doing it before it became a pop culture phenomenon. Hey!" She lifted her hands in the air excitedly. "I'm going to do *Richard III* next year for the Anti-Festival. You would make a great Richard! You're so broody! And your hair is *perfect* for the role. What do you say?"

Jake lifted a single eyebrow. "What do you think?"

Maya, ever the optimist, patted him on the shoulder. "Well, we don't start rehearsals until August, so I have tons of time to work on you."

"So you're sticking with the gratuitous-murder-of-children theme, I see?" Law quipped. "Doesn't Richard murder his nephews?"

"He murders *everyone*," Maya said cheerfully.

Sawyer tuned them out and sipped his beer.

He could tell when Evie arrived before he saw her. Ever since their hotel room encounter, he'd had a strange, extra-sensory ability to tell when she was near. Something happened to his neck. It felt like butterflies in his stomach. Except they were in his neck. Which made no sense, but there it was.

"Hi! Oh my gosh, what a storm!"

She had come from only two doors down, but she was wet. And cold, judging by the way she shivered as she sat down—next to him, because Jake had wordlessly moved one stool over when she arrived to free up the spot. What was up with that? He would find out later. For now he needed to get another question answered. "Why didn't you wear a coat?"

Her brow furrowed. "The Mermaid is a ten-second walk from here."

"And I suppose an umbrella is too much to ask for?"

She made a confused face. "The Mermaid is ten seconds from here." She said it slower this time, like she was talking to a kid. Which annoyed him, but on the plus side, it made his neck butterflies settle down.

"It's on." Law aimed a remote at the TV above the bar and turned up the volume.

Sawyer shrugged off his coat and slung it over Evie's shoulders even though he knew his so-called friends would take note and store it up for whenever they had their next little bro-intervention planned.

"Ben! Can you fix this one, too?"

It was Eiko. She and her husband were sitting at a table with Pearl, Karl, Art, Jamila, and Carol Dyson from the salon. They were clustered near one of the other TV sets across the room. In fact, pretty much everyone who was in the bar tonight was here for the big event.

Sawyer smiled into his beer. This town and its inhabitants might drive him crazy sometimes, but they turned out when it mattered.

"Where's the star of the show tonight?" Karl shouted from across the room.

"She's watching it with her friends," he called back. "I wasn't invited."

"Ahh! Good practice for next year!" Pearl teased.

It was almost Christmas. Which meant it was almost the last semester of Clara's high school career. Which meant it was almost graduation. Which meant it was almost time for her to move away. She and Lynn were constantly texting or Snapchatting or whatever it was that allowed you to turn yourself into a cat, hatching plans for room decor and the introductory science classes they would both need.

Evie laid her hand on his forearm.

It had the effect of settling and stirring up the neck butterflies at the same time, which was technically impossible.

Technically impossible when it came to *neck butterflies*, which were totally a thing?

He looked at her. She wasn't looking back, was just

smiling at the TV as the opening credits played. But she knew. She knew what he was feeling.

All her knowing was both unsettling and a relief. It felt *good* to be understood, but it was also disconcerting. He wasn't used to it.

She did things to him that should have been contradictory. Which was why he was her friend, yet not her friend. The bar erupted into cheers when the host of *The Agenda* introduced Clara. There was so much noise that he couldn't hear anything about the other two kids on the panel.

"*Shhh!*" Evie turned around and shushed everyone!

And then he watched his little sister talk about vaccination policy on TV.

He was so proud, he was fit to bust. He kept switching his attention between the TV and, when he started to get overcome, his beer.

When Evie set her hand on his arm again, he about combusted. It was too much. These women. His sister and his... friend.

"Let me ask you something," he said while one of the other kids—the non-Clara kids—talked. Evie was smart. Maybe she could help him make sense of what was happening to him—when it came to Clara, at least. "Remember *Medea*?"

"Yep."

"I was proud of her then, too. But not like this. This is like..."

"*Medea* times ten?"

"Yeah." Exactly. "What's up with that?"

"It's probably because Medea was a role. Clara's a great actor, but that wasn't *her*. You were proud of her performance. *This* is her talking about her own ideas. Things that came from inside her."

That was exactly right. "How'd you get to be so smart, Evie Abbott?"

She made a dismissive gesture, but he knew the answer. She'd gotten to be so smart because she'd gone to university. She'd followed her dreams.

Was it possible that he could claim a tiny bit of credit for that? The prospect filled him anew with that overwhelming mixture of happiness and melancholy and pride. He took a deep breath. It was almost too much to bear, this onslaught of contradictory emotions.

Just like it would be too much to bear if he did what he wanted to do more than anything—kiss Evie again—and then she went away. That was a contradiction that would *actually* kill him.

"Straight behind you," Law muttered, leaning in close to Sawyer. Sawyer twisted in his seat.

Dammit. Could the world just cut him a break right now?

Charles was standing near the front door, and the whole bar had gone silent, like they were in some kind of cheesy Western movie and a shoot-out was about to take place.

"It's a public place," Jake said quietly. "You're not on duty."

And Charles looked sober.

All of these things were true, but they didn't change the fact that Sawyer's already raw nerves were now screaming.

Charles made eye contact with Sawyer, pointed to the TV closest to where he was standing, and turned his body to face it.

So he wasn't here to make trouble. He was here to watch Clara on TV like the rest of the town. Charles's current address was a room in a sketchy boardinghouse, and Sawyer knew from last time they'd picked him up— after that fight on Main Street—that he didn't have a phone.

So he had probably heard about the show but had no way to watch it.

That was the rational explanation.

The less rational reality was that he was here, and Sawyer was freaking out.

"It's not a public place, actually," Law said, low enough that only Sawyer, Jake, and Evie could hear him. "It's my property. So say the word, and he's out of here."

Sawyer shook his head. He couldn't speak, but he made a point of looking back up at the TV to try to signal that everything was fine.

Of course, everything was not fine.

And of course, Evie knew it.

She waited a few minutes, until the panel was winding down, before saying "Oh! Sawyer! I forgot, I want to have you do some built-in shelves at the inn. Will you come look?"

He shot her a skeptical look. She was going to rescue him *again*?

"I talked to Jake about it, and he said you're the customer service guy." She leaned across him. "Right, Jake?"

She wasn't wrong. Jake was not the person to close a deal. But she was also lying through her teeth. There was no way she and Jake had talked about shelves at the inn.

But Jake grunted vaguely in agreement.

She hopped off her stool and tried to give him his coat back.

He held up a palm. But he got off his stool. "Let's go."

Eve really did want some bookshelves.

There was a big empty wall in her room that called out for some.

Correction: there was a big empty wall in the *first-floor owner's suite* that called out for some. She'd decided that the future owner or manager would be most likely to settle in that room since it was big and on the first floor.

"Hello?" she called, sticking her head back out of the bedroom because Sawyer had not followed her in.

"Sorry." He appeared from behind an unfinished half wall she thought would nicely bracket the front desk. "Why isn't this wall done?"

"I didn't have confidence in my own drywall abilities, and the guys I hired got really busy."

"This little wall will take an hour, tops."

She shrugged. "There was a drywall emergency somewhere else, I guess?"

He frowned and surveyed the space. It was looking more disorganized than usual. She was in a weird spot where a lot of projects were stalled.

Once they were in the bedroom, she swept her arms out. "So I'm seeing this entire wall done with built-in shelving."

"You are not."

"What?"

"You don't want shelves in here. You were just rescuing me again." He wasn't even looking at her. His attention was fixed on one of Lucille's posters, in which a mermaid was towing an unconscious prince through the water. "Just like this. I keep almost drowning, and you keep rescuing me." He leaned in closer to the poster. "Huh."

"What are you talking about? I want bookshelves in here."

He sat on her bed and raised his eyebrows. "For all your books."

"For all the books whoever buys this place will have."

"Because normal people require storage for several hundred books."

"Normal people have knickknacks they need to display."

He snorted. "Right. What this inn really needs is more infrastructure for the display of knickknacks."

She'd been getting a bit indignant, but she couldn't help but laugh at that. "You're a really bad rescuee, Sawyer."

She'd been trying to lighten the mood, but he sighed and buried his head in his hands.

She lowered herself onto the bed and scooted back so she was sitting against the headboard, only belatedly realizing that last time she'd sat on a bed with Sawyer, bad things had happened. Good bad things.

She was so mixed up about that kiss. It should have faded by now. It had been a month, and Sawyer appeared not to have given it a second thought. He seemed to really believe his whole "overcalibration" theory. She…was not recalibrated. In fact, the more time elapsed, the *larger* the kiss loomed. She certainly thought about it enough—if *enough* meant "all the time." But she had learned to live with it, with this kiss forever lurking just below the surface of her consciousness. "Sawyer, can I give you some friendly advice?"

"All right. Friendly advice. Shoot." As he spoke, he uncurled himself and lay flat on his back, but he did it so suddenly and explosively, it was almost like he had meant it literally when he'd said, "Shoot," and someone had complied.

He did not open his eyes, though, which allowed her the freedom to examine him as she spoke. She had grown accustomed to his face. She no longer had the sense that they were hovering between then and now, that he was half boy and half man. He was, now, more familiar than strange.

"Sometimes…" She started slowly, trying to think how to phrase this. "People can end up exerting more control over you than is merited. But the funny thing is, if you really look at the situation, you'll see that it's not them controlling you so much as it's you *letting* them control you. Giving them more power than they deserve."

His eyes popped open, and she jumped a little. He didn't move, though. "Are we talking about me and my dad or you and me?"

"We're talking about you and your dad," she said firmly. She *had* been doing that—giving Sawyer more power over her than was merited—but she wasn't anymore. "I'm not saying he's not a problem, or that you don't have a right to react to him. I'm just saying that objectively speaking, he doesn't have power over you anymore. You grew up. You made something of yourself."

"My sister did, anyway."

"*No.*" He blinked a few times, probably startled because she had spoken so sharply, but that pissed her off. "*You* made something of yourself. Sure, Clara did, or is on her way to it, but so did you." He was trying to object, but she wasn't going to let him. "You grew into a big, accomplished dude. You're the freaking chief of police. You *literally* have all the power. But that's not even the point—that's just a nice little symbolic twist."

"So what's the point, then?"

"The point is, you grew up real nicely, Sawyer." Should she say the rest? Well, why not? "I'm proud of you." He seemed like he was gearing up to deflect, so she kept talking to head him off. "You use your power well. You're fair. Everyone likes you. You're a responsible adult. You *won*. You're a good man."

The way he kept lying there flat on his back was a little disconcerting.

The way a slow, self-satisfied smile blossomed on his face was *a lot* disconcerting.

"You really think I'm a big, accomplished dude?"

She shook her head, tamped down a smile, and changed the subject. "You built me a wall of bookshelves once before, remember?"

"Yes." He sat up suddenly, all signs of laughter gone from his now-serious face. "Upstairs."

She pointed at her blank wall. "So shut up and do it again."

Chapter Seventeen

❧

*S*awyer built Evie some shelves. He was surprised at how much he enjoyed doing it. The canoe, too, which was coming along nicely. Policing was so outwardly focused. He was always talking, persuading, organizing. He'd forgotten how restorative working quietly and steadily could be. How satisfying making something could be.

Of course, he would have liked it better if, like the last time he had done this, Evie had been perched on the bed reading a book while he worked.

But a man could not have everything. And hey, he'd discovered a side gig that could keep him and his empty nest occupied next year—the woodworking business he'd invented was, to his amusement, actually taking off.

After he was done with Evie's shelves, he built her a new front desk.

He built these things for Evie because she was Evie. No further rationale was required.

But maybe also a little bit because he was so grateful for the conversation they'd had that night his dad had come into the bar.

It was funny how a few words from the right person at the right time could make you see things in a new way.

He'd thought about what she said. And about what Clara had said the weekend of the parade, about how Charles seemed more pathetic than dangerous these days.

And then, after all that thinking, he ran into him. It was an uneventful, chance crossing of paths. Charles was headed into the laundromat in the strip mall out on Oak Road as Sawyer came out of the diner next door.

They nodded at each other.

And that was it.

They nodded at each other.

It was unremarkable but, at the same time, a revelation.

The moment he'd caught a glimpse of his dad, he'd braced himself. Prepared for his body or his brain or whatever unholy alliance they had created to trigger the familiar sensation of panic.

But then he thought of Evie and asked himself, *What is actually happening here?*

What was happening was that Sawyer Collins, the chief of police, was walking out of Sadie's Diner laughingly arguing with Sadie herself because she was, as was her habit, trying to press free cinnamon rolls on him since he always insisted on paying for the meal she always tried to comp him. It was a good-natured argument they had every time he ate at her place.

Charles, on the other hand, was coming out of the laundromat, probably because he didn't have laundry facilities in the crappy boardinghouse he lived in, and getting into a waiting taxi because he didn't have a valid driver's license.

Sawyer and Clara were getting ready to spend Christmas with Jake and Art and Jamila, having declined a bunch of other invitations. Whom would Charles spend Christmas with?

It wasn't that he wished bad things on his dad—hell, for a second he thought maybe he should offer to drive him home, but that was going too far. One breakthrough at a time. But he did suddenly see things Evie's way.

The reaction he usually had to seeing his father was a habitual one. There was a groove worn into his psyche that his dad could slip right into, like a kid making a beeline for a favorite slide at the playground. In the past, that reaction, that fight-or-flight response, had been justified by the circumstances. He'd been a child, and his father had been an abusive asshole. You never knew when he entered a room if you—or your kid sister—were going to be safe.

You never knew if, next time the social worker came, she was going to see through your lies. Everything was fine with his dad. No, he didn't mind "helping out" with his sister.

But everything was different now. Maybe it wasn't "fine." That was probably an impossibly high bar when it came to Charles. Evie had said, "You won." That didn't seem quite right, either. It was more that a war had ended without him noticing. He didn't have to let his father slide down that groove anymore.

It was an astonishing thought.

So astonishing that while he stood there marveling as his dad's taxi pulled away, Sadie managed to drop the bag of cinnamon rolls on the hood of his squad car and flee inside.

So yeah, there weren't enough bookshelves in the world to thank Evie for springing him from that particular mental prison. For rescuing him yet again. And since he didn't know how to actually thank her, he just kept building stuff for her.

Well, not *her*, he reminded himself. None of it was for her, as she herself had pointed out. It was for the inn. Which would soon belong to someone else. It might help her sell the place, but it wasn't for *her*.

When she went home to Toronto for Christmas, he missed her. But it was a good reminder of where she really lived. She went *home* for Christmas. That was how she had phrased it.

Also a good reminder? When she started texting him on New Year's eve while he was finishing the front desk.

It started with her usual dry Evie humor. She sent a picture of what must have been a party with her colleagues, because it was a bunch of women sipping drinks inside what looked like a library. Librarians gone wild, she'd written.

An hour later there was another one, of her grinning next to a banner that read "Happy New Year." New Year's EVE! Get it? she wrote. What are you doing?

He put down his paintbrush.

> *Sawyer:* Final coat of varnish on the front desk.
> *Eve:* You're at the in?
> *Eve:* In.
> *Eve:* INN.
> *Eve:* It's North Year's even! Don't be at the inn!

Her next text was a series of wine emojis. He chuckled and glanced at the time. Judging by the misspellings, she was a little toasted.

Sawyer: It's New Year's eve, yes, but it's six p.m.

Eve: Oh, right. Do I know how to party or WHAT? Anyway, don't stay there. Do someone fun.

Sawyer: Hmm. Do someone fun. Who do you suggest?

Eve: SOMETHING.

Eve: Or, whatever, do SOMEONE if that's your thing. I'm sure Pie an hook you up with someone.

Eve: PEARL

Sawyer: I go on duty at seven. Cops don't get New Year's eve off.

He stared at the phone for an embarrassingly long time. She didn't reply.

He sighed and went to the kitchen to rinse his brush. The problem here, he was pretty sure, was that once you kissed Evie Abbott, it was hard to put the genie back in the bottle. A can of worms got opened. Whatever cliché you wanted to throw at it.

Because he was kidding himself with the whole re-calibration thing. There had been none. Evie Abbott was the best woman he had ever met, and he wanted her so badly it made his teeth hurt.

It took three tries for Eve to get the charger cord plugged into her phone.

It was possible there had been a little too much New Year's cheer.

But there! Third time's the charm! Yay!

She got nothing but the battery-charging image, though.

The thing was super dead. She'd turned the ringer off and gone back to her party when she and Sawyer started talking about the possibility of him "doing" someone. Not that he was going to.

But he could.

But he probably wouldn't.

Because he was working.

Which wasn't the same as *because he didn't want to.*

Her thoughts landed on Sadie, the diner owner who supposedly had a crush on Sawyer. Who was Sadie? That she served up homemade hot beef sandwiches that were apparently the best in southwestern Ontario didn't mean anything. That her cinnamon rolls were legendary was not of any concern to Eve. Even if Sawyer supposedly loved them.

Sadie loved Sawyer. Sawyer loved Sadie's cinnamon rolls. Hmm. What was that diagram thingy called, with the overlapping circles?

She lurched toward the corner of the room, aiming for her desk so she could get a pen and paper to actually draw the diagram she couldn't remember the name of, but realized too late that there was no desk in this room because this was no longer her room, she having moved out of her parents' house years ago. It was a den.

She bonked into the bookcase.

Ouch. Okay. Anyway. You know what would prove her point? If she put a picture of Sadie next to a picture of Sawyer in order to showcase how not-good they looked together. Yes! That was better than the Venus diagram or whatever.

The stupid phone was still dead, though, so she got out her laptop. There was a picture of Sadie on the diner's website, and since Eve had visited that website approximately eight hundred million times since Maya had casually mentioned Sadie's crush, Google was not daunted by her drunken spelling and auto-filled the address for her.

Next she google-imaged Sayer Conlins.

Saywee Xolins.

Dang it!

She put her face right next to the keyboard and slowly typed S A W Y E R C O L L I N S M O O N F L O W E R B A Y.

She got some image hits, but they must have been older pictures, because he didn't have a beard in any of them.

All right. Since her fingers weren't working super well anyway, she'd just ask him for one.

And look! Her phone had come back from the dead! A New Year's miracle! Since spelling was too hard for her right now, she went straight to her contacts and called him.

He picked up right away. "Evie. Finally. Is everything okay?"

"I need you to send me—"

"What's wrong? I can be on the road in ten minutes. Do you need me to come get you?"

He was speaking urgently, though she couldn't figure out why. "I'm fine. Can you hang on a sec?"

She switched over to her texts. Uh-oh. There were a bunch from him. Increasingly urgent ones that said things like Hi, I hope you're having fun, but let me know that you made it home okay.

They escalated to Evie, you seemed like you were drunk at 6. It is now 12:30. ARE YOU OKAY?

"Hiiiii," she said when she got back on the call. "My phone was dead. Sorry. I just saw all your messages. Happy New Year?"

She braced herself for a scolding from Mr. Responsible, but it didn't come. He just expelled a breath and said, softly, "Are you home?"

"Yeah." Not that this was home. This was her parents' house. But she supposed it was the closest thing she had to a home in Toronto, since she'd given up her apartment. And Toronto was home.

Right?

Maybe she needed to do a diagram for that, too.

"Did you have fun?" he asked.

"I did. Did you?"

"I'm working. New Year's eve isn't usually as bad as the Mermaid Parade, but it's one of our big nights."

"Right. That sucks. Did you go to Sadie's?"

"The diner?"

"Yeah."

"No. Was I supposed to?"

She smiled. "No."

"So what can I do for you?"

That was...a big question. How long did he have? Because she could make a really long list.

"You started to say that you needed something from me," he prompted.

"Oh! Yes! I need you to send me a selfie."

"Why?"

"Because I need a picture of you with your beard."

"For what?"

"For a diagram."

He laughed. "Now?"

He was working, and she needed him to send her a selfie so she could put it next to Sadie from the diner and prove how not well suited they were—was that unreasonable? She was still pondering the question—it was like she'd decided to give herself a really hard test—when he said, "Okay, hang on a sec."

There was some rustling followed by the chime of an incoming text.

And there he was.

Oh, he was so pretty. It wasn't fair. He was sitting in his cruiser, which appeared to be parked near the little beach. The car's interior light was on, maybe so he could illuminate the shot—so thoughtful! The dim, yellow light made his face glow. There was an odd slice of different, focused light coming from some outside source. It gave the illusion of a white streak in his beard. It made her wonder if he would still have that beard when he was old.

Actually, the real question was, Would she still know him when he was old?

The prospect of *not* knowing him made her sad, suddenly—though maybe that was six glasses of wine talking. But realistically, was she going to keep in touch with him after she sold the Mermaid and moved back to Toronto? They'd moved from not not-friends to genuine friends—with a detour for making out that one time—but were they go-out-of-your-way-to-keep-in-touch-when-you-don't-live-in-the-same-town friends? Probably not.

She cleared her throat to break up the tightness that had lodged there. "You're at the lake?"

"Yeah. Sometimes when I have a break in the action on a hectic shift I come here and look at the water." He paused. "That sounds lame."

"No. I do it, too." What had all her standing in the lake staring at the horizon last summer been, if not that? And she and Maya had done a few more sessions of moonflower-throwing. In fact, they were going to do it again tomorrow. "I'm coming back tomorrow, and Maya wants to throw flowers into the lake. She says even though it's not a full moon, it's a good idea to start the new year with a wish. I'm telling you, there's something, I don't know, soul-calming about that lake."

And…she was officially a maudlin drunk. Enough of that. Time for a mood swing. She put the phone on speaker and swiped back to his picture. Who was she kidding? He would look good with Sadie Cinnamon Rolls. He would look good with *anyone*.

"What are you going to wish for?" he asked.

"I don't know. That's tomorrow. Who knows what I'll wish for tomorrow?"

"Probably for your hangover to go away."

"Touché. But really, who knows? Tomorrow's wishes are for tomorrow." She replayed that statement in her mind. "Wow, that was kind of stealthily deep. Wishing in the moment. Each moment is a wish?" Man, they should give her an Etsy store. She could produce inspirational T-shirts and mugs.

"So what do you wish for at *this* moment, then?"

"At this moment I wish for…" She tilted the phone to try to figure out what was casting that weird chunk of light on his beard. Something squeezed between her legs. "…you and your beard to go down on me."

She clapped a hand over her mouth. Holy crap, *what* had she just said? *Where* had that come from?

Well, she knew where it had come from: a little category called True Things. But how had it gotten out of her mouth?

Six glasses of wine, plus her renegade mouth that never obeyed her brain when it came to Sawyer, was how. She dipped her fingertips into the glass of water she'd brought into the den with her and flicked water at her face. *Look sharp, Abbott. Time to backpedal the hell out of what you just said.*

She was too slow, though. He spoke first. "Why did we never do that when we had the chance?"

Hell, if she could say outrageous things, he could, too. And his question was a lot less outrageous than her bombshell wish. She probably wouldn't remember any of this in the morning anyway.

He, however, was never going to forget it. Suddenly uncomfortable, he unbuckled his seat belt.

"Well..." she drawled. Oh sweet God, was she going to say something innuendo laden? Not that what she had said before was innuendo. Nope, it had been direct as hell.

I wish for you and your beard to go down on me.

He shifted in his seat and reminded himself that she was drunk. Not in her right mind.

"You never had a beard," she said. "I mean, no offense, but I don't know if the hormones had kicked in enough to really make a beard happen for you yet."

He chuckled. So much for more suggestiveness. But he did want to know the answer to his question. "No. I mean, why did I never go down on you? You went down on me. Why didn't I reciprocate?"

"The patriarchy?" she suggested.

He barked a laugh. He might not have said it like that, but she wasn't wrong. "That's it, isn't it?"

"Well, in your defense, I don't know how many teenage boys are, you know, getting right in there."

It was true. Evie had been his first love. That last summer, the summer they started having sex, he'd tried to please her. It always seemed like she was having fun, but from the vantage point of adulthood, and with some more experience under his belt—no pun intended—he could see that things had been a lot more mechanical than they should have been. Although the local high school had had a pretty good sex-ed curriculum, it, too, had been pretty mechanical. How to use a condom and why. Diagrams with parts you were supposed to label—just in case you ever came face-to-face with a fallopian tube in the wild.

No one said anything about pleasure, was the point. No one said anything about female orgasms, specifically.

Had she ever had one with him?

God, it was excruciating to contemplate the notion that maybe she hadn't. But as she'd said, it wasn't like teenage boys really knew what they were doing.

Well, shit. At least that had extinguished the boner her wish had inspired.

It was his turn to talk. "So, beard, eh?"

"I don't know…" She had turned contemplative. She yawned. "I always thought beards were gross."

"Gross!" He feigned outrage.

"I mean, yes. But I was thinking about it purely as a visual thing. I wasn't…" Another yawn. "Thinking with my other senses."

"So you're saying you think my beard is ugly but that it might have other redeeming qualities?"

"Well, not ugly, but maybe good for more than just looking at?" She yawned again. "Would you do it if you were here?"

"Do what?" He was going to hell. He knew what she meant, but he wanted to hear her say it again.

"Would you go down on me?"

He sighed. "No. You're drunk."

"Yeah, but you're not."

"Yeah, but you are."

"So?"

"You can't legally give consent when you're drunk."

"Will you drop the cop thing for one second?"

"It's not a cop thing. It's a human decency thing."

She laughed. "I think it's a Sawyer thing. You're very upstanding, you know."

Why were they even having this argument? It wasn't like anything could happen between them even if she was stone-cold sober and sitting next to him. "Go to bed, Evie." He didn't want to hang up. But she was drunk and tired, and he was supposed to be patrolling.

"Okay." She sighed, a little breathy one that sounded like it might be shading into frustration. It reminded him of the noises she'd made when they'd made out in Toronto. "Sawyer?"

"Yes, sweetheart?" He allowed the endearment to slip out because he was pretty sure she wouldn't remember any of this tomorrow.

"Happy New Year."

He smiled at the dark, cold lake. "Happy New Year, Evie."

Chapter Eighteen

❧

Okay, I'm ready!"

Maya emerged from her bedroom just as Eve found the note on her phone—and screamed.

"What?" Maya rushed over. "What's the matter?"

Eve couldn't breathe as the entire New Year's eve conversation crash-landed into her consciousness.

She turned her phone around and showed Maya the note. Dear Ebe you told Sayer u want him to go down on u [just so youo know happy new yer—Eve lol youself

This was why she had that random, weird—weird but hot—picture of Sawyer from New Year's eve. She'd never really understood why he'd sent her a selfie that night.

Maya shook the phone at her. "What. Is. This."

"I got drunk at New Year's and called Sawyer and told him I wanted him to go down on me and apparently I thought I might forget it—which I *did* until this very moment—so I wrote myself a note for what reason I don't really know, maybe so I could try to do some damage control, but I saved it in my notes and I was just getting my phone out to make a list and I found this and now I am going to die."

Maya did not look as horror-struck as Eve thought she should be. In fact her face went from concerned to amused in the blink of an eye, and she cracked up. "That was the best run-on sentence I've ever heard."

"Don't laugh!" Eve buried her face in her hands. "New Year's was six weeks ago! I've seen him so many times since then, and he hasn't said anything!"

"That's because Sawyer Collins is a gentleman."

"Oh my God!" Eve paused to let another memory surface. "I was getting my hair done at Curl Up and Dye last week, and Sawyer came in to ask CJ about her mom. Remember how Carol Senior had her second hip replaced in January?" Maya nodded. "Sawyer and CJ seemed to have this ongoing inside joke—"

"You know, I think that's what makes Sawyer such a good cop," Maya interrupted. "He has these little schticks with people. He knows stuff about everyone's lives—I mean, just the fact that he was popping in to check on Carol to begin with, you know? It's not like—"

"Will you let me finish my mortifying story of humiliation?"

Maya clapped her hands excitedly. "Yes! Yes, I will!"

"Okay, so she's razzing him about his beard, and he's protesting that he's keeping it. He was talking to her, but he was looking at me—looking at me kind of funny."

"Funny how?"

"I don't know. Funny intense?"

"Yeah, he gets the severe scolding face sometimes." Maya started trying to imitate the face.

"Do you want to hear this or not?"

Maya made a lip-zipping gesture.

"So he's giving me this weird look, which makes CJ look at me, too, and then she asks me what I think, and before I can answer, Sawyer goes, 'Oh, she likes beards, don't you, Evie?'"

"Have you ever noticed that he always calls you Evie, and no one else does?"

She waved dismissively. "That's just always what he used to call me."

"Yeah, but why does he still?"

Eve ignored her. She had to get this out. "So he says, 'You like beards, don't you?' And I say..." Oh, it was so painful. "'Not historically.'"

Maya made a face that was a cross between sympathetic and amused. "Which totally implies that you like them now."

"It does, right?" She'd been hoping there was some other interpretation.

"I think it does." Maya cracked up again.

Eve slumped against the back of her chair and moaned.

"All right." Maya tapped Eve on the shoulder. "Let's go. Maybe you can wish your way out of this."

Eve allowed herself to be led downstairs. Part of her wanted to go home—well, to the inn—and hide under a rock forever. But she'd already seen Sawyer so many times, what would hiding accomplish?

At A Rose by Any Other Name, they chatted with Maya's parents and were given some impostor flowers for their outing.

"I didn't realize your mom worked at the store," Eve said.

"Mom's a nuclear engineer up at the Bruce plant, so she has a long commute. She helps out at the store on weekends, though."

"So your father is a florist, and your mother is a nuclear engineer?" Eve asked. "You don't see that every day."

"I know. Let's just say traditional gender role BS was refreshingly absent from my childhood."

"How come you never work at the store?"

It was Maya's turn to sigh. "Because I want to do my own thing. I want to do theater. Why do I have to be a florist because my dad's a florist?"

"Do we need to talk about this? I think maybe we've been spending too much time lately talking about me." She was a bad friend.

Maya made a sheepish face. "Well, it's the source of some conflict. Am I just going to let my father's empire crumble when he's gone while I make a very poor living playing dress-up? Let's wait and find out!"

"No," Eve said. "Because you're smartly trying to diversify your activities so you can keep doing what you love. That's what the summer camp is for!"

They chatted about Maya's camp plans as they strolled toward the lake in what had become a monthly ritual.

Maya steered her to one end of the pier. "So whatcha gonna wish for?" She performed an exaggerated wink.

"Not *that*."

"You sure about that?"

"I'm sure!" She was going to come up with something else. She closed her eyes so she could concentrate.

Potential Wishes That Had Nothing to Do with Sawyer Collins's Stupid Beard

    1.

She stood there for a really long time. *Come on. Focus.*

"What are you ladies wishing for this time?"

"Ahh!" Eve shrieked.

Maya cracked up. "I think maybe it just came true."

"That right?" Sawyer asked Maya, but he kept his eyes on Eve. Could he tell what she was thinking? One corner of his mouth quirked up. And then. He stroked. His beard.

"We have to…go do that thing." Eve glared at Maya until Maya got the hint.

"Yep, gotta go! Do the thing!" Maya threw her flower in the water and saluted Sawyer. "See you, Chief."

Eve flung her flower over the railing and tried really, really hard to empty her mind while doing so, to not make a wish at all.

She did not succeed.

"Why don't you just do it?" Maya said later when they were settled in at the bar.

"Do what?"

"Do Sawyer."

Eve choked on the Diet Coke she'd ordered on account of the fact that she was *never drinking again*. "What?"

"You." She pointed at Eve. "Sawyer." She pointed at the empty stool next to Eve. "One night of passion." She gestured dramatically between Eve and Imaginary Sawyer.

"Okay, two things." Eve hopped off her stool and picked up Maya's wine. "One. If we're going to talk about this, we're not doing it here." Honestly. Law was seven feet away. She led Maya to one of the booths in the back. This was where they'd retreated the first night Eve had come to this bar. It felt like a lifetime ago.

"And what is two?" Maya prompted once they'd sat.

"Two is did you not see him hoovering Jeannie Wilkerson's face off in front of the entire town?"

"I did indeed see that. *Ten* years ago. When we were *children*."

"Right, but the point is he broke my heart," Eve said quietly. "I can't let that happen again." Saying that out loud, even just to Maya, made her feel way too vulnerable. She pressed her palms against her face.

"Who said anything about your heart?"

Huh? Eve splayed her fingers and peeked through them.

"I don't think you really heard me before. I said you"—Maya pointed at Eve—"and Sawyer"—she pointed at Imaginary Sawyer, who had apparently followed them from the bar—"and one night of passion. *One* night."

Eve spread her fingers wider. "You mean like get him out of my system?"

Maya shrugged. "Wash that man right out of your hair? Or, you know, wash that man's beard hair out of your nether regions—ha!"

"I don't think the 'We're only going to do this once, and then I'll magically be over you' thing actually works outside of romance novels."

"Does it work in romance novels?"

Eve groaned. "No."

"Well, you gotta do you, but it seems like you're torturing yourself. Why not torture yourself *and* get some, is all I'm saying."

Hmm. Was it possible that Maya had a point? "You really think I could...be with him and not get my heart trampled on again?"

Maya glanced quickly at the bar and back to Eve. "Honestly? I don't know."

"Well." Eve harrumphed. "I'll think about it."

* * *

Eve thought about it.

She thought about it all through the next week, which she spent arguing with her tradespeople—when they bothered to show up.

She thought about it when she texted Sawyer. So, hey, not that I ever deserved the special treatment, but did you stop greasing the wheels of my reno?

He didn't reply, but he did do that thing where he showed up thirty seconds later because he'd been over at Law's.

"Hey," he said when she answered the door. "What's happening?"

She stepped back to let him in. "Nothing. That's the problem. I thought you were throwing your weight around so stuff got done around here. Did you stop?"

"I did not." He jogged up the stairs, which were still exposed underfloor. They had sanded and refinished the main floor themselves, but she was having new wood installed on the upper floors. When she arrived on the second-floor hallway, he was coming out of one of the rooms. "There hasn't been any progress on this floor since I was here on New Year's eve."

"Right. And the bathrooms on the third floor have basically ground to a halt in terms of both plumbing and tiling."

"And what do the trades say?" He narrowed his eyes. "What does Dave Pearson say?"

"When I talk to them individually, there's always a good reason. The tile is on backorder, or there's a burst-pipes emergency somewhere else."

He pressed his mouth into a thin line and nodded. "I'm going to take care of this."

* * *

Murder Mystery at the Mermaid.

Sawyer had to admit, it was something. Maya had rigged the place with spooky lighting, and the cast, kitted out to look like they'd stepped out of the board game Clue, was mingling with the audience—which was made of townspeople only, as this was a dress rehearsal Maya had wanted a friendly audience for. They were standing around in clusters, and apparently they would move among a few rooms for different scenes.

The centerpiece of it all was a section of the dining room blocked off with police tape and guarded by cast members dressed as cops. And by one actual cop. He caught Olivia's eye, and she shrugged. He got it. Maya could be very persuasive. Inside the tape was a dead body covered with a sheet.

"I'm surprised you went for this," he whispered to Eve a few minutes before showtime.

"She's trying to get something going for the winter season. I don't think people really get how entrepreneurial Maya is."

He could see that. Maya always had some idea or other.

"All I had to do was clear out some junk to make sure there was nothing dangerous lying around. I figured since the reno is stalled, she might as well use the space."

Yeah. He was monumentally annoyed about that. He'd spoken to the tradespeople who'd been slacking and had been assured they would reapply themselves.

"Maya says the unfinished nature of the space will add to the murderous ambiance," Eve whispered before the lights went out. All of them. So completely that he suspected Maya had flipped the breaker. A murmur threaded through the crowd, and when the power came back on, there was a spotlight trained on the "crime scene." The sheet had been removed from the dead body—and it was a mermaid.

Well, it was actually Jenna dressed in the mermaid queen costume they used for the parade, but close enough.

The show was great. Fun and packed with twists. It was even genuinely scary for a moment, when a second "victim"—Karl Andersen—staggered abruptly out of the kitchen with "blood" gushing out of a wound in his chest.

Eve shrieked and instinctively jerked back, crashing into Sawyer's chest. He tightened his arms around her before she could pull away. He understood the reaction. They all knew the blood was fake, but it was so graphic, and it was *right there*.

What he did *not* understand was why he didn't let Eve go once the moment had passed.

He *did* let her go when his cop instincts felt someone's attention on them. He looked up. Art Ramsey, who was running the spotlight, was perched atop some scaffolding and using a small light to illuminate his own work. But he wasn't watching the play; he was watching them.

He looked away quickly, but instead of returning his attention to the performance, he looked at someone behind Sawyer and winked. Sawyer craned his neck to see who Art was sending secret messages to: Pearl.

He suddenly understood what was happening. Why all the work that he wasn't personally doing on the inn had come to a halt.

Damn them.

Damn *him*. He should have figured it out sooner.

After the play, he cornered them. Sawyer wasn't on duty, so he wasn't in uniform, but he put on his best chief-of-police voice as he pointed to an empty corner—coincidentally, where the hardwood for upstairs was stacked. "I need to speak to both of you. *Now*." He glared at them for a long moment before he spoke. "Are you sabotaging the reno of this place?"

The way Pearl's eyes and mouth opened in a caricature of shock confirmed it.

"Of *course* not," Art said. "Frankly I'm offended that you would suggest such a thing."

"I'm *helping* with the reno," Pearl said, still performing her mock outrage. "How many times have I sent you to help Eve with something?"

He closed his eyes for a moment. When he opened them, his voice had gone cold. Icy. "You were helping her with the reno, back when you thought that was the way to trap her here. Now that you realize that wasn't working, you switched gears and started sabotaging everything."

The shock on her face was real this time. Good. He was *pissed*, and he wasn't hiding it. There was the old folks' cute but ultimately harmless meddling, and there was truly interfering in people's lives. Costing them time and money. Deceiving them.

"Don't you take that tone with me, Sawyer." Pearl shook her finger at him.

"Then stop meddling in Eve's affairs, Pearl."

"The real question here, Sawyer"—the finger made contact with his chest—"is why aren't *you* meddling in Eve's affairs?"

"What the hell are you talking about?"

"Do you *want* her to sell it? Do you *want* her to leave?"

He wanted to scream in frustration. She didn't understand that it wasn't *about* what he wanted. Pearl wouldn't understand the concept of loving someone so much that you gave them up.

"Stop being so goddamn honorable, Sawyer."

See? She didn't understand. She was incapable of it.

"All right, Pearl." Art, who had been watching their spat in silence, put his arm around Pearl and tugged. "He heard you."

Art led Pearl away, but he shot a look at Sawyer over his shoulder. Sawyer would have expected it to be apologetic, sheepish.

But it wasn't. As he shook his head slightly, he looked almost...disappointed?

Well, whatever. He wasn't responsible for the emotional machinations of these people. He was too busy for that—he had tradespeople to yell at. Again.

Chapter Nineteen

❧

*E*ve had never seen a storm like this one, in Moonflower Bay or anywhere. It had been raining all day, but *raining didn't do justice to what was happening out there*. Water was pouring from the sky, but almost horizontally, on account of the wind. Lightning lit up the sky every few minutes, followed by cracks of thunder so loud they made her heart thump. It was the end of February. It should be *snowing*, not raining.

When the power went out, around four in the afternoon, she decided to check in on Pearl. It made Eve nervous to think of her in the dark kitchen by herself.

If she'd been worried about a vulnerable little old lady frightened of the storm, she needn't have been. She found Pearl not cowering in the kitchen but wearing a full-body wet suit.

"Eve! Just the woman I need! Can we take your car down to the lake? There's a rescue underway." She was loading pastries into Ziploc bags.

"And you're going to bring them butter tarts?" Eve was teasing, but when Pearl didn't even crack a smile, she understood that the situation was serious.

"I don't know if it will be any help, or if they'll even be able to stop long enough to eat, but I want to bring some coffee—I got it made just before the power went out. It's freezing out there."

"Of course. The car's out back."

As they inched down Main Street, she started to get scared. For themselves—visibility was down to nothing as rain lashed against the windshield harder and faster than the wipers could deal with—but also for whoever was down at the lake.

"What kind of rescue is happening?" She had to shout to be heard over the pounding of the rain.

"There's a boat out on the lake, and apparently its engine gave up."

"Who would go out on a boat in this?"

"The world is full of people with questionable levels of intelligence."

When they got to the little beach, Eve started to get really nervous. Giant waves that looked like they belonged in *National Geographic* lashed the shore, and the rain was starting to turn to ice. There were two ambulances and several Ontario Provincial Police vehicles parked on the street. Their flashing lights threw out eerie bursts of color in the unrelenting rain.

"Looks like OPP marine units out there." Pearl pointed to the lake, where just barely visible was a big boat with flashing lights that seemed to be anchored and a smaller speedboat coming in to shore. "And Jake," Pearl added, and sure enough, Jake's boat was coming in, too, trailing the speedboat.

"Is that Sawyer on Jake's boat with him?" Or, no, he was actually hopping out of the boat and into the water.

Pearl wasn't looking anymore; she was unloading the coffee urn from the back seat. "Probably. OPP has jurisdiction in the water, but Sawyer will be here somewhere."

Eve, trying to keep an eye on Sawyer, helped Pearl set up the coffee on the trunk of the car and held her umbrella over it. One of the EMTs came over and gratefully accepted a cup.

"What happened?" Eve asked.

"A small cruise ship got stuck about a mile out." He shook his head. "OPP and this guy"—he jerked his thumb toward Jake's boat—"have been shuttling people in."

"Is everyone okay?"

"So far. Some mild hypothermia and a nasty shoulder dislocation in the first batch. We're waiting for the next group."

"But what about the lightning?" Eve was feeling increasingly frantic. "It can't be safe for people out there. The rescuers are putting their own lives at risk."

The EMT shrugged. "Part of the job. Someone has to save these idiots from themselves."

"Todd! The last group is on its way!"

Lightning flashed and illuminated Sawyer, who was carrying someone in his arms. A boy, it looked like, and one of his arms was sticking out at an unnatural angle. Todd handed Pearl his cup and jogged off.

"Oh my God!" Without thinking, Eve followed the medics.

She'd gotten pretty wet in the dash from the bakery to her car, and even more so as they'd stood talking to the EMT. But by the time she reached the beach, she was soaking. Hair-plastered-down, wet-to-her-underwear, water-sloshing-around-in-her-shoes wet.

Sawyer didn't notice her at first. He lowered the boy to a gurney the medics had waiting. "He was unconscious when we got there," he shouted. "The boat has capsized. Maybe he hit his head."

The EMT said something she couldn't hear, and Sawyer turned back toward the lake. Her first instinct was to shout his name, but she suppressed it. He didn't need her distracting him.

But it was like he heard her anyway, heard the silent shout inside her head, because he turned back, and his eyes immediately latched on to hers.

He started toward her, crossing the wet sand in big strides. He looked pissed.

"Evie! What are you doing here?" He *sounded* pissed, too.

"I came with Pearl. She wanted to bring coffee." She looked over her shoulder. Pearl was standing next to a Moonflower Bay squad car with Olivia.

"Pearl, get in the car!" Olivia hollered. "This is no place for civilians. Environment Canada just issued a flash flood warning."

Eve expected Pearl to argue, but she got into the back of the squad car without a peep. Her easy compliance scared Eve. If Pearl was done fighting, it wasn't safe to be here.

"You'll go with them." Sawyer grabbed her arm. "Olivia!" he hollered, but she was already in the car and didn't hear him. "Goddammit."

"It's okay! I have my own car!" She pointed at it, and, not letting go of her arm, he changed course.

Eve got in her car and tried to start it, but the piece of crap engine wouldn't turn over.

Sawyer pounded the roof in frustration as another flash of lightning and crack of thunder let loose overhead.

"I'll walk!" She scrambled out of the car.

"Do you have power?"

"No."

"Go to my house. It's closer, and I could see when I was out on the water that the neighborhood hasn't lost power."

She nodded. It had been stupid of her and Pearl to come, and the best thing she could do now was get out of the way.

He handed her a set of keys. His hands were like blocks of ice. Hers were, too. She hadn't felt cold before, probably because her fear had been distracting her. Now that she was on her way to a warm, dry house, violent shivering kicked in. But Sawyer's hands were *so* cold. She grabbed one of them between hers and rubbed, but it was no use.

"When you get to my place, get in the shower and warm up. You're at risk of hypothermia."

And you're not? she wanted to shout. He'd actually been *in* the lake.

He looked back at the lake. "I gotta go."

"You're not going back in?" The paramedic had said the group coming in—she could see people wading in from the police boat and Jake's boat—was the last.

"There are still a couple more people out there."

"You can't go in the water! What if lightning strikes the lake?"

"There are people stuck out there, Evie."

He pulled away. She wanted to leap onto his back, to physically prevent him from going in the water, but she knew he would only shake her off. He was right: somebody had to go back in, and he would consider it his job. His town; his responsibility.

He was walking away from her, but backward, so he was still looking at her. "Clara's not home. Let yourself in. Get warmed up. Borrow some clothes."

She was so scared. So stupidly scared, it was making her feel unhinged. "Sawyer!" she shouted just as he was about to turn away. He paused, giving her his attention.

She'd intended to say something like, "Be careful," but what came out was, "Come back!"

He pressed a hand over his heart, nodded, turned, and sloshed back into the lake.

Sawyer had never seen anything like that. An emergency that *just kept going*. On and on, it felt like. In reality he'd only made half a dozen trips out, wading to meet the boats and shuttling people to the paramedics, but he was exhausted.

It was the aftereffects of adrenaline, he knew. The crash.

He'd been fine, mostly, or at least capable of mechanically plodding along, until he'd spotted Evie. The fear in her face had ignited panic in his chest. He'd had to get her out of there.

After seeing the last ambulance off and arranging with the marine unit to do some joint reporting tomorrow, he trudged up the beach toward Main Street. He'd lost his phone somewhere in all the chaos, and he needed to find one to call Evie and let her know everything was okay. He could still see that terrified look on her face.

He was about to peek into the hardware store—in addition to a phone, Karl would probably have a good overview of what the needs were in town—when he ran into Olivia coming out.

Before he could speak, she said, "Go home, Chief."

"I'm not off until seven."

"Go home," she said again. "In fact, get in the car. I'll take you."

"But—"

"I have things covered. The storm is waning. Power's

back on the north side of Main. There are crews out working on the rest—Dom's with them. The worst we have is some broken glass on some storefronts and some flooded basements."

He followed to where she was unlocking the squad car. "But we should check on people without power. If power's still out on the south side, Carol Dyson will need help. She won't be able to get up and down the stairs." Carol had one of those automated lifts, which shuttled her from the second-floor apartment to the salon.

"Already done. Joel is driving her to her daughter's place right now."

"But—"

"*Sawyer.* You've done enough superheroing today. Go home. Warm up. I promise we'll call you if we need you. Get in the car."

And so he did. On the short drive, his body just started…deflating. By the time Olivia pulled up to his house, the worst of the storm had passed, but it was still raining steadily. Olivia had said the power was restored to the north side of Main, so he should ask her to drive Evie home. "Can you…"

She looked at him with raised eyebrows as his request died in his throat. The thing was, he didn't *want* to send Evie out to be driven home by Olivia. He was going to crash—soon, and hard. But he wanted to look at Evie first. To see with his own eyes that she was okay.

Or, hell, maybe he could talk her into staying the night. Clara was at a friend's house, and she'd texted him when the flash flood warnings started, saying that she was going to spend the night there. So Evie could sleep in her room. As ridiculous as it was, the idea of Evie sleeping in the next room was profoundly soothing.

So, yeah, though he was usually good at fighting his Evie-related impulses, he was too damn tired to do so right now. If she wanted to go home, he'd rally and drive her. But in the time it took him to do that, he would at least get to be with her for a few minutes.

He was such a goner. He would get a hold of himself soon, though. He would look into her eyes, and then he would tamp this shit back down.

He let himself in and shook off as much water as he could as he scanned the house. The houses in this chunk of town were tiny. Most of them had originally been modest summer cottages. When you stood in the front door of his house, you could see all of it, with the exception of the two little bedrooms down the hall. There was the kitchen to one side with its tiny breakfast nook that was also the lunch nook and the dinner nook since it was the only dining table in the space—and even so, it wasn't used that much for dining because it usually had Clara's homework all over it.

They tended to eat in the small living room on the other side, where there was a coffee table flanked by a worn armchair and a sofa.

A sofa on which Evie Abbott was sleeping.

She was wearing one of his shirts, too, an unremarkable London Knights one so worn it was practically a rag. He could hear the dryer going in the small laundry closet tucked in the kitchen, so she must have thrown her wet stuff in there and heeded his order to help herself to dry clothing. When he'd suggested that, he'd been thinking she would wear something of Clara's. That she had raided his closet instead…did something to him. Something that made him, suddenly, not as tired as he'd been a moment ago.

She had an afghan over her lower body, but it was just a small throw, so he tiptoed to the linen closet to get a proper quilt. He was a little sorry he wouldn't get to talk to her tonight, but clearly the correct course of action was to tuck her in and let her sleep. She would still be sleeping in the next room, which was what he'd just been thinking he wanted.

He didn't want to sleep anymore, though, was the thing.

But he was good at sublimating his own wants. He paused over the couch, poised to settle the quilt over her. She must have sensed his presence. Her eyes fluttered open. He couldn't say he was disappointed.

"Go back to sleep," he whispered, because that was what he was supposed to say.

He remembered, suddenly, that time in the lake when she'd told him her mouth couldn't lie to him. Apparently the rogue mouth problem was catching, but he had it in reverse: his mouth was too damn honorable.

Regardless, she did not go back to sleep. She yawned and blinked her eyes open more fully, and something happened in his chest. It was a strange awareness of a rumbling to come. It felt like his stomach was about to growl, except the sensation was in his chest.

When she sat up fully and said, "Sawyer," with such *relief* in her voice, his heart filled up. He'd thought of heartbreak, all these years, like an emptying. A draining away of some essential life force.

He had not stopped to think about the possibility of the reverse: a refilling.

If he had, he would have imagined it a more orderly process, like filling a water bottle from a tap.

It wasn't like that at all. It was like the storm. Giant, powerful waves full of rocks and debris beat down on his insides, doubling him over with their fearsome, raw power. His breath came in short pants, and his vision started to blur as the blood rushed out of his head and headed south. His dick, it seemed, was as full as his heart. It wasn't a very seemly thought, but nothing about what was happening to him right now was seemly. There was a natural disaster unfolding in his body. The emergency wasn't over, it turned out. It had just moved *inside* him.

"*Sawyer,*" she said again, lower this time, more insistent. "Are you okay?"

He was not okay. Not even close. He knew she meant it in a more immediate way, though, that she was asking about the lake rescue. So he nodded.

He'd already been crouched over her, poised as he'd been to tuck her in, but the tsunami had made him curl in on himself, hunch forward instinctively in a protective crouch.

Which put him within grabbing distance of her.

And she grabbed.

Eve Abbott's Last Three Semicoherent Thoughts As She Threw Herself at Sawyer Collins

> 1. She was exhausted. She probably looked like she was half-asleep. That was her out, when whatever was about to happen was over. It was like sleepwalking. Sleep groping.
> 2. Except... if she was coherent enough to have an excuse preloaded, she probably couldn't claim anything but complete premeditation.
> 3. Well, whatever. Screw it.

And then she was beyond thinking, except as it related to the mechanics of getting what she wanted. Her hands landed on his chest, her palms flat at first, but then she made fists, grabbing handfuls of his sodden Moonflower PD shirt and using them to lever herself up so she was kneeling on the couch. He'd been bent over her, so he was *right there*, level with her, and his lake-blue eyes were wide, like he was shocked. Yes, it was shocking. This was *shocking*.

She kissed him. His lips were cold. That wasn't right. She needed to warm them up, so she set to work on that, moving her own against his, softly at first, because it was like kissing a rock. He was still stunned. Unmoving. But just when she was starting to think she had made an error, that she was going to have to retreat and fall back on the sleep-groping excuse, he came to life. His arms banded around her, and he sucked in a gasping breath, like he'd been drowning and she was his life raft.

He opened his mouth, and she sighed into it. Her head, suddenly heavy, started to loll back, but then one of his hands was there, on the back of her head, the pads of his fingers scraping against her scalp as he anchored her—and *feasted*. There was no other word for it. He fused their mouths together, and their tongues tangled. Slid back and forth across each other, probed deeply. He emitted some kind of humming, growling sound as he tilted her head back and opened her mouth wider. It felt like he wanted to climb inside her. God. She had *never* been kissed like this, not by anyone, not even teenage Sawyer. It was so…dirty. So perfectly, wonderfully, astonishingly *dirty*.

It was also not enough.

She had taken her bra off earlier, along with the rest of her wet clothing, and her breasts felt heavy, swollen. They *ached*. He was already holding her tightly against him, but she was still holding on to fistfuls of his shirt, so her forearms were preventing their torsos from touching. And wasn't *that* a lost opportunity? She started trying to wiggle her arms free, so she could mash her breasts against him and maybe get some relief from all this *sensation*.

But he must have thought she wanted out, because he let go of her immediately. The losses hit her all at once: the loss of his arms around her body, his hand on the back of her head, his mouth on hers. It was all just…gone. Something came out of her mouth that sounded an awful lot like a wail. She should have been embarrassed, but all she could focus on was getting her throbbing breasts some relief, so she pushed him down on the couch and climbed on top of him.

He grunted as she landed on him—she had hurled herself pretty hard. She sighed when her chest finally made contact with his, but it was only partly in relief. Because although she'd gotten what she wanted, it was not enough. She grumbled in frustration as she squirmed on his chest, thinking some friction might help.

He sucked in a breath. "Explain to me what's happening here."

"I'm jumping you." *In case that wasn't clear.*

"Explain to me what's happening *here*." He tapped her temple. "Is this some kind of postadrenaline 'Thank God we're not dead' thing? Because as fierce as that storm was, we were never really in any danger."

There was her out. And she didn't even have to articulate it. All she had to do was nod. Move her head up and down a few inches, and she'd be off the hook. She could peel herself off him, and they'd go back to their usual state of being: friendship with an occasional side of awkwardness.

"No," her mouth said firmly.

He raised his eyebrows. "I notice you're not wearing any underwear."

Right. She'd been singularly focused on the achiness

of her breasts. But as soon as he said the word *under-wear*, it was like a neon arrow lit up in her consciousness, blinking insistently toward the corresponding ache between her legs.

She inhaled a shaky breath. "My clothes are in the dryer."

"You were just lying here on my couch without wearing any underwear."

She wasn't sure if he was merely stating the obvious or if he was trying to convey disapproval. His T-shirt was long. It covered her butt. She didn't say any of that, opting instead to follow his "stating the obvious" lead. "I wasn't planning to fall asleep. I was planning to be dressed by the time you got home."

He grinned. So not disapproval, then. "The best-laid plans…"

"Sometimes turn into plans to get laid?" her mouth said hopefully.

"*This is a bad idea.* Remember that? Who said that?"

"I'll take overly cautious librarians who live in their heads for one hundred, Alex." She wiggled herself so the neon arrow–illuminated area of her body was more firmly on top of his…neon arrow.

"You probably weren't wrong." He groaned as he said it, though. Like she was torturing him, but in a good way.

So she did it some more. "And yet, we're already so far down the bad idea road."

His eyes danced with laughter even as he bit his lip. "If we backed up now, would it really make any difference?"

"Exactly. We've already put the miles on the car. We might as well enjoy the ride." She felt like her face was going to crack from smiling. She loved bantering with him.

He closed his eyes and spoke with them still closed. "*God*, Evie."

She suddenly thought of what Maya had said. "Get it out of our system."

"'It'?"

"*It*," she said firmly. "You know what 'it' is."

"So we do this, and we get 'it' out of our system."

She wasn't sure if that had been a statement or a question—his eyes were still closed, and she couldn't read his face—but she decided to answer it just to be safe. "Yes. Like...friends with benefits." Was that a thing people said in real life?

Whatever. Bantering was fun and all that, but so was *not* talking. His head was still tipped back and his eyes were closed, so this was the perfect opportunity for a little less talk.

Before she could overthink it, she licked his neck.

Which seemed to let the genie out of the bottle. His eyes flew open. There was a single beat while they stared at each other; then, all of a sudden, they were flipped. She was on her back, and he was on top of her. She wanted to cheer, but she was too breathless for that.

But he stopped. Froze in place. What would make him unfreeze? "Sawyer," she said softly. "It's just sex."

And if she'd had any hopes to the contrary, she quashed them, because her reassurance worked immediately.

"All right, but listen, this is how it's going to go this time. You're going to tell me what you like, and I'm going to do that to you until you come."

Oh. There were the tiny gas burners under her cheeks, and someone had just turned them to high. She exhaled shakily. "I think if you keep talking that way, that'll pretty much do it."

He darted down and licked her neck, in a mirror-image gesture of what she'd done to him. Except he kept going lower, pulling down on the neck of his shirt she was wearing as he scraped his teeth gently over her collarbone. "Oh, you like a little dirty talk, do you?"

Did she? Judging by the fact that she suddenly feared maybe she *did* have to worry about the fate of his couch and her underwear-less nether regions, she was pretty sure the answer was yes. So she said it out loud. "Yes." So simple. One word to convey the truth.

Part of why she liked the way he was speaking to her, she was pretty sure, was that it was so different from before. When they'd had sex ten years ago, it had been a mostly silent thing. Not that there was anything wrong with that, but this—*talking*—was better.

"Wait." His head popped up, and an evil smile blossomed. "I think we already know what you want, don't we?"

It should have been impossible, but her cheeks burned hotter. "I don't know what you mean."

"I think you do. But maybe I can remind you." He moved, and like before it was so fast, she didn't really have time to process until he was kneeling on the floor.

Oh God. *He was kneeling on the floor.*

This was really going to happen.

"Sit up," he said gruffly.

If she let it.

She hesitated. Why? Because she was an idiot? Because she was smart? Who knew?

He bent down and kissed the top of a thigh, just briefly, and then rubbed his beard back and forth over it, semiaggressively, like he was making a point of it. Like he was airing a preview of coming—no pun intended—attractions.

She sat up. "I wasn't expecting this."

He merely grunted and opened her legs. He was on his knees in front of her, and from there he could see *everything*. There was nothing subtle about that view.

She laughed nervously—nerves were suddenly at risk of overtaking desire here. "Things are...not super groomed."

He was only the second person she had done this with, was the thing. With the first, an ex, she had always taken so long to come, if she did at all, she would end up stressed that he was going to get lockjaw and all the worrying would end up derailing her.

Sawyer didn't seem to be paying attention to her. Well, not to her face, anyway, or to the words coming out of her mouth. He was staring at her...juncture and—oh God, he was *licking his lips*.

She was struck dumb. Who would have thought, six months ago, when she was locked in the refrigerator at the flower shop with Sawyer kneeling at her feet on the other side of the glass, that she would end up here—but this time with nothing between them except her own fear.

Well. Desire was going to win over fear, she decided. She heaved a huge sigh and felt the tension leave her limbs. As her body grew languid, her legs fell open wider.

He hummed his approval as he looked up at her. "I don't care about grooming. I don't care if this is a bad idea. Honestly, right now I don't care about anything except getting my mouth on you. But if you really don't want to do this, of course we're not going to do this."

The way he spoke, gruffly but clearly, directly and without hesitation, undid all that languidness she had just achieved. She sucked in a breath and her legs came together on instinct, a vain attempt to soothe the sharp spike of need his declaration had sparked.

He must have interpreted it as her shutting things down. He rocked back on his heels and huffed a little sigh. It seemed like a disappointed sigh.

She was going to have to talk if she didn't want this to end. It was scary, but it was also exciting, to say what she wanted. To explain what was happening in her mind. Could she speak as directly as he had? More than just the single "yes" she'd said before?

"I do want to do this." She opened her legs. "I ache between my legs, and that wasn't me backing off, that was just a weird, instinctive instinct to soothe the ache."

Ha! She'd done it! And it wasn't even that hard.

And best of all, it *worked*—it worked immediately. He lowered his head and looped his arms under and around her thighs so he could control them. He brought them in until they were brushing against his cheeks. Until his beard was brushing against *them*. Her skin was damp, and provided some drag as his hair slid across sensitive flesh. He stayed there for a while, kissing one inner thigh, then making a point of turning his head slowly to pay attention to the other. As he turned from one leg to the other, his beard would drag against her center. Every time he made a pass, she moaned. What was the point of holding them in? When you had a man's face lodged between your legs, worrying about what you sounded like suddenly seemed beside the point.

Eventually he started drifting. His passes across her center would last longer. He would pause and swirl his tongue along her opening before heading back to a thigh.

It was so good. So, so good that she was pretty much continuously moaning now. Every nerve ending in her body strained toward her core, strained toward *him*. She didn't want him to go back to her thighs. She wanted him to...

"Stay."

Again, it was so easy! For once her renegade mouth and her body were working together. Her thighs closed tighter, clamping around his head as if to *make* him stay.

He growled again, and she laughed from the pure joy of it. Of this feeling. Of being about to come, but also of just *saying* what she wanted to have happen.

He shifted around a bit and grunted. Was that maybe not a manly sexual grunt but a grunt of discomfort? She glanced down. He'd been kneeling on hardwood for a while now. That couldn't be comfortable.

"Move over there." He nodded at the far end of the sofa.

And...there were the nerves again. "We don't have to—"

"Move. Your ass. There." He gently swatted her hip, which she supposed was as close as he could get to her butt.

She moved. He arranged her so she was sitting against one end of the couch, her legs spread along it. He let his hands linger, drag along the sensitized skin of her inner thighs. There were those calluses she'd thought about before. They were just as potent as she'd imagined.

Too soon—she was getting really into those calluses— he laid himself out on his stomach, so his head was back between her legs.

Her clit pulsed, but she'd lost some of her momentum.

"It usually takes me a while," she warned.

He speared her with those blue eyes. They were doing his signature sparking thing, except...more of it. *A lot* more of it. "You got somewhere to be? I sure as hell don't."

The lamp on the side table illuminated him in a way it hadn't when he'd been on the floor. His beard was wet. From *her*.

It looked *just* like she'd imagined it would, back when

they'd been climbing down from the roof of the Mermaid and the image had randomly popped into her head.

"No," she whispered. "Nowhere to be."

He licked his lips again.

Then he lowered his head and licked *her* lips. A few passes, and she was ramped right back up, fighting competing urges to writhe away from him and to buck her hips against his face to nudge him a little higher.

But wait. She didn't have to nudge, right? She had her newly discovered power. "Higher," she panted, and he moved higher. *Amazing.*

But he must have thought she was instructing him to move on to the main event, because he started tonguing her clit.

That wasn't going to work. "I can't take that much direct pressure. You have to kind of dance around it. Like, on the sides."

And damn if he didn't just adjust. Once he was licking around the nub with a steady amount of pressure, everything inside her started spiraling up and up and up. She was about to say something like *Right there, just like that*, but it was too late. All that came out was a shriek. She clamped her thighs around his head as she'd done before, and he kept working her as she pulsed around him.

When she finally slumped back and loosened her hold on him, he sat up and drawled, "Well, that didn't take long at all." He was wearing the world's most self-satisfied grin.

She grabbed the throw pillow that was scrunched up behind her back and threw it at him. He caught it and winked at her. "Just give me...two minutes." She waved a hand back and forth between them. "To get my limbs working again." Except...something was wrong with this picture. "Wait. You're still wearing all your clothes." And they were wet, too.

Well, of course they were. And of course he was still wearing them: between her grabbing handfuls of the wet fabric of his shirt and him going to town on her, they hadn't stopped to disrobe him.

"Your limbs aren't working, but thank goodness you haven't lost your powers of observation," he teased.

"You should take your clothes off now."

"Okay."

And he did. Another example of the power of using her voice.

"You should, too," he said as he struggled with his wet pants.

She was still wearing his T-shirt. Wow. How was it she'd had pretty much the hottest sexual encounter of her life and he'd been fully dressed and she'd been half-dressed?

"Okay," she said.

And then they were both naked. They eyed each other.

They had been here before, a decade ago. She wondered if he was having the same familiar-yet-not feeling she was. He was the same Sawyer, but more. He had those Mr. Big Virile Policeman muscles now. And he had a pretty good farmer's tan going, which she appreciated, because it had the effect of making him seem less intimidating in all his studliness.

She wondered if *she* measured up to *his* memories. Things were not as...taut as they'd been when she was a teenager.

As if he'd heard her silent insecurities, he wolf-whistled and very obviously ogled her breasts. She did have pretty nice breasts. They were sort of medium size but strangely perky.

You know what else was perky? His penis. Like, bobbing around trying to make its presence known perky.

She sat up straighter. "Hello."

"Hi. Limbs working again?"

She waved her arms in the air to demonstrate that yes, her limbs were working again—*everything* was working again. "Do you have condoms?"

"I doubt it."

"Really?"

"If I do, they're almost certainly expired."

Well...wow. So much for Mr. Big Virile Policeman.

He shrugged. "I've been busy with other things."

She was secretly pleased. Her mind spun up to analyze why in the world a man like Sawyer Collins would have expired condoms. She could sense a list forming. She forced it away. Now was not the time for lists. Now was the time to regroup. Well, she had just been admiring his penis, hadn't she?

She pointed to the other side of the couch, and he moved there without her having to say anything. She used the hair tie on her wrist to pull her hair back. "I think I may be semigood at this now."

"You were always good at it."

"Doubtful. Anyway, I bet you anything I've improved." He shook his head. She was pretty sure it was a fond shake and not a no-thanks shake, but just to be sure, she said, "We good to go here?"

He grinned. "Yes, ma'am."

He should get up and grab the quilt and cover them. He didn't want her to get cold. But that would require getting up off his couch. And *that* would require getting out from under Evie, who was currently sprawled all over him, looking very pleased with herself.

As she should be. He wasn't sure if she was "better" at blow jobs than she used to be. He remembered them extremely fondly. But then, he'd been eighteen, and she had been the first person other than himself to touch his dick at all, much less put her mouth on it. He'd wanted to give her a medal every time she did.

But he'd never said anything back then about enjoying himself, not explicitly anyway. Oh, they'd cuddle and all that. He was pretty sure she knew that she turned him on. But why had he never *said* anything?

Fast forward ten years, and Evie was still pretty damn spectacular when it came to blow jobs.

She was also better at talking.

He loved that.

So he would be, too. "That was fun."

He was understating it entirely. The truth was closer to *You have ruined me for anyone else for all time.* But there was embracing the idea of talking, and there was scaring the lady away.

"Mmm," she agreed, her voice muffled by his chest. She was limp. He liked it. Later he would remember what a huge mistake this had been, but for now he was in no hurry. He banded his arms around her.

They lay there for a minute, but then her head popped up. Her eyes, inches from his, were open wide like a thought had just landed in her head. "Remember how we said friends with benefits?"

He remembered how *she* had said friends with benefits. But..."Yeah?"

"Can one of those benefits be that you jump-start my renovation? I know I questioned earlier why you were helping me, but, dude, I need you to help me. Everything has just ground to a halt."

He sighed. "Yeah, about that."

She wiggled out of his embrace, and he had to force his

arms to go lax. He didn't want her to go yet. But she was wrapping the afghan around herself and moving toward the dryer, which had long since stopped. She paused with the dryer door open and looked at him over her shoulder. She was waiting for him to speak. He'd mucked about too long in his own head. That was the real danger here, confusing the world in his head—the world he wanted— with the world he had in front of him.

"I thought I was greasing the wheels of your reno—and I was—but it turns out the old folks were, too, except with the opposite aim."

Her jaw dropped. "You mean Karl and Pearl and everyone are *sabotaging* my reno?"

"I just found out—the night of the murder mystery play. I'm getting it straightened out."

"But why would they do that? I thought they were trying to help by sending you over all the time."

"They changed tactics. I think they really don't want you to leave town."

She tilted her head like she was considering. "Is that really sweet or really infuriating?"

"Maybe a bit of both?"

She sighed and pulled on her jeans.

"I'm going to take care of it." As much as he didn't want to. As much as he suddenly got what Pearl had been saying about how he shouldn't be helping hasten Evie's departure.

"Thanks, Sawyer." She pulled her shirt over her head. "You're a good friend."

A good *friend*.

Right.

Chapter Twenty

❦

*H*ello, friend, I need some benefits. Eve cracked herself up. But honestly, she was onto something with this new philosophy of just asking for what she wanted.

The reply came right away. Are you sexting me?

Oh! Now she *really* cracked herself up. She'd been joking, but she *hadn't* meant it that way. But of course it had come across as a booty call. No! Not on purpose, anyway. I need to talk to you about my flooring situation.

She wasn't actually sure if they were going to have sex again. Did their negotiation extend beyond just the one time last night? Did she want it to? Yes, of course she wanted it to. The man was a magical sex god. But was it wise? No, of course it wasn't wise. But where was the balance between those two statements?

Anyway, it wasn't up to her. He hadn't said anything, as he'd driven her home that night, about a repeat performance. Was he even interested?

Sawyer: Well, that's disappointing.

Well, okay then. She smiled.

Sawyer: Because I was thinking of sexting you.
Eve: Really?
Sawyer: Can I?
Eve: Sawyer, are you asking permission to sext me?
Sawyer: I think I am. This isn't the right way to do it, is it?

Ugh, he was just so adorable. And upstanding and charming. And now she very much wanted to see what he was going to say.

Eve: Hit me.
Eve: That came out wrong. Not literally. Sext me.
Sawyer: I think we're both really bad at this. But okay. Are you ready?
Eve: I am ready.

She was so ready, she was starting to get the tinglies.

What came through cracked her up anew. It was a photo of a box of condoms. Before she could reply, another one came in. It was a close-up of the expiration date, a date several years in the future.

Sawyer: I drove to Grand View to get these.
Eve: Why?
Sawyer: When you're chief of police in a

> place like this, you can't really do anything
> on the down low. I have people commenting
> on my purchases all the time. I shouldn't be
> wasting my money on organic. I'm not get-
> ting my oil changed frequently enough. I
> have to be stealthy if I want to keep a secret.

A secret. He wanted to keep her a secret. That put a damper on her excitement.

But he was right. If anyone in this town got even the slightest inkling that they were spending time together, the matchmakers would have a field day.

> ***Sawyer:*** So, not to be too utilitarian, but I just
> got off a shift, and I have an hour before I
> have to go see a client Jake and I are doing
> some work for.

So he wanted to come to her place for a quickie. Well, what did she expect? Romance? No. She didn't expect that, and, more to the point, she didn't *want* that. If they were going to keep having sex, and it seemed like they were, it had to be just that. Sex.

> ***Eve:*** Well, you'd better get a move on then.
> ***Sawyer:*** We'll leave time to talk about flooring.
> ***Eve:*** Wow, you *really* don't know how to sext.

This was all wrong. As Sawyer parked behind the Mermaid, he considered hiding the condoms in the trunk and saying he'd forgotten them at home.

After he'd driven her home last night—no, after he'd

driven her back to the inn, which was *not* her home—he'd talked himself into driving to Grand View to buy condoms, repeating to himself the *Sawyer, it's just sex* disclaimer she'd fed him.

He had told himself that if she could think of it that way, he could, too. And if it was just sex, he could let her go when the time came. Did he want to never have sex with her again, or did he want to turn off his emotions and enjoy her while she was here? Now that he'd had a taste of grown-up Evie, there was no question.

So why did he feel so squicky all of a sudden?

Maybe it was the quickie aspect of things. Even if this was just a physical thing, Evie deserved more than a hurried tumble between other obligations. That was what they had done—out of necessity—when they were teenagers. Finding places to have sex had been a challenge. They would wait until Lucille was out and lock themselves into Evie's room, mostly, but the fear of getting caught had always loomed.

All right. So they'd talk about her flooring problem and schedule another time to have meaningless—but unhurried—sex. Problem solved. He knocked on the door.

Maya opened it. "Hey, Chief!"

"Hi, hi!" Evie appeared over Maya's shoulder. She made a face that was at odds with her chipper greeting and mouthed, "Sorry."

"What's up?" Sawyer said to Maya. What he meant was *Why are you here, and how can I get you to go away?* Even if they weren't going to have sex, he wanted Evie to himself.

"I'm trying to get Eve to go to Toronto for her job interview."

Wait. What? "Job interview?" he echoed.

"She was going to do it over *Skype*." Maya snorted.

"They already know me!" Eve protested. "Everyone on the hiring committee knows me."

He was trying to catch up. "Is this the collections development thing?"

"Yes. The job was posted last week. I have a Skype interview set up for four o'clock today."

"And I keep *telling* her," Maya said, "it doesn't *matter* if they know you. You're not going to make your best impression when you're a two-dimensional image on a computer screen. You need to demonstrate that you're taking this seriously."

As much as he wanted to schedule that unhurried yet meaningless sex for as soon as possible..."She's not wrong, Evie. If you really want this job, you should *show* them that."

Did she really want this job? Was there any chance she didn't?

She looked at him for a long moment. Blinked. Turned to Maya. "You're right."

Damn.

"And I haven't seen my parents since Christmas," Evie said. "And Hot Docs is going on."

"Hot Docs?" he asked. "Sounds like medical porn."

Her lips quirked. "Documentaries. It's a film festival. I was reading the listings kind of wistfully the other day." She nodded decisively. "Yep. I'll stay the weekend in Toronto. It will be good to go home for a few days."

Home. There was that word again. Sawyer swallowed the protest rising in his throat. This was good. It was a well-timed reminder that her life—her parents, her dream job—was in Toronto.

Also, Sawyer had never in his life seen a documentary.

He clapped his hands. "Great. Is there anything I

can do while you're gone? You wanted to talk about flooring?"

She looked at him for what felt like a long time. Finally she sighed. "Yes. I saw the Bluewater Flooring truck at Curl Up and Dye."

"Carol is having the floors in the apartment upstairs refinished," Maya said. "She's staying with CJ temporarily."

"Right, but the dude from Bluewater Flooring told *me* he wasn't taking any work in Moonflower Bay until at least July. The actual flooring has been here for months, but every time I ask him, he says he's too backed up with work in Grand View."

Well, that got Sawyer's dander up. As much as he wanted to lay himself at her feet and beg her to stay forever, it annoyed the hell out of him that people were playing her like that. He cracked his knuckles. "We'll just see about that."

Toronto was fun. It was like being on vacation, which was a little weird, because Eve had spent her whole life there. It probably just felt like a holiday because she didn't have to work and therefore didn't have to fight the rush-hour crowds on the subway.

She did a lot of texting with people from Moonflower Bay. Maya was aflutter about the casting for *Richard III*. I got a grant, so I could bring in a B-list Toronto actor for the lead. I do that sometimes. What do you think of this guy?

A series of pictures came through.

> *Eve:* He seems fine?
> *Maya:* But just fine, right? He's not blowing you away.
> *Eve:* Well, these are just headshots. I have

no idea if he can act. But yeah, he's not as
broody as Jake.
Maya: I'm never going to get Jake. Sigh.
There's not a natural Richard in this town.
Eve: Hey, here's an idea. You know how the
Stratford Festival did a whole bunch of
gender-swapped Shakespeares a few
seasons ago?

It was true. It turned out she and Maya had seen one of
the same productions.

Eve: Why can't "Richard" be a woman?
Maya: OH. MY. GOD. You are a genius.
Eve: What about Pearl? Or Eiko? I mean, you
want a natural schemer, right? Or play it yourself.
Maya: COME BACK. WE NEED TO DIS-
CUSS. Will you be assistant director?

She loved Maya, but she wasn't about to get entangled in
one of her bonkers plays. Also...

Eve: I won't be in Moonflower Bay by the
time the Anti-Festival rolls around.
Maya: Even though I'm the one who talked
you into going and doing that stupid interview in person so you can get your dream
job and leave me, I don't like this answer.

Eve sort of didn't, either. It left her with a strange
hollowness inside. But honestly, she needed to calm down.
It wasn't like she was moving to Timbuktu.

> *Eve:* I'll come back and see it! I'll lead the
> standing ovation!
> *Maya:* No. Anti-Festival is for Moonflower
> Bayers only.

Well, that stung.

The next day she got a text from Pearl. Sawyer said I have to apologize for sabotaging your renovation. So I guess I apologize.

Eve chuckled. She was annoyed, but Pearl was funny.

> *Pearl:* I only did it because I want you to
> stay.
> *Eve:* Thanks, Pearl.
> *Pearl:* Lucille did, too, you know. That's why
> she left you the place.

Eve sighed. No one really knew why Lucille had done what she'd done. If she'd confided in Pearl, Pearl would have been all over Eve with that news early on.

More importantly, Pearl didn't understand the complexities of the situation. Her life was pie and scheming and *Fortnite*. That wasn't reality.

And then the pictures from Sawyer came. Got things going again. Read a bunch of people the riot act, and now they're working overtime to make up for their "scheduling oversights."

The pictures he sent made it look like the inn had undergone a jump forward in time.

> *Eve:* It looks like the second floor is basically
> done?
> *Sawyer:* Yep. All that's left is baseboards.

Some more pics came through.

> ***Sawyer:*** Third floor's a little rougher. Bathroom guys are coming tomorrow. Flooring up there will take a little longer. They have another job in Bayshore—I checked, and they legit do. They've sworn they'll be back within two weeks. I'm going to clear out the bits and pieces of junk up here so it's all ready for them.
> ***Eve:*** There's still furniture in 3C.
> ***Sawyer:*** Your old room. It's padlocked. Is there a key somewhere? If not, I can get a locksmith and clear it out for you.

She had been in denial about the room. His offer should have been tempting. Why wouldn't she want someone to just…handle it? She could return to town, and the Pink Room of Pain would be gone. Well, it would probably still be pink. But the stuff inside it would be gone.

And was it even painful anymore? She and Sawyer had gotten past their junk. She smiled. They'd gotten *way* past it. She no longer felt like memories were assaulting her when she walked through town—these days, she could bend over and drink from the fish fountain no problem. So didn't it follow that the room would also have lost its power over her?

> ***Eve:*** I actually was going to leave that room alone. I know it looks like a seven-year-old dipped it in cotton candy, but…

Ugh. How to explain when she couldn't make sense of it herself?

Sawyer: But maybe the new owner will have a seven-year-old who likes cotton candy?

She smiled.

Eve: I guess I'm just attached and had told myself that it would be a fun owner's room. Or it could be storage—it's so tiny it's barely useable as a proper guest room. But I'm being an idiot. So, yeah, have at it—thanks. The key is in the silverware drawer in the kitchen.
Sawyer: No, if you don't want to touch it, we won't. Anyway, it's small enough that if the new owner doesn't like it, it will be easy to change.

The new owner. The idea of a new owner had, for so long, been theoretical. But it was getting closer.

Sawyer: How's Toronto?

She replied reflexively.

Eve: Great.
Sawyer: How was the interview?
Eve: Great.

Right? It *had* been great to see her old professor. Eve had told her about Moonflower Bay, and they'd agreed that inheriting the inn was almost like something that would happen in a Hallmark movie.

Eve: I think I'm going to get the job.
Sawyer: When would you have to start?
Eve: I don't know. Since it's a new position,
they said it would be flexible.

On paper, everything was working out better than she could have dared hope. When the year was up, she'd sell the inn and be back in Toronto with a pile of cash and the spanking new job of her dreams. If she had to go back early to take the spanking new job of her dreams, she could do that. Sawyer would probably keep cracking the whip on the reno, and she could check in on the occasional weekend.

But, damn, she was going to miss...

The lake. She was going to miss the lake.

Eve: I want to go for a swim. I wish it was
summer and we could swim in the lake.

He didn't reply for a while. No wonder—that had been a random change of subject. Her fingers had taken over for her brain there.

Sawyer: What documentaries did you see?

It was his turn for a random change of subject, apparently.

Eve: Just one. It was about Dr. Ruth.
Sawyer: The sex lady?
Eve: Yep.
Sawyer: Did you pick up any tips?
Eve: Are we sexting now?
Sawyer: Nope. When are you back?
Eve: Tomorrow morning.

Sawyer: Great. I'm on overnight, so I'll take a quick nap and then see you midday—for the real thing, not the digital version.

She grinned. She was excited to see Sawyer. But not just Sawyer. Maya, too, and even meddling Pearl.

Sawyer: If you want to, of course.

He had probably added that disclaimer because she hadn't answered.

Eve: Oh, I want to.

Chapter Twenty-One

❧

*E*vie was lugging her stuff inside the Mermaid when Sawyer started texting.

Sexting, really. Or at least their version of it, because what came through was a picture of his smiling face next to a box of condoms. Are you back yet?

> *Eve:* I thought you were napping. It's only
> ten.
> *Sawyer:* Couldn't sleep. Can't imagine why.

She could feel herself blushing.

> *Sawyer:* I'm at the community center. Can
> you meet me here?
> *Eve:* Isn't it closed on Sundays?
> *Sawyer:* Not if you're the chief of police.
> Bring a bathing suit.

Her gasp was audible. She had idly mentioned wanting to swim, but it seemed he'd made it happen.

> *Eve:* I just have to grab something to eat,
> and I'll be over.
> *Sawyer:* I have lunch here. Just come.
> *Eve:* Actually, maybe I should wait and do
> that there, too?

She snickered at herself.

> *Sawyer:* Yes. Several times.
> *Eve:* You know what? I think we're getting
> better at this sexting thing.

Sawyer stood inside the doors of the community center waiting for Evie, and when she got out of her car in the parking lot, he was overcome. There was no other word for it. His throat thickened. She had only been gone a couple days, but he had missed her.

He wasn't sure why. Life was the same as always. If anything, it was full of more distractions than usual. He'd had a mountain of paperwork to do after the rescue in the bay. He had driven Clara to the mall in London to shop for dorm room stuff. It was only February, but she wanted to "get a jump on things."

But now Evie was here, and all the distractions fell away. He couldn't speak as he opened the door to let her in.

She did not appear to be similarly affected. "Hi!"

"Hi," he managed to croak.

"Did you have a good weekend?"

He had so much stuff saved up to tell her—about Clara's

questionable dorm room decor decisions, about how Joel had caught a couple getting it on in the lane next to Lawson's Lager House, but it had turned out *not* to be Art and Jamila. But he couldn't make his mouth work.

But that was okay, because a chorus of sea creatures had taken up residence in his brain, and they were loudly reminding him that talking wasn't the only thing mouths were good for.

He kissed the girl.

And the girl kissed him back.

They were both smiling as they kissed, laughing almost. He didn't know what was up with her, but for his part, he was just so happy to be here.

"So, VIP swimming?" she said when they separated. "How amazing is this?"

"Don't get too excited. It's still just the Moonflower Bay Community Center." He led her to the locker rooms.

"Oh my gosh! I can go in the men's locker room since the place is closed!"

"You can, but again, I feel the need to manage your expectations. It's the men's locker room, not the Ritz."

"I remain delighted." She grinned as she pushed through the door. "Ahh!" She jogged past the lockers and swung her head around to gape at the urinals. "Transgression!"

His heart was light as he followed her onto the pool deck. She immediately started shedding her clothing. Instead of the blue one-piece she'd worn for their swimming lessons so many months ago, she was wearing a bikini. The top was purple with a "shell" over each breast. The bottom was shimmery green. It was an Ariel bikini. She was going to *kill* him. Both because that suit was inherently sexy as hell and because it was so *her*.

He moved toward her. He'd only been going to hug her.

He just needed to hold on to her for a second. But she must have misread his intent—probably on account of the groan he couldn't hold in. "So we're getting right to it, are we?" she teased as she slid her hands up his shirt.

"Not necessarily." She had wanted to eat. He pointed to a beach blanket he had set up in one corner. The effort required was Herculean, but he managed it. "Lunch." He'd come with takeout from Sadie's.

She skipped over—but she ignored the lunch and laid back on the blanket. Her hair fanned out all around her, and her eyes were bright with mischief. "Lie back and look at the sky, right? That's what you tell all the girls?" She cocked her head as she contemplated the ceiling. "Lie back and look at the community center ceiling? I bet you've never used *that* line on any other girls."

"There aren't any girls." *There's only you.*

"Currently?"

"Correct."

"But I bet there have been hordes. Since me, I mean."

Were they really going to do this? He'd been willing to call a halt to the proceedings if she wanted lunch, but he wasn't so keen on derailing them to have this discussion. But still. He had to correct the record. "There have been two."

"Two girlfriends?"

He studied her face. She didn't seem upset. And it wasn't like he was going to lie to her. "Yes."

"But probably more than that who have laid back and looked at the sky."

Ah, he saw where she was going with this. "Are you asking me what my number is?"

"I guess I am."

"Including you?"

"Yes. Total number."

"Five."

Her eyes widened. Yeah, it wasn't a very manly number, he supposed, but he didn't see any need to lie. "So me plus two girlfriends. Who were numbers four and five?"

"Tourists." Just like he couldn't make purchases in town without everyone commenting on them, he couldn't make other transactions, either. Occasionally opportunities had presented themselves. Even less occasionally, they had presented themselves when he hadn't been on duty or needed by Clara. He'd always intended to get on one of those apps, but life got in the way. It just never seemed urgent enough. Unlike now, when he suddenly started to feel like if he didn't get inside Evie Abbott *right now*, he was going to lose his mind.

"So I'm the sixth," she mused.

"No. You're the first."

You're the only.

Sawyer flipped them so he was on his back and she was lying on top of him. Surprised, Evie squealed. His eyes sparked with a mixture of amusement and lust.

"How about we talk about this some more later, if you still want to?"

She didn't want to. She angled her face for a kiss, and he obliged. It was slow. Lazy, almost. But deep, so deep. She sighed into his mouth as her body relaxed. When his lips left hers and roamed across her cheek, she said, "So there's not a weekend janitor who could pop in at any moment?"

"Nope." His lips tickled her ear as he spoke.

"Lifeguards looking to brush up their skills?"

"Nope." His beard slid along her neck—he was doing that on purpose—as he moved down her body. "But do you want to stop?"

She responded by undoing the front clasp of her bikini top. This suit was ridiculous—she had bought it online at a post-Christmas sale but hadn't had a chance to wear it. As they had at his house, her breasts ached, and she needed him to touch them.

He read her silent message, moved down her body, and used one hand to cup each breast. And while she appreciated that he knew what she wanted, she also kind of wanted to stick with the whole talking thing she'd discovered last time. It had been such a revelation. And so hot.

"Will you put your mouth on my breasts, Sawyer?"

"*Yes.*" He lowered his head and sucked, sharp and quick, on one nipple. A bolt of lightning extended from his mouth through the nipple to her center. He pulled back and examined her. "I love how hard your nipples get."

"The other one's a lot more sensitive for some random reason. Always has been."

The hand on her left breast moved up and grazed that nipple. "How come I never knew that?"

"I never told you," she said quickly, not wanting to make this about his perceived shortcomings. "But I'm telling you now."

He smiled, slow and predatory but somehow still infused with the lightheartedness that seemed to be all around them. "I wonder if beards work on sensitive left nipples, too."

There went the burners in her cheeks. She inhaled automatically, sharply. Held her breath for a moment and on the exhalation said, "There's only one way to find out."

Then he went to town on her. There was no other way to say it. All of his attention was focused on the one breast. He licked and sucked and kneaded and rubbed his beard on the hardened nub. And he just *kept going*, the sensations piling up inside her until they became almost painful. She squirmed, but he was relentless. The pressure built and built, both in her breast and between her legs.

"I think I could come just from this," she gasped as he did a swirling thing with his tongue.

He stopped just long enough to say, "I'm going to take that as a challenge."

It was a challenge he won.

"Oh my God," she panted when she'd come back to earth.

"Did you come when we were together when we were younger? Generally speaking?"

Oh no. Here they went. There was no good way to answer that question.

He must have taken her silence as an answer, because he lowered his head to her neck and said, "I'm sorry."

She grabbed his cheeks and forced him to look at her. "Sawyer. We were *teenagers*."

"Still. I should have asked."

"I should have *said*." She wasn't even that good at masturbating back then. "I hardly knew how to make myself come. There was no way I ever would have had the guts to try to show someone else how to do it. I love my parents, but they sort of flunked the birds-and-the-bees talk."

"Then maybe we shouldn't have been having sex."

"I loved having sex with you. You turned me on."

"I just never finished the job."

"Not never." He raised his eyebrows skeptically. "I would sometimes sort of…hump your leg and surprise myself with an orgasm. A stealth-gasm." She was trying to lighten the mood, but it wasn't working. She could tell he was going to object some more, so she shoved him off her, rolled him onto his back, and straddled him. "We were *children*. Neither of us know what we were doing. But look at us now."

There. She'd cracked him. He rolled his eyes, but she could see the beginnings of a smile. So she hammed it up, gesturing at her naked chest. "I mean, really. We are winning at this friends-with-benefits thing. I'm topless and writhing all over you in semipublic." She writhed to make the statement true, squirming around until she was lined up with his erection. "I had an orgasm without even using any of those condoms." That got her the full smile. "That's what life is, right? Or what it should be, anyway. We learn things. We get better."

His arm floated up and made contact with her cheek. "I—" He swallowed whatever he'd been going to say. For a second she thought his eyes had gotten teary, but it must have been the harsh fluorescent lighting making them look shiny, because when he said, "Maybe we should use one of those condoms?" his voice had gone all low and sexy.

It was her turn to smile. "We wouldn't want them to expire."

"*Two* boxes of expired condoms would probably be a greater blow to my manhood than finding out that the only orgasms my teenage girlfriend ever had in my presence were accidental."

"So maybe we should stop talking."

"About this, anyway." He swatted her butt playfully. "Take this off, Ariel."

She laughingly started squirming out of it. "So this is like the porno version of *The Little Mermaid*? What would Walt say?"

"Yeah." His eyes were riveted to her hands as she slid the bottoms over her hips. "Except you know how in the movie all the sea creatures are singing to the prince and telling him to kiss the girl?"

She nodded. "I seem to remember that. As established, I have seen the movie once or twice."

"Right, but in this version, he's going to *fuck* the girl."

God *damn*. Sawyer loved how much Evie loved it when he talked dirty. All that time he had spent *not* talking dirty to Evie almost seemed like as much of a crime as all those missed orgasms.

He watched her closely to make sure he hadn't gone too far. The way her pupils dilated, even under the bright lights, and the way she sagged in place, like her spine had gone limp at the bold suggestion, indicated that he had not. She had climbed off him in order to get her swimsuit bottoms off, but he had been enjoying the view when she'd been straddling him, so he reached over his head for his backpack, extracted a condom, and grabbed her hand. "Come back here."

She settled herself back on his upper thighs and started stroking his dick. He shuddered and forced himself not to close his eyes. He didn't want to miss anything. Her nails were painted pale blue, like the sky, and he was riveted by those little splashes of blue against his reddened flesh. A breathy little sigh had him transferring his attention to her face to make sure she was okay. She was staring at his dick, too, and she bit down on her upper lip and did the sighing thing again, as if she liked what she saw.

He reached up for her left breast—she was right when she'd said *We learn. We get better*—and was rewarded with one of those moans he loved. He was afraid he wasn't going to last very long, so he used his other hand to find her clit and press along the side of it.

"Sawyer," she gasped as he pressed against her.

"Put the condom on me, Evie."

She looked dazed as she lurched forward, reaching for the foil packet next to him on the towel. He adjusted as best he could to keep his ministrations continuous.

She was clumsy as she unrolled it on his length, and as she sighed and said, "Oh my God, I can't wait," his heart turned over.

This was so good. He loved making Evie Abbott clumsy and limp. "Climb on and ride me, Evie."

And he was inside her. Inside Evie Abbott. Like no time had passed *and* like a lifetime had passed.

We learn. We get better.

He kept going with both nipple and clit the way he'd learned she'd liked.

"That's right, Evie. Come all over my dick, and then I'm going to come inside you."

And she did.

And he did, too.

Chapter Twenty-Two

⌒

*I*f the sex hadn't already undone him, their postcoital chat would have.

After Sawyer got rid of the condom and Evie slumped on his chest with what he was pretty sure was a happy sigh, she suddenly said, "Do you know why I was always afraid to swim?"

"No," he said carefully. "I wondered, but it never seemed like you wanted to talk about it." In truth, he'd been desperately curious, but it had seemed like the topic was off-limits. And as they'd established to his great chagrin, they weren't always so great about talking back then.

"When I was three, I fell into a pool at a party."

His body tensed, which was stupid, because obviously she was fine. She was right here. In his arms. He forced those arms to loosen. He wasn't sure what the protocol was here. If they were friends with benefits, there was probably no call for cuddling. He would let her lead the way on that front.

She slid right off him—okay, then. But he didn't have time to get maudlin over it. She looked him right in the eyes and said, "My dad had to jump in and get me. They didn't notice right away, though. Apparently I just slipped in. So I wasn't actually breathing. They called 911, and one of the guests did CPR on me."

He whistled. "That'd do it."

"I don't remember any of it, though."

"I bet you do, in some kind of visceral way."

"I must, right? Why else would I have been so freaked out by water for so many years? They tried to make me take swimming lessons after that, but I would just scream bloody murder. I *do* remember that. Standing on the pool deck and honestly thinking I would die if I had to go in. Everyone kept telling me to calm down, but I felt like I couldn't breathe just *looking* at the water. Eventually they gave up."

His heart was breaking at the image of young Evie terrified and screaming. "Why didn't you ever tell me?"

"I was embarrassed. Who lets their life get derailed by an event they don't even remember?"

"Your life didn't get derailed. You just couldn't swim. It wasn't that big a deal."

"It kind of was in a lakeside town. But I appreciate the sentiment."

"No one cared," he said, wanting to put her at ease. But that wasn't actually true, was it? And they were telling the truth these days—at least when it came to sex. But she'd opened up to him about this. Could he do the same? "You remember when we were dating?"

"No, Sawyer. I don't remember that at all." She rolled her eyes at him but grinned as she did so.

He pushed a lock of hair out of her face. But only because it looked like it was bugging her. Then he made himself stop touching her. Again. It was harder this time. "We'd hang out at the beach, but you'd never go in."

"And you never pushed me to. You found other stuff for us to do. Picking berries. Breaking into lighthouses. I always appreciated that."

He nodded. That's why he'd been building her the canoe, too. He wondered if she remembered it. He almost mentioned it, but then he thought about it sitting in his garage. He had no way to explain—to her or to himself—why he had suddenly decided to finish it. There was no way to say, *Hey, remember that canoe that I was making for you as a giant-ass symbol of my teenage devotion? Guess what? I'm back at it!* That wasn't in the friends-with-benefits script.

So he said nothing.

So much for their new era of talking.

How many times do you think we had sex your last summer here?

The next day, Eve was at the library when Sawyer started texting her. Unlike her branch in Toronto, it was actually quiet, so when she snickered, she drew the attention of nearby patrons.

"Sorry," she whispered, scrambling to silence her phone when another text arrived. Like, not actually that many when you think about it, right? It was hard to get any privacy.

What was going on here?

> *Eve:* I guess it depends what you mean by
> sex. Like, are we talking penis-in-vagina
> only?
> *Sawyer:* Hmm. Good point.
> *Eve:* If so, yeah, between Clara and Lucille, it
> wasn't like we had that many opportunities.

He didn't reply right away, so she sent another one.

Eve: You're still really bad at sexting, Sawyer.

He ignored her joke.

Sawyer: What I'm actually talking about is opportunities for orgasms. So not just penis-in-vagina. Heavy petting counts.
Eve: Heavy petting!? Hello, did we back-to-the-future ourselves to 1956?
Sawyer: Humor me. I'm doing some data collection here.
Eve: Wow, REALLY bad at sexting.
Sawyer: It's not sexting. It's data collection that happens to be on the topic of sex.
Eve: I don't know, Sawyer, I wasn't making notches on my bedpost. I didn't have a spreadsheet.

She had been, however, writing about it in her diary in the Pink Room of Pain and could probably pretty accurately come up with the number he wanted, or at least a ballpark. But she wasn't about to tell him that. She *was* going to have to deal with the room. One of these days.

Sawyer: Listen. I have this idea. You're in town for what, six more months?

She paused. Was this a bad time to tell him she'd found out this morning that she'd gotten the collections development job? There was nothing stopping her from moving back to Toronto and starting the job right now.

She could come back on the weekends to deal with
inn stuff.

In the time she spent pondering how or whether to say
this all, another text arrived: Regardless, my plan is to use
whatever time we have left to make up for all the orgasms
you didn't have that summer. That's why I'm asking for
a number.

She cracked up. "Sorry, sorry," she said when a woman
she didn't know glared at her.

She'd better take this outside. And not just because of the
laughing. She was getting a little warm.

> *Sawyer:* Are you still there?
> *Eve:* Yeah. I was at the library. I laughed
> so hard at your last text that I kicked my-
> self out.
> *Sawyer:* I'm not sure you should be laugh-
> ing. It's going to mean a lot of orgasms for
> you.

He was serious.

> *Eve:* That's such a man thing, to get all
> fixated on some artificial number.
> *Sawyer:* Let me say this again: it's going to
> mean a lot of orgasms for you.
> *Eve:* So I would be stupid to scoff at this
> plan, is what you're saying?
> *Sawyer:* You said it, not me.

Okay, so what was her hurry? She could hang around a
little longer for Orgasm Fest.

> *Eve:* You know what, the selection at this library sucks. I could do so much better with my own Little Free Library.
>
> *Sawyer:* Are you trying to bargain with me to get me to build you a Little Free Library? Because you don't have to do that. All you have to do is ask.

She had not been. But now that he mentioned it...

> *Eve:* Sawyer, will you build me a Little Free Library?
>
> *Sawyer:* Done.

Ten days later, the orgasm count was up to thirteen, there was a Little Free Library in front of the Mermaid, and Evie was about to do something stupid.

Her phone rang at ten sharp.

"Professor Chen, hello." They were having a call to discuss details of the job offer.

"You have to stop calling me that. We'll be colleagues now. It's Linda."

"Linda, then!"

"You got the formal offer?"

"Yes. Thank you. I'm thrilled."

"There's not a lot of room on salary. Provincial budget cuts have been punishing."

Eve was more than happy with the salary on offer. It was much higher than her current one—well, than the one she was on leave from. Currently she was living on her line of credit, adding to the pile of debt that had her so freaked out.

But, she reminded herself, when she sold the Mermaid, she would wipe that all out.

But she was probably supposed to bargain. That's what people did in these situations, right? If you didn't know your own worth, how could you expect your employer to? Or something. She racked her brain. Vacation days were set by the union, so there was no leverage there. "I'm fine with the salary as is, but I need some accommodation on the start date." That was true. Even if she did the weekend commuting thing, she couldn't get her act together in the standard two weeks. She still had the pink room to deal with. She needed at least a month.

"How much accommodation are we talking about?" Linda asked.

"Six months."

What the hell? Where had that come from? She did not need six months.

But...how high could Sawyer's number get in those six months?

And the swimming. Lake swimming, not covert community center swimming. It would be June before the lake was warm enough.

There was silence on the line. Linda and the hiring committee knew she was on leave from her branch job. She'd been open about her situation, and they'd said they would wait for the right candidate.

But would they wait six months? Should she backpedal? She should backpedal. This was the dream job.

"Okay," Linda said.

"Really?"

"Well, they're new jobs. I'll get your colleague up to speed, and she can help train you. I'm taking a lot of holidays this summer anyway. So you get your affairs in order, and we'll start fresh in the fall. You can start after Labor Day?"

"Yes."

Okay, then. She was making an atypically irresponsible decision, choosing a sex-and-swimming summer vacation over a salary.

But that's all it was. She was choosing sex and swimming. Not Sawyer.

Right?

Chapter Twenty-Three

❧

I never want to look at another raspberry," Eve said as she plopped down next to Sawyer and Clara on a blanket at Sandcastle Beach.

"You went picking?" Sawyer asked. He had tried to pay her a conjugal visit early that morning, but she'd replied to his texts from the raspberry patch—the Raspberry Festival was in full swing.

"Yep. With Maya. I think I ate my weight in them as we picked. Then we had raspberry pancakes at Sadie's." She paused and wrinkled her nose. "They were delicious."

"Delicious raspberry pancakes upset you?"

"No. *Anyway.* Then Jenna lured me into the store on my way here and made me sample a bunch of different kinds of raspberry smoothies. Amber did the same thing with raspberry beers—she's manning the bar while Law plays in the sand." She glanced over at the sandcastle competition that was underway. "I couldn't take two steps down Main Street without someone pouring a raspberry beverage down my throat."

Sawyer chuckled. "You should try the raspberry lemonade at Legg's." He gestured to the beachside stand. "They only do it this weekend."

"Nope. If I drink any more raspberry-themed beverages, I will float off to sea. It'll be like *James and the Giant Peach*, except with a raspberry."

"So I guess you don't want one of Pearl's famous raspberry ricotta hand pies?" Clara dangled a perfectly golden pastry in front of Evie, then snatched it away.

"Hang on now, I think I'm getting a second wind." She grabbed the pie, took a big bite, and started pulling one arm out of her shirt. "Are we swimming?" She transferred the pie to her other hand and extracted her other arm from her shirt. "I wore my bathing suit."

It was a black one-piece, not the *Little Mermaid* bikini. Which was disappointing. But he couldn't stay anyway. "I go on duty in less than an hour, so I can't."

Which was also disappointing. But, he consoled himself, in the month or so since the lake had been warm enough to swim in, he'd gotten to see lots of Evie in all her bathing suits.

And out of them.

He was really enjoying the whole friends-with-benefits thing they had going. Mostly.

"I'll swim with you," Clara said. "I'm going to miss the lake so much."

Evie glanced at him. Probably to check on his well-being. She knew he was freaking out as the time ticked down to Clara's departure. But maybe that *wasn't* what she was thinking of, because she said, "I'm going to miss the lake, too."

"Are you *kidding* me?" came an indignant shout from over by the sandcastles. Sawyer was glad for the distraction. The less he had to think about departing women, the better.

It was Maya. She was working on an elaborate sandcastle. Or she had been. She was currently standing over Law's plot, where he was working on one of his own, and pointing at some shiny blue things he was using to edge a turret.

"That is sea glass," he said.

"That is *not* sea glass. That is some kind of polished rock you brought in, and you know that's not allowed. Natural materials found on the beach only."

"Nowhere in the rules does it say the materials you use must be found on the beach the same day. I collected this glass all year."

Maya gasped as if he'd announced he had decided to close the bar and become a professional puppy murderer. She waved Karl, who was one of the contest's judges, over.

"I think that's your cue to leave," Evie said, grabbing the pie back from him. "Unless you want to get stuck in the middle of that. Go enjoy your last few minutes of being off duty."

"Agreed." Clara got up. "Let's hit the lake, Eve."

The two of them wove their way through the various sandcastles in progress. Clara didn't know that Evie had ever been afraid of the water. She'd been too young to remember it, and Sawyer had kept their recent swimming lessons to himself. He watched them step gingerly over the pebbly stretch of beach and laugh and chat as they waded in.

It was funny to see them like that. Evie had always been kind to his sister. He had the idea that other girls might have resented boyfriends who came with little kids attached, but not her. She had always made room for Clara, both literally and figuratively. She would organize berry picking outings and present Clara with a special kid-size bucket emblazoned with whatever cartoon character was Clara's current favorite. She would let Clara help with the resultant jam making, even though Clara's "help" was anything but.

To see them together today, with Clara all grown up, plucked some tender, loose part of his insides he hadn't realized was so vulnerable. If he and Evie had stayed together, maybe they would've ended up exactly here, getting ready to send Clara away for school.

But no. Those were useless thoughts. He reminded himself how happy he had been to hear that Evie had gone not just to college but to grad school. That she'd become the librarian she'd always wanted to be. That would not have happened unless she'd left.

He reminded himself how she always kept referring to them as friends with benefits. She would text him booty calls with that line she'd accidentally used that first time, *Hello, friend, I need some benefits.*

So if he was getting grumpy about having to say goodbye again soon, that was his own doing. He sighed.

The lake was crowded, and Evie and Clara stopped to talk to Eiko and Pearl, who were in the water even though he was pretty sure they were supposed to be helping Karl judge the contest.

After a few minutes, they extricated themselves and continued out. Soon they were just two heads bobbing in the waves. Getting farther and farther away from him.

As metaphors went, it was pretty heavy-handed. But that didn't make it any less apt.

"I have a favor to ask," Clara said to Eve after their swim.

"Sure." Eve was still marveling that here she was, casually toweling off after a swim like it was no big deal.

"You know how Sawyer is taking me to Toronto at the end of August?"

"Yep."

"He's moving me in and staying the night in a hotel. I was kind of hoping he'd drive back the same day, but he says he'll be too tired. Which I get, but..."

"You don't want him to stay overnight?"

"I just...I think it's going to be hard for him to say goodbye."

"Ah." Sweet Clara. She wasn't wrong.

"I wish we could say goodbye, and he could teleport back here. I mean, I'll be sad, too, but I'll have Lynn, and we'll be busy working on the room."

"But Sawyer will be alone in his hotel room brooding."

"Which is why I was hoping you'd come with us. You're a local. I had so much fun when we hung out there. You could take him to that cute café. Or, you know, just...distract him."

She sure could. Eve bit back a smile. But also, he *was* going to be upset, maybe more than he realized. "Have you told him yet?"

Clara heaved a sigh.

"Just tell him! I promise he's not going to care. His eyes will get really big and he'll be shocked for a second, but then he'll realize that it all makes sense in retrospect."

"So what are you saying? You'll only come with us if I tell him?"

"No! No!" Eve didn't understand why Clara kept putting this off, but it wasn't for her to understand. "I'll come with you regardless, assuming it's okay with Sawyer."

"Will you ask him? I think he'll take it better coming from you. I don't want to damage his sensitive masculine pride."

Eve laughed. She was pretty sure he was going to jump at the chance to have other sensitive masculine parts of him tended to in a hotel room in Toronto. She had gotten really good at that, if she did say so herself. Nearly five months of sleeping together—as adults who didn't have to hide from Lucille and had an entire empty inn at their disposal—had afforded her lots of opportunities for practice.

It was a little jarring to think of how little time they had left. But it was for the best. She'd had fun, but her new job and her debt-free future loomed.

"I'll ask him. But just think about telling him before you leave, okay? I think it will be a relief."

"Okay." Another big sigh. "I'll tell him. Soon."

Eve had her chance to ask Sawyer later that day, when he walked by the inn while she was outside eating more raspberry things.

"Try this." She handed him half a sandwich.

"This is great. What is it, and where did you get it?"

"It's a raspberry-brie-honey grilled cheese, and Law is selling them at his stand outside the bar. He has a panini press going."

"That's quite a step up from crappy frozen pizza."

"He told me he's thinking of expanding the food options at the bar."

"He did?"

"You don't think it's a good idea?"

"No. It's a great idea. He's classed the place up since his dad retired. It's becoming known for wine and craft beer, so food is probably a logical next move."

Sawyer had been pretty open about the fact that he was dreading the emptying of the nest, but she also didn't want to make it seem like she thought he needed babysitting. In

the end she decided to just blurt it out. That had been working well in...other contexts. "So Clara asked me to come
with you guys to Toronto for the big move-in."

"That would be great. I'm going to be a basket case. You
sure you don't mind?"

Well, that had been easy. "Nope. Everything's basically
done here. Just waiting for the Realtor to decide when to
make the listing live. She has a big theory about timing—
I'm just doing what she says."

"Well, as long as she writes this thing into the purchase
agreement." He moved to the Little Free Library and shook
the post, like he wanted to make sure it was holding.

"I saw one went up at Jenna's."

He ducked his head. "That might have been my doing."

"Really?"

"Well, I'm kind of getting this vision of Main Street."
He faced the street and lifted his hands like he was an artist
contemplating his masterpiece. "Moonflowers and Little
Free Libraries."

God, was he *trying* to torture her? "You'd better be
careful. People might get their sickeningly adorable small-
town traditions mixed up and start throwing books into
the lake."

He turned back to her library and started rummaging
through it. "What have people been leaving?"

"I've actually been doing quite a bit of curating—
removing some titles I don't think reflect well on my little
library, adding others."

"Collections development," he said.

"Yes! Though it's actually more of a hybrid of that and
my old job, because I still get to interact with people. See
them delight in finding a book." She was going to miss
that, actually.

"You know, this inn could easily slide into a book-themed place. You have the mermaids—fairy tales. You could have a library inside for guests. An actual room. Coordinate with Maya and her kids' camps and do story hour..."

He trailed off, probably because he was realizing that he was doing the same thing she kept catching herself doing—forgetting that she was leaving. Selling the inn. Going back to Toronto to take the job she'd been working toward for so long.

"So was this one yours?" He held up a book. *The Joy of Lesbian Sex.*

She grinned. "That was not mine, but I gave that one a lot of thought. It's extremely outdated. For some reason, they updated *The Joy of Sex* in 2008, but they left the lesbians in the 1970s." She eyed him closely. Clearly Clara had not alluded to anything, or he would have said something. "Outdated sexual health information can be dangerous," she added. "But I also feel like on balance, it has the potential to do some good."

Sawyer smiled goofily at her. "I love...how much you've thought about this. I bet you're going to be really good at that new job." He transferred the smile to the book.

"Put that back! Some young lady's mind is just waiting to be blown." Maybe Clara's Miss Not Theoretical would wander by. Although Eve hadn't seen her—with or without Clara—for months.

Sawyer did not put the book back. He started flipping through it. "Hmm. I feel like there's some stuff in here that is more widely applicable." He looked up and raised his eyebrows. The goofy smile was gone. "I need to work on my numbers."

"You're on duty!" she whispered urgently. She wasn't sure why she was whispering. The street was full of people, but the festivities were generating a lot of noise and no one was paying attention to them.

"We don't have that much time left."

"You're on duty!" she said, like maybe he hadn't heard her the first time?

"I can be *really* quick. I won't even take off my clothes." He cracked his knuckles.

He cracked his knuckles. Well. Who was she to turn her nose up at the offer? But she did sort of want to tease him, so she said, "But I'm not done with my sandwich."

"You can keep eating it while I make you come."

Wow. She had no comeback for that. Also, she would really like to see that. Feel that. Taste that?

Wordlessly she turned and led him inside. Neither of them spoke as they walked through the finished main floor to her room in back. He slammed the door behind them, walked her toward the dresser and started unbuttoning her jeans.

Which left her staring at the ledge with the sad mermaids and the childhood photos. She'd left those alone even as she'd renovated the rest of the room. She and Sawyer had had sex in this room many times in the past few months, but on the bed. There was something deeply unsettling about the prospect of doing it while looking at these mementoes of the past. *Their* past. What they were doing now was categorically different from what they'd been doing then. That had been love. This was friends. And sex. "I can't face this way," she panted as he shoved his hand down her pants.

Thankfully, he didn't press her as to why. He spun them both around, his hand in her pants the whole time, sat on the dresser, and pulled her back against him.

"Better?" he rasped.

She didn't answer, not in words, anyway. She just

inhaled sharply, because he was getting right down to business. Usually he drew things out, but he was making good on his promise to be quick, using his fingers to stroke around her clit with the perfect amount of pressure. Pretty soon he would start whispering filthy things in her ear.

And…yep, as if on cue, he said, "I shouldn't be doing this while I'm on duty, but the honey in that sandwich made me think of this honey."

Normally a line that cheesy would have made her roll her eyes. But as she was learning, context was everything. He dragged his fingers down her opening before returning to her clit. "I'd like to have my face in there tasting you, but this will have to do for now."

She was so close. She arched her back and writhed against him. He was hard, but she knew he wasn't going to concern himself with that right now. He was so singularly focused on her, it was intoxicating.

"Come for me, Evie. Can you do that?"

She could, and she did, on a moan so obscene she was a little shocked it had come from her.

He gently pushed her off him. Panting, she started to reach for his belt, but realized she was still holding the sandwich with one hand. She'd had an orgasm while holding a grilled-cheese sandwich. She cracked up.

But when she moved to put it down and used her other hand to start to undo his belt, he shook his head and stepped away. "I gotta go back to work." He stilled the hand that was in the process of setting down the sandwich. "You eat up, and I'll catch you later."

She rolled her eyes. "You are the worst."

He smoothed his beard and saluted her from the doorway. "Yeah, but I'm also the best."

Chapter Twenty-Four

❧

The day before their departure for Toronto, the count was up to 133. Sawyer was inwardly gloating.

Or inwardly...something. He would replay their latest encounter in his mind, and it would start like gloating. But then it would turn into something less fun than gloating.

Half of him wanted to press fast-forward. To have it over and done with—to have Evie gone. Clara, too.

His phone dinged, and he rushed to look at it. She was right about them being bad at sexting, but his body reacted to his text notification chime as if it were the smuttiest sound he'd ever heard.

But it wasn't her; it was Law. Where are you? We went ahead and loaded the canoe into Jake's truck.

Right. He'd been living in his head so much, he'd forgotten they had plans to transport the canoe to the cove for its test voyage. Sorry. Got caught up at the station. I'll meet you on Locust.

The spot at which Locust Street met Sarnia Street was the closest a person could park to Paradise Cove, and it was where Jake left his truck. From there you had to walk the rest of the way.

Or maybe it was more like portage the rest of the way, when you were carrying a canoe.

"You want me to help?" He got out of his car as the others hoisted the boat.

"Nope, just lead the way," Jake said.

Soon they were wading into the water in front of Jake's cottage and paddling out.

Well, the other two were paddling. They were seated on the canoe's two seats and had relegated Sawyer to sitting on the floor in the middle, like he was their kid.

"Maybe we should have tested this with one person first," Sawyer said, mentally estimating their combined weight.

"You lacking faith in your own work?" Law needled.

"Well," Sawyer said, "I started this thing ten years ago and we finished it by watching YouTube videos." Which sounded better than teaching yourself to swim from a book, but only just.

"But look, it's fine." Law, who was seated in front of him, pulled his oar out of the water. He heard Jake, behind him, doing the same. As the boat slowed, they stayed silent, rocking gently in the waves.

Well, damn, they'd built a boat. Evie's boat.

Just in time for her to leave.

He twisted around to look at Jake. "So I guess we can start selling canoes now."

Jake didn't say anything, which wasn't inherently un-usual. But there was something about the *way* he was not saying anything that made Sawyer feel like maybe this wasn't *just* a canoe-testing trip.

"We wanted to talk to you," Law said.

Shit. He had let himself get suckered into Bromance Intervention: Nautical Edition. He should have seen this coming.

He didn't even have an oar. He tipped his head back and sighed. He needed to start paying attention to what was happening around him. Well, he needed to start paying attention to something other than Evie.

"You've been distracted lately," Law said.

No kidding. He didn't bother saying anything. They had him in their clutches, and they would be determined to speak their piece. Or Law would. Jake would probably just grunt in agreement.

"You've been sleeping with Eve, haven't you?"

There was no point in hiding it. "Yep."

Law didn't jump all over that like Sawyer had expected. "I heard she's coming with you when you drop off Clara at school."

"That was Clara's idea." That had come out a little too defensive. He cleared his throat and tried again. "I think she thinks having a local there will be helpful."

"It's almost like you guys are married. Dropping your kid off at school," Law said.

"Okay, whoa. It is not like that. We're just sleeping together until she leaves."

"But you like her," Law pressed.

"Of course I like her. I don't make a practice of sleeping with people I don't like."

Law looked over his shoulder. "So you're friends. And you're sleeping together. And she's coming with you to drop your sister off at university."

"That's right."

"So basically you *are* a couple, but you won't cop to it. Is that because of you, or does she share this delusion?

"We are *not* a couple."

"Why not?"

That, surprisingly, had come from Jake. Sawyer twisted around to look at him. "Because she lives in Toronto. She's been here under duress. She's *leaving*." God. Were they being obtuse just to irritate him, or were they really this dumb?

"But so is Clara," Jake said.

"So?"

"So you can leave, too."

Sawyer wasn't sure what he was more gobsmacked by, what Jake had said or the fact that he'd said it at all. "I can't just... do that."

"Why not?" Law asked.

"My life is here. My job is here." His voice was rising. He ordered himself to calm down. "*You* assholes are here."

"You've done your time, man," Jake said quietly. "Clara turned out great, and that's to your credit, but you can be done now."

Sawyer sucked in a breath. The thing about the bromance—historically, anyway—was that they helped each other without needing to analyze everything to death. That was why Law and Jake came to all of Clara's plays and science fairs. Why they'd babysat when she was younger. Why Sawyer and Clara spent every holiday with Jake or Law and their extended families.

So on the one hand, what Jake was saying wasn't a surprise. Jake and Law had been there. He just hadn't really grasped how much they had *seen*.

But if they had seen all that, really *seen* all that, they should understand that it wasn't like he could just shed his life like an old skin and skip merrily off to Toronto after Evie. "You guys don't understand. It's too late. She's from another world."

"Toronto is three hours by car!" Law objected.

"Not just geographically. She's into documentaries and…collections development."

"She's into what?" Jake said.

"Exactly." He could see Law ramping up again. "Look. You guys have made your point. But it's too late." Unlike Ariel and the prince, they couldn't live—not forever, not happily ever after—in each other's worlds.

Law still looked like he was going to object, but Sawyer was done with this conversation. "I'm done talking about this. You assholes want to paddle this thing back to shore or do I need to jump out and swim?"

They rowed back, and when they dragged the canoe onto the beach, it was to find that its pink stripe hadn't held up to the boat's maiden voyage.

"Needs more varnish," Jake said.

"Nah," Sawyer said. "Don't bother. This was a stupid idea anyway."

Eve had kind of been hoping the Realtor would leave before Sawyer and Clara arrived to pick her up for the trip to Toronto. No such luck, though. They pulled up as she was installing the for-sale sign out front.

Eve wasn't sure why, but the overlap was making her uncomfortable. She and Sawyer had been doing an excellent job *not* talking about her upcoming departure, and though it was nonsensical, she didn't want to present him with visual evidence. She wanted to keep living in denial, she supposed. Denial and orgasms.

There were worse places to be.

"Eve!" Clara called as she got out of the driver's seat. "I'm driving, so you should call shotgun!"

Eve laughed but refrained from doing so. The siblings should sit up front with each other on a historic day like this. "Jessica, do you know Sawyer Collins, our chief of police?" Eve had recruited Jessica from Grand View, way back when she first came to town and needed an estimate. She'd been trying, back then, to use nonlocals, because she'd been so paranoid about the fine citizens of "Matchmaker" Bay poking their noses into her business. So much for that. "And his sister, Clara. Sawyer, Clara, this is Jessica Hacking from Remax in Grand View."

Sawyer shook Jessica's hand and nodded at the for-sale sign. "Hard to believe it's been a year."

Eve didn't know what to say.

Jessica stood back to admire her handiwork. "Here's my thinking, Eve. I'm leaving town tomorrow, back on Labor Day. My plan is to run an agents-only open house this evening, get some buzz going, then the listing will go live. We'll hold back offers until after the long weekend, both because I think that's the right strategy but also because then we can sit down and go through them together. My question is—"

"Hold up," Sawyer, uncharacteristically, interrupted. "What happened to the Little Free Library?"

Jessica blinked. "We had to take it down. It was interfering with the sightlines to the sign."

Annoyance flashed across Sawyer's face. "We can put it back up after the sale," Eve said, wanting to smooth things over. But then she realized that she wouldn't be here for that. Even if they got an offer over the weekend, the sign would probably stay up until the closing date. Maybe she could ask Sawyer to put the library back up without her.

And hope the new owner wanted to keep it.

"So," Jessica continued, drawing Eve out of her unsettling thoughts, "are you okay with me having one of my colleagues handle any showings while I'm away?"

"Sure. We're leaving town, too." She gestured at Sawyer and Clara. "Right now, in fact. But I'll be back tomorrow sometime, probably in the afternoon?" She looked at Sawyer, who nodded.

"I'll give my colleague your number so she can be in touch if there are any issues. I'll be reachable by phone, too. But I don't foresee any problems."

"Sounds like you're on top of everything," Eve said.

"I am. Of course I can't guarantee anything, but I'm almost certain that by the time we see each other again, you'll have papers in front of you that will start the process of getting rid of this place. You'll be free."

Free.

She looked at the building. It was looking good. The windows were sparkling, the door had a fresh coat of paint, and she and Clara had planted some moonflowers in pots. Her gaze wandered up to the roof. It felt simultaneously like a lifetime ago and like just yesterday that she'd been stranded up there. She had wanted to escape Sawyer's notice so badly that she'd semijokingly thought of rappelling down the building.

Now she had that freedom she'd so desperately wanted. This... was not what she'd thought it would feel like.

Clara dropped the bomb in the car.

In the car.

"Sawyer," she said, "Remember how you said it's easier to talk about serious things in the car?"

Eve sat up so abruptly that her seat belt engaged.

"What's up?" Sawyer said casually.

Oh boy.

"I'm gay."

"What?"

"I'm a lesbian. I like girls. I mean, I like boys, too, but I like-like girls. You know what I mean."

Clara glanced at Eve in the rearview mirror. Eve nodded encouragingly. This was not how she would have delivered the news, but then, it wasn't her news to deliver.

There was a long silence. She couldn't see Sawyer, but she could *feel* him reeling. "Is *this* why you never dated?" he finally asked.

"I dated. I just didn't date boys."

"What?"

Clara chuckled. "Relax. I didn't really date girls, either. I thought I might have a little thing with Lily Markerville, but it didn't last. And really, that's mostly why I didn't tell you. It's not like this town is exactly teeming with teenage lesbians."

You never knew. Eve herself had witnessed a young woman—not Clara and not Lily Markerville, who she assumed was Miss It's Not Theoretical—taking *The Joy of Lesbian Sex* from the Little Free Library several weeks ago.

"That's *mostly* why you didn't tell me?" Sawyer asked quietly. "What's the rest?"

Good job, Sawyer. That was the right question. Not that this needed to be a huge production—Eve was *hoping* for not a huge production—but Clara was trying to gloss over this too quickly.

"Well...you know." Clara sighed. "Why didn't we start talking about Mom and Dad until this year?"

It was Sawyer's turn to sigh. "Because talking about this stuff is hard."

"But marginally easier in a moving vehicle!" Clara said with exaggerated cheer.

Sawyer turned around in his seat and speared Eve with a severe look. "Did you know about this?"

Her wince must have answered for her. He turned back to Clara. "I hope I'm not the last to know because you thought I would react poorly."

"No, no. I don't know. I just…let it get away from me. I…didn't want to lose anyone else." Her voice had gone high. Eve recognized it as a sign that she was about to cry, so Sawyer must, too. "I can't lose you."

"That's right," he said vehemently. "You *can't* lose me."

Clara glanced over, and the siblings shared a long look before Sawyer snapped his fingers at the windshield, indicating that he wanted Clara to pay attention to the road. Once she had done so, he said, with the same intense tone, "You think you're rid of me because you're in school in Toronto, but I'm going to be texting your ass constantly. And they'd better have some kind of fall parents' night or something or I'm gonna declare my own. You are *never*"— his voice cracked—"getting rid of me."

Clara emitted a single sob but got herself under control quickly. "I'm sorry I didn't tell you."

"No." Sawyer shook his head. "I'm the one who's sorry. I didn't know this big thing about you. I should have seen it."

"No, you shouldn't have."

"Yes, I should have." He paused. Eve couldn't see his face, but he tilted his head like he was thinking about something really hard. "I totally should have."

Clara met Eve's eyes in the mirror again, but this time she looked more at ease. "Eve said you were going to go through a slideshow of the past to try to see what you'd missed."

Sawyer snorted. "Well, Eve doesn't know everything." He turned, and there was both annoyance and affection in his expression. It felt like they'd all come through something together.

"She kind of *does* know everything," Clara said.

Sawyer rolled his eyes even as affection won out over annoyance and faced forward. After a few moments, he said, "Yeah, she kind of does."

They rode in silence for a while, and as they turned off the Bluewater Highway onto a country road, they passed fields of corn ready to harvest.

"What did you mean 'a thing'?" Sawyer suddenly asked.

"What?

"You said you thought you had 'a thing' with Lily Somebody—who I've never even heard of, by the way."

"Lily Markerville. She was new in town this year." Clara blew out a breath, and her shoulders slumped. "We started hanging out around the time of the Anti-Festival, and it seemed like she was really into me, and then she..." Her voice hitched, but she regained control. "She stopped replying to my texts and acknowledging my existence entirely—like, wouldn't even make eye contact with me at school."

"Well," said Sawyer. "Then fuck her very much."

After two hours of hauling boxes up three flights to Clara's room in the muggy heat of a Toronto August, Eve was beat. When her phone rang, she jumped at the chance for a break. She would yak the ear off a telemarketer if she could do it sitting down in the shade.

It wasn't a telemarketer, though; it was Maya. "Hey."

"Where are you?"

"I'm in Toronto helping Sawyer move Clara. Where are you?"

"Outside the back door of the Mermaid to pick you up for antiquing."

"Oh, crap." She'd totally forgotten that she'd agreed to go shopping with Maya for furniture for the set of her

Anti-Festival play. "I feel like Richard needs an antique chest in which to keep his dagger between murders," Maya had said.

Eve waved to Sawyer to indicate that she needed to take the call and walked to a bench and plopped down. "I'm so sorry. I stood you up."

There was a long pause. Eve felt terrible. She was ramping up to apologize again when Maya said, "You fell in love with him."

What? "I'm not in love with him!"

"Oh, so you're just there performing manual labor on behalf of his little sister as a gesture of friendship."

"Correct."

"Is that why you're sleeping with him, too?"

"I am *not* sleeping with him!"

"Eve. Come off it. You took my advice, I guess, but you didn't bother to tell me about it."

That last part was true. She'd thought about telling Maya. She'd meant to. But Maya had suggested she have sex with Sawyer once, in a get-it-out-of-your-system way. She hadn't known how to tell Maya when *once* became...six months. And Sawyer himself was hiding it, so she'd defaulted to following his lead. She sighed. "How did you find out?"

"I have my sources."

"Oh my God, that town." It was maddening.

"You know what I think? I think you love this town, and you love Sawyer."

"I do *not*." She was aware that she sounded like a petulant child, but she didn't care. "And even if I did, which I *don't*, it doesn't matter. The listing for the inn goes up today. I start my new job in less than a week. My parents are converting the den back into a bedroom until I can find a new apartment." She got up. It was instinctive. She needed to move. This was what she'd felt like that day on the roof. Restless and caged. Like she needed to flee.

"Right," Maya said. "Okay."

She was hurt. Eve could hear it in her voice. "You want to wait for me to go shopping? We'll be back tomorrow."

"I can't. I'm doing the day camp."

"Right." Maya was doing a kids' theater one-day camp, a test run of her idea for a longer one next summer.

"Anyway, it wasn't really about the antiquing. I just thought it would be...a fun outing." She cleared her throat. "I'm really going to miss you, okay? I had a whole last-hurrah day planned." Her tone had become defensive. It startled Eve to realize she knew Maya well enough to know that she masked negative emotions like fear and sadness with combativeness.

"I'm really going to miss you, too. I—" Her eyes and throat started burning in tandem.

"I know," Maya said softly. "Me, too."

Chapter Twenty-Five

❧

Sawyer expected moving Clara into university would churn up a lot of emotions. He just hadn't expected awkwardness to be one of them.

But there they were, crammed into her small room, staring at each other. All the boxes were moved in. Many of them were already unpacked. Evie had made both girls' beds.

There was nothing left to do.

His stomach growled. Maybe that's what was left to do—dinner. They could walk somewhere—Evie would know where to go—and have some food. Put off saying goodbye.

Lynn's mother appeared in the doorway. "We're going to head back to our hotel, sweetie. We'll pop by and see you in the morning before we head to the airport."

So he should probably offer to take Lynn to dinner, too? He liked Lynn a lot, but he kind of wanted Clara to himself for one last evening. Well, Clara and Evie, of course.

Lynn hugged her mother. "You know you can come with us to the hotel if you want, have dinner and spend the night," her mom said.

"Thanks, Mom, but there's a bunch of people from the floor going for dinner."

"I know. I know." Lynn's mom pulled back, and her eyes were suspiciously bright. Sawyer's eyes started to sting like they wanted to get in on the action. "You should go with your new friends."

Sawyer looked at Evie. He must have succeeded in transmitting his question via ESP, because she gave a little nod. Lynn walked her parents out, and Sawyer turned to Clara. "You going to that dinner, too?"

She looked torn. "I don't have to. Why don't the three of us go somewhere to eat?"

"No, no. You should..." His voice cracked.

"You should go make new friends." Evie's voice was firm but kind.

Clara looked at him. He nodded, but he was faking it. God. Clara looked so *young*. How could he just *leave* her here? What had *happened*? One minute he was sneaking into her room at night to perform tooth-fairy duties, and now she was *here*. Now she was a person who wrote essays about vaccination policy and was majoring in engineering and was going out to dinner with her friends in Toronto.

"I'll see you in a month," she said, as if she could read his mind. "At the Anti-Festival." She had informed him that she'd read up on the topic and thought it best that she not come home for a month, that giving in to homesickness too early on could prevent proper socialization.

What could he do but agree?

But then her face crumpled, and she threw herself into his arms.

He felt like he was floating above his body. Which wasn't the worst thing in the world, because otherwise he was pretty sure he would start openly weeping. He hugged her tight. "I'm so proud of you, and I love you so much." He wasn't crying, but his speech was clogged with unshed tears. Thinking back to the bomb she'd dropped in the car that morning, he added, "I love *everything* about you."

"Thank you for everything, Sawyer," she whispered.

He forced himself to let her go. To make a dismissive gesture. "Okay, we're being melodramatic. I'll see you in a month."

She nodded overly vigorously and took a step back. Turned to Evie and hugged her.

Evie. Evie who was looking at him over Clara's shoulder, her eyes bright with moisture but steady like beacons.

Evie would get him out of here.

And she did.

She propelled him out of the room, and as soon as they were on the stairwell—Clara had hovered in her doorway waving at them as they walked down the hallway—Evie grabbed his hand. Held it tight and led him down three flights. When they got to the van he'd borrowed from Jordan's auto shop, she held out her hand and said, "Keys."

He gave them to her. Once inside, he slumped forward and let his head hit the dashboard. "Today my sister came out and moved out. That's a lot of out."

She didn't answer, just started the van. "What do you want to do? Stop for dinner somewhere?"

"No. My whole body hurts. I'm not sure why—she didn't have that much stuff. I just want to grab some takeout and crash at the hotel. Maybe hit the hot tub." He had made sure the hotel he booked had a pool.

"Perfect." As she pulled up in front of the hotel, she said,

"You get checked in, and I'll go in search of provisions and be back soon."

He started to protest, reflexively—she should go to the room and crash and he should go find food—but she pointed at the passenger-side door before he could marshal the words. "Go."

So he decided to just let her take care of him.

When she returned with heavenly-smelling Thai food, he wanted to kiss her. Well, he always wanted to kiss her. But he *extra* wanted to kiss her. He'd changed into swim trunks, so she went into the bathroom and changed, too. They bolted back some curry and a spring roll each and hit the hot tub.

Forty minutes later his skin had turned pruney and he felt considerably better. He heaved a sigh. "Can I ask you a question?"

"Shoot."

"Do you think Clara and Lynn..."

She grinned. "You're going to have to learn to talk about it, Sawyer."

"Do you think they're a couple? Or might become one? I mean, I'm cool with the whole gay thing. I am. I'm *not* cool with the whole *sex* thing. I wouldn't let her room with a boy."

"Okay, one, you can't control what Clara does. There's no 'letting' or 'not letting' anymore. She's gonna do what she's gonna do. All *you* can do is trust that you did a good job. And you *did*." She patted him on the arm. "And two, Lynn is straight."

"How do you know that?"

"Clara told me."

God, he was glad Clara had had Evie to talk to this year. "Does Lynn know Clara's gay?" Because if Lynn wasn't going to be cool with it, that was going to be a problem. And he didn't care how much control he was or wasn't supposed to be exerting, he was going to make it *his* problem.

"She does, and she's fine with it. They're friends, Sawyer. They're leaning on each other as they make this big transition. It's all good."

Right. "Okay."

She huffed a laugh. "Look at you. You went from hating Lynn because she might be deflowering your sister to hating Lynn because she might be disapproving of your sister."

"So?"

"You're cute."

"I am not cute."

"Yes you are." She splashed him. He rolled his eyes. He was too tired to splash back. But she had him smiling.

"Time for dinner part two?" she asked. "And maybe some trashy TV?"

That sounded great. "Yeah."

She started to climb out, but he stopped her progress with a hand on her arm. "Evie."

"Yeah?"

God. He didn't even know what he wanted to say. And he was so tired. So he settled for ripping off Clara's line from earlier. "Thank you for everything."

She smiled—a big, incandescent, guileless smile. He wasn't sure if it made him feel better or worse.

When they got back to the room, Sawyer flipped through the TV channels until he found an underwater documentary. "It's not *The Little Mermaid*, but it will have to do." He grabbed one of the takeout boxes. "Why don't you shower first?"

When Eve emerged from the bathroom a few minutes

later, he was asleep in a chair. Poor guy. She laid a hand on his shoulder. "Sawyer."

He blinked his eyes open. "Oh, man. I am wrecked."

She tugged his arm to get him on his feet and pointed him toward the nearest of the two beds.

He flopped down on his stomach. "Give me two minutes, and we'll work on our numbers some more." His voice was muffled by the pillow his face was mashed into.

"Nope. Time for sleep." She picked up his backpack and set it next to him. "Put on something dry first, though."

"Uhhh." He rolled over. It looked like a huge effort. "I'm sorry."

"Don't be sorry. You've had quite a day. I'm tired, too." She hadn't hauled as many boxes as he had, or been through nearly the same emotional wringer, but she was beat. "I'm going to go brush my teeth and hit the sack as well."

When she reemerged from the bathroom, he was under the covers breathing deeply. She paused for a moment. There were two beds in the room. They had been sleeping together—frequently and enthusiastically—but they'd never *slept* together.

Because they weren't *together*. Sleeping in the same bed was something you did next to your boyfriend, not your friend with benefits.

She moved around the room quietly putting a few things in order before slipping into the other bed and turning out the light.

"Evie?"

She'd thought he was asleep. "Hmm?"

"Will you sleep with me?"

Oh boy.

He scooched to the far side of his bed and held back the covers.

Well, crap. How could she say no after this day? Worse, she didn't *want* to say no. She slid in next to him. "This is a bad idea."

He tucked her against him, sighing as he spooned her against his chest. "I know."

When Eve awoke the next morning, her first thought was that she was so cozy. It should probably be illegal to feel this cozy.

But then she realized *why* she was feeling so cozy. She was spooned up against Sawyer's chest. She felt warm and safe.

But only for a moment.

As she woke up more fully, she started to feel decidedly *un*safe.

Panicky, even.

She hadn't ever woken up with Sawyer. It hadn't been possible when they were teenagers, and friends with benefits, especially a friend with benefits who had custody of his teenage sister, didn't do sleepovers. So they'd spent six months sleeping together but not *sleeping together*.

She had spent six months telling herself that she could do the friends-with-benefits thing. That she could have some fun, then hightail it out of town with a full bank account and an intact heart.

Had she been kidding herself?

This was a bookend. The first bookend had been that day on the roof.

This was the *closing* bookend. The end.

Today, like on that day, she was panicking. But unlike then, she wasn't angry. She didn't have anyone to blame this time but herself.

No, this time, she was sad. So sad, she was afraid she was about to start crying.

Very slowly, she started to inch herself out from under Sawyer. He continued breathing deeply. She reached for her phone on the nightstand. It was next to his—and there was a notification on his.

She hadn't been trying to snoop.

Well, she hadn't been trying to snoop until she saw it was a text from Law. Jake and I fixed the pink stripe on Eve's canoe.

What? Her canoe? *What?* That was as much of the text as the preview notification would let her see.

"Hey." Sawyer. She set the phone down and turned. Her adrenaline was surging, but he was yawning, so she didn't think he'd seen her messing with his phone. He reached for her, but she sprang off the bed before he could make contact.

"We should get going!" she said, hearing the high weirdness in her tone.

"Why? I'm off all day."

It was Friday. He'd taken off specifically so they wouldn't have to hurry home.

Reasons Eve Had to Get Home Right Now

1. She had to go into the Pink Room of Pain. She had to finally face it.
2. No. She had to face herself. So she could decide how brave to be. How much she was willing to upend her life. How twisty she could stand to be.

That second entry was so many items, and she'd just jumbled them all together. Her list-making skills were breaking down.

"I was hoping we could talk," Sawyer said. "Among other things." He wagged his eyebrows.

"I have to get back!" she practically shouted. She had gone from sounding a little weird to sounding totally unhinged.

"Why?"

"I have to talk to Maya!"

"Now?"

"Yes! It's important." It had been a line to get them out of here, but as soon as it came out of her mouth she recognized it as a *true* line.

He sat up. She had alarmed him. "Use my phone."

She gave a momentary thought to accepting his phone. Getting him to unlock it, taking it into the bathroom, and opening that text. Reading the whole thread.

But it didn't really matter, did it? If she'd learned one thing this year, it was that she had a voice. That she could ask for what she wanted.

She just needed to figure out what that was.

"I need to talk to Maya in person." She made an apologetic face. "Sorry. I know you were planning to spend the morning here."

He got out of bed. "Give me five minutes."

In less than ten, they had checked out and retrieved the van and were on the road. Ten more and they were on the highway headed west.

As they drove in silence, Eve watched the familiar landmarks of Toronto recede. She went back over the mental list she'd composed this morning to see if, now that that immediate sense of panic had receded, she could do a better job unjumbling everything.

Reasons Eve Had to Get Home Right Now

Home. She hadn't done that on purpose.
But it *did* feel like she was going home.
Holy crap, she was so confused.

Chapter Twenty-Six

❦

*S*omething was wrong. Sawyer couldn't say exactly what it was. Well, that wasn't true. He knew what it was in a general sort of way. He just didn't know what had triggered it.

It wasn't like there weren't several options. His insistence that they sleep—literally *sleep*—together, for one. That had probably been a step too far toward the kind of emotional intimacy Evie didn't want. Or how about the fact that she'd witnessed him slowly lose his mind over the course of yesterday?

Or maybe it had nothing to do with the Toronto trip. Maybe it was the fact that the Mermaid Parade was tomorrow.

Whatever it was, the question was, could he fix it? Was he too late?

Why hadn't he listened to his friends? Why hadn't he listened to his *heart*? He had truly believed that it was too late for him and Evie, but he could see now how wrong he had been to not even give it a shot. To not give *them* a shot.

It had taken last night for the realization to hit. It had taken the knowledge that he needed her with him. That lying down next to her, holding her, made everything better.

That he would be a fool not to try to follow her back to Toronto.

He glanced at her as they hurtled down the 401. She was looking out the window.

He looked at her again as they left Kitchener behind. She was still brooding.

"Everything okay?" Clearly everything was not okay, but he wanted to hear her speak, to break this awful silence.

"Yep." She kept looking out the window.

All right, then. He should just take a hint. They needed to talk. Well, he needed to talk, and he could only hope she would listen. But now was clearly not the time or the place. He'd wait until they got home. To the inn. Whatever.

Eve hadn't even really registered that it was the weekend of the Mermaid Parade. Well, she had, but it didn't have the same weight as last year. So she had temporarily forgotten, until they rolled into town Friday afternoon to find that the mermaids had taken over. As Sawyer slowed on the approach to the inn, she took in a group of young women—tourists, she suspected, because she didn't recognize any of them—in elaborate mermaid getups posing for pictures in the gazebo. And there was Karl Andersen wearing a T-shirt that featured the "man" symbol you saw on public bathrooms, but instead of legs, it had a tail.

When they pulled up to the inn, the front door was ajar, and the lockbox on it was open. "There must be a showing happening."

Sawyer parked and tried to run around to the passenger side to help her out, but she rushed to beat him. As in the morning, she couldn't let him touch her. Couldn't bear any more of his chivalry and attentiveness.

She turned and tilted her head up to contemplate her inn. *Her* inn?

She took several steps back so she could see the whole thing at once. She took in the same improvements she'd noted when they were here yesterday: the door, the moonflowers. But today they felt like *her* improvements. Things she had done to her aunt's inn with help from her friends.

And there were those balconies. The ones she and Sawyer had spent so much time on as kids. The one they had almost kissed on as adults.

Tears threatened again, but unlike this morning's, they felt like...happy tears.

Yes, this was her inn. *Her* inn. She smiled.

And then Jeannie Wilkerson walked out the front door.

Eve inhaled sharply. Or maybe that sound had come from Sawyer, because actually, Eve couldn't breathe.

Jeannie handed a business card to a fortysomething man in a business suit. "As I said, offers are being held back until Tuesday. But please don't hesitate to be in touch if you have any questions. I'll get you the information about the zoning variance."

Breathe, Eve ordered herself. Breathing was a necessary precondition to whatever was going to happen next.

Jeannie, who looked essentially the same except skinnier and blonder, turned to put the key back in the lockbox.

Breathe.

She did, finally, but it came on a gasp.

It drew Jeannie's attention. But not to Eve.

"Sawyer? Sawyer Collins? Oh my God!"

She started down the stairs. Objectively speaking, she was probably moving pretty fast—she seemed really excited to see Sawyer—but Eve felt like she was watching a car crash in slow motion. Sawyer recoiled, physically stepped back from Jeannie, but the van behind him prevented him from dodging the incoming hug.

"I was hoping I'd run into you," Jeannie exclaimed.

"Jeannie." His voice was flat. "What are you doing here?"

"I'm back!" she said. "Well, I'm in Grand View. Just off a spectacular divorce, returning to my roots, you know, the whole clichéd thing. My dad has had a couple minor health scares, and even though when I was growing up here all I wanted to do was escape, bam, I'm suddenly all nostalgic for this place." She swatted his chest. "So I just thought, screw it, I'm making a change. I quit my job, got my real estate license, and here I am."

"Here you are." He was still speaking in a stilted, sort of robotic way. It was awkward enough that Jeannie looked around, like she thought there might be some external explanation for why Sawyer was acting so oddly.

Eve, calmer now, looked around, too. She could have sworn they had an audience. She felt like everyone was watching. Just the same as that day in the parade. But although there were people on the street, no one was paying them any attention.

"Oh, I'm sorry!" Jeannie exclaimed. She held her hand out to Eve. "I don't think we've met. I'm Jeannie Wilkerson."

Eve allowed her hand to be pumped up and down. *We may not have met, but I'm familiar with your work.* Ha!

Look at her. Running into Jeannie Wilkerson had been her worst nightmare, but here she was cracking jokes to herself.

It turned out that Jeannie Wilkerson was just a person. A divorced real estate agent with a sick dad. A regular sort of person.

"This is Eve Abbott," Sawyer said, still in the flat, robot voice. Was it possible Jeannie's appearance was affecting him more than it was her?

"Oh! Eve!" Jeannie clapped her hands. "I think that guy is going to make you a *very* good offer. I have another showing this afternoon, but I don't think we're going to do better than that guy."

"Who was he?" she asked.

It no longer mattered. But she was mildly curious.

"He works for a development company. They want to gut the place and do condos. They're very motivated."

"What does that mean, gut the place?"

"Well, I know it's a little disconcerting, because you've done such a lovely renovation, but they'll probably keep the facade so the shell looks historic, but take it down to the studs inside and start over."

Eve hoisted her bag on her shoulder and went inside without a word. *Like hell they will.*

After Sawyer watched Evie go inside the Mermaid, he knew what he had to do.

He walked over to Lakeside Hardware, hoping that most, if not all, of the old folks would be there.

He was in luck. Four sets of eyes swung toward him when the bell on the door jingled to announce his arrival.

"Hi, Sawyer. I was going to—"

Whatever Pearl had been planning to say, she thought

better of it. Her eyes widened. Did he look as unhinged as he felt?

"Sawyer, son," Karl said. "What's wrong?"

"I need to throw the mer-king and mer-queen competition."

He grinned. "You came to the right place."

Eve went right upstairs to the Pink Room of Pain. Unlocked the door, stepped inside, and looked around. Really *looked*. Did a slow circle, taking in the walls studded with mementoes of who she used to be. The one *Little Mermaid* poster she'd left up. The Eiffel Tower prints. The painting Jake's mom had given her.

She walked over to the window and opened the blinds. The inn was taller than the houses on the block behind it, so she saw a big swath of blue sky.

What had she been so afraid of? It was just a room. It didn't have any power over her that she wasn't giving it.

Just like Jeannie Wilkerson was just a person.

Just like *Sawyer* was just a person. A person who had made a mistake, maybe?

But more importantly, *she* was a person who had made a mistake. Many mistakes.

A List of Mistakes Eve Abbott Had Made

Nope. No list.

How about, instead of making a list, she just tried to ask for what she wanted? Using the voice she'd gradually discovered this past year?

She pulled out the stool at the dressing table, sat, and opened the drawer, suddenly wanting a glimpse of who she used to be. She'd kept all kinds of junk in here—nail polish and hairbrushes, but also photos, fortunes from fortune cookies, and Hogwarts letters she'd written and mailed to herself. The detritus of a girlhood.

It was all still there. But lying on top of it was a big manila envelope.

It had her name on it, in the spidery scrawl she recognized as Lucille's.

With shaking hands, she opened the envelope. It contained a letter and a copy of the will.

Dear Eve,

Just kidding! Here's the real will.

I'm sorry I played such a mean trick on you. I know you probably went into a panic after you met with Jason (who, by the way, was innocent in this scheme). Hear me out, though.

I think you made a mistake when you ran away from this place. I think you made a mistake when you ran away from Sawyer. (Mind you, I think he made a mistake with that hurtful stunt he pulled, but I suspect he had his reasons.) I'm not sorry I didn't let you turn your back on university, but I didn't realize your absence was going to be permanent.

I also think I made a mistake not telling you all this sooner. I'm writing this from a hospital bed. Yes, I know: so melodramatic. But I am fully in my right mind. You'll see that the will enclosed is more recent than the one Jason gave you. I am assured by the fancy Toronto lawyers I hired to draft it that it will stand up to any and all legal scrutiny. This is just a regular will. You get the inn. You can do whatever you want with it, whenever you want.

I was hoping, though, that you might think about staying. Maybe not running the inn. I know that might not be your thing. But staying in town. I feel like you love it here, in your heart, and it hurts me to see you leave what you love behind because of…what? Pride? Hurt? Fear? Because I made a mistake?

I don't know, and I'm sorry I never asked you about it.

But I thought maybe if you were presented, just for a little while, with the idea—if I backed you into a corner—you might sit with your discomfort and discover a truth underneath it. I knew you'd be up here within hours of arriving, so I hope you weren't freaking out for too long.

I haven't told anyone yet about this heart attack. For all I know, I'll recover, everything will be fine, and I'll change my mind about all this. But I don't think so. Regardless of what happens right now, I'm old and sick. I don't have a lot of time left. But it turns out that as you get old, you learn some things. One of the things I learned pretty late in the game—and partly by watching you, my Eve—is that you can be a sad mermaid, or you can be a happy one. You can twist yourself into a mold you think you should fit into. You can give up yourself in the process. Or you can swim with your friends, and sing. And maybe meet a prince. Or maybe not. But regardless, singing is better than crying, isn't it?

So you have a choice. You can bust me. You can show Jason this will. He's smarter than he looks, and I have no doubt he'll figure it out. Or you can rip up this will and this letter and stick around for a while and see what happens.

I will love you either way, my Eve. I always have, and I always will.

Lucille

The tears fell, hot and silent. Eve closed her eyes. Tried to make sense of the swirling sensation inside her chest. It felt like sorrow. But also like hope. Those two things should have been contradictory.

How many times this past year had she thought about how Sawyer, with his rough hands and his soft beard, inspired contradictory emotions? About how this whole town did?

She kept her eyes closed. Her eyeballs physically hurt. Okay. This was going to be okay. This letter felt like a bomb exploding in her lap, but it wasn't actually telling her anything she didn't already know.

This was her dream job. This inn with the Little Free Library. The fairy tales they both held.

This was her dream, *period*. This town. Her old—and new—friends.

And maybe, if he would have her, Sawyer?

She took a deep breath and opened her eyes. She blinked, thinking at first that tears were making her see things. But no, there was something there, in the mirror. It was angled so she could see out the reflection of the window.

She leaned forward, squinting.

Balloons. It was Maya's camp.

Dozens of balloons were floating up, up into a sky as blue as the lake.

And they were all shaped like mermaids.

Chapter Twenty-Seven

❧

*T*he next morning, Eve woke to a pounding in her head. "Oh," she groaned.

"Ugh," Maya said. "Seconded."

They were in the pink room. After her revelation last night, Eve had summoned Maya. And Maya had come with wine. So much wine. They hadn't even talked. She'd shown Maya the letter and burst into tears. Maya had poured wine down her throat, and held her while she cried ten years' worth of tears. Tears for lost opportunities but also for found ones. Tears for lost voices and found voices.

Eve rolled over so she was face-to-face with Maya. "I'm staying here. I'm keeping the inn."

Maya smiled. "Of course you are."

"I think what Lucille was trying to say was that in the end, the Disney version is the right model, you know?" Eve paused, trying to make the swirling thoughts of yesterday coalesce into a plan of action. "Better than the tragic version, anyway? So I was thinking. In the movie, Ariel is trying to figure out where she belongs, right? She wants to be part of the human world, but she doesn't feel like she fits." She blew out a breath. Man, this was going to sound corny. "Well, this is my world. This silly town is where I want to be."

Maya patted her arm. "I totally appreciate the sentiment. But I think you're wrong. I don't think any version of 'The Little Mermaid' is the right metaphor here. I mean, Ariel suffers so much, even in the Disney version. Clearly, if you're going to get all deep and metaphorical, *Splash* is your source material. Tom Hanks swims off to live happily ever after in the underground kingdom with Daryl Hannah."

"Okay, but if we're going with *Splash*, it follows that I *don't* stay here," Eve said. "Sawyer goes back to Toronto with me. And *that* doesn't make any sense, because clearly Moonflower Bay is the underwater kingdom. I mean, we have the mermaids and everything."

"I *might* concede your point, but if this is *The Little Mermaid*, what does that make me? That stupid fish sidekick?"

Eve giggled. "No, because I already have a tree named after Flounder."

Maya raised an eyebrow. "So, what? I'm either a seagull or a crab?"

Eve snuggled into Maya's shoulder. "Maybe everything doesn't have to be so aggressively metaphorical."

"What?" Maya gasped theatrically. "Now you're just talking crazy. What is life without aggressive metaphors?"

"Regardless, what I need now is a plan. I have to actually talk to the prince. Or Tom Hanks. Or whoever he is. And I have no idea how to do that. Because you know what? This *isn't* a story. It's real life." She sat up, wincing at the pain in her head. "I also need Advil."

"Oh, oh!" Maya waved her hands in the air. "You should do it at the parade! Return to the scene of the crime! Reclaim the parade!"

Eve slid off the bed. "I think after the parade is better." Sawyer would be getting ready for the parade now. In the meantime she needed a hangover breakfast. So she was just going to take herself over to Sadie's and eat her weight in pancakes.

The river was about to take a big twist, and she couldn't see around the bend. But she was, amazingly, okay with that.

The first weird thing about the parade was that Sawyer wasn't driving the squad car, Olivia was.

But what did Eve know about the modern-day Mermaid Parade? Just because Sawyer had driven the mermaid-ified cop car last year didn't mean he did it every year.

The second weird thing about the parade was that Maya had disappeared. She had come to Sadie's with Eve, but once there, she'd gotten a text that had sent her running. "Mer-queen duties call," she'd said. "Good luck with your prince."

And so Eve found herself standing outside the Mermaid Inn watching another Mermaid Parade. She was surprised by how many people marching or perched on floats she knew. She waved at Carol Dyson from the beauty salon as she gave her daughter CJ a blowout on the back of the Curl Up and Dye float. And at Eiko, who was weaving in and out of the floats taking pictures for the newspaper.

And there was Jordan from the auto shop, driving the

members of the Bluewater Quilting Guild, who were smiling and waving from the back of a pickup truck that was covered in a quilted truck cozy complete with openings for windows, mirrors, and exhaust pipe.

By the time the high school marching band appeared, Eve was grinning from ear to ear. What they lacked in skill, they made up for in enthusiasm. This year, unlike last, the trident-throwing majorettes made her laugh and clap.

And then it was over—or almost over. She craned her neck to get a look at the garish monstrosity that was the final float of the parade. It was covered in streamers and bric-a-brac and papier-mâché sea creatures. It was like one of Lucille's knickknack shelves come to life—on a gigantic scale. Poor Maya.

Except Maya wasn't there. Neither were the two giant clamshell thrones on which the mer-king and mer-queen traditionally perched.

There was a mer-king, though, a bare-chested mer-king with a crown and a trident and a tail.

And that mer-king was Sawyer.

And he was sitting in a canoe painted with a pink stripe.

"And Ariel and the prince lived happily ever after."

Eve whirled. Maya. "What are—"

Maya snapped her fingers and pointed to the float. "Don't look at me. I'm just here fulfilling my cartoon-seagull-sidekick duties—I've decided on the seagull, by the way. *Crab* just has bad connotations."

When Eve returned her attention to the float, it had stopped moving. She felt her jaw drop as Sawyer got up out of the canoe. Or tried to. His tail made it difficult. While the entire town watched, he wrestled with the thing, eventually reaching behind him and undoing a zipper and stepping out of it entirely. He was barefoot and bare-legged under there. So when he climbed down and made his way over to her, he was only wearing shorts. And a crown. And carrying a trident.

Maya whistled as he approached.

Eve turned again, and Maya did her impatient snapping-and-pointing thing again, directing Eve's attention back to Sawyer.

He was aiming blue laser beams at Eve. Then he started talking. "You weren't the only one who paid attention to Lucille's fairy tales. That 'Little Mermaid' story—the original—is *dark*. She gives up her voice and her legs for the prince. And guess what? He's not worth it."

Speaking was impossible. Eve opened her mouth, but nothing came out.

But no. Screw that. She had a voice. So she tried again. "Maybe he *is* worth it." It came out as a whisper. But he heard her.

"I didn't want you to give anything up for me. Stopping you from doing that seemed like the most important thing."

It was hard to know what to say to that. Because he was right. She would have given up anything. She would have been waiting tables with Sadie as her boss, probably, and who knew if she and Sawyer would ever have learned to talk to each other?

He took a deep breath. "Here's the thing, Evie. I love you. I've always loved you. It's only ever been you for me. I've made mistakes. I'll own that. Sending you away wasn't one of them. Maybe my method was problematic. I've apologized to Jeannie, by the way, but she's unbothered by the whole thing. But I don't regret that you went on to school, to travel, and to a career."

"But—"

He held up a hand—a hand holding a trident, which made her smile. "But you did that, and now you're back. And it feels like a second chance. I should have seen it as that a year ago. But...I don't know. It felt like what I had done was irreversible. You doing everything you were supposed to do and then *coming back* wasn't in my play-book. And then we..." He looked around, for the first time seeming to register that they had an audience. "And then I should have seen it as a second chance several months ago when...things changed."

When they started sleeping together, he meant. She chuckled.

"But you had the big job in Toronto. You were leaving again. It felt like if I didn't put boundaries around what was happening, history was going to repeat itself. I couldn't be with you—*really* be with you—and lose you again."

She wanted to interrupt him, to tell him that he hadn't been the only one struggling with the boundaries of their relationship. He hadn't been the only one afraid of getting hurt again. But he wasn't done with whatever he was trying to say.

"But then I realized that's all bullshit. That's just fear. Clara's gone. She's grown up. So I can do *whatever the fuck* I want to do."

Her stomach dropped. The lightness she had been feeling was gone.

"And what I want to do is be with you. So let's go to Toronto. I know some people who have connections on the Toronto Police Service. Or I'll get a security guard gig. Or I'll harass Clara part-time and become a Little Free Library installer the rest of the time."

"Oh my God. This is totally *Splash*!" Maya gave Eve a little push toward Sawyer, who was still standing a few feet away.

"This is what?" Sawyer's brow furrowed as he turned to Maya.

Maya pushed Eve again—hard. Right. Now it *was* her turn. "I don't want to go back to Toronto." Her voice was shaky and quiet—almost a whisper—but that was okay, because she was talking only to him. "I mean, I love Toronto. I'll miss it. But I already told Jessica to take the Mermaid off the market."

Sawyer inhaled a sharp breath.

"I'm staying. I was so focused on what I thought was my dream job, but I didn't realize that what I have here is my dream *everything*. I got my dream back." Her voice hitched, and she had to swipe away a few rogue tears, but she didn't care. "I got my love back."

"Evie." That was all, just her name. He seemed to have lost his voice. But that was okay. She had one now.

She cleared her throat. "So, yeah, I guess I'm an innkeeper now." She turned to Maya, who was beaming.

"You're also the mer-queen!" Maya held up a teal-sequined monstrosity. "You can use my tail. I cut a hole in the bottom last year, because I refuse to be jailed. So you can walk in it. Kind of."

Eve accepted the tail but turned to Sawyer, because there was more to say. "I'm sorry I didn't have the guts to tell you earlier how I felt. But I love you."

He bent down and picked up the crown that had fallen off his head. "Do you love me enough to put on that ridiculous tail and be my mer-queen?"

She pulled on Maya's tail. "I do. I can swim now and everything." She pointed to the float. "Is that my canoe?"

"It is. I realize that you don't need it now that you can swim, but..."

"It's good to finish things. To read all the way to the end of the story."

"Yes." He took her hand. "Exactly."

Sawyer and Evie walked back to the float. The sun had come out, and he watched it shine down, as it had so many times before, on his Evie, the queen of the mermaids.

As they approached the base of the float, he boosted her up, and the marching band broke into "Kiss the Girl."

So he followed the girl up onto the float, put his own tail on, righted his crown, and did exactly that.

Epilogue

～

A month later

They waited for Maya to arrive before starting the official tour. When she did, everyone broke into applause. Sawyer ushered her into the kitchen of the Mermaid and noted with amusement that she still had "blood" on her hands—she had played the title role in the fall play herself.

"Yeah, yeah, thanks." She found Jake in the small crowd. "It would have been much better with you as Richard, but whatever."

Evie made quick introductions. "Maya, this is my mom and dad." Her parents had come for the opening of the Mermaid and had already met everyone else. Evie was using the Anti-Festival as a dry run before the grand opening next week. Last night had been the town sleepover, and tonight her parents would stay as the inn's first official guests.

They were staying on the first floor, so maybe he and

Evie could retreat to her old room two floors up, which was still pink.

But no. No pink room action tonight. Clara was home. He had temporarily forgotten, even though she was right there. Look at him, getting all accustomed to his empty nest.

As Evie led the group—her parents, Pearl, Maya, Jake, Law, and Clara—out of the kitchen, he tried to see the inn through fresh eyes.

It was much less overtly mermaidy than it used to be, but there were little touches here and there, sometimes when you least expected it. The tile on the floor of the entryway, for example, was tiny blue and green scales. The place reminded him of Lucille. But also of Evie: there were plants everywhere, and she had turned one of the second-floor rooms into a library where she was going to run book clubs and story times for the town.

The tour ended on the third floor. "That's it," Evie said. "The last room, around that corner, isn't done yet. Shall we go downstairs?"

Evie was bringing back Lucille's cocktail hour tradition and had talked Law into making some of his fancy grilled-cheese sandwiches for the first one—and she had commissioned some mermaid pies from Pearl.

"Let me get the food going," Law said, "and we can meet in the dining room in fifteen minutes. Pearl, you want to come get the pie ready?"

"I'll show you to your room," Evie said to her parents.

"Jake and I can do it." Maya swooped in. "I'm going to run home and change out of my costume before we eat." She turned to Jake. "And I need you to help me move Richard's throne off the stage outside. It's going to rain, and that thing is an actual antique." She took Eve's mom's arm without waiting for an answer from Jake. "I gotta tell you, I'm not sure how I survived in this town before your daughter moved here."

"This place looks really great, Eve," Clara said.

Clara. She had arrived midmorning. Jake had picked her up at the bus station because Sawyer had been on duty, so he hadn't really gotten a chance to see her. He hugged her. Hard.

"Ow, Sawyer!"

"Sorry, sorry." He was just so happy she was here. "How is everything going? How's chemistry?" Chemistry was her hard class.

"It's good. Still almost impossibly hard, but good."

"How's Lynn?"

"Better at chemistry than I am, which is handy."

"Anything else I should know about? Any*one* else I should know about?"

"Sawyer." She swatted him. "No."

"You mean the ladies aren't all lined up for a chance to study with you?"

"*Sawyer.*" She started toward the stairs.

"Okay, okay, but hang on. I have something to talk to you about."

"I *told* you I'll let you know when I go on a real date, okay?"

"Not that."

Clara turned, her brow furrowed. She could sense that he was having trouble with this. Which was dumb. It wasn't that big a deal.

"I'll leave you two alone," Eve said.

"No. Stay." He softened his tone. He needed her. "Please." Here went nothing. "With your birthday coming up, I decided to speak to Charles." Both women's eyebrows shot up in tandem. "Last year he wanted to give you a birthday present, and I didn't let him." He waited for a reaction—indignation, maybe, or more shock, but none came. "So now that we're all, like, talking about our feelings and stuff"—he gestured to encompass both of them—"I thought I should probably stop being the gatekeeper. I'm not going to apologize for doing what I felt I had to do to keep you safe, and I'm never going to have a relationship with him, but that doesn't mean you can't. I spoke to his AA sponsor, and he's been sober for two years now. So I asked him if he wanted to pass that present on this year, and he said yes. I told him I'd see what you thought."

"I…" Clara's eyes were darting around like she wasn't sure what she wanted.

"Maybe a good way to start would be to let Sawyer give him your email address," Evie said. "That way you could control when and how you digest anything he has to say."

"Yes," Clara said softly. "I think that's a good idea."

He cleared his throat. "All right, then."

Clara threw herself into his arms. Surprised, he hugged her back.

"I love you so much," she whispered.

More throat clearing was required. "I love you, too, Clare Bear."

After a moment she sniffed and pulled away. "I'm going to run to the bathroom and pull myself together." She gave him a little wave as she descended the stairs, and he felt like a huge weight had been lifted from his shoulders.

"Sawyer." Evie started to speak. "That was—"

He stopped her mouth with a kiss.

A long one. He needed it. Evie was his center. *She* was the reason he'd been able to do all this—get over his junk with his father, send Clara to school and not die.

Also, he really loved kissing her. He wondered if he

would ever get over this. If he would stop being delighted by the way her body tensed slightly when their lips first touched. The way she always followed that by opening her mouth, doing one of her signature breathy moans, and relaxing in his arms.

He pulled back just as things were getting good. "I'm sorry. I interrupted you. You were saying something?"

She pointed down the hall toward the pink room.

"I'm sorry, what?"

"Let's go work on your number."

He laughed and followed her.

"I really have to redo this room," she said as they entered. She'd cleaned it up a bit, but it was still, elementally, the same. Still a pink shrine to the things she had loved as a girl.

"No you don't." He'd been arguing for keeping it. He liked it. It was a memory of happy times. And of sad times. Of all the times, and all the stories, that had gotten them here.

"But it's so *pink*. Who's going to want to be in here?"

"Us."

Oh, crap. He hadn't meant to say that. Not yet. Well, okay, he could backtrack. He could spin it to mean "us" as in right now. "Us" as in "Let's go in there and work on our number."

He opened his mouth to do that, but what came out was, "It can be an owner's suite. For us. Not that I'm the owner. You're the owner. I'm just the owner's boyfriend."

She blinked rapidly.

It was too soon to bring this up. It had only been a month since the parade.

But also, it had been eleven years and one month since the parade. And today was a day for breakthroughs, apparently.

He took her hand. "I don't want to pressure you. So tell me to back off, and I will. But I want to wake up with you every day, or crawl into bed with you after a night shift." He sighed. He was making a mess of this. "Evie, you came back. I never thought that would happen, but at the same time I feel like I've been waiting so long for *exactly that* to happen. I just...I think we should move in together. I don't want to wait anymore."

She smiled. "I don't want to wait anymore, either."

His breath caught. Before he could say anything, she added, "But what about your house?"

"I hear Jeannie Wilkerson is a really good Realtor."

She rolled her eyes at him, but it was a loving roll. "You're not emotionally attached to the place?"

"I'm emotionally attached to *this* place."

"Even if it's going to be like living inside a piece of bubble gum?"

"Hey, don't knock this room." He patted the pink wall. "I lost my virginity in this room."

"What about the canoe?"

He loved how into the canoe she was. They went out on it almost every day. "We can keep it at Jake's."

"Okay, then," she said through a noise that seemed like it was half laugh, half sob.

"Okay, then," he echoed. He almost marveled over how easy that had been, but he stopped himself. They were due for some easy.

"What time is it?" she asked.

He glanced at his watch. "Six twenty-five."

"So that's like five minutes until Law is ready for us." She raised her eyebrows, issuing a silent challenge.

He raised his eyebrows back, pretending he didn't know what she was getting at.

"I was just thinking about last time I had one of Law's grilled-cheese sandwiches. You remember?"

"Oh, I remember."

"You told me then you could be fast." She pressed her lips together like she was trying not to laugh. "But five minutes? That's probably asking too much, even for you."

He pointed to the bed. The time for talking was done.

It was not asking too much for Sawyer, it turned out.

As they entered the dining room, Eve felt like everyone knew what had just gone down in the pink room. And to be fair, Maya, Jake, and Law probably did.

Hopefully, though, her parents did not. Her mom waved her over. "Honey, we saved you a spot." It was between her mom and dad, and she went and sat, her heart full.

"This place is lovely," her mom said.

"Turns out Lucille knew what she was talking about." Eve turned around and let her eyes find one of Lucille's sad mermaid posters. She'd kept some of the sad mermaid stuff and some of the happy mermaid stuff. Enough to keep some continuity with the past but not enough to weigh the place down. With the addition of her plants and her books, it felt like the perfect mix. She was a bit worried about money—as in, she had none. But she'd sat down with her parents, Sawyer, and a spreadsheet, and they'd figured that between a small mortgage on the inn and the higher rates she'd be able to charge for the new rooms, she'd be okay. And Maya, ever entrepreneurial, had some ideas for more theatrical events in the inn that would bring in income they'd split.

And hey, maybe she'd start charging her boyfriend rent now that he was going to be living here. She grinned and raised her glass. "To Lucille."

"To Lucille," everyone echoed.

After dinner they walked to the lake with a basket of flowers. It was only a half moon, but as Eve had learned this past year, Maya wasn't one to let a detail like that stop her.

Maya and Eve led the way onto the pier, arm in arm. "Whatcha gonna wish for?" Maya asked.

Eve looked over her shoulder. Her parents and Pearl were chatting with Clara.

Law and Jake were talking, too. Well, Law was talking. Jake was his usual silent self.

But Sawyer, who had been bringing up the rear, was looking at her. Just like he had that night more than a year ago, the first time she and Maya had come out here to make wishes.

She held a flower out over the lake and considered.

Wishes Eve Abbott Considered While Sawyer Collins Stared at Her Back

1.

Nothing. She had nothing.

And for once, she was completely fine with that. You didn't need wishes, or lists, when you had a voice you knew how to use and a town full of crazy people to be your backup singers.

So she stepped back to let her friends do some wishing. She had another agenda, anyway.

Everyone threw their flowers in. Her parents exclaimed over the charm of the tradition. Clara went on about how she had missed the Lake Huron sunsets. Pearl and Law were talking about *Assassin's Creed*.

Eve moved over to the far side of the pier, wanting to do

this alone for some reason she couldn't articulate. But she didn't think Lucille would mind. She pulled the urn from the shoulder bag she'd been carrying, mouthed, "Thank you," and upended it into the lake.

Sawyer came up and put his arm around her shoulder. If he'd seen what she'd done, he didn't let on. "I have to take Clara to a party some of her friends from the grocery store are having."

She cleared her throat. "Yeah, and I should spend some time with my parents."

"And then I should stay at the house with Clara tonight."

"Of course."

They sighed in unison.

"But she goes back tomorrow," he said, reading her mind.

"They all do." In fact, her parents were driving Clara back to the city. "The time will go fast," she said, to herself as much as to him.

"No, it won't." He kissed her and stepped away.

"Sext me later?" she called after him.

He winked. "I'll do my best."

**DON'T MISS THE NEXT BOOK IN THE
MATCHMAKER BAY SERIES!**

Jake Ramsey has a broken heart—one he never
expects to heal. When a new doctor arrives in
town, he offers to help get her practice up and
running, and it's the first time in years he feels
comfortable with someone. Nora Walsh is definitely not looking for a relationship... despite the
efforts of the town matchmakers. But when Jake
starts to see how much the community needs her,
he joins his neighbors in trying to convince her to
stay permanently. Except he's having a hard time
convincing himself it's the *town* that needs
her... not him.

**READ MORE IN PARADISE COVE,
AVAILABLE IN SUMMER 2020!**

About the Author

Jenny Holiday is a *USA Today*–bestselling and RITA®-nominated author whose works have been featured in the *New York Times*, *Entertainment Weekly*, the *Washington Post*, and on National Public Radio. She grew up in Minnesota, where her mom was a children's librarian, and started writing at age nine after her fourth-grade teacher gave her a notebook to fill with stories. When she's not working on her next book, she likes to hang out with her family, watch other people sing karaoke, and throw theme parties. A member of the House of Slytherin, Jenny lives in London, Ontario, Canada.

Learn more at:

Jennyholiday.com
Twitter @jennyholi
Instagram @holymolyjennyholi
Facebook.com/jennyholidaybooks

FOR A BONUS STORY FROM ANOTHER AUTHOR
YOU MAY LOVE, PLEASE TURN THE PAGE TO
READ *MEANT TO BE* BY ALISON BLISS

Sidney Larson always thought dark-haired, blue-eyed Brett Carmichael was sinfully sexy, to say nothing of the muscular mechanic's talent with his hands. But Sidney *so* didn't have time for Brett's overbearing tendencies when they were together, so she broke things off. Now a chance encounter brings Brett back into her life, and Sidney can't help but notice intriguing changes in her ex. So what's stopping her from revisiting their scorching-hot chemistry?

Since Sidney dumped him, Brett's made major life adjustments, thanks to therapy and a long, hard look at himself. Sure, he's still intense, but he knows how to focus his energy on his career, not on trying to control a fantastic woman like Sidney. Brett finds the sweet, generous brunette more seductive than ever, but now that he's finally worthy of her, will she be willing to give him a second chance?

Chapter One

Brett Carmichael blew out a huge sigh of relief.

Not only had he just clocked out after another busy day at the garage where he worked, but after almost a year of long days and miserable nights, things were finally starting to look up.

Thank God.

For months, he'd been scouring the entire Granite, Texas, area looking for an old building that he could buy and turn into an automotive repair shop. After all, he'd been dreaming of opening his own garage since he was fifteen years old. Back then, he used to spend hours tearing old car engines apart and then putting them back together again just for the hell of it. Now, at age thirty, he actually got paid to do it.

Brett was a damn good mechanic. Always had been. Which was probably why almost everyone in town brought their vehicles to him when they needed work done. He had a great customer base, but oftentimes he was so busy that he had no choice but to pass some of the repair jobs off to another mechanic in the shop. He hated doing that though because he couldn't guarantee the other guy's work like he could his own.

Sadly, not all mechanics took pride in their work like Brett did. He didn't randomly guess at what was wrong with a vehicle without doing some kind of research to make sure he was on the right track, and he didn't take shortcuts just because doing so would be easier or faster. He believed in finding the actual problem and repairing it correctly the first time rather than doing a half-assed job.

That was one of the reasons he wanted to open his own business. The moment he found a suitable location, he planned to open a garage and hire a couple of great mechanics who held the same beliefs as he did and who would do things the proper way. But Granite was a small town, and finding a place for sale that met his needs hadn't been easy.

Brett didn't need anything big and fancy. He was used to working in cramped quarters and spent most of his time crawling around under a hood or sliding beneath a car on the cracked wooden creeper that his boss was too cheap to replace. But there were a few requirements on which Brett—unlike his boss—refused to budge.

The structure of the building needed to be large enough to house a separate waiting area for the customers in order to keep them safe and out of the mechanics' way. Also, the parking lot needed to have enough lighting to be secure and have enough space to store vehicles overnight, if necessary. The last thing he wanted to worry about was a customer getting hurt or their vehicle getting stolen or broken into. So as far as Brett was concerned, these things were nonnegotiable.

Unfortunately, that only made it harder to find a place.

At least until his best friend had called this morning. Logan had apparently overheard a conversation at his bar the night before about a used car lot a couple of miles outside the city limits that was now up for sale. The old man who owned it had passed away a few months ago, and it had closed down for good. Although the owner's only son had inherited the business, the man didn't live in the area. The middle-aged son had instead flown in from Arizona only long enough to sell off the remaining used car stock at auction and officially put his father's property up for sale. Both of which he had already done.

That meant Brett had to move fast.

So after hanging up with Logan, Brett had immediately called the phone number his friend had given him and spoken with the son about the property. The lot sat on five acres and was located on the main road between Granite and a neighboring community. Not a bad location, if you asked Brett. It would be close enough to Granite for Brett to serve his regular customers, yet near enough to another town to gain some new clients.

The building was divided into two sections. The front office would come fully furnished and had a large, air-conditioned waiting area for customers, while the shop had three huge bays with galvanized steel doors and a separate room for storing car parts. Not only that, but according to the son, the parking area was well lit and had several surveillance cameras already installed.

All of that sounded perfect and was exactly what Brett had been looking for. But the thing that caught his attention the most was when the son told him that he was willing to throw in the hydraulic vehicle lift, electronic diagnostic equipment, a welding machine, and several upright toolboxes filled with hand tools...for free.

Brett hadn't expected that. Who in their right mind would give away thousands of dollars in equipment like that? Not that he was complaining or anything. That equipment would come in handy, and although Brett already had his own set of hand tools—most mechanics worth their salt did—it never hurt to have extras on hand. He never knew when he might break off a wrench and need another in a pinch.

But something bothered him about all of this. While the place seemed like a perfect prospect and was definitely in his price range, the deal sounded almost too good to be true. Maybe the owner's son was just in a hurry to relieve himself of his father's business and get back to his own life. Or maybe he just really needed the money from the sale of the property. But Brett couldn't let the idea of fulfilling his long-held dream persuade him to make rash decisions that he'd regret down the road. Lord knows he'd already done enough of that to last him a lifetime.

In order to be sure of what he was getting himself into, Brett needed to see the place in person and inspect the building for any major issues. Unfortunately, that in itself

was a problem. The son had already booked his return
flight back to Arizona in the morning, and the only time
he could show the property was tonight. Otherwise, Brett
would have to wait to see it until the man came back in a
few weeks to clear out his father's home.

But he worried that if he didn't jump on this opportunity, there was a good chance someone else would. So
he'd agreed to meet the guy at the used car lot around
seven o'clock.

That should've given him enough time to run home,
grab a bite to eat and a quick shower, and then make
it to the dealership on time. But as usual, things hadn't
panned out according to his plan. Just as he started
to close up shop, an elderly woman had pulled in and
asked him to check her alternator belt. It had been
squealing, and she was leaving in the morning on a
gambling trip with her bingo friends.

Closed or not, Brett hadn't been able to refuse her.
But by the time he'd replaced her belt and sent her on
her way, he was now running late himself. He would've
called the guy to let him know, but in his rush to get
there, Brett had accidentally left his cell phone in his
toolbox back at the garage. Along with the guy's phone
number. Just great.

Brett peered up from the road long enough to check
the position of the sun, which had already descended
behind the trees. It was getting dark, and he hadn't had
time to get a shower, much less eat anything. But it
looked like, as long as he hurried, he would make it to
his appointment only a few minutes late. Well, if the son
hadn't given up on him and left already.

As Brett's gaze lowered back to the road, he noticed a dark smudge on the side of his hand attached to the steering wheel. He had washed up before leaving the shop, but he always seemed to miss a spot. Sighing, he rubbed the offending mark against the thigh of his jeans to remove it. That was just something that came with the territory of working in a dirty environment.

And with as many hours as he'd put in lately? God, he'd never be able to get all the oil stains off his hands and black grease out from under his nails. Unless, of course, he scrubbed them until they were raw... which always hurt like hell.

Didn't matter though. It would all be worth it when he finally had a garage of his own. That was the only thing he'd ever wanted. Well, maybe not the *only* thing. There had been something—*or rather someone*—else. Unfortunately, that relationship hadn't panned out as he'd hoped, and the two of them had parted ways last year.

No, idiot. She dumped you. There was nothing mutual about it.

Brett cringed at the familiar stab of regret slicing into his chest. The same one he'd felt many times before. But the last thing he needed right now was to think about the woman he lost and wonder what could've been. So he let out an exasperated breath and shoved the guilt and pain into a mental storage locker and kicked it to the back of the closet in his brain to be dealt with later. He didn't have time for that shit right now.

After spending almost an entire year being miserable, he was finally close to getting the only other thing that had ever truly mattered to him. He needed to keep his focus on the here and now. He'd worked hard for months to make his dreams come true, and he was proud of how far he'd come. He wasn't going to allow anything to stand in the way of that. Especially when it came to his past.

Brett motored down the window, allowing the cool evening breeze to whip through the interior of his over-sized truck. Though it was the beginning of January, winters in South Texas were considerably different than in northern regions. Unless a frontal system blew in, it wasn't actually all that cold. Especially during the day. If anything, this kind of weather was what most people referred to as "nice fall weather." But once the sun fell below the horizon, the temperature would usually drop considerably.

Glancing down at his cargo jeans and stained white T-shirt, Brett shrugged. He didn't have a jacket with him, but he wasn't planning on standing outside in the night air very long anyway. He'd be fine.

No sooner had the thought run through his mind than he noticed a little silver Pontiac Solstice up ahead parked on the shoulder of the road. The emergency flashers blinked off and on like crazy, and a figure was bent over near the back tire. It didn't take a genius to know that they probably had a flat, but Brett shook his head. While the stranded motorist had managed to park their car completely off the road, it was dangerous to change a tire on the side of the vehicle nearest traffic. Especially at night when other motorists' visibility was limited.

But Brett also knew from experience that it sometimes couldn't be helped.

As a courtesy, he immediately slowed down and veered over the center line to go around the little sports car at a safe distance. Normally, he would've pulled over and offered his assistance to someone stuck on the side of the road. After all, he was a mechanic and almost always kept tools in his truck. But tonight he couldn't really spare the time. So instead, he mumbled to himself, "Sorry, buddy. Better luck next time."

But as he drove slowly past, the person bending over near the back tire straightened into an upright position, and he immediately realized his mistake. Although Brett had assumed the person was a man from a distance, the long dark locks and pristine white pant suit clinging to lush curves confirmed that she was very much indeed a woman.

Damn it.

Maybe it had something to do with growing up with a younger sister or being raised by a single mom, but Brett had always had a soft spot for women. Especially ones who seemed to be in trouble.

Without hesitation, he pulled onto the shoulder of the road in front of the silver sports car and turned off his engine. Then he glanced at his watch and gritted his teeth. God, he didn't have time for this right now. But there was no way in hell he could drive past a stranded woman and not stop to ask if she needed some assistance. His dad had taught him better than that.

But that didn't mean he had to be happy about it.

Disgruntled by the inconvenience, Brett shoved open his door and climbed out before heading directly for the woman, who had apparently gone back to work on her tire using a small flashlight that she had lying on the ground next to her. Hell, as far as he could tell, she hadn't so much as even looked up when he stopped. Hopefully that meant she had things under control and was almost finished putting on a spare. If so, he might be able to still make it to his appointment.

Not wasting any time, Brett walked right up behind her. "Do you need some help with your tire, miss?"

Her head snapped up, and her posture stiffened as if a metal rod had been shoved into her spine, but she didn't turn around or respond.

Worried that he'd somehow frightened her, he cringed and took a nonthreatening step back. She hadn't looked back at him yet, but if she decided to, he didn't want to seem like he was towering over her. He was a pretty built guy, and it wouldn't be the first time that his appearance alone had intimidated someone.

He purposely softened his tone to keep his deep voice from sounding too harsh. "I was just driving past and saw you stranded here. I'm a mechanic so I thought I might be of some assistance."

The woman rose slowly to her feet and cocked her head back slightly as she released a sound of annoyance from the back of her throat. Though it was barely audible, the quiet noise reverberated through him as if her vocal cords were two cymbals crashing together.

His body stilled. *No. It couldn't be.*

The moment she turned around to face him, his

mouth fell open. Probably due to the whirlwind of emotions that were bitch-slapping him in the face.

She shook her head. "It doesn't take a genius—or a mechanic—to change a flat tire, Brett."

He blinked rapidly, not believing his eyes. "Sidney?"

She huffed out an irritated breath. "Oh, come on. I don't look *that* different."

No, she didn't. Actually she was just as gorgeous as ever. But the last person he expected to come face-to-face with was his ex-girlfriend of all people. Not only that, but it had been almost a year since he'd last laid eyes on her, and he hadn't known she'd grown out her brunette hair.

He'd never seen Sidney with long hair before, but the short, choppy do she used to sport while they were dating was now trailing down her back with lighter-colored pieces framing her heart-shaped face. It looked great. The flattering style really brought out the rich color in her warm brown eyes.

But that crisp white pant suit she was wearing? *Holy hell.*

Sidney had always dressed in a classic, conservative style that included tailored clothing, high-quality fabrics, and lots of neutral colors. In fact, he hadn't even thought it possible for her to look any more sophisticated and elegant than she had back when they were dating. Yet the woman never failed to surprise him.

Brett didn't know exactly what it was about her modest attire that always sent his tongue wagging. Most guys he knew went for women in low-cut tops and high-rise skirts. Those were nice and all. But give him Sidney in a tailored blouse and a pair of pressed pants, and he'd be hard for days.

It was like she had a pureness about her that called to him, an innocence that he'd lost years ago and would never get back. Every time he was around her, all he wanted to do was roll her onto the nearest bed and muss that polished hair as he soiled her cleanliness with all the dirty things he wished to do to her body. And this time was no exception.

Brett glanced down at his oil-stained hands though. Great. She was going to think he hadn't washed them. Even though he had. Twice. Shoving his hands into the pockets of his jeans, he realized he still hadn't responded to her yet. "You look as great as always, Sid." *Damn. Took you long enough, dumbass.*

"Um, thanks. You too," she said, turning away from him. "But you can go. I have everything under control."

Her dismissal hit him like a punch to the gut, and he winced. Okay, so maybe he deserved it after what he'd done to her last year. But it was almost completely dark outside, and he would be damned if he was just going to leave her stranded in the middle of nowhere all alone. Even if she did have a flashlight.

Brett shook his head. "Sorry to disappoint you, but I'm not going anywhere."

* * *

Damn it. The last person Sidney Larson wanted to be rescued by was her ex.

After the stunt Brett had pulled last year, she'd broken up with him and told him she never wanted to see him again. And she'd meant it at the time. But the past year had been a real struggle for her. Part of her wanted to prove to him—and maybe a little to herself—that she didn't need him in her life. While the other part of her had contemplated running back into his arms to make up for lost time. So she'd purposely avoided running into him... well, up until now.

She had a feeling that seeing him again would bring back all of those feelings and memories that she'd tried so hard to suppress. She was right. The urge to fling herself back into his arms—and his life—was as strong as ever. But after the crap he'd pulled last year, she just couldn't do it.

No matter how good he looks.

Actually, he looked better than good. Brett was sexier than ever. He had always maintained a great physique, but after one glance at those arms of his, she had no doubt he'd been putting in some extra hours lifting weights at the gym. Not only that, but the man had always pulled off a grungy, bad boy look without even trying. And it completely suited him. Because he was the type of guy that fathers had been warning their daughters about for years.

But just because Brett was rippling with more muscle than ever didn't mean she needed him to do her dirty work for her. She could change her own tire, thank you very much. A fact he should know because he was the one who'd taught her how to do it. "You always were a sucker for a damsel in distress," she said, rolling her eyes. "But I don't need your help, Brett. I know what the hell I'm doing."

He grinned but planted his feet firmly in place and crossed his bulky arms over his broad chest. "That's fine. Then I'll just stay here and keep you company until the spare is on."

God, no. The last thing she wanted was him standing right behind her while she was bent over with sweat dripping from her temples as she panted heavily. That reminded her way too much of that time when he'd taken her over the back of the couch and had...Jesus. Never mind. This was exactly what she was afraid of.

She huffed out a breath. "Well, maybe I don't want your company. Have you thought of that?"

He nodded. "I have." Then he shrugged one strong shoulder. "But that's just too damn bad. Because until that spare tire is on your car and you're pulling away from me, I'm not going anywhere."

Damn it. She had a feeling he would say that. "God, Brett. I'm not afraid of the dark."

"I didn't say you were," he replied, a smidgeon of irritation leaching into his voice. "But I'm not leaving you out here by yourself, Sid. So either you put the tire on or move your ass aside and I'll do it for you."

His demanding tone sent shivers over her skin, and her mouth went dry. It was strange that, after almost a year later, he still had that effect on her. "Fine. But I'll do it myself. I don't need your help."

"All right."

Sidney turned back to her flat tire and kneeled down on a space blanket she'd borrowed from her emergency kit. It crinkled as she tried to reposition herself, and rough pieces of gravel poked through the thin silver material into her knees. But it was at least keeping her pants clean, which had been the overall idea anyway.

Sidney adjusted the beam on the flashlight directly onto the tire and then sat back on her heels and looked over the tools in front of her. She knew what she needed to do, but it was a little nerve-wracking having a certified mechanic, who also happened to be her ex-boyfriend, standing over her watching her do it. Who needed that kind of added pressure?

Brett must've noticed her hesitance. "What do you need to do before jacking the car up?" he asked, prompting her.

"I know what to do," she told him. "I have to use that four-arm metal thingy to loosen the bolts."

He chuckled. "It's called a four-way lug wrench."

"Close enough," she said, reaching for it.

Flipping the tool around, she tested each end of the wrench until she found the correct size for her lug nuts. Once the end was snugly slipped over the nut, she tried to turn the wrench. It wouldn't move, so she rose up onto her knees and leaned over the tool to give herself more leverage and then tried to twist it again. No such luck.

Damn it. Why is this not working?

"Need some help?" Brett asked.

Sidney shook her head. "Nope. I can get it. It's just a little tight."

So she used the trick Brett had taught her. She slid one of the heavy jack stands under the opposite end of the wrench to hold it up in place. Then she rose to her feet and kicked off her black heels. Keeping one hand on her car for balance, she placed one foot on the left side arm of the wrench and stepped up onto it.

Well, that wasn't supposed to happen.

Instead of standing on top of the wrench several inches off the ground, her weight was supposed to break the lug nut loose. But for some strange reason, it didn't work.

Weird. Especially given that she had put on a few pounds since Brett had last seen her. It wasn't like she had been all that thin back when they'd dated, but she couldn't help worrying that her most recent weight gain only reflected how miserable she'd been for the past year.

Brett cleared his throat, as if reminding her that he was still standing there and watching her. "You sure you don't want my help?"

"I've got everything under control," she replied, bending her knees and bouncing a little on top of the wrench. Still nothing happened. So she did the only thing she could do. She bounced a little harder, hoping she didn't break something. Including herself.

Sidney did everything in her power to force that stupid lug nut to move because there was no way she was going to admit that she needed Brett's help. Even if, in this instance, she clearly did. So much for proving to him that she was capable of handling any situation thrown at her. That was kind of hard to do while sitting on the side of the road as helpless as a baby bird that had fallen from its nest.

"Okay, stop that," Brett ordered. "You're either going to damage your car or wind up hurting yourself. Get down from there and just let me take a look."

Sidney hopped down and moved out of his way as quickly as she could, but she hadn't been fast enough. As he maneuvered past her, a familiar scent wafted straight to her nose. In the past, he'd always smelled like this when he had gotten off work, and even then, she couldn't get enough of it. Sure, it was probably just a mixture of sweat and grease, but the earthly, masculine notes always took on more of a smoky, charred wood quality and made her mouth water.

But she couldn't think about that right now. She had more important things to worry about. "I don't understand. I did it the way you showed me."

Brett glared at her. "What? I never told you to climb on top of the wrench. You were only supposed to put some weight into it to break the nuts free. Not stand on it."

"Yeah, but that didn't work...and I put *all* of my weight into it." And Lord knows she had plenty of that.

He squatted down and tried to crank on the wrench himself. When it wouldn't turn, he pulled it off and checked the others. When they wouldn't turn either, he looked closer at the lug nuts. "Damn it. I think whoever put these tires on this vehicle tightened the lug nuts too much. Probably used a pneumatic impact wrench."

"Okay, so what do I need to do to fix it?"

Brett stood and dusted his hands off, probably more out of habit than anything. "Nothing."

Confusion swept through her. "What do you mean, nothing?"

"What I'm saying is that *you* won't be doing anything. I'll have to fix it myself."

"Why's that?"

"Because I'm most likely going to have to cut the lug nuts off and replace them. Otherwise, the lug bolts could break off inside the wheel, which is more expensive and complicated to fix. But I'm thinking these might have an aluminum cover so I can just chisel off the aluminum part in order to get to the metal inside. That would make things a little easier for me."

"All right. So what are you waiting for? Let's get to work then."

Brett ran his fingers through his hair. "It's not that simple, Sid. I don't have those kinds of tools with me."

Figures. "So now what?"

"I'm going to drive you home and then come back with the tow truck to pick up your car. That way I can take it back to the shop, where I can work on it."

Her eyes widened. "Are you crazy? I'm not leaving my sports car out here on the side of the road in the middle of nowhere."

"It's not like we have a choice."

"Sure we do. I'll stay with the car while you go get the tow truck."

His head snapped to her, and his blue eyes narrowed. "Sidney, if you think I'm going to leave you out here all alone, then you're the one who's crazy. You should know me better than that by now."

Oh, she did. But he should know her better than that too. In the past, she'd never agreed with him just for the sake of doing so, and she wasn't about to start now.

And just because he wanted her to do something didn't mean she would actually do it either. "Well, I'm not going to risk coming back to my car sitting on blocks because someone stole my tires. They're expensive, you know."

He squinted at her. "If *we* can't get the tire off, then how the hell is someone trying to steal it going to?"

Oh. Right. Good point. "Well, I don't want them to take my entire car."

"I'm certain we don't have to worry about that either. The car has a flat tire. It isn't going anywhere."

"Yeah, maybe. Unless the car thief has a tow truck."

Brett rubbed at his temples and groaned, as if a sudden headache was coming on. "Sidney."

"What?" She shrugged. "I'm just saying."

Brett smiled with the same adorable lopsided grin she'd always loved so much. "Just get into the truck. It'll be fine, I promise."

She sighed. "Okay, fine. But if my car gets stolen before you get back, I'm holding you personally responsible."

"Yep. I figured as much."

They picked up all the tools and the space blanket and locked them inside her car before heading to his red GMC pickup. Sidney couldn't believe she'd been defeated by a stupid lug nut, and she wasn't necessarily talking about the one on her car. Unfortunately, she had no choice but to accept Brett's offer...even if she wasn't all that happy about it.

She hated being this close to him. It was bad enough that his mere proximity set her on edge and had her stomach doing back flips. But his intoxicating scent forced her to hold her breath just to be able to think straight. Even just being back inside his truck stirred up old memories of the last time they'd been together like this. Only, that time, the windows were fogged over, their clothes were on the floorboard, and she was trembling with pleasure as he thrust inside her repeatedly.

Damn lust-filled memories. Although she'd spent the past year trying to forget them—*forget him*—the vivid recollections still haunted her daily. And being this close to him was only making things worse.

Chapter Two

Brett was seriously annoyed.

The fact that Sidney—who apparently was just as stubborn as that damn lug nut—would stand on a tire iron, bouncing up and down, rather than ask him for assistance really pissed him off to no end. But for the woman to admit that she would willingly put herself at risk just to try to stop someone from stealing her car? Insane. He hoped like hell she never got mugged because the person robbing her was going to have a hell of a time convincing the stubborn-ass woman to let go of her purse.

At least he'd managed to convince her to get into the truck without putting up too much of a fight. Because he'd definitely meant what he said. He wouldn't have left her. If that meant spending the night with her in the middle of nowhere, then so be it. He'd have sacrificed himself to the cause.

Yeah, like spending time with the woman I'm still in love with is much of a sacrifice.

Either way, he was glad he was the one who had

found her on the side of the road. Although he'd missed his appointment to look at the used car lot and probably lost his one shot at finding the perfect place for his new garage, it was all worth it as long as Sidney was safe. They might not be together anymore, but that didn't mean he wanted to see her get hurt. Hell, he'd hurt her enough already.

As he pulled out onto the road, he glanced over to see Sidney rubbing her arms. "Are you cold?"

"A little."

He flipped the heater on and pointed his vents in her direction. "Let me know if you get too warm, and I'll turn it back down some."

A slight smile lifted her cheeks. "Okay, thanks."

He nodded to her and drove on in silence. But after a while, when the sounds of her slow, rhythmic breathing started to arouse him, he figured he better make small talk or he was going to end up with an embarrassing problem on his hands. "So how long have you had the sports car?"

"Oh, I got it a little over two months ago. Do you like it?"

"Yeah, it's nice. I bet it runs great too."

"It does." She glanced over at him. "So you hadn't heard I'd gotten a new car? I thought for sure by now that everyone in town had."

He shook his head. "I've been working a lot so I guess I've been out of the loop lately."

Which was mostly true. But he was still surprised that he hadn't heard mention of her new sports car. After all, he was a guy who liked cars, and they did live in the same small town where any kind of gossip was fair game. Then again, they didn't exactly travel in the same circles. Never really had.

Sidney had always been out of his league. It had just apparently taken her longer to realize it than he had. But once it finally got through to her, she'd hauled ass out of their relationship and never looked back. Yeah, avoiding him for the past year had spoken volumes.

Brett couldn't really blame her though. He didn't have the best reputation, and the last thing he wanted to do was soil hers any more than he probably already had. That was why he hadn't bothered asking her out the first time he'd met her.

She'd walked into the shop wearing a pink blouse and a knee-length tan skirt that matched her high heels. Unfortunately, he'd been busy with one of his regular customers, and another mechanic had walked over to help her. Or so he had thought.

The moment he overheard the other mechanic recommending unneeded services to her and quoting marked-up prices, all because she was a female customer who probably didn't know the difference, Brett stepped forward and offered to take over. Lord knows he'd seen plenty of mechanics pull that dick move on unsuspecting women, and surprisingly even on a few men, and it wasn't at all something Brett condoned. In fact, once he finally managed to open his garage, if he found any of his own mechanics pulling that kind of a bullshit scam, he was going to fire the asshole on the spot.

He was just glad that he had been there that day to save Sidney from the jerk who tried to screw her over. And she had seemed pretty grateful about it too. The moment Brett had come over and declared that he was taking over, she seemed a little surprised and not entirely sure of what was going on. But within minutes, she must've figured it out because she'd smiled and mouthed a thank-you to him under her breath.

She'd come in for a tune-up, and that was the only thing she was charged for…and not a penny more. Brett had made sure of it. But after that, things had started to get a little weird.

The following week, she'd returned to the garage and asked for Brett specifically. She requested that he replace her air filter, though hers looked brand new. The next week, she'd come back by to ask him to check the pressure in her tires. Little did she know that he had already done so the week before since he thought one had looked a little low. But he went ahead and checked them again anyway, even though none of them ended up needing air. But by the time the fourth week rolled around and she once again showed up at the garage where he worked, Brett couldn't take it anymore.

He hadn't planned to ask her out. Not only because she was one of his clients, but because they were just too different.

Sidney came from money. He'd learned that she'd grown up in a nice home where she was surrounded by fancy things and never had to want for anything. Although she'd always claimed to be a spoiled brat, Brett had never seen any real proof of it. She was warm and kind and funny, as beautiful on the inside as she was on the outside. And she was way more sophisticated than any girl he'd ever dated.

Brett, however, was only twelve when his father passed away, leaving big shoes to fill, and he tried to do so in as many ways as possible. He watched his little sister while their mom worked, earned extra money to help pay bills, and made sure that the two women in his life would never want for anything. But when he got busted for hustling pool, his reputation went downhill fast. And so did his attitude. He was moody and belligerent and rough around the edges. Not the kind of guy you take home to meet the family.

Honestly, he didn't know what the hell Sidney ever saw in him back then.

But when he finally asked her out, she just smiled and said, "About damn time." And then another strange thing happened. Her car suddenly didn't have any more issues.

Guess mechanics and pool hustlers aren't the only ones who run cons.

The thought had Brett chuckling to himself, which prompted a glance from Sidney. "What's so funny?"

He cleared his throat and immediately straightened his face. The last thing he wanted to do was tell her that he'd been reliving the day they met in his mind. "Ah, nothing. Sorry."

But there was something he wanted to talk about when it came to their past. One specific event that replayed over and over in his mind on a regular basis. Valentine's Day of last year. The day he royally screwed everything up between them.

That day, he'd shown up at the bank with a dozen red roses, hoping to invite her to dinner, where he'd planned to propose to her. But when he walked into her office and found an irate man berating her for not approving his loan, Brett had lost his cool. Sidney had shaken her head at him, clearly wanting him to stay out of it, but he hadn't listened.

Instead, he'd stepped in front of her and jumped down the guy's throat. At the time, he hadn't known that the asshole was the bank manager's brother. Nor had he realized that Sidney would be so upset with him that she'd end their relationship over it. But he'd found out both of these things the moment she pulled him outside into the parking lot.

Brett hesitated to bring up the past incident, knowing it would probably anger her all over again. They needed to talk about it though and at least clear the air between them. But he didn't want her to feel as though he was forcing her into conversation while stuck in a vehicle with him so he waited until his truck rolled to a stop at the curb in front of her home.

She opened her door to get out, and the interior light flicked on above their heads. "Thanks for the ride, Brett."

"Sidney, can you hold on for a second? I'd like to talk to you about something before you go."

Her face morphed with confusion, but she nodded and closed the door, plunging them back into darkness. "Okay."

He rubbed his sweaty palms on his jeans and took a deep breath. "I wanted to talk to you about last year . . . when you broke things off with me."

She shook her head. "Brett, I don't think—"

He raised his hand to stop her. "Just hear me out. Please." She nodded reluctantly but he could tell she wasn't expecting this to go well. "When you broke up with me last year, I was not in the right head space to do this so I'm doing it now."

Her hand held on to the console, and she looked as though she was bracing for impact. "All right. Go ahead, I guess."

He nodded and continued on. "At the time, I thought you had gone a little overboard by breaking up with me over something so trivial."

"I—"

"Just wait. Let me finish before you say anything."

He had no doubt that she expected him to give some pathetic excuse for his ridiculous past behavior, but that wasn't what he was doing. He'd never gotten the chance to apologize for what he had done, and now seemed as good a time as any. Maybe she would never forgive him, but he at least wanted her to know that he regretted the incident and knew how badly he'd messed up.

Swallowing the guilt he felt, he breathed out slowly. "I just wanted to say I'm sorry. I understand why you walked away from me. Maybe at the time I couldn't see it, but now I know for sure you were right in doing so."

Sidney's gaze fell to her hands as she picked at her fingernail. "Well, I'm sorry too."

He shook his head adamantly. "You don't have anything to apologize for."

Her eyes rose, meeting his. "Sure I do. I hurt you, didn't I?"

Brett nodded solemnly. "Of course I was hurt. Valentine's Day was the worst day of my life. But honestly, it changed me for the better and made me realize what a jackass I've truly been."

"What do you mean?"

"You know all about my overprotective tendencies and my need to control everything. Well, after losing you, Valerie and I had a similar incident."

"Oh, you mean the bar fight with Logan?"

Damn. Gossip sure traveled fast. "Yep, that's the one. I came unglued when I found out my best friend was sleeping with my little sister."

She nodded. "I had a feeling that would happen. I once saw them in the movie theater looking pretty cozy and wondered if you knew that something was going on with them."

"I didn't at first. When I found out, I hit the roof, and it caused problems between the three of us. So much so that Valerie threatened to disown me. But after losing you and hearing you say that you never wanted to see me again...well, I couldn't bear the thought of losing another important person in my life. That's what saved my relationship with my sister and my best friend."

Sidney smiled. "I'm glad to hear that everything worked out for you."

He shrugged. "Well, not *everything*. I still lost you in the end. But you walking away made me realize that *I* was the one with the problem. Not you. Not Valerie or Logan. It was all on me. So I started seeing a therapist to help me work through my issues. It's been a big help."

"That's great. I'm happy you're finally talking to someone about these things. You needed that."

Brett rubbed at the back of his neck. "Yeah, I did. Especially after you were out of my life. You were the only person I told a lot of that stuff to. When you left, I didn't have anyone to talk to about my problems anymore."

"I'm really sorry, Brett. I just figured a clean break would do us both good. I figured that once we got past our feelings for each other, we could try going back to being just friends. But I... well, I've been busy and haven't crossed paths with you up until now."

Brett wanted to laugh at that, but he didn't. The only way you wouldn't cross paths with someone in a town as small as Granite was if you were purposely avoiding them. He wasn't stupid enough to believe that he hadn't ran into her for almost a full year by coincidence. No way. He had no doubt she'd made that happen herself.

"I just wanted you to know I've changed. I'm not at all the same guy from before. And I have you to thank for that. If you hadn't broken up with me when you did, I would probably still be that same asshole you dated back then. So thank you for breaking up with me. You did me a huge favor."

* * *

Sidney was so stunned that she didn't know what to say.

Who in their right mind thanks someone for breaking up with them?

While she appreciated the heartfelt apology, she

couldn't help wondering if her weight gain had anything to do with his being so glad that they were no longer together.

Maybe that was just her insecurities bubbling to the surface though, since he never seemed to have a problem with her size before. Then again, he'd clearly been spending a lot more time at the gym, bulking up all those hard-packed muscles, while she'd spent the past year drowning her sorrows in pints of rocky road ice cream.

Sadly enough, it was easier to believe he had a problem with her weight than to believe Brett was a changed man. Old habits die hard, and it wasn't like the incident at the bank was the first time Overprotective Brett had reared his ugly head. According to his sister, Brett had been that way since his father's death. Valerie probably put up with it out of some sense of loyalty—after all, they were family—but Sidney wasn't willing to do the same.

Still, although she hated to admit it, she couldn't pretend that hearing him say he'd changed didn't intrigue her. Sure, he had been too overprotective and had a jealous streak a mile long, but he had always treated her well. Not only that, but she had never stopped loving him and . . . well, last year's Valentine's Day had been the worst day of her life too.

She still remembered it as if it were yesterday. Brett had come barging into her office unannounced and interrupted a heated meeting she was having with the bank manager's brother. Sure, the guy was an ass, but he was a client nonetheless, and it was her job to deal with him. Besides, it wasn't like it was the first time she'd dealt with a difficult man before. She'd dated Brett, for goodness' sake!

The moment she spotted him in the doorway of her office, she knew there would be trouble. That was why she gave him the look—the universal one that signified that there was more to the situation than met the eye. After her subtle warning, Brett should've backed off and let her handle things in a professional manner, one befitting a place of business. But he hadn't.

No, instead he'd caused a huge scene in front of her coworkers at the bank that embarrassed her to no end. Not to mention that she almost lost her job over it. So yeah, she'd broken up with Brett and told him that she never wanted to see him again.

Sidney gave him a tight smile. "I'm glad you're doing well, Brett. It's good to hear."

"Thanks."

She glanced toward her house. "Well, I should probably go inside. Thank you for your help tonight. I really appreciate it."

"No problem. I'll have your car ready in the morning. Would you like me to swing by here and pick you up before I head to the shop?"

"Um, no. I think it's better if I find my own ride. Thanks for the offer though. If you can just call me to let me know when it's ready, that would be great."

"Sure."

She opened her door and climbed out of the truck. "Thanks for the ride home."

"You're welcome," he said, smiling.

Chapter Three

The next morning, Brett called Sidney to let her know her car was ready to be picked up. While he was still disappointed that she'd refused a ride to the shop, he understood that she wanted to keep her distance from him. They weren't together anymore, and she clearly wanted to keep it that way.

Just because he'd thought about her every day for the past year didn't mean she'd done the same. If the new hair and new car didn't state the obvious, then the fact that she'd been avoiding him for so long should've told him what he needed to know. She had moved on.

Serves me right. She deserves better anyway.

Though Sidney had never acted like the spoiled brat she claimed to be, Brett didn't exactly make a ton of money. That was usually what happened when you worked for someone else. But he was tired of killing himself by working twelve-hour shifts, only to collect a measly hourly wage while the owner of the business kicked his feet up on his desk and counted all the dough his employees brought in for him.

Maybe the other mechanics in the shop were okay with that, but Brett was no longer willing to work his ass off to make someone else rich. Screw that. It was just like his therapist told him. If he didn't put value on his own worth, then who the hell was going to? She probably hadn't been referring to his monetary worth, but as far as he was concerned, the same rule still applied.

So Brett picked up the phone and dialed the number Logan had given him once again, in hopes of leaving the guy from last night a message. Chances were good that he would already be on his flight, but Brett hoped that he would return his call once he landed back in Arizona...if he was even still willing to entertain an offer from Brett, of course. After Brett hadn't showed up for their scheduled meeting and wasn't able to call to let him know, he wouldn't be surprised if the guy wasn't interesting in calling him back. After all, no one wanted to do business with a flake.

But Brett had to take the chance of getting turned down. The place sounded too damn perfect to pass up.

The phone rang twice, and then the man answered. Brett hadn't expected that, since this guy should've already been on his flight back to Arizona. But apparently, the airline had somehow overbooked the flight, and this fella happened to be the unlucky bastard who got bumped from it. Though that probably sucked a lot for him, it was great news for Brett, and he planned on taking full advantage of the situation.

The guy wasn't at all happy with Brett for not showing up or calling last night, which was apparent in his attitude. But Brett managed to keep his cool. Once he explained what had happened and how he'd left his phone at the garage, the man said he completely understood that things sometimes happened out of anyone's control. Maybe getting bumped from his flight had given him that perspective. Or maybe he was just a nice guy. Because then he offered to show Brett the lot later in the afternoon since his next flight wasn't leaving until tomorrow.

Brett couldn't believe his luck. Just as he opened his mouth to accept the man's offer, Sidney strolled through the bay door wearing beige slacks, a cream-colored top, and a pearl necklace that dipped inside her shirt between her breasts. Momentarily distracted, all Brett could think was, "God, yes!" But when the man on the other end of the line chuckled, Brett had no doubt he'd said the words aloud.

Feeling like an idiot, he promised not to leave the guy waiting once again and then hurried to get off the phone before heading to the counter, where Sidney stood waiting for him. "Hey," he said, staring into her rich brown eyes to keep his gaze from following the trail of shiny white beads leading inside her shirt. "Your car is out back next to my truck. I didn't want to leave it up here, where someone could accidentally put a ding in it."

She flashed him a bright smile. "Thanks. I always worry about that too. So how long did it take you to fix it?"

"Well, not counting the time it took to tow your car back to the garage, I'd say about four hours. An hour or so per tire. By the way, you have the most stubborn lug nuts I've ever seen on a vehicle."

She cringed. "Oh no! That practically took you all night. Did you get any sleep?"

He shrugged. "Yeah, some. When I finished up with your car earlier this morning, I crawled into the backseat of my truck and slept for a few hours."

"God, I'm so sorry. I didn't realize it was going to be such a huge task to get those things off."

"It happens. Sometimes a big job turns out to be a small one, and little jobs turn out to be a mechanic's worst nightmare. You just never really know until you start working on something."

She grinned. "So you're saying this job was your worst nightmare?"

"Not really. But if you had heard the way I was cussing up a storm this morning while trying to get those damn nuts off, you probably wouldn't believe a word I just said."

Sidney laughed as she pulled out her debit card. "I'm just glad you managed to fix it. How much do I owe you?"

Brett pulled her keys from his pocket and slid them across the counter in front of her. "Nothing. You're good to go."

She shook her head and shoved her debit card toward him. "What? No way. I'm paying you for the work you did."

He put the card back into her hand and closed her fingers around it. "I don't want your money, Sid."

"Then what the hell do you want?"

His fingers tightened around hers. Hell, that was a loaded question if he'd ever heard one. He grinned for a second as several sexy scenarios ran through his head, and then he forced himself to blow out a slow breath and behave himself. "Look, Sid. The way I see it, I owed you one after how I screwed up our relationship. So just let me do something nice for you, and we'll call it even."

"That's not us being even. *I* broke up with *you*, remember? So this would put you one ahead of me."

Brett rolled his eyes. "Humor me, okay?"

But she wasn't having it. Sidney shook her head adamantly and tried to hand him her card once again. "No, I don't feel right about you working for free after hours. And I'm certain your boss wouldn't like it either. After you went out of your way to help me last night, the least I can do is pay you for your time. Besides, you don't owe me any favors. What happened between us is in the past, and that's where it's going to stay. It has nothing to do with this business transaction."

He cringed at her words but covered it by glancing at his watch. It was already eleven o'clock, and he had only a few hours before he had to be at the car lot. The last thing he wanted to do was spend them arguing with her. "Sid, I don't have time to argue with you about this. I have somewhere I have to be in a few hours, and I still need to clean up and grab lunch. Call it a favor or a random act of kindness or whatever you want, but I'm not taking your money. Got it?"

Brett didn't wait for her to respond, since chances were good that she would've just continued to argue with him. So instead, he turned and walked away. He didn't want her to pay him for his help, damn it. He hadn't done any of it for the money. Didn't she get that? He had done it because he loved her with every fiber of his being.

And that wasn't something you could put a price on.

* * *

Sidney watched in disbelief as Brett walked away.

He stopped to talk to another worker briefly before he moved toward the small sink across the room and began soaping up his grimy hands. She had a profile view of him, which meant all he had to do was turn his head slightly in order to see her. But as far as she could tell, he hadn't so much as looked back once, and she had a feeling he was avoiding her on purpose.

As if ignoring me is going to work. He should know better than that.

She stood there watching him scrub the dirt away for so long that her gaze accidentally drifted to his left bicep, which was flexing and tightening against the sleeve of his dark blue T-shirt with every motion. She swallowed the hard knot forming in her throat. Damn, he'd really bulked up.

Sidney was so mesmerized by the movements of his muscles that she didn't even notice when another worker approached the counter. "Can I help you, miss?"

Startled, she jumped and grasped her chest, turning to see the young worker whom Brett had stopped to talk to on his way to the sink. She had met some of the other mechanics in the past, but this one must've been hired sometime in the past year. "Oh goodness, you scared me."

The young guy grinned. "Sorry about that."

Yeah, he looked real sorry with that huge smile on his face. "It's okay. I should've been paying closer attention to my surroundings."

He motioned across the room to the sink where Brett was still standing. "I saw you staring. Were you waiting for Brett to help you with something? Because if so, I hate to tell you this, but he's not on the clock today."

"What do you mean? He's right there."

"Yep, but it's his day off."

Oh great. Now she felt like a real jerk for not paying him. "But what about the car he worked on early this morning?"

The young worker shook his head and waved his hand in the air. "That was just him helping out a buddy. Besides, I'm pretty sure he just wanted to get a look under the hood. It's a sweet-ass ride." She grinned with pride, but he must've thought it was the curse word that gave her that reaction because he followed up with, "Oh, sorry. Pardon my French."

Sidney giggled. "I've heard the word *ass* before. Even used it a few times myself," she said with a wink. "And you're absolutely right. It *is* a sweet-ass ride."

The worker laughed and nodded in agreement. "Are you sure there's nothing I can do for you, miss?"

"No, I'll just…wait around until I can have a word with Brett." He couldn't possibly ignore her—or wash his hands—forever.

"All right. But you better do it soon. He's about to leave. Has some appointment later to look at a used car lot that went up for sale recently."

Her head snapped up. "What in the world would Brett want with a used car lot?"

"He's hoping to buy it and turn it into his new auto repair business."

Her eyes widened. "Brett's opening his own garage? Oh my God. That's wonderful news!" He had told her about that particular dream of his a long time ago, but she hadn't known he was actively trying to fulfill it. Good for him.

The worker nodded in confirmation. "Yeah, he's working on it. But he's still not sure he'll qualify for the loan yet. I think he's hesitating to fill out the forms."

She gazed across the room and spotted Brett drying his hands off. "Really? Well, that's…uh, interesting. I might be able to help him with that."

When Brett finally glanced up, she motioned for him to come back over. But he shook his head. So Sidney did what she had to. She rounded the counter and headed into the garage, straight toward Brett.

One of his brows rose in question. "What do you think you're doing?"

"I need to talk to you."

"Not here, you're not. You can't be back here. Didn't you read the signs?" He pointed to the closest one on the wall nearby. "It says no customers allowed in the work area."

She grinned smugly. "Good thing I'm not a customer then."

He tilted his head in confusion. "Huh? How do you figure?"

"Customers pay for your service, right? But you wouldn't let me pay you. So that means I'm not one of your customers." That was her story, and she was sticking to it.

He gave her a *yeah, right* look and pointed to a different sign. "Well, this one says 'Employees Only,' and the last I knew, you don't work here."

She shrugged. "Apparently, neither do you. At least not today. Why didn't you tell me it was your day off?"

"Because it didn't matter." He glanced around the garage. "Who the hell told you it was my day off anyway?"

She ignored his question. "It does matter when you're working on my car and not getting paid for it."

Brett waved his hand dismissively. "It's not a big deal. Let it go already," he said, walking past her toward a rear exit.

Sidney followed him outside. "Fine. If you won't let me pay you for your time, then let's at least make a trade. You did something for me, now it's my turn to do something for you."

His feet stalled beneath him, and he turned around slowly to face her. His heated eyes resembled the blue flame on a welding torch, and they zeroed in directly on her. "Sidney, if you're even close to insinuating that you'd sleep with me in exchange for fixing your car, you're seriously going to piss me off."

Wait, what? She blinked at him in confusion, not understanding where the hell he'd gotten that cockamamie idea from. "Oh dear Lord, of course not. That's not at all what I was getting at." But she couldn't help giggling. If he thought having sex with him would be doing *him* a favor, he was seriously underestimating his skills in the bedroom.

Her reaction only annoyed him more. "What's so funny?"

"Uh, nothing." She bit her lip to contain the laughter bubbling in her throat. "I just meant that I wanted to help you get that loan you're going to apply for so you can buy that used car lot and open your garage."

His eyes widened. "Jesus. How do you know all of that? Just who the hell have you been talking to? My sister? No, I bet it was that stupid husband of hers. He can't keep a secret to save his own life."

Sidney chuckled. "Actually, I heard it inside while I was talking to one of the workers at the counter. I didn't know it was supposed to be a secret."

"It had to be Kyle."

She shrugged. "I don't know his name. Young guy with a big smile. Super friendly. Piercings in both ears."

"Yep, that's him. He's a good kid and all, but he spreads gossip faster than a teenager."

"Well, I'm glad he told me. I think it's great that you're finally going after your dream of opening your own garage. You've wanted that for so long. I just wish you had told me the good news yourself last night."

He shook his head. "There's nothing to tell. I'm not even sure if I'll get the loan, and I still have to check out the property to see if it's worth the asking price."

Did she dare ask? "Uh, so which bank are you planning to use?"

His eyes met hers. "Not yours, if that's what you're thinking. I didn't want to put you in a weird position since we have a past."

"I appreciate that, but it wouldn't have been a problem. I take my job as a lending officer seriously, and the loan process would've been the same for you as any other client."

He nodded in agreement. "I figured as much. But I think I'll go ahead and stick with the other bank I chose. I wouldn't want to get approved for a loan through you and anyone in town to question your integrity just because we used to be a couple. I think it's better this way."

"That's fine. But at least let me help you out by giving you some tips on how best to get approved for a loan. If you want, I can even look over your finances and credit score to make sure everything is in order and walk you through the documents you'll need to fill out. Being prepared could really help your chances of getting that approval."

"You don't mind?"

"Of course not. You did me a favor, and I'd like to repay it. Do you have mobile banking on your phone so that we can bring up your statements online?"

"Yeah."

"Good. Well, if you have some time right now, maybe we could grab a bite to eat and go over your records." She motioned to his favorite fast-food eatery—a little locally owned hot dog stand across the street from the shop. "I know how much you love that place. Why don't we just go there?"

"You want me to go to lunch...with you?"

Heat crept up her neck. "Um, yeah. I mean...as friends only, of course."

He seemed to hesitate with an answer, which only made her feel even more self-conscious about her curvier figure. Was he afraid people would see them and assume they'd gotten back together? And if so, why did she even care? It wasn't like it was any of their business anyway.

Finally, he gave a nod of approval. "All right. Let's do it then."

Jeez. Took him long enough.

Chapter Four

Brett had found a small table off to the side where they could have some privacy during lunch as they went over his finances and discussed his credit report. It was bad enough that Kyle was spreading his business around town. He didn't need the two of them doing it inadvertently as well.

They started off making polite small talk as they looked over the documents on his phone, but it wasn't long before they were sharing a few laughs and reminiscing about old times. And that only had him missing Sidney more than ever.

He'd been reluctant to accept her offer, knowing every minute he spent with her was only messing with his head and giving him false hope of renewing their relationship. But the temptation of spending more time with her was just too much to resist.

Sidney had always oozed warmth and goodness, and he missed having her in his life. Even though she was very clear about their "friends only" status and showed no interest in anything other than repaying a favor, he'd

take what he could get. Because he'd rather have her in
his life as a friend than nothing at all. And if she could
help him get that loan for the garage, then that was just
an added bonus.

Caught up in their conversation, neither of them
seemed to notice that they had a visitor approaching
until the man was practically on top of her and already
leaning in for a hug. "Hey, Sidney. How are you?"

Her mouth fell open, but she managed to snap it shut
in time to hug him back. "Oh, um...hey, Charles."

Brett didn't miss her uneasy tone or the way she
cut her eyes over to him, as if she was worried about
what he would say after seeing another man hug her.
But she was a free agent, and it wasn't up to him. She
could damn well hug whomever the hell she wanted,
and there was nothing he could do about it. Sure, he
didn't like it, but that didn't mean he had to vocalize
his feelings.

Besides, Charles wasn't at all Sidney's type. He
looked like a golf nerd in his pink polo shirt and khaki
shorts, as if he was some kind of country club caddy
or maybe a frat boy. He was tall, dark, and probably
good-looking by most women's standards, and he had
a perfect set of brilliant white teeth. But he didn't at all
have that rough edge and intensity that he knew Sidney
loved so much.

Sidney glanced at Brett and then back to her friend.
"Uh, so what are you doing here?"

Charles shrugged lazily. "Someone said this place
sells the best hot dogs in town so I thought I'd come try
them out. But I didn't know you were here. I was sorry

we had to postpone dinner last night because of a flat tire, but I'm looking forward to our date tonight."

Wait, what? Brett's head snapped in Sidney's direction, and she immediately cringed. Even though she tried to smile a little, the guilty look on her face told Brett everything he needed to know. She'd had a date last night. Damn.

He guessed this explained what she had been doing out there all alone and why she had dressed up. He hadn't even thought to ask her since he figured that she would've told him if she wanted him to know. Apparently, she hadn't.

"Um, yeah. Me too," Sidney said quietly.

"I didn't even see your car out front," Charles told her.

She nodded. "That's because it's not. It's still parked at the garage across the street."

Charles shaded his eyes like a pansy and gazed across the road. "Sounds like you need a new mechanic. How hard can it be to change a flat tire?"

Irritation swept through Brett, and he ground his teeth together to keep from saying anything.

Sidney's face paled instantly, and she sat a little straighter. "Uh, actually, the car is fixed already. I just need to go pick it up when I'm done."

Charles nodded. "Well, that's good. Hopefully they don't charge you an arm and a leg. Mechanics are crooked like that, you know?"

Brett blew out a breath and counted to ten in his head. Charles was lucky that Brett was seeing a therapist who had given him tools to control himself in this kind of situation. Otherwise, Brett would've already ripped off this guy's arm and leg and beat him with them. The dickhead.

The three of them sat in uncomfortable silence before Sidney finally said, "Well, I guess it's time for me to get going. I've got some errands to run before I head home."

Charles smiled. "Same here. Hopefully you won't have any more problems with that tire. Of course, that all depends on whether the mechanic knew what the hell he was doing when he fixed it."

Brett rose from his chair, and Sidney stiffened instantly, clearly worried about what he planned to do. Charles was completely oblivious though and didn't even seem to notice the thick tension hovering in the air around them.

Of course Brett didn't like knowing that the woman he loved was dating again. Who the hell would? But he was sickened to no end as he watched her stiffen, all because she wasn't sure how he would react to the news. He'd done that to her, damn it.

In the past, he'd always gone off the deep end. God, he was such an idiot. No wonder the woman left him. At least now he had finally learned to recognize his insecurities for what they were and had learned to control himself. In fact, he was more confident in his behavior than ever, and he was extremely proud of the progress he'd made over the past year. He only wished he'd made these changes sooner. Maybe then he wouldn't have lost her.

Especially to this guy, of all people. Christ.

But Brett didn't want to draw this out any longer than he had to. So he sucked in a slow, deep breath and steadied himself as he offered his hand to the other man. "It was nice meeting you, Charles. I'm Brett, one of Sidney's friends."

The guy shook his hand. "Great to meet you too, Brett. Sidney's one heck of a woman, isn't she?"

Brett glanced over at Sidney, who was sitting there with wide eyes and an open mouth. "That she is," he said, smiling at her. "Thanks for all your help today, Sid. You two have fun on your date tonight."

Then he did something that surprised even him. He turned and headed back to the garage to get his truck, leaving the woman he loved alone with another man.

* * *

After dinner at the Gypsy Cantina, Sidney slid into the passenger seat of Charles's car and stared out the window. She'd been quiet most of the night and was certain that she'd been terrible company as far as first dates went. But she couldn't seem to stop thinking about Brett.

Actually, she didn't know what to think. There was no mistaking the shocked look in his eyes when Charles announced that he and Sidney had a date. Brett's head had swiveled in her direction so fast that she was surprised it hadn't fallen off his shoulders. She hadn't really planned on mentioning the date to Brett, but once it was brought up, it wasn't like she could keep it from him.

Thanks a lot, Charles.

Unsure of how Brett would react, Sidney nearly panicked when he suddenly rose to his feet and faced the other man head-on. Her breath had stalled in her lungs, and her nerves had fired a warning shot to each of her limbs in case she needed to react quickly. Even though Brett had told her that he was in therapy and has changed his ways, she'd seen him in action too many times in the past to expect anything but the worst.

But then he'd surprised her.

Maybe it's true. Maybe he really has changed, after all.

After saying good-bye to Charles at the hot dog stand earlier in the day, she'd headed directly for the shop to talk to Brett. She didn't know why she felt the need to explain herself, but she did. Too bad she didn't get the chance. By the time she arrived, Brett had already left.

She'd worried that might happen, damn it. Now she couldn't stop wondering what it had all meant. Had he been upset about her date? Or did he not care at all? Maybe that was it. Maybe he was completely over her and didn't give a damn who she went out with. After all, he had told her to have a good time on her date tonight. God. Had he really meant that? She just didn't know.

"It's starting to rain," Charles told her, turning on his wipers to clear the splatters of rain drops from his windshield. "I don't think it's supposed to get bad until later tonight though."

"That's good," Sidney replied absently.

"You okay? You're not sick or anything, are you?"

She badly wanted to fake some stomach pains and

ask him to take her home, but she couldn't bring herself to do it. "I'm fine. I think the weather is just making me a little tired." She crossed her mental fingers, hoping he would take that as a hint.

No such luck.

Charles winked at her. "Don't worry. I have something that is going to wake you right up. I hope you're thirsty," he said, pulling into a parking lot.

Sidney glanced through the windshield and gazed up at the Bottoms Up sign on the front of the bar, and her stomach twisted. As Charles pulled into an empty slot, she quickly scanned the surrounding vehicles until her eyes landed on a red pickup a few rows over. Damn it. Not only did Brett's best friend and sister own this bar, but his truck was in the parking lot. The last thing she wanted to do was make anyone uncomfortable...including herself.

She wiped at her brow. "Um, I don't know about this."

"Oh, come on. It'll be fun. We can grab a few drinks and cause a bit of a ruckus."

Exactly what I'm afraid of.

While Brett had been nice to Charles during lunch, she didn't want to push her luck. One incident of Brett controlling himself was hardly what she considered proof that he had changed his ways. He might've just been on his best behavior earlier. Who knew? But if he was inside drinking, that might make things a little more tense. Alcohol always had a way of complicating things.

Still, it was a small town, and they wouldn't be able

to avoid each other forever. The lug nut incident proved that already. They would both eventually have to get used to seeing each other around, even if they were with someone else...

Oh, dear God. She hadn't even considered that before since she'd been so busy avoiding him. But now that she had, the thought of Brett with another woman made her chest ache. She peered up at the bar again and bit her lip, wondering if he was inside with a date at that very moment.

Unfortunately, there was only one way to find out.

She sighed. "All right, let's do it."

Chapter Five

Brett hadn't planned to stay long.

He'd stopped by the bar only long enough to tell Logan and Valerie all about the used car lot that he'd checked out earlier in the day. Beyond needing a new paint job and a little fixing up, Brett couldn't dream of a better place to open his garage. And that alone had him dying to rush home and fill out the loan application. But his sister and her husband insisted that he hang out and tell them more about it. So he had.

Although he was still worried about not getting approved for the loan, they both seemed genuinely happy for him and said that, if he didn't, they would be happy to cosign for him. His chest swelled with emotion. It was nice having family in his corner who believed in him and had his back. The only thing that could make his night any more perfect was—

As if on cue, the entrance door to the bar swung open, and Sidney stepped into view. Brett's gaze flickered over her, and his throat tightened. She was wearing black slacks paired with a white button-down. He didn't know how she did it, but she always managed to look like she'd just come from a business meeting. Maybe it was strange, but something about that always aroused him.

But that problem corrected itself when he noticed the guy behind her. His stomach dropped, and the awesome mood he was in went to shit. The last thing he wanted to do was spend the rest of the night watching the woman he loved canoodling with some other guy. Fuck that.

Knowing Logan was in the storeroom breaking down liquor boxes, Brett began making his way to that side of the bar. He made sure to give Sidney and her guest a wide berth and stayed on the opposite line of foot traffic to keep from being spotted. He didn't need another uncomfortable meeting like they'd had earlier in the day. If you asked him, once had been enough.

But before he made it to the hallway in which the storeroom was located, someone grasped his arm. "Hey, where are you going?"

He glanced over his shoulder at Valerie and then turned to face her. "I'm going to see if your husband needs any help."

"Oh, he's probably close to being finished by now."

Brett shrugged. "That's all right. I'll just go hang out with him then. Anything as long as it gets me out of this room."

Valerie's eyes filled with concern. "Why? What's wrong? Did something happen?"

"Yeah," he said, grabbing her shoulders and turning

her toward the area where Sidney was sitting with her date. "That happened."

"Oh. That sucks."

"My sentiments exactly."

His sister glanced back at him. "Did she see you?"

"Not yet. I was trying to escape before that happened."

Valerie crossed her arms. "Go on then. I'll cover for you, if necessary. I can always say that I borrowed your truck."

He squeezed her shoulder and smiled. "Thanks, Val. This is why you're my favorite sister."

She laughed. "The competition isn't real stiff. I'm your only sister, dork."

Brett grinned at her and then slipped down the hallway to get out of sight. He didn't look at it as running from his problems. It was more like he was removing himself from a difficult situation rather than reacting to it.

He'd learned that in therapy.

Over the past year, his counselor had given him some great tools that really improved his overall behavior and attitude. Like when he was struggling with a difficult situation, she'd suggested that he head to the gym and take his frustrations out on a boxing bag or work up a good sweat on the weights. He'd taken her advice, and not only had it enhanced his body, but working out had become therapeutic when something was troubling him.

Like seeing Sidney with another man.

Unfortunately, he didn't have access to a gym this late in the evening. But the good news was that he now knew how to handle the uncomfortable situation like a grown man rather than the immature idiot he once was.

Brett shoved open the door to the storeroom and found Logan sitting on a crate. "Hey, dillhole. Need any help?"

"With what? Sitting on my ass?"

"You're supposed to be working. I know you don't know what that is, but I thought maybe by now you would've figured it out." Brett shrugged one shoulder. "Guess not."

Logan grinned wide. "Says the guy who shows up *after* the work is done."

Brett sat down on a crate and leaned back against the wall, making himself comfortable. He would probably be here for a while. "Only proves I'm smarter than you."

"And lazier too," Logan said with a chuckle. He kicked his feet up on the box in front of him. "So what are you doing back here? Did your sister get tired of you already?"

"Not this time," Brett told him, smirking.

"Then what's up?"

"Nothing."

Logan gave him a *yeah, right* look. "I know you better than that, Brett. Start talking."

He sighed. "Fine. Sidney's in the bar."

"All right. What's wrong with that?"

"She's on a date."

"Oh." Logan rubbed his chin as if he were in deep thought. "So I take it that you're hiding back here to keep from running into them?"

"No, I'm avoiding them to keep from running into them."

Logan squinted at him. "Isn't that the same thing?"

"Probably, but saying I'm avoiding them sounds a lot better. Doesn't make me feel like such a loser."

"Oh, come on. You're not a loser, man. You can't help how you feel." He leaned forward, his face serious. "Does she at least know that you're still in love with her?"

Brett shook his head. "No. I didn't tell her."

"What? Why the hell not? What are you waiting for?"

"Logan, she avoided me for almost an entire year, and now she's on a date with another man. What would be the point? She's obviously over me and has already moved on."

Logan's eyes widened. "So that's it? You're not even going to fight for her?" When he didn't get a response, he shook his head with annoyance. "God, you're such a loser."

Brett couldn't help grinning. "I thought you just said I wasn't one."

"Yeah, well, I lied."

* * *

Sidney should've known better.

She had a feeling that coming into the bar would be one giant mistake, and she was absolutely right. She and her date had been sitting at the bar for nearly two hours, and she hadn't seen a single sign of Brett beyond his truck in the parking lot. And that only made her consider that he'd met someone and gone home with her in her own vehicle. Why else would he leave his behind?

She scanned the entire bar again, hoping to spot him in some dark corner, but he was nowhere to be seen. Damn it. Why was she torturing herself like this?

Charles stumbled toward her, his eyes glazed over. "I still can't find my keys," he slurred drunkenly.

Great.

Instead of watching for Brett for the past few hours, she should've been keeping an eye on her date, who apparently drank like a fish. After having a few too many, he was now in no condition to drive. Which really didn't matter since he couldn't find the car keys that he'd lost somewhere in the bar anyway.

Sidney caught sight of Valerie passing by and flagged her down. "Hey, Valerie. Did anyone turn in a set of car keys? We seem to have lost some."

"Hmm, I can double-check with my head bartender, but I haven't heard about anyone finding any car keys. I'll let you know if I do though."

"Okay, thanks. But if they turn up, can you just hang on to them until tomorrow? It's getting late, and I think we're about to leave."

"No problem. But how are you getting home? Do you need me to call you a cab? We have the taxi company on speed dial."

She nodded. "Sure, that would be great. Thanks."

Charles placed a hand on his stomach and hunched over a little. "I don't feel so good."

Sidney glanced at Valerie. "Uh, maybe we should

step outside and get some fresh air while we wait on that cab."

"I'll go call them right now and tell them to look for you two out front."

"Thanks, Val."

Sidney grasped Charles's arm and led him out the exit. It was still sprinkling a little so they stayed under the covered area and sat on a wooden bench. He immediately leaned forward with his elbows propped on his knees and hung his head. Guess those four Irish Car Bombs he'd chugged had hit him all at once. Idiot.

She was seriously annoyed. Not only had Charles drunk himself to intoxication like a frat boy at a kegger, but he hadn't seemed at all concerned about how she was going to get home since he'd picked her up. And what really frustrated her and had her stewing in silence was the one thought that replayed over and over in her mind.

Brett would never have done this.

A few minutes later, Valerie stepped outside. "Just checking on you two. I would've came out sooner, but I went around asking all the bartenders and waitresses if anyone turned in a set of keys. No luck yet."

"That's okay. I'm sure they'll turn up at some point." She'd barely finished the sentence when a pair of headlights turned into the parking lot. "Oh, good. There's our ride."

Sidney helped Charles to his feet and walked him out to the sidewalk as the cab pulled to a stop in front of them. Light rain pelted the top of her head, but she opened the door and waited patiently as her date stumbled forward and crawled inside.

She turned back to Valerie, who was still standing under the covered area and waved. "Thanks, Val."

Once Valerie had waved back, Sidney ran around to the other side of the taxi to hurry and get out of the rain. But when she threw open the door, she froze in place. A horrible retching sound came from inside the car, and the rancid smell of hot wiener smacked her in the face. Oh, God.

She'd never been able to handle the sounds and smell of someone throwing up and immediately covered her nose with her hand. She liked hot dogs, but not the kind that had been partially digested and thrown back up. Gross. To make matters worse, Charles had thrown up on her part of the seat. Great. There was no way she was going to sit in vomit, much less smell that odor all the way home. No doubt she would end up puking herself.

She sighed and glanced to the driver, who looked as annoyed as she felt. "Um, I'll just wait for the next taxi."

"I am the next taxi, lady. It's a small town. Not enough business to run more than one taxi a night."

Ah, crap. "Okay, then I'll just find another way home." She pulled out a twenty-dollar bill and passed it to the driver as she rattled off Charles's address. "This should cover his fare." Then she handed him another twenty. "And this is for your trouble. Sorry about the mess."

The driver shoved the money in his shirt pocket and grinned. "Wouldn't be the first time that has happened. But thanks for the tip. I appreciate it."

"No problem." She gazed at her date in the backseat. "Charles, I hope you feel better soon."

He only groaned in response so she shut the car door, and the cab pulled away.

Valerie looked as confused as ever. "Hey, what happened? Why didn't you get into the cab?"

"Because Charles decided to throw up all over the backseat."

"Oh no. Well, you could've ridden in the front seat, I suppose."

"And smell that all the way home? No thank you. I'm just going to walk."

Valerie shook her head. "But it's late. And it's cold and rainy."

Sidney shrugged. "It's not that bad. I'll live."

"I have a better solution. Stay right here, and I'll get you a ride home."

"Val, you don't have to do that. I don't want to trouble anyone."

"No trouble at all. Trust me, he won't mind."

She sighed. "Okay, but if Logan's busy, then don't bother him. I only live a mile or so down the road. I don't mind walking."

"No worries," she said with a grin. "I promise I won't bother Logan."

Valerie disappeared inside the bar, and a few moments later, the door to the bar flew open so hard that Sidney thought it might break from its hinges. Brett stood in the doorway, his face twisted with anger and his hands fisted at his sides.

She didn't know why he was so mad, but she'd forgotten how intimidating he could look when he was worked into a frenzy. Although she'd never felt intimidated by him in the past herself, she could understand why others would feel that way. And just seeing him like that again only made her doubt his earlier declaration.

Changed man, my ass. Looks like the same old Brett as always.

Annoyed that she had started to believe him, she crossed her arms defensively. "What are you doing out here?"

Valerie stepped out from behind him with a huge grin spreading her face. "He's your ride home."

Chapter Six

Damn his sister.

When Valerie had showed up in the storeroom and told Brett that Sidney needed him right away, she'd scared the hell out of him. The panic that had run through him when he thought she was hurt or in trouble had sent him flying down the hallway and through the bar like a runaway freight train. He hadn't been able to get to her fast enough.

Valerie could've just told him that Sidney needed a ride home. It's not like he minded. "What happened to your date?"

Sidney didn't reply right away so Valerie answered for her. "He got wasted, lost his car keys, threw up in the cab, and then he left."

Brett's eyes narrowed onto Sidney. "He just left you here?"

She shook her head. "Um, not exactly. I volunteered not to go."

He couldn't help grinning. Sidney always had a weak stomach when it came to certain smells. She'd once gone through four different car fresheners before she found one that didn't make her sick to her stomach. "I can take you home."

She shook her head. "It's okay. I can walk. It's not that far."

"I was heading home anyway. It's on the way. I don't mind. Besides, you really shouldn't be out walking this late at night. Especially in the rain. It's not safe."

Sidney sighed, as if she didn't seem too happy about his offer. "Okay, fine."

Valerie smiled. "Good, it's settled then. You two have fun," she said, heading back inside the bar.

He shook his head. Like it wasn't obvious what his sister was trying to do. But he didn't need her interfering in his love life. Especially since she hadn't appreciated it when he'd done it to her. Guess now Valerie was giving him a dose of his own medicine. The little matchmaker.

Brett and Sidney ran to his truck and quickly climbed into the cab to get out of the rain, which had started coming down faster. He offered to turn the heat on for her, but Sidney told him not to bother worrying about her. He didn't know why she was so irritated with him for giving her a ride home, but that was definitely the vibe he was picking up from her.

To be honest, he wasn't in the best of moods himself. While he was still irritated that her date had gotten drunk and left her to fend for herself, he was glad that he was the one who was making sure she got safely home...and alone. He didn't know how long she'd been seeing this other guy, but the thought of her being intimate with another man was eating at him. Not that he could tell her that.

They drove in silence. When he pulled up at the curb, he shut the engine off, and the heavy rain instantly blurred the windshield with a sheet of water. He gazed over at her. "I'll walk you to your door."

She shook her head persistently. "No need. I'll be fine."

"All right."

An awkward tension sat between them, but she didn't move to get out of the car. Instead, she gazed up at him and said, "Where were you tonight?"

"At the bar."

"I know that but...where at the bar? I didn't see you in there."

Damn it. Why was she asking him that? Did she think he was there spying on her or something? "What does it matter?"

"I just...want to know."

He hadn't intended on telling her any of this, but he refused to lie to her. "The moment I saw you and your date come into the bar, I hid out in the storeroom."

She blinked at him. "Why would you do that?"

"Because I couldn't bear the thought of another man kissing or touching you...the way I used to."

She closed her eyes. "Brett, I..." Her voice trailed off.

His chest tightened, and he cringed. "It's okay. You don't have to say anything." Because hearing her say she couldn't be with him again would hurt just as much now as it had a year ago. "I understand."

"Do you?"

"Sure," he said, trying to soften his voice to hide the pain.

He sighed inwardly. He was pining away for a woman who clearly wanted nothing to do with him. And sadly, it was his own fault. He could kick himself in the ass for ruining things with her, but that wouldn't make him feel any better about it. So, as a man resigned to his own fate, he instead would do the one thing he really didn't want to do. He would wish her the best and let her go.

Brett cleared his throat. "Look, I don't know how long you've been seeing this new guy, but if he's the one who makes you happy, then I wish you both all the best. That's all I ever wanted for you."

A look of confusion warped her shocked face, and she shook her head at him. "I . . . uh, don't know what to say. I thought—"

"You don't have to say anything back, Sid. I just wanted you to know that I want the best for you. Always." He glanced at the windshield. "The rain stopped. You better get inside before it starts up again."

"Um, okay," she said, blinking at him.

"Good night, Sid."

When Brett leaned over the arm rest to give her a peck on the cheek, Sidney turned her face up to his and kissed him directly on the mouth. The gesture was so unexpected that it froze him in place. Her lips were touching his, but he was so stunned by it that all he could do was sit there like a damn corpse. What the hell was wrong with him?

The moment Sidney didn't get a favorable response, she pulled away and mumbled an awkward apology. He could tell how embarrassed she was that he hadn't kissed her back, but before he could explain himself, she reached for the door handle so she could escape the humiliation she felt.

But he wasn't about to let that happen. Not after she'd kissed him.

Brett reached for her and pulled her back to him before ratcheting her up in his arms and covering her mouth with his. Her lips parted in surprise, and he took advantage of the moment by thrusting his tongue inside and deepening the kiss. God, he'd missed this. The taste of her lips. The scent of her skin. The feel of her soft, curvy body pressing against his. Lord help him, he couldn't get enough of her.

And apparently, she felt the same way.

Her tongue rolled against his with a hunger he hadn't felt before, and her insistent hands roamed over him with a passionate fury. If it hadn't been for the middle console keeping them apart from the waist down, he was pretty damn sure she would've already straddled him.

"God, I want you," she whispered, nipping at his bottom lip as she pulled at his belt to undo it.

Stupid fucking console.

Brett was prepared to rip the damn thing out of his truck right then and there, but then he remembered that she'd just been on a date with another man. Damn it. Talk about a mood killer.

He was so confused that he didn't know what to do.

He thought she had moved on with her life and gotten over him. After all, in the past few days, she'd refused his help, told him they were just friends, and gone out with another guy. What else was he supposed to think? Yet now she was kissing him and trying to take off his clothes.

She almost had his belt completely unbuckled, and he knew that if her hand went anywhere inside his pants, it was all over. There was no way he could—or would—stop things at that point.

He put his hand on top of hers and pulled his mouth back slightly. "Sid, wait."

"Why? Do you want to get into the backseat first?"

Holy hell. He closed his eyes. *Be strong, man. You can do this.*

"No. I think we need to talk first."

She trailed her tongue over his lips. "No, we don't. Let's not ruin anything by talking."

He licked his lips, tasting her on them. "I'm serious, Sid. What is this?"

"It's called sex," she said, blowing out an aggravated breath. "But I'm pretty sure you already knew that."

"Look, things have changed between us, and I don't want anyone to get hurt. I think we should slow this down before that happens."

The stunned look on her face made him feel bad, but she hadn't said anything about them getting back together, and the last thing he wanted was a meaningless one-night stand with her. Sidney had never been that kind of woman, and he sure as hell wasn't going to treat her that way.

Yeah, he'd slept with her before. Sure, he would probably kick himself in the ass later for not allowing himself to have her. But she'd just been out with another man, for goodness' sake. So at this point, he needed to make sure she was all in. Because *he* definitely was.

He'd lost her once and didn't want that to happen again. If that meant taking things slow and showing her that she could trust him to be the man she needed—the only one she needed—then that was exactly what he was going to do.

He gave her an encouraging smile. "Why don't we go out to dinner tomorrow night so we can spend some time together? It's been a while since we did that."

"Uh, okay. I guess so."

Brett nodded. "Great. I'll pick the place."

Because it was going to have to be somewhere public where he wouldn't be tempted to rip her damn clothes off and slide her under him.

* * *

Sidney didn't know what the hell was going on.

She'd spent the entire night lying awake, wondering why Brett had put the brakes on when it came to last night's make-out session and whether her new figure had anything to do with it. After she'd offered herself up on a platter and he still refused her, what else could it be?

He'd said he wanted to take things slow. But weren't things like that something guys said when they weren't all that interested? She'd read *He's Just Not That into*

You before. Even saw the movie. Now she felt like she was living the scenario in her head.

If he'd rather take you to dinner than to bed, he's just not that into you.

Then again, this was Brett she was talking about. *Her* Brett. And he'd never once treated her like that before. So maybe he really did want to take things slow like he'd said. And if that was the case, she appreciated the notion. Honestly, that was probably for the best anyway.

She'd called Charles that afternoon to let him know that Valerie had texted her that she'd found his keys and he could pick them up at the bar. Then she broke the news that she just wasn't that into him...except she did it much more nicely than that. He hadn't really seemed all that worried about it, which actually was a little insulting since he had been the one who'd acted like such a dumbass on their date.

But whatever. At least she wasn't nursing a hangover. Karma sometimes had a way of righting the wrongs of the world.

The faint roar of an engine rumbled in the air, and her heart flatlined.

That had to be Brett since she wasn't expecting anyone else, but he'd arrived a few minutes early. She glanced in her full-length mirror and smoothed the wrinkles out of her white silk blouse and black pencil skirt before sliding into her strappy heels and heading to the door.

The moment she opened it, her breath caught in her throat. Brett leaned against the doorjamb with both hands, wearing a pair of distressed jeans, a fitted black Henley, and a pair of steel-toed work boots. Even the wicked smile he wore screamed of a bad boy who was about to deflower a virgin... which only made her wish she was still a virgin.

"Hey, Sid. You look great."

She smiled. "Thanks. So do you."

He nodded a thank-you. "Ready to go?"

"Yep." She waited for him to move aside and then stepped out the door, pulling it shut behind her. "So where are we going to dinner?"

"You'll see," he told her, grasping her hand and leading her out to his truck.

A thrill coursed through her. He was holding her hand like he always had, which she thought was a pretty good sign. Or was that just her being ridiculously naive and reading into something all because she hoped that it meant more than it did?

Jeez. Stop it. Or you'll drive yourself crazy all night long.

Brett opened her door for her but gazed at her with a funny look on his face. "Everything okay?"

Crap. He was picking up on her nervousness. "Yeah, I'm fine."

"You sure?"

"Of course," she said, climbing into the cab. "Let's go eat."

He nodded and shut her door before strolling around to the driver's side and getting in. They made small talk as he drove, although he didn't take her hand again like she'd hoped he would. But he was driving so she tried not to read into that too.

When he pulled into the Gypsy Cantina's parking lot, Sidney sat a little straighter in her seat. "Uh, is this where we're having dinner?"

"Yeah, is that okay?"

"Sure, I just...well, you know who owns this place, right?"

"Jessa."

"Well, yeah. But you know who she's married to, don't you?"

"Oh, you mean Max. Yeah, what about him?"

"You two don't get along."

He smirked. "Sure we do. Whenever we aren't in the same room, we're fine."

"That's my point exactly. You know Max is most likely going to be here. This probably isn't the best place for us to have dinner."

Brett pulled into an empty parking space anyway. "It'll be fine."

"You sure?"

He took her hand in his and rubbed his thumb in circles over her palm. "I am. Trust me, there's nothing Max can say or do that is going to rile me up."

Sidney rolled her eyes. "Okay, if you say so."

Brett grinned as he got out of the truck and came around to open her door. He seemed really confident that Max wasn't going to upset him tonight, but Sidney knew how relentless Max could be. She'd seen him in action before. Max was a good guy, but he liked to see people squirm. He would push every button Brett had until he found the one that would detonate.

As they headed inside, Sidney could only hope that

Max's taunting wasn't going to cause Brett to overreact as he always had in the past. *Guess we'll see what happens.*

Although the place wasn't completely packed, it was still pretty busy for a Sunday night. Dining guests were scattered around the room, but there were a few empty tables available. They were seated at one of them directly below a gorgeous chandelier that hung in the center of the room.

Sidney loved the gypsy caravan feel that the decor provided. A canopy of red fabric draped from the ceiling. Colorful glass lanterns lit every table. Mixed print throw pillows accented the room with their rich hues and bold patterns. It was all so different from any other restaurant in the area...as was the wonderful gourmet food Jessa served.

The hostess provided them each with a glass of water and a menu and told them their server would be with them in a moment. A few minutes later, when the server finally appeared, Sidney was still looking over her menu, but Brett's chuckle had her glancing up to see what was so funny.

Max stood there with an apron wrapped around his waist and a tablet in his hands, ready to take their order. He glared at Brett. "Laugh again, and I'll spit in your food."

"Max!" Jessa came from somewhere behind him and stood at his side. "You can't say stuff like that in here."

"Oh, I was only kidding...mostly."

Jessa grabbed the tablet from him and turned her attention back to Brett and Sidney. "Don't mind him.

He's just cranky because he's having to wear an apron. He's filling in for one of my waitresses while she's on maternity leave, but I promise he won't touch your food. What would you like?"

"I'm not the least bit worried," Sidney said with a smile. "I'll have the pan-seared halibut with the lobster risotto and sautéed asparagus. No parmesan, please."

Brett shrugged. "Well, I guess I'll take my chances," he said with a laugh. "I'll have the beef Wellington with mushroom sauce, bacon mac 'n' cheese, and roasted Brussels sprouts. No saliva, please."

Max grinned. Probably because he knew he had Brett worried. "You're so lucky I'm not filling in for one of the chefs."

Jessa elbowed him and whispered, "If you keep saying stuff like that, you're going to be lucky if I don't make you sleep on the couch tonight."

He threw his hands up in surrender. "Okay, okay. I'll behave."

She rolled her eyes. "No, you won't. We all know you better than that." Then she winked playfully at Brett. "If he gives you too much grief though, let me know, and I'll put him on dish duty."

Brett laughed. "I'm sure it'll be fine. I can handle anything Max throws my way."

Max lifted one brow. "I hear a challenge calling my name."

"Give it your best shot, buddy."

"Oh Lord. I'm going to go get started on your order. You two behave yourself," Jessa said to the guys before heading for the kitchen.

Sidney bit her lip. The last thing Brett needed to do was egg Max on. He'd always been able to rub Brett the wrong way in the past. She just hoped that Brett wasn't asking for anything he couldn't handle.

Max pulled up a chair and sat backward on it as he glanced back and forth between them. "So are you guys back together now?"

Oh, dear God.

Chapter Seven

Brett watched as Sidney quickly grabbed her water and took a sip to keep from having to answer Max's unexpected question, and frustration surged inside him. Was that her way of saying they weren't getting back together?

And if so, then why agree to go on a date with him?

Brett sat back in his chair. Great. Now he didn't know how to answer the question himself. So he gazed over at Max and calmly replied, "What's it to you?"

He shrugged. "Just a question. Didn't know you were going to get defensive about it."

Sidney stared at Brett with a blank, unreadable expression, and he had no clue what she was thinking.

"I'm not defensive."

"Maybe," Max said, grinning. "But you didn't answer the question either."

Sidney visibly cringed at the remark and then tried to cover it by taking another sip of her water. Brett's eyes met hers over the top of the glass, and the unrelenting tension between them made him want to crawl in a hole.

Thanks for pointing that out, asshole.

He needed Max to stop with his questioning before things with Sidney blew up in his face once again. So he shot him one of his blue-eyed glares. "All right. That's enough. Unless you want me to go in the kitchen and ask Jessa when you two are going to start having babies, I suggest you knock it off."

Max's eyes widened. "You wouldn't dare."

Brett grinned smugly to assure him that he definitely would.

Shaking his head, Max glanced at Sidney. "So what have you been up to?"

She tilted her head and released a sigh, clearly relieved that he'd changed the subject. "Um, not much."

"I heard you had some car problems a few days ago."

Damn. Word certainly travels fast around here.

"Oh, that?" Sidney nodded. "Yeah, I had a problem with my tire. But it's all taken care of now."

"Glad to hear it," Max replied. "In fact, maybe you can help me out. I need someone to check out a tapping noise coming from under my hood. Know any good mechanics around here?"

Amusement forced Brett to smile. He couldn't help it. The comment was funny. "Good one," Brett said, offering him a fist bump.

Sidney looked as confused as Max did, but after a moment, he lifted one hand and returned the gesture. "Thanks," Max said, laughing.

Brett had done plenty of maintenance on Jessa's food truck in the past so Max must've known that Brett was a damn good mechanic. She'd even had him replace all the tires on it before she sold it as the new delivery truck for the Sweets n' Treats bakery.

"If you're serious about the tapping, it could be a lifter or an exhaust leak. Bring your truck into the shop, and I'll check it out for you," he said without hesitation.

Surprised by his reply, Max's head snapped toward him. "Really?"

"Yeah. And if you can't bring it in during work hours, just give me a call, and I'll set up a time after hours to meet with you."

"Thanks, man. I appreciate it," Max said, offering his hand.

Brett shook hands with him like they'd been friends for years. "No problem."

Max stood. "I'll leave you guys alone now. Your food should be out soon." He started to walk away but stopped and turned back to Brett. "By the way, I heard that you were thinking about buying that old car lot that went up for sale and turning it into a garage. If you do and you need any electrical work done, let me know. I'd be happy to return the favor."

"That would be great," Brett said with a nod. "Thanks a lot."

As Max finally walked away, Brett sat there dumb-struck. What the hell had just happened? Had they actually become friends? Weird.

But Brett was proud of the way he'd handled things with Max. As usual, the guy had tried to push his but-tons. It was exactly why he'd chosen to have dinner at the Gypsy Cantina in the first place. But Brett had been confident in his ability to stay calm and handle whatever Max dished out. Like a real man would. Besides, what better way to prove to Sidney once and for all that he was a changed man than to face his nemesis and let her see that he could control himself?

Funny thing though. He hadn't realized how good letting go of the animosity toward Max would make him feel.

* * *

Who is this new Brett?

It was as if he'd gone from being a caged tiger to a cuddly teddy bear. Sidney could plainly see how hard he had worked to become a better man, and that only made her fall even more in love with him. It also left her wondering if things between them could work out after all. Well, if it wasn't for one little problem.

Does he feel the same?

As they strolled out to the truck after dinner, Brett slid an arm around Sidney's waist and held her body against his. She stiffened a little but tried not to move away. She couldn't help being a little worried that he might be turned off by the extra pounds on her already curvy figure. Especially since he hadn't answered Max's question inside about the two of them getting back together.

But she was still grateful. The warmth of his arm provided her with some comfort and relief against the chill in the air and the cold drops of rain that fell from the darkened sky. Fortunately, they both made it into the truck before the spattering of rain turned into a full-blown downpour.

Brett drove her home and then parked at her curb. "Look at that. I managed to get you home at a respectable hour. It's only nine o'clock."

Yeah, almost too respectable to be considered a date.

She could tell he wasn't planning to stay since he hadn't turned off his engine, but she thought maybe she'd give it a shot anyway. "Would you like to come inside for a little while?"

He didn't hesitate. "I don't think that's a good idea."

"Oh. Okay," she mumbled, embarrassed that she'd even asked.

"But I'm happy to walk you to your door to make sure you get inside."

She peered out the front windshield at the substantial amount of rain water sliding down the glass. It was a freaking monsoon out there. "No, that's all right. There's no point in both of us getting wet."

"I'm not scared of a little water."

Little? She'd be lucky to make it to her front door without drowning. "Seriously, I'll be fine. Good night, Brett."

He wrapped his hand around the back of her neck and pulled her face to his, stopping only centimeters from her lips. "Good night, Sid," he murmured, his tone deepening as his warm breath wafted over her closed lips. Then he leaned forward and brushed his mouth lightly over hers.

Her lips trembled against his, and her heart began to race. With each swipe of his firm mouth, tingles erupted throughout her body. But he was barely touching her, and she wanted more. So she tilted her head to the side

and parted her lips to give him better access and invite
him to take the kiss further.

But instead, Brett broke the kiss and pulled away.
"Uh, we need to slow down."

What? Not again.

She hadn't been intimate with anyone since they'd
broken up a year ago, and her sexual frustration had
been catching up with her ever since she'd first run into
him. Her patience was wearing thin, and she couldn't
take it anymore. She was desperate to have his hands on
her body, touching her like he used to. Like she ached
for him to.

"Why? It's not like we haven't had sex before."

"Yeah, but we were together at the time. Things
were...different then."

Her heart sank. He didn't say the words out loud,
but he didn't have to. She could read between the lines.
In other words, I was a little thinner and sexier back then.

Even though he'd told her more than once that he
wanted to take things slow, Sidney knew something else
had been holding him back. Brett hadn't taken things
slow a day in his life. Now it all made sense.

Maybe he hadn't wanted to hurt her feelings, but she
had no choice but to accept his reluctance for what it
was. Rejection.

Brett was a good guy. Better than most people realized or gave him credit for. That was partially his own
fault since he had a tendency to wear a tough-guy mask
and keep his circle of friends tight. Unfortunately, not
many others got to see the real man behind the curtain.
Sidney was just grateful that, at one time, she'd had her

own personal backstage pass. Even if those days were clearly over.

Without saying a word, Sidney reached down and slid both of her heels off. Then she snagged them by the straps with one finger and rose back to a sitting position. "Good night, Brett. Thank you for dinner."

Brett stared at her with a confused look on his face. "What's wrong? Are you mad at me for something?"

Clutching her shoes in one hand, she flung the passenger door open and slid out of the truck. Her bare feet splashed into a puddle of cold water as large drops of hard rain pelted against her body. She was getting soaked, but she turned back to him anyway. "No, I'm not mad. I'm hurt. There's a difference."

"I don't understand."

"Well, I do." She shoved a wet strand out of her face. "I understand perfectly. I get that you're not attracted to me anymore. But you should've said so from the beginning rather than inviting me to dinner."

Brett blinked at her. "What are you talking about?"

"I know I've gained some weight, but that doesn't change who I am." Her voice cracked as tears welled up in her eyes.

He stared at her blankly, not saying a word.

God, this is so embarrassing. She turned to leave.

"Sidney, wait."

But she didn't. With tears in her eyes, she slammed the door and sprinted through the storm toward her home.

Chapter Eight

Lightning struck in the distance, but it was Brett who felt like he'd been hit. He sat there in shock, unable to move.

Sidney doesn't think I want her because she's gained a few pounds? Is the woman fucking insane?

Not only did she have a gorgeous figure, but he'd been torturing himself by not touching her. He just didn't want to be intimate with her until he was sure they were back together for good...because he loved her and didn't want to screw things up again like he did the last time. But there was no way in hell he was going to let her keep thinking that he wasn't attracted to her. That was ridiculous.

Brett turned off the engine and catapulted out of the truck as fast as he could, his boots sloshing in the water running off the curb. Cold rain beat down on him, but he didn't even bother trying to cover his head. It was pointless. Within seconds of being out of the truck, his clothes and hair were already completely soaked through.

He dashed for her house and caught up to her before she was able to unlock the door and get inside. "Sidney."

She glanced up at him with her wet hair hanging in her face and shook her head. "Go away."

"No, we need to talk."

She put her key into the lock and twisted it. "No, we don't."

"Just hear me out, okay?"

She threw the door open but didn't step inside. Instead, she pivoted on her bare feet and glared at him with eyes of fury. "I don't need you to console me. That's only going to make me feel worse."

"That's not what I'm doing. I'm just trying to explain—"

"God, would you just stop already? I don't need to hear some lame excuse as to why you don't want to be with me. I get it, okay?"

"Apparently not," he said, running a hand through his dripping wet hair. "I never once said I didn't want to be with you."

Rain water dripped off the tip of her nose. "No, but you still rejected me...twice."

"Not for the reason you think." He wiped water from his eyes and took a step closer. "Sid, I didn't know you were insecure about your weight. You never have been in the past. But I promise that wasn't the reason for me putting a halt to things between us."

She fisted a hand on her hip. "Why then?"

"I wasn't sure where we stood or if you even wanted to get back together. I mean, you went on a date with someone else. What was I supposed to think?"

"But I kissed you last night. I wouldn't have done that if I was with someone else. You should know that about me."

"I do know that about you, but...well, it's been almost a year. Things sometimes change. I didn't want to make false assumptions about us and where we stand. Basically, I didn't want to get hurt."

"Well, I didn't want to either, you know? I believe you when you say you've changed. I can see it in your attitude, your behavior, even the way you carry yourself. You're different. And I want to believe that you're still attracted to me, Brett. I really do. But it's hard for me when I don't look the same as I did before."

Brett's eyes gazed over her. Her makeup was smeared down her face, her long hair was plastered to her head, and her skin had broken out in goose bumps from the cold. She looked like hell. But he knew how beautiful she was—inside and out—and there was no one else he would rather be with.

Then he glanced down and realized something else. Her thin white blouse was soaking wet, and she looked like she'd just participated in a wet T-shirt contest. One she would've easily won, seeing how she wasn't wearing a bra. Christ.

"You're going to have to trust me, Sid."

Her bottom lip trembled. "I...don't know if I can. Not when it comes to this."

Brett moved toward her until he had her backed up against the doorjamb and their bodies were touching. Determined to convince her how wrong she was, he rubbed himself against her, letting the hard ridge in his pants speak for itself. "Does that at all feel like I'm not attracted to you?"

Her breath hitched, and the sound made him even harder.

Unable to help himself, he bent his head and kissed her, his mouth taking hers with a fierce hunger that he'd never felt before. She responded immediately by parting her lips and pressing more of herself against him, and his heart beat wildly. God, he wanted her. But he still needed to know if she was all in.

With a growl of frustration, he forced himself to pull back. "I love you, Sid. Always have. But I need to know you feel the same. Otherwise, we need to stop this right here and now before one of us gets hurts."

Her chest heaved with every breath. "Of course I'm still in love with you. I've been miserable without you. I never stopped loving you."

Thank God. His heart squeezed. "Let's go inside and get out of the rain."

"I don't think I can move yet. My legs are shaky. Give me a minute."

Not happening. He wasn't waiting that long.

His hands slid down her sides to the hem of her wet skirt, and he tugged it up high on her thighs. Then he lifted her, wrapping both of her legs around his waist. The move only pressed her more firmly against him, and the feel of her took his breath away. The only thing separating them was his jeans and her panties, and if he had it his way, both would be coming off as soon as they got inside.

Her arms clung to his neck as he moved through the

door, kicking it shut behind him. There were no lights on inside, but he knew where the bedroom was located. In addition, the lightning flashed through the window and allowed him to see well enough to keep from running into any furniture she might've moved since he'd last been there.

They must be leaving a trail of water from the front door to the bedroom, but neither seemed to care. When his knees came into contact with her bed, he laid her down gently onto her back and immediately tugged off her damp panties.

Brett stood and stripped off his wet shirt. Then he reached into his pocket for a condom before unbuttoning his pants. His pants were soaked, and it would take way too long to get them off so he left them on. He needed to be inside her right now, damn it. So he rolled the condom on his length and lowered himself on top of her.

"I'm not going to last long this first time, Sid, but I promise to make it up to you on the next round."

"No need to promise anything. I know you, Brett. And I'm going to enjoy every second of this. I always have." She smiled and hooked her legs around his waist, pulling him into her.

Fevered passion exploded between them as she threw her head back, moaning loudly. Beads of liquid rolled down his neck, though he wasn't sure if it was from the rain in his hair or the sweat he'd accumulated on his skin with every motion. He couldn't get enough of all of her lush curves that he remembered so well. And a few new ones that he was enjoying immensely. He loved her no matter what. A few pounds didn't change a person's heart and soul... and that was what meant the most.

Moments later, her body surged with its first spasm, and he was finally able to let himself go. Thank God. But as he did, one single thought ran through his mind.

So much for taking things slow.

* * *

Sidney couldn't uncurl her toes. Not that she cared much after the mind-blowing orgasm. Brett had just gifted her. Her body still tingled from the explosions he'd caused inside of her, and her legs had gone numb.

He hovered over her, eyes closed and breathing like he'd just run a marathon. She reached up and rubbed her hand along his strong jaw, and he immediately turned his face toward her palm and kissed it before collapsing next to her. He lay there only a moment before getting up and going to the bathroom to dispose of the condom. When he returned, he kicked off his boots and then lay down next to her. He pulled her against his side, and she snuggled in as she laid her hand across his chest.

He released a hard breath. "Sorry about that. It's been way too long."

"I don't know why you apologize every time. You act like I didn't enjoy myself. Trust me, that isn't the case." She smiled. "And in case you're wondering, it's been too long for me too."

He kissed her forehead. "I was afraid to ask. I know we weren't together, but I hate the idea of another man touching you like I have."

"Brett, no one could *ever* touch me the way you have."

He leaned over and kissed her gently on the lips. "Same here, Sid. No one has ever made me feel the way you do."

Her heart swelled. "I'm glad to hear it."

She traced her finger over his broad chest before moving lower to his gloriously tight abs. He'd always been in great shape, but now his body was even harder and stronger than before.

"You get any lower, and you're going to have a big problem on your hands."

She giggled. "Don't you mean *in* my hands?"

"With any luck," he said with a loaded grin. "But if you're ready for round two, all you had to do was say so. I'm up for the task." He glanced downward. "Literally."

"Ding, ding, ding," she said with a smirk.

He laughed. "All right."

Brett made quick work of peeling his wet jeans off his legs and tossing his socks onto the floor, leaving him completely nude. The man had hardly ever worn underwear while they were dating so she wasn't surprised he didn't have any now.

He lifted up onto his knees and began unbuttoning her blouse. With every motion of his arms, all those hard-packed muscles of his flexed and tightened in the moonlight. She couldn't hear the rain anymore so she assumed it had either stopped or lightened up enough that it had become soundless.

Once Brett had removed her blouse and slid her skirt

off her legs, he reached into her nightstand and pulled out a condom. "Still in the same place," he said with a smile.

"Yeah, because that's where you left them."

He lay down next to her, facing her. "Turn over," he commanded, helping her roll over with one hand on her hip.

She faced away from him but could hear the crinkling of foil as he opened the condom. Once it was in place, he settled in directly behind her and lifted her leg over his and entered her.

They both moaned loudly.

She moved against him, meeting each thrust with one of her own as heat radiated through her, warming her from the inside out. Need pooled in her gut, and she twisted her neck to gaze over her shoulder at him.

Their eyes met. Lit with desire, his baby blues focused intently on her as he pulled her mouth to his.

God, the man could kiss.

His tongue slid between her lips and rolled against hers with a purpose as he explored her mouth thoroughly. Her fingernails dug into his muscular thigh, and she melted into him. An immeasurable amount of heat built inside of her before detonating into a full-blown explosion, and she cried out...

He swallowed her cries of pleasure and continued kissing her as he ground against her, sending electricity humming through her veins. Once her convulsions finally subsided and her body tingled with contentment, he held himself deep inside of her and came, groaning her name.

Sidney closed her eyes, enjoying the sensation of his muscles vibrating against her. Sweat coated their skin, and they both could use a shower. But the last thing she wanted to do was move. With Brett beside her, she had everything she needed.

Chapter Nine

Two weeks later, Brett planned a do-over.

Maybe he was a glutton for punishment since they hadn't been back together long, and the last time he tried to propose to Sidney, things didn't go quite as planned. But it was Valentine's Day once again, and he wanted to spend the rest of his life with this woman. If that meant taking a risk of it all blowing up in his face once again, then so be it. He wasn't waiting another year.

Once again, he strolled into the bank where she worked with a bouquet of red roses in hand and a diamond ring in his pocket. The same ring he'd bought for her last year and never got to give her. They didn't make it to dinner the last time so he wasn't taking any chances. He was going to propose to her on the spot and finish what he'd set out to do last year...before anything bad could happen.

But unfortunately, Sidney wasn't in her office when he arrived. She stood behind the front counter, helping a teller with a customer, and everyone looked up at him as he entered the bank. The moment Sidney saw Brett coming toward them, she gave him "the look"— the same one she'd given to him last year—and then cut her eyes to the male customer she was helping.

Brett had learned his lesson the last time this happened. He had no doubt that Sidney could handle herself in any situation, and if she did need his help, she would ask for it. So he got behind the gentleman and waited patiently for his turn at the teller window.

When the guy glanced back over his shoulder at him, Brett nodded a friendly hello and asked him how he was doing. But the man ignored him and turned back to Sidney and the other teller, who both wore looks of frustration. Yep, they were clearly dealing with an asshole. Figures.

He couldn't hear what the man was saying to them since he was whispering as if he was afraid Brett would overhear his account number, but he was obviously being a jerk about something. Sidney's eyes kept glancing back at Brett, and it set him on edge. Was she worried that he might say something?

So as he waited for the guy to finish his transaction, Brett glanced around the bank, noting the light gray walls paired with the darker gray carpet on the floor. They looked good together, and he wondered if he shouldn't have the same look in his customer waiting area once he opened his garage.

After a few moments, the guy in front of him finally turned to leave, and the relieved look on Sidney's face told Brett that she was glad to be done dealing with the jerk. Brett hated that the guy had given her a rough time, but he hoped that what he was about to do would change her day for the better. And his too, if everything went right.

Brett set the roses on the counter and then kneeled down on one knee. Then he quickly pulled the ring out of his pocket and opened the box, holding it up to present it to her. "Sid, I—"

Sidney turned away from him, and Brett froze. Did she not want to marry him? But then he saw her running around the counter as fast as she could, and he realized that she just couldn't contain her excitement about his proposal. Smiling, he waited for her to run over and fling herself into his arms. But instead, she ran right past him without even glancing at the ring and headed for the doors of the bank.

Damn. His heart stopped beating, and his chest ached. That was brutal. If she didn't want to marry him, all she had to do was say no. No reason to make such a dramatic exit.

He rose to his feet, closed the ring box, and turned to leave. But he saw Sidney locking the front door with her keys before returning to the counter. Her hands were shaking almost as much as her voice as she lifted the roses from the teller window and said, "I'll be in my office. Let me know when the cops arrive."

Brett blinked at her as shock rocketed through him. *She locked me inside the bank and called the cops on me? All because I was going to propose to her? That's taking things a bit far, don't you think? And what was she doing with the roses…using them as evidence? Jesus.*

Sidney walked toward him. Not knowing what her

intentions were, he braced himself. Was she going to throw the roses in his face and slap him? My God, she was really taking things to an extreme level. What happened to a woman just saying no to a proposal?

But instead, Sidney grabbed his hand and tugged him down the hallway toward her office. The moment they got inside, she closed the door behind them and let out a huge breath that she'd apparently been holding in.

Brett shook his head in annoyance. "You know, if you didn't want to marry me, all you had to do was say no. There's no reason to lock me in the bank and call the cops on me. It's not a crime to propose to the woman I love." Her pale face broke with a smile, and that only annoyed him more. "Go unlock the doors, Sid. I'll leave willingly."

She laid the roses on her desk and laughed. "You big, lovable goof. I didn't lock the doors because of you. I locked them because the guy in line in front of you robbed the bank."

He stilled. "What?"

She grinned again. "Yeah, the guy you were trying to make polite chitchat with was a bank robber. He had us put all the cash from the teller's register into a bank bag for him and then he walked out with it."

"Jesus. Are you okay?"

She nodded. "I'm fine. Just a little shaken up."

Brett couldn't believe it. He was right there and could've helped her. "Why didn't you signal to me? I was right behind him. I could've easily subdued him and held him until the police got here."

Her head snapped up. "I *did* signal you. I gave you 'the look.'"

"Yeah, but the last time you gave me that look, you wanted me to stay out of a situation. How was I supposed to know it meant something different this time?"

She glared at him. "God. We really need to work on our signals if I'm going to marry you. I don't want my own husband not understanding what I'm trying to tell him."

One of his brows rose. "Your husband, huh? So is that a yes?"

She shook her head. "Well, technically, you haven't asked me a question yet."

He grinned and pulled out the ring box, lifting the lid and turning it toward her. "I love you, Sid. Always have and always will. I promise I'll work every day to make you happy and be a better man, one you can be proud to call your husband. Would you do me the honor of marrying me and allowing me to spend the rest of my life with you?"

She didn't even look at the ring. Her eyes were on him and filling with tears as distant sirens rang in the air. "Yes! I love you too, and I've never wanted anything more. You've always been in my heart, Brett, and that's where you'll always stay."

He pulled her to him and kissed her, long and hard. When he finally pulled back, he said, "By the way, I got the loan I applied for so it looks like I'm going to be opening my own garage."

She bounced in place. "That's wonderful news. Congratulations! I'm so happy for you. I knew you could do it."

"Well, I had a little help from you."

"No, you deserve all the credit. You worked so hard for your dream, and it's finally coming true. That's the best thing ever."

He tightened his grip around her waist. "No, you are. I'm going to make you happy, Sid. I can't promise I'll always be perfect, but—"

She put a finger over his lips. "Hush. You are perfect...for me."

If you loved this story, read more in Alison Bliss's A Perfect Fit series, sassy rom-coms celebrating curvy women:

Size Matters
On the Plus Side
More to Love

And don't miss:

Out of the Blue
Coming in early 2020

About the Author

Alison Bliss is a bestselling, award-winning author of humorous, contemporary romances. A born and raised Texan, she currently resides in the Midwest with her husband, two kids, and their dogs. As the youngest of five girls, she has never turned down a challenge or been called by the right name. Alison believes the best way to find out if someone is your soul mate is by canoeing with them, because if you both make it back alive, it's obviously meant to be. She writes the type of books she loves to read most: fun, steamy love stories with heart, heat, and laughter. Something she likes to call "Romance...with a sense of humor."

To learn more, visit her at:

authoralisonbliss.com
Facebook/AuthorAlisonBliss
Twitter @AlisonBliss2